Confederate Gold
The Missing Treasure

by

Bill Westhead

© 2002 by Bill Westhead. All rights reserved.

No part of this book may be reproduced, stored in a retrieval system, or transmitted by any means, electronic, mechanical, photocopying, recording, or otherwise, without written permission from the author.

ISBN: 0-7596-6852-3

This book is printed on acid free paper.

1stBooks - rev. 03/13/02

FOREWORD

Confederate Gold is first and foremost a novel. While the major and many minor characters are fictitious I have tried, as far as possible, to set them among historical figures who were involved, no matter how indirectly, in the event and its aftermath. I would, however, point out that the physical descriptions and dialogue of some of the lesser known historical figures involved are based entirely on my imagination.

The events leading up to the robbery and the torture of the Chennault family, as recounted by Mary in her letter to Clarrisa, are based on fact. For this I offer grateful thanks to my long time friend and colleague Mr. Ralph L. Hobbs for his verbal permission to draw on his painstaking research into the whole affair. The result of this research was published by him in 1976 under the title "The Fate of the Two Confederate Wagon Trains of Gold", Library of Congress Catalog Card Number 76-27020.

My thanks are also due to Jennifer Williams for her continued help and guidance in the publication of this novel.

Finally any similarity between the fictitious characters in the story and any person, alive or dead, is purely coincidental.

Confederate Gold
The Missing Treasure

CHAPTER 1

1912 - Tom Byars

Tom Byars. That is me. A twenty two year old reporter on the staff of the Daily Post. But this is not my story. It belongs to another and it all began the moment I entered the newsroom one Monday morning in September.

"I need you in here, Tom," Harry Hopkins shouted from the small glass cubicle that served as his office.

I went in and stood silently facing the portly figure seated behind his cluttered desk. His vest was undone and his shirt sleeves, rolled up to the elbow, displayed pudgy arms. "Ever heard of the gold train robbery of '65?" he said, looking up at me through thick glasses that made his deep brown eyes seem enormous.

I hesitated. Although I had only been with the paper for a few months I had learned to be wary of this fifty year old editor of our local newspaper and his renowned temper.

"Well!" he snapped, scratching his bald head with the end of a pencil. "Have you or haven't you?"

"Yes," I said. "I've heard my grandfather talk about it. Supposed to have happened near Washington, Georgia but I always thought it was just one of his stories."

"That's what I might expect from the likes of you." Hopkins smile held no warmth. "Don't know what reporters are coming to these days. No nose for a mystery."

"Mystery?"

"Believe me that robbery happened and, what's more, there's still a lot of that treasure missing. Now don't you wonder where it might be? Particularly if I tell you it's said to be worth twenty million today."

I gasped. "How do you know all this?" I demanded, throwing my earlier caution to the wind.

Bill Westhead

To my surprise he remained calm, tapping the side of his nose before pulling three folded sheets of paper out of a drawer and tossing them on his desk. "Read that if you don't believe me," he said twisting one end of his waxed moustache. "Not now," he snapped, as I picked up the yellowed sheets and began to unfold them. "I want you to go talk to Josh Singleton."

"Who?"

"Josh Singleton. Lives at Hayes farm about five miles south of Rome. I believe he was a guard on that train. I've already written him so he'll be expecting you. On your way."

I shuffled from foot to foot. I wanted to tell Hopkins I had plans for the evening but knew better. To put a girl before a story would see me unemployed in a trice. I reckoned I could find another girl but would never find another newspaper job in my home town. I left clutching the three pieces of paper.

Seated at my desk I smoothed them out taking care my sweaty hands did not smudge the ink. I saw it was a letter and my heart leaped when I saw the address 'Washington, Georgia' and the date 'October 14, 1865'. I started to read.

My dearest Clarissa,

I have so much to write about since my last letter, nothing of which makes for good telling. Ever since that fateful night of May 24, when the Confederates (God bless them) charged the gold train, we have been cruelly and unjustifiably treated by the Yankees and General Wilde in particular.

But pray let me start at the beginning. We, along with our good neighbors, were housing our gallant, sick and wounded soldiery. They were a pitiable sight, dressed in rags, dirty and starving. The agonizing groans of those suffering from dysentery were almost unbearable but, above all, I shall never forget the vile smell of rotten meat that leapt from their gangrenous

Confederate Gold
The Missing Treasure

wounds. There were so many that dared not return to their own homes, for fear of arrest by the Unionists, that we had to sleep them in the outhouses, all the big houses being full. Of course we had little food but did what we could to strengthen them for their several journeys. Then the gold train was charged. General Wilde, hearing about the money being taken, came straight to Washington with more Yankee soldiers than I knew existed. As soon as they arrived, Angelina (you remember the negro Grandma raised and who had been the family nurse for years) ran off and told them that Pa had some treasure hidden in the house. Pa did have a little money and Ma a little jewelry they had managed to save during the war. We can only think Angelina must have seen some of Ma's poor trinkets.

When General Wilde rode up to our house on his big horse followed by his soldiers our dog, Jefferson Davis, ran out and barked at them. Unfortunately Pa shouted at the dog and when the Yankees heard his name they all laughed and shouted "Kill Jefferson Davis". Despite Pa's pleas they shot the poor thing to death in front of our eyes and then thrust their bayonets into him. It was horrible. Not satisfied with that they arrested Pa, along with my brother and uncle, and took them away. We did not know if we would ever see them again.

After the men folk had gone more crude soldiers came and searched the house, all the while cursing and abusing Ma and the older children. Fortunately the little ones had run away and hidden in the fields. The biggest insult we had to suffer was when the Yankees made us strip off all our clothes and sent Angelina into the room to search us. Finally they found the little parcel of gold Pa had saved and before we could say anything we were forcibly taken into town and locked up.

The following day the menfolk returned and were locked up with us. Their hands were terribly swollen and black as our kitchen chimney. It was days before they could use them again. Pa was very pale and sobbed as he told us how the soldiers had taken them to the woods, tied their hands behind their backs and strung them up by their thumbs. Only when Pa fainted were they let down. Altogether they were strung up three times and each time asked where the gold was. Of course, they could not say because they did not know.

In the end Pa managed to get Mr Barnett and another lawyer. One of them went down to Augusta and got an order from the General there for our release. Then a gentleman by the name of Colonel Drayton came and sent us all home. In the end Ma's trinkets were returned to her and Pa got his money back. Still it cost us a sight more to pay all our expenses. So, my dear, we were robbed by the Yankees after all.

When we got home we heard they had taken Tom, Pa's body servant, and hanged him because he would not say where Pa's money was, as if he knew. Angelina never shed a tear. Can you believe it, her own son hanged, and she never mourned. She is a very strange person.

I do not think Pa will ever get over his torture. He has become so particular about keeping the family in the clear that it has become an obsession with him. He also tries to persuade our neighbors to give up any valuables they have hidden, even though these are their own possessions. It is not surprising that these good people now avoid him, which is very sad as he is a good, kind man.

No one knows what happened to the gold taken that night. Perhaps one day some one will find it but I cannot, in my heart, wish them good fortune in their discovery.

My dear, I seem to have written of nothing but our family woes. This war has treated us all very badly, but we will survive, although our lives will never be the same again. I do hope that you and your beloved husband have started to overcome the outrages committed in Atlanta by the cursed Sherman and that your beautiful house is now restored to a habitable state. We know, from painful experience, how hard it is to try to regain, even a little, of that which we have lost.

Confederate Gold
The Missing Treasure

Please write soon. Your letters are always so cheerful and still cause Pa to smile, which he does very rarely these days.

Your ever loving friend

Mary

Here was positive proof that the gold train had been robbed. Questions tumbled and crashed into my mind until I began to wonder if there were enough grey cells to hold them all. I jotted down the major ones, pushing aside minor details for later. What happened to those Confederates after that night of May 24? Did they escape or did they suffer the same fate, or worse, than the innocents in the letter? Above all what happened to the gold? More and more unanswered questions continued to come. Finally, armed with six pages of hurriedly scribbled notes, I left the newspaper office and dashed across the dusty, dirt road to the little town library. I hoped they would have documents in their archives which might answer some or all of these questions.

It was dusk when I left the library little wiser than when I had entered. My major source remained Josh Singleton.

So it was that on September 26th, 1912 I crunched up the stone-strewn path to the columned porch of a modest farm house in north Georgia. I was dressed, as I thought befitted a newspaper reporter, in blue suit, white shirt and grey tie.

An old man in worn overalls stared down at me from the top of the steps. By now the newspaper story had become of secondary importance. If I could get Josh Singleton to talk I had high hopes I could recover the gold myself, start my own newspaper, and leave the pompous Harry Hopkins for good.

"Tom Byars, reporter for the Daily Post," I announced by way of an introduction. "Harry Hopkins, my editor, suggested I talk to you."

Bill Westhead

"Oh yes,' he replied, his unwavering eyes continuing to stare at me. "Got his letter yesterday morning saying you would be calling. Well you'd better come up and sit yourself down," he continued, pointing to an empty wicker chair.

I accepted his invitation.

"Well Tom Byars what can I do for you?" he said in a pleasant but firm tone, as he settled himself into an old wooden rocking chair opposite me.

"I was hoping Mr. Singleton," I began tentatively, "that you might be able to tell me something about life around here during the Civil War. This is living history and we need to record it before it's lost forever."

My instincts told me to be cautious of this man. If I came straight out and asked him about the gold I sensed the interview would end abruptly. The few references I had found in the library regarding the gold train and its hazardous flight from Richmond had been of little value. Nowhere had I found his name mentioned, but then the documents had only listed a few of the officers involved. Despite my dislike of Harry Hopkins, I knew him to be a good newspaper man. His sources always proved uncannily reliable. I had to believe Josh Singleton knew of the gold train and had knowledge of the resting place of, at least, some of the stolen fortune. I could not afford to offend him.

"That's a tall order," he said.

There was silence. I glanced at my large, ungainly feet encased in shiny black boots, before looking at him again. For the first time I took in the wiry frame, the craggy features above the steel grey beard and the twinkling blue eyes that bored through me to focus on some distant object. His stubby fingers drummed on the arms of the rocking chair and the semblance of a sad smile twitched at the corners of his mouth. I sensed he was back in yesterday's world recalling the triumphs and, more particularly, the tragedies of the war. Perhaps General Lee's surrender at Appomatox Court House, or the fateful flight of

Confederate Gold
The Missing Treasure

President Jefferson Davis and his family ending in their capture at Irwinville, some miles south of where we now sat. But there was also something secretive in that stare and I wondered if it might relate to the gold train. My excitement mounted as I fought the urge to ask the one vital question uppermost in my mind.

"I appreciate we can't cover everything in one meeting," I said, breaking the silence, "so let me try and clarify my particular interest."

The fingers stopped their tattoo and, while the eyes still twinkled, the smile had been replaced by a furrowed brow and quizzical expression.

"All right, tell me what you want to know and I'll see if I can help you. Of course the mind isn't what it used to be, but I'll try. People ought to know what went on at that time so they'll never make the same mistakes again."

I thought for a moment. His changed look worried me and, before speaking, I reminded myself again to choose my words carefully.

"It's not so much the details of the battles that were fought. Those have been covered in numerous books," I said, hoping he did not notice the tension in my voice.

He nodded. Although he still stared into the distance, I sensed he was watching me closely.

"Let me put it this way," I continued. "There are very few accounts of a personal nature. Suppose we talk about how you first got involved in the war and then how you fared during and after it was all over." That should eventually get to the gold train, I thought, pleased with my subtlety.

He leaned forward, his eyes narrowed as though reading my thoughts. I wondered if he sensed what I was really after and feared I might have lost my opportunity of finding a fortune? But after a few seconds, which seemed like hours, he relaxed back in his chair. "Hm!" he mused.

My spirits rose. It seemed he had fallen for my ploy and, given time, I would get the information I wanted. Still I continued to sense that, despite his age, his wits were a match for mine and again I warned myself to stay on my guard.

"Even now you have narrowed down your request there's still a lot to talk about," Josh Singleton said.

I nodded.

"Well let's see what I can remember of those days. You ask the questions and I'll answer them best way I can."

This suited me as it gave me a chance to lead the discussion in the direction I wanted it to go. I had cleared my first hurdle in my search for the gold.

"Let's start with your childhood," I suggested.

"Seems as good a place as any to start," he said with a deep, manly chuckle. I imagined that laugh in victory at First Bull Run, but could also hear it in defeat at Vicksburg. It had the quality of a man who willingly braved danger and laughed in its face.

"Right," I said, producing the note book and pencil I had brought with me in expectation of writing down every detail of the interview. "Let's get the preliminaries over. Where you were born? Who your parents were? What they did? You know the sort of thing, background for the story."

"Typical of a reporter," he said. "Start at the beginning and stop at the end. Then take all that's been said and twist the facts into a good story with little truth."

I had to admit he was right. Suddenly I felt overcome with guilt at trying to deceive this old soldier who had given his youth in the service of the Confederacy. I hoped Harry Hopkins would publish what I wrote, despite the fact that now my main reason for being here was to find the gold. I could feel the handle of the shovel in my hands as I dug.

"Josh Singleton, this is the story of your life!" I said, trying to break the tension that knotted my stomach.

Confederate Gold
The Missing Treasure

Thus began the most intriguing story I have ever heard. I have tried to reproduce it just as Josh Singleton told it. I hope I have done both the story and the man justice. I make no apologizes for what is written. He would not have wanted it so. He was a man's man. He lived that way and told his story that way. Georgia was his home and the Old South his nation.

CHAPTER 2

"I was born on a plantation in north Georgia," Josh Singleton said, "name of Strong's"

"Never heard of that one," I said, "and I'm pretty familiar with most of the old plantations. Did a study of them a couple of years ago."

"Then you probably know it as Hampton's," he replied. "By the time I was born Mr. Strong's son-in-law, Mark Hampton, had inherited the place. He was the very devil of a man. Tall, lean, sour faced, he was the second son of an English aristocrat. Always regretted coming to the Americas. He made his fortune here but always thought the world owed him a living without him having to work for it.

He married Mr. Strong's only child, Jane. Many said it was just to get his hands on the plantation, which was probably true. She was a dumpy woman, plain of feature who persisted in dressing in, what she called, the latest fashions from Europe. I can tell you she always looked like an overdressed porker, but I thought the world of her. So different from her husband."

"Was she your mother?" I asked.

"Good God, no!" he exploded. Then silence.

He avoided my gaze for several minutes, seemingly lost in thought. At last he took a deep breath, started to say something, then hesitated. It appeared he wanted to speak but yet was afraid to do so. Finally, in a whisper I only just heard, he said "My parents were never married."

I looked in amazement at the old man sitting in front of me, not sure I had heard him correctly.

"You look surprised," Josh Singleton continued, "but it's true. Mr. Hampton would not allow it."

"Would not or could not?" I said without thinking.

"Both I suppose."

Confederate Gold
The Missing Treasure

"But why? What had it to do with him?"

Suddenly his whole body started to tremble and I could see beads of sweat breaking out on his forehead. I wondered if he was sick when, suddenly, an incredible thought struck me. The man opposite me was as white as I was but could it be that one of his parents had been black, maybe a slave on the Hampton plantation. His embarrassed eyes and turned head suggested he knew what I was thinking. Wondering where to put myself I stared at a bee, working a circuitous path through the rose that adorned the porch, and waited for Josh Singleton to continue.

"You're right," he said finally, fighting to control his feelings. "My mother was a slave in the plantation house. A beautiful, kind woman, but none the less a slave. My father was the white overseer. Offspring of a poor family he had worked his way up. When I was born he had complete control over all the slaves. Even when Mr. Hampton was there, which was not often, he hardly ever interfered with my father's decisions."

"I didn't realize that sort of thing went on back in the old plantation days," I answered naively.

"You didn't?" he said. "I thought you just told me you'd studied the plantations. Still I suppose they'd leave such little indiscretions out of any plantation family history."

I heard the sarcasm in his voice and saw the hurt in his eyes. Afraid he would see the confused look on my face, I lowered my head and scribbled furiously in my notebook.

"My father always claimed he was the best overseer in the state," Singleton continued. "Maybe he was but I don't really know. I do know I thought his treatment of the slaves was harsh but I think he tried to be fair. Still that was the way in those days. Slaves were money and, although you worked them hard, you kept them healthy. He wasn't really cruel, he just did as everyone else did working them day in and day out from sun-up to sun-down in the fields. Looking back I think he was probably more cruel to his family than the slaves. From the outset he believed my mother tried to trap him by becoming pregnant.

Although not a big man he was lean and strong and, when drunk, would beat the both of us. He was always sorry afterwards and often times cried. I think in his strange way he loved us. Anyway, enough of that. To cut a long story short, there I was in the year 1840, the offspring of unwed parents."

He paused while I finished writing.

"Did you work on the plantation?" I asked him.

"Of course, everyone worked." he answered. "I did those jobs which were too good for the slaves and too degrading for the white folks. You must understand that I was not treated as a white boy and yet I was not a slave. I sort of fell between the two. The white people at the big house would not accept me as they did my father. I could use the kitchen with my mother but neither of us were allowed in any other part of the house unless the Hamptons said so. On the other hand the slaves didn't want me with them because of my father. In a nut shell I was an outcast."

"But weren't other children in the same situation?" I asked, having got over my initial shock.

"Oh yes," he said.

"Well didn't you band together and make your own amusement?" The answer seemed so obvious I wondered why I had bothered to asked the question.

"No," he answered sharply, "and you wouldn't have done either. There was a hierarchy among the blacks as well as the whites. My mother, being a house slave was above the field hands. My father, being the overseer was above the poorer white folk. This put me in the top class of the unwanted. The whites didn't want me, the blacks wouldn't have me and my father refused to let me associate with the so-called lower class of mixed folk because it would undermine his position."

There was silence as I tried to imagine the utter loneliness of growing up with no friends of your own age.

"It must have been a miserable childhood," I said lamely.

Confederate Gold
The Missing Treasure

"Yes it was," he agreed. "But it helped me in later life. I suppose I've always been a loner. Maybe I was born that way or maybe I just grew up that way, I don't really know. But loner I am and a loner I shall remain although loneliness has scared me at times. That's why I took the name Singleton."

"That's not your real name?" I gasped in surprise.

"Oh no," he said with a knowing smile. "I took that name later in life. Seemed to fit. I am a single one."

He gave me a look as though daring me to pursue the origin of his name further.

"I suppose you were relieved when the war came?" I suggested, trying to move the story along and get to the real purpose of my visit.

"Oh I'd left the plantation long before the war came," he answered. "Ran away to sea when I was twelve."

I was stunned. Ever since I had heard of Josh Singleton I had assumed he had been a soldier during the war. Yet here he was running away to sea. Now, for the first time I began to have serious doubts about his connection with the gold train. Maybe there was another Josh Singleton. But the man intrigued me and, as I sat there and watched him take a pinch of snuff, I still felt deep down there was some hidden secret in his past even if it was not the gold.

"I thought you were a soldier during the war," I said, in an attempt to clarify his earlier statement.

"That's what a lot of people around here think," he answered, the twinkle back in his eyes. "But they're wrong. I ran away to sea at the age of twelve and that's where I served most of the war, blockade running. Never fought on land at all. You know," he continued, leaning forward to emphasize his point, "few people really know how important blockade running was to the Confederate cause, because so few of our exploits have ever been recorded. Ah," he sighed, "those low, sleek, grey painted ships were a pretty sight every time they slipped through the northern blockade and into a southern port. Everyone assumed we were a bunch of cutthroats willing to sell anything to the highest bidder. But, I'll have you know, we shipped in over half a million rifles during the war not to mention precious manufactured goods. We fought as hard for the South as any soldier in the field. But then I'm jumping ahead of myself."

I wanted him to jump ahead to the end of the war, but he was determined to tell his story in his own time and in his own way. Pencil poised over my notebook, I listened as he continued.

"The best job I had on the plantation was to help ferry the cotton down the river to Savannah at the end of the season. Savannah was a great place in those days. Everyone was always friendly and the large buildings bustled with activity. There was always a feeling of wealth and power about that city. But above all it was the wharf and river that thrilled me. When I had time, which wasn't very often, I would wander along the waterfront, fascinated by the tall ships and the sailors even taller yarns of foreign lands." He paused and his eyes again became distant as if remembering those far off days.

"One day I left home, if you could call it that, on one of the cotton ferry boats heading for Savannah," the old man said, picking up where he had left off. "By then I had made up my mind I was going to sea. Once the boat was unloaded I hid in the back streets until it had left the dock. Then I went hunting me a sailor's life with visions of captaining one of those great ocean going ships. The fearless imagination of youth, I suppose. Anyway I soon came down to earth. It took me three days and nights begging up and down that waterfront before finding a ship that would take me on. At last I got a job as cabin boy aboard the clipper *Bountiful* that plied the Atlantic. When we sailed that night I knew I was finally out of reach of Hampton and his plantation."

"Did you ever see your folks again?" I interrupted.

That same distant look came into his eyes. Then his hand reached into his vest pocket and slowly drew out a battered pocket watch. Opening the cover he peered at it for some moments, closed it and returned it to his pocket.

"I only saw my father once after that," he said a touch of sadness in his voice. "Having run away I daren't go back to the plantation, even for a visit. Despite my father, I knew Hampton would have made an example of me by having me flogged in front of the slaves. It was not until Georgia joined the cause, that I dared return to make peace with my folks. Only my father was alive when I got there, my mother having died of a fever during my first voyage. We spent the day together and as I was leaving he gave me his blessing. The only time in his life he ever did. Never saw him again but heard, much later, he'd been killed at Vicksburg."

"So you spent the war years at sea?" I ventured, working feverishly to get my notes straight.

"Most of them, yes," he said raising his bushy eyebrows.

"When did you leave the sea?" I asked.

"When the end was in sight," he said. "Then, like thousands of others, I wandered around here and there trying to stay alive. Those were the worst of days when you couldn't trust a single soul.

"You mean the time of Yankees and carpetbaggers?" I prompted.

"That's right," he said. "The damned blue-bellies were bad enough but some of the Southerners, who became their puppets, were even worse. Between them they ran everything. There was nothing you could do without their permission and only then if you had their price. They were lining their pockets at our expense and it was hard for loyal Southerners to accept that their way of life had gone forever. Of course mine had gone with it, but then mine was not much anyway." He laughed. "Well I drifted around for a while before finishing here where I have farmed these few acres ever since. Never been real wealthy but I've managed to make enough to see me through."

Bill Westhead

He levered himself out of the chair and limped over to light two oil lamps on the porch. I had not realized how quickly the time had slipped by and had failed to notice the sun slowly disappearing behind the rolling terrain.

"It's too late for you to set out tonight," Singleton said kindly. "Besides you haven't heard the story you came for, just the start. You'll stay here the night and we'll finish it tomorrow."

It was not so much an invitation but an order, as though he needed me to stay.

"Thank you Mr. Singleton," I said.

"Everyone round these parts calls me Josh, so you'd best do the same. Don't go in for all this false politeness. Josh I was born and Josh I'll die." he said, his eyes narrowing in a look which dared me to contradict him.

"Well thanks again," I said, then added "Josh." I felt uncomfortable calling him Josh, not only because of his age but also because I did not feel anywhere near the equal of this strange man.

He beckoned me to follow as he led the way into the clapboard house. The entrance room floor was a beautifully polished hardwood with an exotic rug in the center. Could be Persian, I thought. The drapes were of an old fashioned brocade which shouted of by-gone wealth, while the antique furniture seemed out of place in a farm house. Yet, despite the heaviness of the furnishings, there was a strange freshness about the place.

We crossed the room, out the back door, and along a narrow walkway to the a wooden outhouse which served as a kitchen. Clearly this place had been built at a time when kitchen fires could menace the whole house.

"You'll have a bite to eat?" he said, as we entered the outhouse.

"I'd appreciate that," I said, the familiar smells already tickling my appetite.

He lit two oil lamps before starting to cook over a wood burning stove, all the time talking about the hardships of farming

Confederate Gold
The Missing Treasure

today. The war years were forgotten as he turned his hand to preparing the food. In no time I was faced with a full plate of corn, black-eyed peas, ham and biscuits which I attacked like a starving hobo.

Immediately the meal was finished and the plates and pans washed, he turned out the oil lamps and, candles in hand, beckoned me to follow him back to the house. Without a word we crossed the main room and ascended a narrow staircase leading to the upper storey. In the flickering light I could see that the steps and hand rail were of rough hewn pine in stark contrast to the polished hall floor of the main room. He noticed my roving eyes and laughed that deep and powerful laugh I now imagined it to be that of a sailor enjoying the threat of an approaching storm.

"Wondering where I got some of this stuff, eh?" he said.

"Well yes," I replied, embarrassed that he had seen my searching gaze.

"Carpetbaggers weren't the only ones that knew their way around here my boy."

Again I had the sense of something mysterious about the man.

"And don't forget I knew where the old plantation house was," he said, giving me a knowing wink.

There was no need to ask more. I knew that, even in those dark days, he had somehow managed to salvage some of the old plantation furnishings for use in his own home.

He ushered me into a bedroom which, even in the dim candlelight, confirmed my suspicions that the wealth of the house was on the ground floor. The room itself was about ten feet square with floor and ceiling fashioned out of the same rough hewn pine as the stairs. A glassless opening at the far end let in the soft light of a crescent moon. On each side of the opening were strong iron hooks on which hung two boards which acted as shutters in the event of bad weather. The only furniture was a small wooden bed covered with a lumpy pallet

Bill Westhead

and a well worn quilt while a chipped bowl and water jug sat at an angle on the floor. Although clean, there was a slightly musty smell about the room indicating that Josh Singleton rarely had guests staying in his house.

"'night," he said, as he closed the door.

For some time I sat on the edge of the bed lost in thought. If Josh Singleton had been a guard on that train he must have known what happened to the gold, I reasoned. So why had he not tried to recover it? If he had recovered it, what had he done with it? He had certainly used very little, if any, on this part of the house.

I undressed down to my underclothes and climbed onto the bed, covering myself with the quilt. Thoughts churned through my mind as I closed my eyes. Perhaps Harry Hopkins' information had been wrong after all, but my instincts continued to tell me otherwise. I wondered how much longer I could stifle my curiosity. I felt so near and yet so far from that old Confederate treasure.

CHAPTER 3

Breakfast the next morning was plain fare, a plate of grits mixed with eggs and large thick slices of home cured ham. I was amazed at the amount of food my host put away. He did not seem to have a care in the world, while I nibbled at my fare. At every bite my stomach contracted as jumbled thoughts of the Confederate treasure whirled through my mind.

"Well my boy," he said, wiping his plate clean with a huge piece of hoe cake. "A few household chores and then we'll get back to my story, for what it's worth."

A fortune, I thought, but refrained from saying so. Instead I simply said "Sounds good to me."

The few household chores turned out to be a full morning's work. The downstairs of the house was cleaned from top to bottom, the pigs fed, eggs collected and the few surrounding fields inspected. We had eaten lunch before I found myself, once again, sitting on the porch facing Josh Singleton.

He slowly lowered himself into his rocking chair, took a quick pinch of snuff, sneezed and then asked, "Now where did I get to last night?"

Quickly I referred to my notes. "You were telling me you had been a blockade runner during the war," I answered.

"Ah yes!" he mused. "I remember now." That distant look was back in his eyes. "I spent those years on the *Carolina II*, one of the fastest two-masted, Bermuda rigged schooners afloat. She'd could outrun any Yankee ship. Never got caught although we came close on several occasions when running in food, rifles and ammunition from foreign ships anchored out to sea. Occasionally we'd bring in a few trinkets for the ladies. We made landfall in coves and inlets all along the coasts of Georgia and the Carolinas, always landing cargo at night. The darker the night the better. I tell you we came to know that coastline like

Bill Westhead

the backs of our hands. Our Captain was the devil himself, one James Sangster."

Something stirred in my subconscious and my hands shook. Suddenly I could hear my grandfather's husky voice talking of a Captain Sangster who had been involved in the robbery. I wondered if a piece of the jigsaw had just fallen into place?

"He'd lead us anywhere at any time and what's more, we'd follow," Singleton said, without any indication he had noticed my reaction.

"What sort of man was Captain Sangster?" I coughed to hide the quaver in my voice.

"How do you describe a mixture of devil and man?" Singleton mused. "At times he was wild and fearless as though the devil himself sat on his shoulder. Other times sullen, staying in his cabin for hours not speaking to a soul. During those moody periods he could be dangerous particularly if he thought you might try to take over his command. He had to lead. He could never follow. Despite this I will always remember two things in his favor, he was honest and he never forgot a good deed.

I remember one night in the spring of '63. We'd taken on a cargo of rifles earlier in the evening and were running before the worst storm I'd ever been in trying to make landfall south of Savannah before midnight. As first mate I was on deck while Sangster took a turn below. The wind was so strong that instead of riding the waves, the bows of the little ship were being driven under. Our staysail and foresail were already ripped to shreds before I sent a message begging the skipper to shorten sail to save the ship. But Sangster was in one of his wild and fearless moods and forbade it. So we continued plowing through towering waves which constantly enveloped our bedraggled foremast and threatened to swamp us. Each time the stern reared up I could see nothing but pounding waves slashing over the bowsprit. Pitch darkness would suddenly turn to bright daylight as great flashes of lightening ripped the sky. What with the

Confederate Gold
The Missing Treasure

pounding of the sea and the crashes of thunder you had to shout in the next man's ear to make yourself heard. It was nature gone mad, raving mad. I don't mind telling you I prayed, as I had never prayed before, that the Almighty would see us through. Even after all these years the terror of that night still haunts me.

Suddenly I felt a hand pressing down on my shoulder and there he was. His piercing eyes were shining and his mouth was set in a ferocious grin.

"Great night," he shouted in my ear. He was actually enjoying the storm.

In my amazement I must have loosened my hold on the wheel for suddenly the little ship heeled hard to port. I fought to bring her back but at that moment a mountain of a wave exploded over the side. It hit me with the force of a cannon ball and would have knocked me over if I had not had a firm grip on the wheel. When I recovered my breath I realized his hand was no longer on my shoulder. I glanced to one side. At the same moment a flash of lightening forked through the sky and I saw an arm, in a familiar sleeve, flailing away like a rag doll. Instantly I knew the skipper had been swept overboard and was clinging for dear life to the far side of the rail. I was the only one aware of his plight and knew it was up to me to save him. All thoughts for my own safety vanished. Ideas flashed through my mind, faster than the howling gale, only to be discarded. I daren't leave the wheel for fear the ship would founder and none of the crew were near enough to hear my shouts. Although I could still see the dismembered arm waving through the sheeting rain I knew Sangster could not last long in his perilous position.

At that very moment the ship again heeled hard to port and, to hold our position, I instinctively scrambled to the starboard side of the wheel laying all my weight on the spokes. As I did so my foot caught on something and looking down I saw a coil of rope. My prayers had been answered. Moving back in front of the wheel I stuck my right arm through the spokes and grasped the wheel post."

Bill Westhead

There was pause as Singleton seemed to relive the moment. "It's amazing how much strength ultimate fear generates," he finally said. "I hardly felt the pain of the spokes cutting into my flesh. With my free hand I managed to lash one end of the rope around the post and then, with all my strength, hurled the other end towards the waving arm. I watched in dismay as it was carried away on the wind and fell short. With difficulty I recoiled the rope and tried again. Again it fell short. I can't remember how many times I hurled that rope into the wind until, at last, I got it to fall over the rail close to the flailing arm. The arm disappeared. Dragging my own aching arm from between the spokes, I wondered if I had been in time. Minutes seemed like hours as I waited. Then, to my relief, a silhouette-like apparition clambered over the rail, fell back on the deck and lay deathly still. Eventually one of the crew came aft and seeing the skipper, dragged him below. Now I could concentrate again on fighting nature's fury. Pain seared through me but it was not until we gained the shelter of the island I found my arm was broken.

By then that devil Sangster was up and about as though nothing had happened. He never mentioned the incident or even thanked me for saving his life. But I know from later events that he knew he was in my debt."

I stopped writing at this last remark, fighting to control my curiosity, for I sensed that pressing the point now might well lose me information not gain it. Instead I asked him how long he had been a blockade runner hoping, in his own good time, he would tell me what these later events were.

"Until early '65" he answered.

"What made you change?"

"We were ordered to scuttle the ship," he said. "By then our cause was lost and there was not much we could do. We continued to do what little we could and to make the best of things but with the fall of Vicksburg and Sherman's march through Georgia the supply lines to our armies were cut. Landing rifles in Georgia or the Carolinas was no use. There was no way

Confederate Gold
The Missing Treasure

to get them to the men who needed them. We tried landing them further north, but the number we got through was so small as to be worthless. Most of what we landed fell into Union hands and finished up being used against our own boys. So we were ordered to pull the plugs on the *Carolina II* to prevent her falling into enemy hands. It was a sad sight to see that gallant ship go down to Davy Jones' locker. We had to sink her ourselves 'cause no matter how hard they tried the damned Yankees couldn't. After that I found myself in Richmond."

"So you found yourself in Richmond," I repeated lamely. I wanted to add 'and then what' but quickly put the phrase out of my mind. We were making progress towards my goal although I was finding the going excruciatingly slow.

"Right. I remember I went to church the first Sunday I was there," Josh Singleton said, his voice barely audible. Clearly he was still thinking of his ship.

This surprised me. After what I had heard I would never have suspected him of being a religious man. Why, I wondered, would he suddenly go to church? Then I recalled that at the time the war was almost over and the South finished. Still I reckoned it must have been a rare occurrence for him to have remembered it all this time. I was about to frame a question, but as I looked up I saw his eyes closed.

I sat there chewing the end of my pencil and pondered over what I had learned so far from a man who had known Captain Sangster. Not only known him, but saved his life. I suddenly realized I would never have had this opportunity to talk about the gold train if the *Carolina II* had not made landfall that spring night of 1863. Suddenly his eyes opened. He stared at me knowingly. Then, without further delay, he continued to relate his story which, I still hoped, would ultimately lead me to my fortune.

CHAPTER 4

1865 - Josh Singleton

St. Paul's Episcopal Church was packed on that first Sunday morning in April. The famished populace of Richmond were crammed into every pew while the overflow stood in the aisles and along the back. The clammy smell of fear, coupled with the stench of unwashed bodies, pervaded the airless nave. Those unlucky enough not to be able to get into the church crowded outside, although they could hear nothing from where they stood. I guess we were all there for the same reason, praying for a miracle. The war was going from bad to worse for the South. Defeat stared us in the face. It was only a question of time, and a short time at that. Jammed shoulder to shoulder we listened as the preacher extolled the righteousness of our cause and exhorted the dejected congregation to even greater efforts in defense of that cause. He did not seem to understand, or accept, the plight of the South on that day.

Suddenly a murmur arose from the crowd outside, which quickly increased, sweeping into the back of the church and rolling down the nave like a giant wave breaking on rocky shores. Every head turned as a man, dressed in the tattered semblance of a Confederate officer's grey uniform, forced his way into the crowded church and down the center aisle. Although he held himself erect his sunken eyes, hollow cheeks, unkempt beard and sallow complexion spoke of utter weariness. He typified the South in her final agony.

The preacher halted his sermon in mid-sentence as the officer fought his way to the front pew and passed a piece of paper to the man sitting there. Having delivered his message the officer stood to attention and saluted. The recipient rose unhurriedly to his feet, adjusted his tail coat and bow tie then

Confederate Gold
The Missing Treasure

bent to pick up his hat. He was shorter than the officer, with a mop of greying hair neatly brushed across a wide forehead. He nodded in acknowledgment of the salute and, with an imperious wave of his hand, beckoned those with him to follow. The preacher stood in the pulpit open-mouthed while the packed aisle parted like the Red Sea before the group. As they approached I noticed the man's neatly trimmed goatee beard which seemed to lengthen his haggard face. But it was his eyes that held my attention. Deep set and tired though they were, I will never forget the determination that blazed out from under those bushy eyebrows. Looking neither left nor right, he swept by me, followed by the rest of the group who looked as though they had not slept for days.

Suddenly I realized why there had been no move to stop this sudden exodus. The man was Jefferson Davis, President of the Confederacy. I was awestruck as the Kentuckian strode through the doors, every inch a soldier and a statesman.

"I don't like the look of that," I said turning to my companion, Simon Price. "Wonder what disaster has overtaken us now?" Although I tried to put a brave face on things, the quiet desperation in my voice was only too apparent.

"Don't know," said Price slowly, his brows furrowed under an unruly shock of blonde hair. "I can't believe it possible but the situation must be getting worse if the President has to be called out in the middle of a church service. Obviously whatever the cause it seems it can't wait another half hour so I guess it must be a major disaster."

I gulped. I had hoped for a more cheerful response and, for the first time since coming to Richmond, I felt the chill of fear run up my spine. In earlier days I had controlled my own fate. Now I realized my fate was in the hands of others. Since the beginning of the year news from all the battle fronts, both north and south, had told of defeat followed by defeat in rapid succession. The gallant Southerners who, for the last four years had defied the might of the Unionists, were almost spent and the

Bill Westhead

end was very near. Starvation was rampant. A barrel of flour, if one could be found, now cost four hundred and twenty five dollars.

Although we all continued to pray for a miracle that would turn the tide and restore the Confederacy to the days of its former glory we never seriously thought it would happen. In our hearts we knew the final catastrophe was imminent.

Everyone in the congregation seemed to sense the same impending doom. Many were in tears, while others openly bemoaned our lost cause and made wild guesses as to the latest calamity which had occasioned the sudden departure of Jefferson Davis. It was several minutes before the preacher could regain control of his flock. A final hymn, a prayer for the safety of our gallant boys in grey and the service was abruptly over.

Outside the church restless groups thronged the sidewalks and streets anxiously waiting for news. It was not long in coming as rumor of the South's pending surrender started to run through the city like a forest fire.

Realizing we could do nothing by simply standing around with the populace, Simon and I set out for our headquarters. Pushing our way through the milling crowds we were mounting the steps leading to the main doors when we heard the sound of distant thunder.

"That's strange," said Simon, looking up, "the sky's as clear as a bell."

Together we looked in the direction of the rumbling. Immediately the cause became clear.

"Artillery!" I said, a fraction of a second before him.

We froze on the headquarter steps as the noise of the firing grew louder, borne in on the light winds which blew from the north and west. Suddenly a small ruddy glow lit the sky. We stood rooted to the spot, unmindful of the danger, as shell after shell descended on the city until the noise of the explosions became continuous. The ground shuddered with each impact and the air filled with dust as walls and roofs started to topple. The glow we had noticed a few minutes earlier rapidly increased in intensity. The sky became a myriad of colors as flames leaped upwards to mingle with the sun's rays which were now struggling to penetrate the flying debris.

"Looks as though the fire and brimstone the preacher called down on our enemies a little while ago is being brought down on us," said Simon, his mouth set in a grim smile.

I nodded, unable to put thoughts into words, as I watched this unforgettable brutality rain down from the sky. Women screamed for their children while several men shouted conflicting orders which, even if heard above the din, were ignored. People scrambled for cover. Chaos reigned. It was several minutes before either of us could tear our eyes away from this airborne destruction and turn a deaf ear to the wailing panic of the populous.

Inside the headquarters the scene was little different but, at least, we learned the truth, although this proved to be little better than the rumors we had heard outside. The only good news was that the South had not surrendered. But even this report was offset by the knowledge that General Lee had sent a message advising Jefferson Davis to abandon Richmond by evening as it could no longer be defended against the likelihood of an all-out Union attack. It was this message that had caused the commotion in the church.

Next we learned the President and his cabinet had already met and unanimously agreed to move the government to Danville, one hundred and forty miles to the south.

That orderly arrangements were being made inside headquarters for their departure was not immediately apparent. Men stood around in small groups lost in their own thoughts and fears, while others disappeared behind closed doors only to reappear and continue their headlong dash down the crowded corridors. Orders were given, some obeyed, some ignored. The scene resembled an ant's nest suffering the effects of boiling water. I waited with my own group, resigned to the fact that, sooner or later, the boiling water would hit me.

"You there sailor!" a voice broke in on my thoughts. "Report at once to Captain Parker, naval commander of the *Patrick Henry*."

"Yes sir," I answered automatically, then added "Where is he?"

"Up the stairs, second door on the left."

Relieved to have something to do, I fought my way up the stairs, knocked on the door and entered.

A bearded man with greying hair dressed in the uniform of a Captain in the Confederate navy sat behind a table. "Name?" he demanded before I was half way into the room.

"Singleton sir," I shouted above the increasing noise of the bombardment. Despite feeling dejected in my tattered naval clothing, I sprang to attention and saluted smartly.

"Join that group over there," he commanded, nodding in the direction of some twenty men standing in the far corner.

Together we watched as men of all ages streamed into the room. Many of the older ones came quietly, their bloodshot eyes, drawn features and mud spattered uniforms bespeaking months and years of suffering in the cause. Others, fresh complexioned and radiating an air of excitement, showed themselves to be newly recruited for the great, but now rapidly dying, adventure. The group I had been assigned to grew to about sixty, while a smaller group of about a dozen, lounged on the other side of the bare room.

Finally the Captain rose from behind the table, stooped to pick up a small pack and approached us.

"My name is Parker, Captain Parker," he said, pacing back and forth in front of us. "You men have been selected to guard a train that will leave Richmond shortly carrying our President and his cabinet, along with members of his staff. Your duty, as if I have to remind you, is to defend that train to the last man. Pick up your weapons and report to the railhead immediately."

Confederate Gold
The Missing Treasure

A few enthusiastic 'Yes sir' from the new recruits answered this call, while the rest of us remained silent. Those of us who had anything, began to bundle together our personal belongings. Like the rest in our group, I was only too pleased to be leaving this fast developing hell-hole. By now everyone seemed well aware that death or capture, which if tales were true might be worse than death, were our only alternatives should we stay.

"You won't be taking those things with you," the Captain shouted, seeing us shoulder our packs. "Only take those essentials which you can carry in your pockets. The rest will be left here."

A stunned silence greeted this order. No one had very much but we were now being ordered to abandon everything in the world we possessed.

"Here are your rations," Parker said, as he handed each man two pieces of mouldy looking bread covered in a fine layer of dust and a thin slice of something that resembled meat. With derisive laughs we stuffed the food in our pockets.

This done he strode over to the second group. "Report to Rear Admiral Raphael Semmes," he commanded, loud enough for all to hear. "You are to destroy the *Patrick Henry* and the rest of the Confederate ships in the James River to prevent them falling into enemy hands." He paused then added, "Like the others you will only take your rations and what you can carry in your pockets. After destroying the ships you are dismissed. Make to your own home, wherever that might be, and may God protect you."

From the look on the faces of the second group, it was clear they would rather have fought their ships and lost than simply destroy them. As for going home few, if any, knew if they had a home to go to and all were fearful of discovering the truth.

For some minutes no one moved. Then slowly we began to unpack our pathetic bundles and stuff our pockets with what few items we could carry all the while muttering at the incompetency of the headquarters staff.

Bill Westhead

"Move," shouted Parker from across the room, as he saw the lethargy with which we were storing our precious items. "Follow me."

Leaving the room we followed the short, broad shouldered Captain down the stairs and out onto the dusk lit streets. During the time we had been in the building conditions outside had continued to deteriorate. The glow to the north and west of the city had increased and now skeletons of roofless buildings could be seen outlined against leaping tongues of fire. Dust and smoke hung in the air drying my throat, causing me to cough continuously. Each breath filled my nostrils and lungs with the acrid smell of gun powder.

Civilians and troops alike, loaded with what belongings they could carry, scuttled from one building to the next in an effort to gain protection from the bombardment. As we left the headquarters a vast column of white smoke rose into the sky immediately followed by a deafening roar. The ground shook under our feet and large chunks of debris rained down from the sky.

"What the hell was that, sir?" I asked, as we flattened ourselves against a wall.

"Our troops have orders to blow up the magazines," Parker shouted above the din. "That was one of them. They all have to be destroyed before the damned Yankees get here. There'll be more before we make the station."

Some braver, or more mercenary, souls were rushing in and out of houses loading carts with household effects. Small groups of skulking men and coarse looking women could be seen breaking into the few remaining undamaged stores. It was a world gone mad.

As we struggled through this human chaos towards the railhead fires, newly lit by the retreating Confederate troops, added to the pandemonium. Dodging or pushing aside anyone who got in our way we had just reached the station when another deafening explosion shattered the few remaining windows of the

Confederate Gold
The Missing Treasure

building. The plume of grey smoke that billowed into the sky over the James River confirmed that the Confederate fleet was no more.

Part of the station building had already suffered from the bombardment and the entrance was littered with broken bricks and stone. Added to this were shards of glass ankle deep in places which, if we were not careful, would cut our poorly shod feet to ribbons.

Clambering over the debris, as fast as we dare, we headed for the appointed platform where the Presidential train waited. There were no signs of pomp and ceremony as in the past. Instead of comfortable carriages the train had been hastily made up of freight cars and flat bed trucks which now blended into the deepening shadows thrown from the shattered arches overhead. The only sign of life came from the locomotive where a trickle of smoke indicated the engineers were ready to leave at the first opportunity.

Cabinet members and others appeared along the platform, ushering wives and families in front of them. We watched in disgust as some of the men arrogantly strutted between the freight cars fussing about their own belongings, while we stood there, our worldly wealth in our pockets. Many of the women were no better as they too fluttered up and down the platform more concerned about their hair and make-up than the evacuation of the city.

We stood raggedly to attention watching this self-centered exhibition. Then the unmistakable figure of the President appeared. There was no sign of fuss or panic in the man. He approached us with a weary, but measured, stride.

"We place ourselves entirely in your hands," he said simply. "May God be with all of us in the days ahead."

Even at this catastrophic moment he continued to maintain an aura of authority and, unlike most of his cabinet, had no need of arrogance. Instead he treated everyone as equal in these final hours of our struggle.

Captain Parker saluted and, as if by unspoken command, the rest of us straightened up and followed his lead. A smile flitted around the corners of the grim mouth and, for a moment, the fatigue on the President's face was replaced by that look of determination I had first seen in the church. Without further words he turned and quietly entered one of the freight cars. The rest, with their families, quickly followed.

"Take up your positions," Parker commanded, pointing to the flat bed trucks that were interspersed between the freight cars. Thankfully we climbed aboard.

A motley collection of boxes and bags filled with earth or sand had been placed around the perimeter of each flat bed to protect us from rifle fire. We settled down our backs against the hastily constructed barricades, rifles across our knees. The snorting of the locomotive increased and steam billowed from the tall smoke stack, throwing black, oily grit over freight cars and flat beds alike. The giant wheels began to turn and we started out on, what many believed, would be our final journey through the dying Confederacy.

Confederate Gold
The Missing Treasure

CHAPTER 5

Slowly the train gathered speed seemingly reluctant, even now, to leave Richmond. To a man we stood and looked back, eyes riveted on our burning capital. The continuous sound of exploding magazines coupled with the gun fire reverberated in our ears. No word was spoken. We continued to stand until the last magazine was blown. By then only a vivid red glow lit the darkening skies and marked the location of our beloved city. Unashamed tears washed down our grime covered faces as we settled back behind our barricades. The train continued to move steadily southward. Despite its snail-like pace every turn of its giant iron wheels carried us further into the Confederacy and safety. But individually we dreaded what might await us at the end of our journey.

Throughout the night the train rattled and swayed along the poorly maintained tracks, throwing us from side to side of the flat bed and preventing that deep sleep for which we all yearned. Intermittent stopping and starting, as the crew were forced to switch tracks, added to our misery. A dank mist held us in its ghost-like hand and the wind, that whistled through every small crack in our barricade, penetrated our thread-bare clothing. Confined space made physical exercise impossible and the few that tried were roundly berated. Cold and miserable we huddled together, each trying to draw warmth and moral support from his neighbor.

"I'm sure a Yankee prison can't be worse than this hell hole," I said to the figure pressed next to me.

"You're right." He paused, then with a humorless chuckle added, "Reckon we'd have been better off taking our lot in Richmond. At least we'd have been warm with all those fires around."

Bill Westhead

"Hell fire and damnation you prattling sons of bitches. You don't know what you're talking about." The voice exploded from somewhere among the bunched forms at the far end of the flat bed.

"What the hell's it got to do with you," I shouted, my temper rising. "It's none of your damned business what I think and say."

"It is when I hear talk like that. Have you any idea what it's like in places like Rock Island and Elmira," the voice continued. "You've only got to look at our own camp at Belle Isle. The prisoners there are walking skeletons and I don't doubt that our boys in northern camps are just as badly off, if not worse. You linger in any prison camp until you die of disease or starvation. It's a living hell with death a welcome relief. I for one would rather be here or dead than in one of those blue-belly prison camps."

In the silence that followed the whistling wind and irregular clatter of iron wheels on uneven tracks persisted uninterrupted. My stomach began to rumble, reminding me that I had not eaten all day. Rummaging in my pocket I found the moldy bread and meat. Knowing that some of my companions might kill for food, even these lousy crumbs, I twisted round until I faced the barricade before stuffing as much as I could into my mouth. It did nothing to assuaged my hunger. Blessedly exhaustion finally overcame my suffering and I drifted off into a fitful sleep.

Dawn broke and with it the mist turned into a steady drizzle. We were already so cold and wet that even this added nothing to our misery. Our faces, hands and arms were streaked with grime from the smoke which continued to billow back from the locomotive and our eyes were bloodshot from the grit, wind and lack of sleep. Looking at my companions' blackened faces reminded me of the plantation slaves and I wondered how they had fared over the years and where they were now. I felt sure that even the field hands must be better fed and clothed than me. Try as I might I could not push these disquieting thoughts aside

Confederate Gold
The Missing Treasure

and, far from helping, the coming of daylight merely increased my depression.

The train kept up its sluggish pace through the dreary and desolate countryside. Small and apparently deserted homesteads, now visible in the watery dawn light, slipped by. Earlier such discouraging sights had been hidden by the kindly pall of night. Even the sun, trying to fight its way through the heavy overcast, did nothing to brighten my mood. Occasionally we rattled through a small town where there was some sign of life but the people, distractedly going about their routine daily tasks, paid no attention to the Presidential train.

"All this for our precious cabinet and their upstart families," one of the group muttered, summing up the feelings of most of us. "As though we haven't done enough already."

"There's more than the cabinet on this train," said another with a quiet air of authority. The complaining stopped as he continued. "Did any of you notice those boxes they were carefully stowing in the front two freight cars last night? And did you see how they locked and barred the doors when they were finished?"

"Yea, I noticed that."

"What do you know that we don't?"

"Yea. Tell us what you know. Come on don't hold back."

"We're all in this thing together."

Everyone started shouting at the same time, eager for any news that would help take our minds off our present situation.

"I'll bet it was gold" he whispered, his eyes sparkling.

"Gold!" The word was repeated up and down the flat bed as each envisioned the treasure that might be lying but a few feet from us. Wealth that could take us out of our present, and possibly future, misery for none of us knew what our end might be.

Suddenly a voice from the far end put everyone's thoughts into words. "If it's gold it's Confederate gold, our gold. We haven't been paid for months and if the Yanks get their thieving hands on it we never will be. What say we take it first chance we get? I reckon we're entitled to it."

The flat bed quickly became divided into two groups, one opting to take the gold and go home, while the other chose to protect it and continue the fight. Arguments raged back and forth all morning and, but for the confines of the flat bed, would have become violent. Even so a few fists flew as each side tried to persuade the other. I was for taking the gold but, as the day wore on, loyalty to the Confederacy slowly prevailed among us and by early afternoon thoughts of stealing the gold had been abandoned, at least for the time being.

After fourteen interminable hours the train finally chugged to a halt on the outskirts of Danville on the border of Virginia and North Carolina. It was late afternoon as we painfully climbed down onto the tracks, thankful for any movement that would loosen our cramped limbs and add an element of warmth to our bodies.

Although only twenty-five, I felt like an old man. My aching bones and stiff joints cried out for the soothing motion of the rocking chair back in the old plantation house kitchen rather than the further aggravation of a rocking flat bed. Slowly we limped back and forth along the length of the train giving a poor imitation of guarding the passengers. As each of us approached the engine we glanced at the two bolted and chained freight cars and wondered.

The drizzle had stopped and a watery sun offered some degree of warmth. Gradually my spirits rose as I chewed on the last of my meager rations while the pain in my limbs lessened. Now I was prepared to go on when the order came. But no order came. The train remained stationary on the outskirts of the town and my feeling of well-being started to sink with the setting sun.

"Looks like we're going to spend another miserable night trying to sleep on those damned flat beds," Ben Parsons, a grizzled veteran of thirty, muttered as we ambled from one end

Confederate Gold
The Missing Treasure

of the train to the other. "But by the looks of things they won't be moving which might prove a small blessing."

"Guess you're right," I said.

As if our mutterings had been a catalyst for action, no sooner were the words out of our mouths than we were ordered to board the train. The huge driving wheels skidded on the damp rails then gripped and at a slow walking pace we pulled into Danville. Somehow the driver managed to avoid the congestion of broken down rolling stock, before finally bringing the train to rest in a siding. Here Captain Parker gave us permission to wash in a nearby water tank.

To a man we leapt off the flat bed and, ignoring the gasps from the ladies on the train, stripped off our clothes. Naked, we plunged in, frolicking and splashing about like a group of school kids. The grime dropped from our hands and faces and the breathtakingly cold water revived our spirits. With no means of drying ourselves we ran up and down rails, stepping on the cross ties to avoid the gravel beds, until dry enough to don our old rags.

"That should give those stuck-up women something to talk about for the rest of their lives," drawled a skinny, bearded Tennesseean who answered to the name of Elijah. "Bet they've never seen anything like what we've got between our legs. Must have given them a fair old thrill."

The laughter that greeted this remark was cut short by Captain Parker who, returning from the city at that moment, had witnessed our display.

"You disgusting rabble!" he exploded. "You're not fit to wear the uniform of the Confederacy. I will personally shoot the next man that brings such disgrace on the uniform. Have I made myself clear."

The awkward silence that followed clearly showed that he had. In the short time we had been under Parker's command we had come to realize he was a strict disciplinarian and did not make idle threats.

Bill Westhead

"Form file," he said. His voice was again that of a man in complete control and we jumped to obey.

"We are to stay here the night," he continued, as we faced him. "You will stand guard, fifteen men at a time. Each detail will spend two hours on and six off. Time off is for sleep. Let me not catch any one of you prowling the streets of Danville."

Guard details were quickly organized and the first group despatched about its duties. Being in the third group, I had four hours before call and within a few minutes was sound asleep, despite the hard, uneven flat bed floor. It was as black as a mine shaft when we were awakened and reluctantly climbed down onto the tracks to face two hours of drudgery.

"Do you really believe this train is carrying gold?" I asked Ben Parsons, as we trudged towards the front of the train.

"Not only believe, but know," the Virginian said. "It's right there in those two cars." He pointed forward to the now infamous freight cars. "I saw them load it."

"You did!" I said my voice rising in surprise.

"Quiet you idiot. You don't want to wake the whole train," he said, punching me on the shoulder. The blow was light but, I guessed, as hard as this frail, hundred pound man could deliver.

"Sorry," I whispered. "You know I really thought we were guarding the President and his cabinet."

"So we are my friend," Ben said, "so we are. Jefferson Davis intends to fight on but he's going to need all the money he can get. I for one haven't been fighting these last four hellish years to quietly surrender now. Not even for all the gold up there," he added, as we drew level with the freight cars. "We're going to use that gold to continue the fight and woe betide anyone who tries to take it while I'm alive."

I was silent. Any lingering ideas I might have had of helping myself to a little of the treasure lying behind those bolted doors was squashed by Ben's vehement outburst.

The following day we waited, expecting at any moment to be ordered to continue our journey. Nothing came that day or the

Confederate Gold
The Missing Treasure

next. The train sat silently in the siding as though exhausted by its flight from Richmond. When not on guard duty I lay around thinking, wistfully, of gold and my own future.

Even the arrival of General Breckenridge, which in earlier times would have been an occasion for a military parade, did nothing to stir us out of our apathy. Only when he ordered the opening of one of the two freight cars did we show any interest. The sight of two officers staggering across the siding carrying a large wooden box between them would become a major topic of discussion in the days that followed.

Seven days later we were all still in Danville when, like wild horses, rumor ran through the town that General Lee had surrendered. No one believed it. It had to have been put about by the blue-bellies for there was no way the General, the saviour of the South, would surrender. We did not learn the truth of it until General Breckenridge made his announcement later in the day. My stomach lurched into my mouth as I listened to the dull-voiced statement. There was no need for words the tears said it all. The war was over. With the South finally crushed, we were now at the mercy of the victors.

"We need to get out of here and save ourselves," Elijah said, as the two of us wandered listlessly along the tracks. "There's nothing left to fight for but our own scrawny necks. I'm heading home."

"I'm with you," I answered.

If Captain Parker had been a few minutes later his command would have been reduced by, at least, two guards. But at the very moment we were about to leave he rushed out from behind the engine.

"Board," he ordered, as he hurtled past and continued his headlong flight along the tracks, becoming more and more breathless each time he repeated the order.

"What a great commander he is," Elijah said, nodding in the direction of the disappearing Captain. "We've been here for days doing nothing. Now disaster strikes he suddenly decides to take action. God help us if we run into any Yankees. We'll be dead before he'll give the order to fire."

"Not his fault," I said. "He's under orders just like us, but his come from the President. Jefferson Davis is the one that's caused us to dally here, meeting up with his family and trying to organize and open government offices."

"Suppose you're right," Elijah grumbled, as we settled once more into our, now familiar, positions on the flat bed and waited for the train to continue its crawl south. We knew at the outset this journey would be hazardous but now, with the South's surrender, the Yankees would be looking to roundup every Johnny Reb they could. The danger to everyone on the train had suddenly increased ten-fold.

Unlike the journey from Richmond, the second stage to Greensboro, North Carolina was short and uneventful. Even the weather cooperated. By nightfall we were thankful to be holed up in yet another railroad siding. Compared with Danville, our arrival in Greensboro was a triumph. Compatriots surrounded the train as it groaned to a halt and raised a ragged cheer as Jefferson Davis stepped down. A man in a resplendent, though well worn, general's uniform ceremoniously stepped forward. In contrast to ourselves his face was clean shaven, except for a neatly trimmed moustache and goatee beard.

"Welcome to my headquarters Mr. President," he said, his hand raised in salute.

"We thank you General Beauregard for your hospitality, more particularly under our present trying circumstances," the President replied, taking the General's proffered hand. "However, we regret our stay must, of necessity, be short. It is essential we continue our journey as soon as possible."

As the President and General continued to exchange words we tumbled down from the flat-bed hoping we too might shake the hand of the man who had directed the bombardment of Fort Sumter back in '61, the first military action of the war.

Confederate Gold
The Missing Treasure

"I understand the situation Mr. President," Beauregard said. "But in the meantime if you and your party will follow me we will repair to my headquarters."

At this the two men strode across the tracks towards a large house followed, at a distance, by the Cabinet members and their families.

That night and the following morning we spent on endless and, we reckoned, futile guard duty. Ben Parsons and me were about to finish our detail when a disheveled force of armed soldiers, wearing tattered Confederate uniforms, ambled into the siding. We, along with the rest of the guards on duty at the time, stopped and stared at the oncoming troops, unsure of their purpose. It seemed to us unlikely they were looking for the President or any of his party. So why were they here?

Suddenly my heart started to pound in my chest and the small hairs on the back of my neck stirred as the thought struck me that this group intended to rob the train.

"I reckon you're right!" Ben said, as I whispered the thought in his ear. "We must rouse the rest of the lads. That gold's ours."

Constantly yelling, "The freight cars are being robbed," we stumbled along the uneven tracks to the front of the train. Hearing our shouts the reserve details, including Captain Parker, tumbled to the ground and followed, like a family of ants protecting the queen.

By the time we reached the locked and barred cars the unkempt group of Confederates had wheeled towards them. There was no longer any doubt in our minds that their objective was the gold. I, along with several others, crawled under the front car. With my eyes sighted along the barrel of my rifle I watched, with mixed emotions, as the ragged band approached.

The threat of imminent bloodshed, particularly my own, rekindled the old fears that had lain dormant in me for some months. An involuntary shudder swept through me and I wriggled closer to the iron wheels for protection. There was something sinister and yet pitiable about the men. I imagined them, less than two years ago, swinging northwards heads held high and a purpose in their step. Now, on poorly shod feet, they shuffled towards us shoulders stooped and eyes downcast. I had seen slaves adopt a similar posture after being beaten by my father. The appearance of these once proud soldiers seemed to epitomize what had become of the once proud South?

A few yards from the freight cars they stopped and we held our breath. Whether or not we fired on our own side would be decided by their next move. I glanced in Captain Parker's direction. He lay, seemingly immobile, his revolver aimed at the tall, thin man who appeared to be in command of the column.

"Lay down your arms. I am here to open that freight car," the man said in a voice that tolerated no argument.

There was no answer from our side.

"I am Colonel Jackson in command of this detail. I am here to open that freight car and I order you to lay down your arms."

At this Captain Parker found his voice. "By whose authority?" he shouted back.

"By the authority of General Beauregard signed by the President," said Jackson, waving a piece of paper in the air.

"Cover me," Parker said, as he slowly crawled out from beneath the freight cars. With his revolver still aimed at the Colonel, he approached the column. My eyes watered as I continued to squint along the barrel of my rifle, ready to fire should anything go amiss. If we could not have the treasure no one else would. The Captain read the paper twice, then gave the signal for us to lower our rifles.

Taking a bunch of heavy keys from his belt Parker handed them to Jackson who immediately marched up to the front freight car. Without a word he opened the locks and removed the chains. Then he ordered four of his men to pass down two large chests before bolting and chaining the doors again. As the two chests were unlocked we gaped at the sight that met our eyes. The chests were filled with sacks. As first one and then another was opened, the sunlight glinted on the silver coins inside. There

Confederate Gold
The Missing Treasure

was more silver in those two chests than I imagined to be in the whole world.

"Whoever said those chests contained gold, lied," I whispered to Ben.

"What d'ya mean?"

"That looks more like silver to me," I said, as the Colonel handed out a given number of coins to each bedraggled man in his column.

"So what," Ben said. "All spends the same way."

"Yes," I said, wondering how many more chests were still in the two freight cars. There was no longer any doubt that the train was carrying more than just the Presidential party.

What little news trickled through to us in Greensboro merely confirmed our plight. General Stoneman's Yankee cavalry was now raiding through the heartland of the Confederacy destroying the railroads, our railroads, the railroads we had to travel if Jefferson Davis was to continue the fight. As each report came in it became more and more certain that within the next day or two we would have to abandon the train and take to our own flat feet.

"I'm a sailor," John Arnold grumbled. "Prefer the rolling deck under my feet not hard tramped earth. My feet weren't made for marching."

"Nor your body for a prison camp," I said, slapping his thin shoulder. "Remember what was said on the train. I'm a sailor too but better we march than fall into Yankee hands."

"Suppose it is," he said reluctantly, brushing back his dark hair. "Course if we'd been allowed to keep moving instead of hanging around all day we'd probably have been there by now, wherever there is. Not sitting here worrying about damned Stoneman and his cut throat, nag-riding rabble."

A few hours later our suspicions were confirmed when Captain Parker was heard requisitioning the Commissary Department of General Beauregard's army for wagons and ambulances, sufficient to move our entire group cross country should this become necessary. All available flat beds in the

Bill Westhead

Greensboro yard were added to the train but there were still not sufficient to carry the requisitioned vehicles. Even when the barricades from our own flat beds were removed to make more space some commandeered vehicles had to be left behind.

With every wagon crammed full the engine was clearly overburdened. It moved so slowly that all of us aboard wondered if it would ever make our next destination. A new sport now presented itself as the slowness of the train allowed us to jump down onto the tracks, jog along for a short time, then climb back. Stupid though this action might appear it broke the monotony of our agonizingly slow flight south. "Stoneman will never catch us at this rate," Elijah said sarcastically as, for the umpteenth time, we jumped down from the flat bed.

"No," I answered in like tone. "I guess we're walking faster than they can ride."

Although there had been no confirmed sightings of Yankee cavalry during our twelve hour trek to Charlotte there had been several false alarms which added to our nervousness. The Charlotte stop, like the previous ones in Danville and Greensboro, proved to be another frustrating delay broken only by news received on the second day.

As we lounged around the siding trying, in vain, to keep out of the blazing heat of the afternoon sun the quiet was suddenly shattered by tremendous cheering and shouting from the direction of the town square.

"What the hell's that about?" I asked Ben.

"Don't know," he said, "but I suppose we ought to go and find out. We could do with some good news for a change."

The nearer we got to the noise the more crowded the streets became. Pushing forward we finally arrived at the square only to stop dead in our tracks at the sight that met our eyes. Soldiers and civilians mingled together, dancing about like dervishes and hurling anything they could lay their hands on into the air..

"What the hell's going on?" I shouted to a young woman nearby, who was whirling about frantically. Her skirts, billowing

Confederate Gold
The Missing Treasure

out from a hand-span waist allowed sight of a shapely leg and fine ankle which, in an instant, became of more interest than any news.

"Lincoln's dead," she shrieked. "The devil's gone where he deserves."

Not sure I had heard correctly I grabbed her round the waist and pulled her towards me forcing her to stop her gyrations. Suddenly she threw her arms round my neck. "What did you just say," I shouted above the din while, at the same time, my arms automatically moved to encircle her waist.

"Lincoln's dead," she said, repeating the phrase again and again like a child learning to read. Each time her voice rose until it finally became an hysterical scream. Then she broke my embrace and danced off into the crowd.

It was difficult to believe what I had just heard but after months of disaster following disaster any good news was welcome, no matter what. Without even a glance at Ben I followed the girl into the crowd, shouting and waving my arms like everyone else. By now it had dawned on me that if, indeed, Lincoln was dead our troubles were over. With him out of the way I had no doubt in my mind the South would rise again. Little did I know at the time that what we were fervently celebrating, far from offering us salvation, heralded even worse disasters.

Towards sunset I found Ben and, exhausted from the days affair, we returned together to the siding.

The following morning I watched as yet another treasure chest was unloaded to pay the troops in the town.

"Go on like this there won't be a damned thing left for us," Ben grumbled, as we saw the now empty chest hurled onto the side of the track.

Returning to our flat bed we were surprised to find Parker standing atop it, arms folded and a smile lighting his usually stern features. "Grab yourselves a shirt while you can," he said, pointing to a pile of blue shirts under the wagon.

"You'll look like a damned Yankee boy in that shirt," Elijah said, as we eagerly obeyed the Captain's orders. "Likely as not I'd kill you if I didn't know you." A huge, friendly hand slammed into my chest sending me staggering into the side of the wagon.

"I'd get you first," I answered, picking myself up.

The good hearted banter continued. With Lincoln dead and a change of clothing, even if only a shirt, our spirits soared. We were far from defeated.

"We make for Chester, South Carolina tonight," Parker said, as he climbed down and started towards the head of the train.

"Thought we were going north again to win this damned war," we shouted after him.

"Not yet me boys," Parker said jovially, then added philosophically, "but who knows what the future will bring."

Fortunately we did not.

Confederate Gold
The Missing Treasure

CHAPTER 6

"Where do you think you're going with that thing?" a soldier standing at the side of the tracks yelled as the train, with a last gasp effort, chugged into Chester. The mists of early morning swirled about his tall, lean frame giving him a wraith-like appearance. Like those around him, he was clad in the remnants of what had once been a Confederate uniform. The left sleeve, knotted at the shoulder, indicated his own physical contribution to the cause.

"We're heading south to continue the war," I replied from my vantage point astride a wagon shaft atop the flat bed.

"Thought the war was north of here," he drawled.

By now we were all lined up along the edge of the flat bed staring down at the rabble walking alongside the ever- slowing train.

"We'll be going back north again very soon," we shouted above the derisive laughter and taunts of the unknown soldier and his comrades.

"Sounds a good idea," they yelled in unison, "'cause that thing's no good here. We ain't got no railroad tracks. So you'd best be off north."

As if by mutual agreement we turned and stared steadfastly to our front, trying to ignore the sarcastic jeers that continued to come from the group.

"Does this thing go cross country on its own wheels or does it need danged tracks?" The jibes persisted. "We're telling you there ain't no tracks south of here. The blue- bellies have torn them up so we reckon you'll all be walking if you're going south. Go north and fight."

Although we did not want to show this rabble their last taunt had struck home we were, nevertheless, stunned. More particularly as it had been delivered with a strong sounding element of truth. We had loaded the wagons expecting to have to walk part of the journey, but not as soon as this. It was the first clue we had of the havoc being wreaked by marauding Union cavalry. The thought of trying to protect a slow moving horse drawn wagon train, through country now in the hands of a merciless enemy, filled us with dread. I had visions of the Yankees helping themselves to our gold, while I lay there choking on my own blood. It seemed so real that a violent shiver shook my body from head to foot. To cover my embarrassment at this outward show of fear, I leapt down from the train and approached the tattered troops who were now lounging in the damp grass.

"What the hell would you know about the tracks being destroyed," I demanded.

They looked up at me with lifeless eyes as I plunged on, not caring now what I said. "Doesn't look as though you've done a danged thing to stop the blue-bellies judging by the way you're lazing around here."

The tall, lean man who had started the taunts rose, unhurriedly, to his feet. By the time he had uncoiled to his full height of over six feet I found myself staring directly at his chin. Without warning his right hand shot out and grabbed me by the shoulder. Strong boney fingers dug into my flesh. The quick whip of his wrist took me unawares and I found myself spinning round before finishing face down in the grass, a foot in the middle of my back.

"Don't come here telling us what we've done or not done for the South." The voice above me was low and menacing. "We've seen more action these last three weeks than you've ever dreamed of, guarding these damned tracks and repairing them as fast as we could. We've been shot at, bayonetted and plain ridden down by that bastard Stoneman and his blue- bellied gang. Of the seventy men that started out on this mission you can count those that are left."

Confederate Gold
The Missing Treasure

The foot was removed from my back and a swift kick in my side rolled me over. Fortunately the foot was not booted, merely covered in rags. Recovering my breath I sat up and took a closer look at the group. I counted fourteen.

"Sorry, I didn't know," I muttered. The tall soldier nodded as if accepting this weak apology while the group turned their backs on me and slouched off across the fields in the direction of the town.

"Best get back to your own job," the big man said, as he offered his hand to help me to my feet. "See if you can do any better than we did."

"Thanks," I said, turning to leave. As I did so a large foot in my rear propelled me on my stumbling way. I felt like a child being chastised by an irate parent.

While this confrontation had been going on the train had finally come to rest in yet another siding. From some distance away I could see the area was a hive of activity with the wagons and ambulances being off-loaded and lined up alongside the tracks.

"So it's true is it?" I shouted to the first man I saw.

"Is what true?" he said, pushing a wagon to the edge of the flat bed before helping man-handle to the ground.

"There are no tracks south of here?"

"You've got it. From now on we walk. And what's more you'd best be seen working not standing around if you know what's good for you."

Dodging through a melee of men and wagons I finally found my own group and for the next two hours sweated through the unloading of the train, obeying an endless stream of orders and counter orders. Despite the apparent chaos everything, including the boxes from the two freight cars, had been transferred to the wagons by mid morning. But problems in commandeering horses delayed us and it was early afternoon before we finally set out on our trek southwards.

Bill Westhead

As the heavily laden wagons began to move out of the siding it was apparent the horses, many in poor condition, would be hard pressed to make Newberry. But the slow, early going was nothing compared with what lay ahead. To avoid detection by the Union cavalry we immediately took to the back roads on leaving Chester. At best these were little more than cart tracks. Now the recent heavy rains had turned them into a quagmire of cloying mud that stuck like pine resin to feet, hoofs and wagon wheels alike. Hour after hour humans and horses alike struggled to keep the column moving through the incessant ooze. Progress was so painfully slow that our earlier journey by train began to seem like an enjoyable gallop. While we fought and swore our way through the stinking morass we became increasingly aware of our vulnerability and by late in the day many wished the Yankees would attack and put an end to our misery.

As dusk fell over the miserable landscape we drew up at a large building where a sign above the main entranced announced it to be the Woodward Baptist Church. Immediately orders were given for the families and senior officers to take refuge inside the building. The rest, excluding those detailed for guard duty, were ordered to bed down in the wagons. Only too thankful that the day had finally ended we stretched our pain-racked bodies between treasure boxes and family possessions. Dazed by hunger and exhaustion we slept undisturbed by the continuous rain splattering on the canvas covers, which boded ill for the morrow.

By morning the rain had turned to a fine, soaking drizzle and by mid day the clinging mud and slime brought the column to a halt. As weakened horses and spent men strained to free the wagons Mrs. Jefferson Davis took matters into her own hands. Climbing down from the relative comfort of her own wagon, she lifted her youngest child onto her back, hoisted her skirts up to her knees and squelched off on foot through the grasping sludge. Other ladies with their children, shamed by this action, followed her example. With the wagons lightened the convoy was again able to struggle forward.

Confederate Gold
The Missing Treasure

Up to this moment I had thought of these women as mere trappings of their husbands' positions. Now, as I watched them stagger through the mire alongside the wagons, my admiration for them grew with every step they took. At times they sank up to their knees in the muck but there was never one word of complaint throughout the day. By the time we camped for the night, they had gained the undying respect of every male in the column.

Rains caught in canvas buckets provided a steady supply of drinking water but food was quickly becoming a prime concern. As soon as the new camp site was established a number of the guards, despite their exhaustion, volunteered to form a foraging party while the rest of us tried to get some rest. Although it seemed I spent the whole night in fitful sleep it could not have been more than two hours before the sound of hoarse cheers woke me. Through sleep-filled eyes I saw the foragers return with somebody's precious hog slung from a rough cut tree branch, blood still dripping from its slit throat. For a moment I thought it was a dream but when I felt someone trip over my outstretched feet I knew it was real.

Eagerly I joined the troops who, unmindful of any enemy that might be in the vicinity, had started to build a fire. Like children we milled around the flames our wet clothes steaming in the heat. The smell of roasting pig the likes of which we had not tasted in months made our mouths drool. We rooted in the embers and, ignoring burns, scratched for the bits that fell from the sizzling meat. Women and children were rudely shoved aside in the increasing frenzy.

It took the officers, using whatever weapons they could lay hands on, some time to regain control of this madness. Finally a line was formed, women and children at the front followed by the officers then the men. There were so many heads in front of me I felt certain nothing would be left when my turn came but, eventually, a piece of meat was thrust into my hands and I sprinted towards the trees stuffing my mouth as I went. Even

Bill Westhead

now I feared someone might butcher me for this tidbit. My few good teeth bit into the hot, succulent flesh. Constantly I wiped my hand across my chin then licked the grease from my fingers so as not to waste any part of this juicy morsel. While it was the best food I had ever tasted it was not long before my stomach rebelled at this delicacy viciously thrust into it and I was violently sick.

This night the officers and families slept in the wagons while we found cover under the wagons or in the woods on either side of the track. Finally the rains stopped and a cloudless sky greeted us the following morning. The sodden ground steamed in the drying rays of the sun, enveloping the convoy in a ghostly mist. The musty odor of rotten vegetation hung in the still air. As each hour passed the going became easier, but the effort exerted by everyone the previous day had taken its toll, especially on the women and children. By early afternoon it was clear that many, including the gallant Mrs. Jefferson Davis, would never make Newberry on foot.

"You must rest in one of the wagons Ma'am," I heard Captain Parker say politely but firmly, as the President's exhausted wife once more sank to her knees.

"I will do no such thing sir," the lady protested, as she struggled to her feet. "There are others more in need than I. Let them ride. I will walk."

"Ma'am," Parker insisted, "without you rest you will not make Newberry and, as we cannot abandon you, nor shall we. I hate to give you a direct order, but if needs be I must. Again Ma'am I ask you to ride for all our sakes. Will you be kind enough to do as I bid."

Realizing that further argument was useless the courageous lady and her family reluctantly climbed into their wagon.

A few minutes later I was ordered to check that the President's wife and family were safe. Lifting the back canvas cover of the wagon I saw that, overcome by exhaustion, she and the children had fallen into a deep sleep. Even the pitching of the

*Confederate Gold
The Missing Treasure*

vehicle as it lurched from rut to rut did not appear to disturb them. They were still sound asleep when our party staggered into Newberry that evening.

As the column came to a halt every man collapsed. Some slid down the mud covered wagon wheels their backs propped against the spokes, some sank to their knees simply too weary to take another step, while others lay flat on the ground. The horses, heads hanging low and legs trembling, looked as though they too were on the point of collapse. It seemed only the wagon shafts and harnesses held them upright. A sorrier group I had never seen or wished to see again.

From my position, propped against a wagon wheel, I watched in wonder as the indefatigable Parker strode off in the direction of the railroad station. Like us he had spent the last three days slogging through all embracing mud but, unlike us, he seemed tireless. Even now, I suspected, he was planning the next stage of our journey. Could this be the same man, I wondered, who had dawdled in Danville, Greensboro and Charlotte delays which, I felt sure, had resulted in the our present plight? Watching him disappear round the corner of the station building, I prayed that whatever lay ahead would not be as exhausting as the trek we just completed, for I doubted I could live through it again.

I must have dozed off for it seemed only minutes before he came marching back across the square shouting as he went. I guessed that our rest, if it could be called that, was to be short lived and I was right.

"No time to rest boys," I heard him yell while still some fifty yards away. "The tracks are intact from here to Abbeville and we must move at once before they too are destroyed. Come, we've a train to load."

Without a word we struggled to our feet and shuffled off to the appointed siding.

"The Presidential party will follow us to Abbeville on horseback," Parker said, seeing our bewildered faces as we stared at the three freight cars and three flat beds that made up this new train. "They will be escorted by our cavalry."

Working like zombies throughout the rest of the night we loaded the treasure into the two front freight cars and what wagons we could stack onto the three flat beds. Just before dawn the loading was finished and we were ordered into the third freight car.

"Guess we're riding in luxury this time," Ben Parsons said, as we hastily scrambled aboard.

The locomotive gave a long piercing whistle, the iron wheels skidded on the wet track then grabbed and, with a clatter of couplings, the train lurched forward. It was not long before the gentle swaying of the freight car had an hypnotic effect and, free from the wind and grime of our earlier train journey, we slept the sleep of the damned.

We were awakened by the sound of the freight car door grating on its rusty runners. Reluctant to return to the misery of the real world, I opened one eye in time to see Captain Parker leap down onto the tracks. In a daze I wondered if he was deserting us and the thought brought me to my senses. If he was going, so was I. Staggering to the open door I glanced out to see a group of elderly men huddled together on the station platform. Despite their well worn frock coats and crumpled tall hats it appeared they were there in some official capacity. Any idea of deserting vanished. I lounged against the side of the freight car and watched Parker march towards them.

"Good day to you gentlemen of Abbeville," I heard him say as he approached. "We crave your services in defense of our beloved Confederacy."

At Parker's words a look of abject fear swept across the face of every individual in the group. If Parker noticed he chose to ignore it.

"We have on board," he said, pointing to the train, "monies to continue the war. We need your help to keep them safe from the thieving Yankees for a short period of time."

Confederate Gold
The Missing Treasure

"Much as we would like to we dare not help you," the officials chorused to a man, holding up their hands as if fending off evil spirits.

For a moment Parker seemed utterly speechless and I saw his fists clench as if fighting to control of himself. "You cowards," he finally spluttered. "You're refusing to help our cause. You're prepared to let your President and his family suffer, as though they haven't suffered enough already. You'll let our gallant boys continue to die without even one of you lifting a rotten finger to help. I can tell by your faces you think the South is finished?"

The city officials bowed their heads at this tirade and backed away as Parker, his temper thoroughly roused, moved towards them. Finally one of the group, shame showing on his shrunken features, shuffled forward.

"We're not cowards," he said, his voice cracking with emotion. "but the Yankee cavalry is raiding near Pendleton. If they found out we were hiding Confederate money what chance would you give the people of this town? We daren't let you unload the train here. You must take it on to wherever you're going." Having spoken his piece the man shuffled back to the group.

Parker turned on his heel. His face was flushed as he climbed back into the car and his beard twitched as he muttered under his breath.

"I bet those mealy-mouthed cowards cheer when the President arrives. Perhaps he can make them change their tune," he said, storming up and down the freight car.

Parker was still fuming when, two hours later, the presidential party rode into town. "See what I mean," he said, as ragged cheering greeted their arrival. "Those bastards will applaud the man but I doubt will chance their scrawny necks to help him. What's more," he added, "I bet they won't have the guts to tell him to his face." Face still flushed he climbed down and marched out of the station to make his report.

Bill Westhead

He was back within the half hour.

"Unload the train and hitch the wagons." he commanded, as he strode down the platform. "The President refuses to endanger this cowardly lot and orders us to make for Washington as fast as possible."

"Washington!" Elijah said, his eyebrows almost touching the peak of his grimy cap. "Thought we were going south."

"Washington, Georgia, fool," Parker snapped.

We could not know that this order and successive counter orders would result in a cat and mouse chase across the hills and plains of north Georgia as, in the days ahead, we strived to evade an ever increasing number of Yankee cavalry troops.

We struggled across the Savannah River on a swaying pontoon bridge hastily erected by civilians but, on arrival in Washington, learned the likelihood of capture increased by the minute. We were ordered to reload and head for Augusta by rail. Finding ourselves in even greater danger there the train was immediately turned round and sent back to Washington. Here some nameless high ranking officer decided we had a better chance of avoiding capture if we continued on foot. Again we transferred the treasure to the wagons and in time finished back in Abbeville. In the ten days that had elapsed since our last visit we had covered over two hundred miles, eaten little except what we could beg or steal, exhausted ourselves with loading and unloading trains, fought our way along mud-splattered roads and not progressed one mile further south.

"Why the hell are we back here?" Ben voiced the question that was on everyone's lips as we pulled in. "They didn't help us before, why should they now?"

"We're just running round in circles going nowhere," Elijah grumbled, pushing long fingers through his red hair. "As God is my witness I'd rather stand and fight those bloody Yankees than work myself to death like this."

Confederate Gold
The Missing Treasure

"I reckon we're going to have to sooner or later," I said, without conviction. Truth to tell, I was so hungry and exhausted that I had no stomach for anything, least of all a fight.

"How long do you reckon we're going to be here this time round?" Elijah asked.

It was clear no one, not even those in command, knew the answer to this question. What had started out from Richmond as a great crusade to enable the South to continue the war, had now degenerated into a desperate race for survival.

To our surprise Jefferson Davis and his party were still in Abbeville along with their escort of four skeleton brigades of cavalry. While we had been running round the countryside in circles the President, it appeared, had put his time to good use for now the city officials were willing to let us store the treasure in a warehouse on the edge of the square. That night, for the first time since leaving Richmond, we all got a good night's rest.

Everyone expected us to be on the move again the next day but nothing happened. Despite our situation growing more desperate as each day past, no one seemed ready or willing to decide the fate of the gold which remained stored in the warehouse under guard.

"As sure as hell that gold ain't going nowhere unless it sprouts wings and flies," Elijah complained, on the morning of our fourth day of inactivity. "I don't know why we don't just load it up and drive it to the nearest damned Yankee camp leave it there and all go home," he continued. Then, as an after thought added, "Those of us that have a home left."

It seemed as if fate now took a hand, for less than an hour after Elijah had given vent to his feelings, Captain Parker summoned the guards.

"Midshipmen," he began. A chill ran through my spine. We knew he only used that address when he had something of great import to say. I stood with the others and waited. "A squadron of cavalry have recced the countryside south of here," he continued, "and determined a safe route for the Presidential party. The treasure has been handed over to the care of General Duke and is to go with them. The President dismisses you with thanks for your loyalty and wishes you God's speed as you journey home to your loved ones."

"If we have a home and loved one's to go to," a voice behind me mumbled.

Having delivered his last order Parker strode off. Many, including me, wondered if we would ever see him again. No one spoke and it was several minutes before men who had faced death every day for years began unashamedly to hug each other and openly wipe tears from their eyes. I was no different as Elijah and Ben left to go their separate ways.

At last only six of us remained, lost souls with nowhere to go, wondering what the next few hours might bring. There seemed little point in thinking any farther into a future as the only choices offered were starvation, disease, capture or death. Finally deciding there was only one action we could take we asked permission to remain as guards. Better to die fighting with comrades, we argued, than to be shot or worse, tortured and killed on some lonely southern road.

With permission reluctantly granted we were again ordered to reload the wagons. This time the people of Abbeville rallied to assist us. Their relief at our removing the gold was apparent for all to see and the nearer we got to completing our task the more polite smiles replaced sullen frowns.

Poor fools, I thought. They think the danger will pass as soon as we move out. They don't know the danged Yankees.

The troop of cavalry that was to accompany us was a poor sight to behold, no longer the pride of the south. The glossy coated, prancing horses and proud owners of yesteryear were now nothing more than under fed nags wearily carrying unkempt riders. Many of the men had lost limbs while others bore the marks of poorly healed injuries. Despite this I still recalled their earlier invincibility and clung desperately to that thought. I even

Confederate Gold
The Missing Treasure

deluded myself that, with them to guard us, the gold would finally reach its destination.

"Where to this time?" I shouted to one of the cavalry soldiers, as he trotted by our sweating loading party.

"Washington, Georgia."

"Washington!" I yelled, echoing the cry that went up from the rest of the loading gang. The jovial mood of those around me fizzled faster than a sputtering candle in a gale. Mentally and physically we sagged. What a moment before had been light work suddenly became a burdensome task. It was a despondent crew that finally finished the loading.

Within the hour we found ourselves trudging back along the same dreary road we had traversed only a few days earlier. As we passed the same neglected homesteads, I was again filled with a feeling of hopelessness. Nothing had changed. It was as if the clock had ceased to tick and time had stood still in sympathy with our lost cause. We passed the same unattended cattle which, I swear, had not moved since we had last seen them. The route seemed even longer and more deserted than before as we plodded forward.

By the second night out our feeling of desperation gave way to one of rebellion which came to a head the following morning when General Breckenridge arrived.

"Why are we running round in circles with this damned gold train?"

"Where are the bloody Yankees?"

"When do we get paid. Our families need the money?"

"This paper stuff is worthless. Where's the real money?"

"Where is the President?"

We hurled these and many other demands at him, while he sat his horse, his deep set eyes scowling at the motley gathering hemming him in on all sides. Suddenly he raised an imperious hand and a brooding silence, more ominous than the recent shouting, fell over the group. I felt the tension in the air just as, years ago, I had felt the uneasy quiet before a storm at sea. But this was not Mother Nature speaking, it was human beings driven to extremes of mental and physical endurance.

"Gentlemen." The General's educated but icy voice cut through the threatening silence. "In this our time of greatest adversity let us remember those who have given their lives for our gallant cause. Let not our actions shame their names and deeds. We are, and always will be, Southerners and gentlemen."

We stood like puppets waiting for someone to pull the strings as Breckenridge continued, hardly pausing for breath.

"Even now, with our great Confederacy at its lowest ebb, you are still the flag bearers of our cause. Your names and deeds will be recalled by future generations if you maintain the honor and trust reposed in you. Lose your honor or violate your trust and your names will be forever erased from the pages of history. You ask for payment for your services. Gentlemen your request is reasonable, although your method of address is scurrilous. Nevertheless you have my word, as a Southern officer and gentleman, that when this train reaches Washington fair payment will be made to every man present."

"General." A corporal in the cavalry stepped forward. Breckenridge glared at him, but said nothing.

"We will maintain our honor and will violate no trust placed in us. We will continue to guard this train to the last man if such be necessary. But—." The corporal paused, his eyes downcast. There was no sound, save that of his boots scuffing the ground as he shuffled from one foot to the other before continuing. "there is no assurance we will ever reach Washington. While we do not doubt your word we would ask that payment be made now and not upon arrival in Washington."

I held my breath, wondering what Breckenridge's reaction would be to so bold a speech.

"Gentlemen," he finally said, his voice calm. "If you wish me to comply instantly with my promise, so be it. Paymaster make out your payrolls immediately and deliver them to me."

Confederate Gold
The Missing Treasure

There was an explosion of pent up breath and hoarse cheers as the General turned his horse and trotted off towards a nearby house.

While the lists were being prepared we laughed and joked about our imminent fortunes. Thoughts of being able to buy food, however little, was enough to make our mouths water.

"Bring the wagons up to the house and report to the Paymaster," ordered Major Thompson, who wore an insignia announcing him to be a veteran of Ferguson's cavalry brigade.

With more speed than we had mustered in the last two weeks the horses were harnessed and the wagons moved as ordered.

"Unload the first two wagons and stack the boxes in the living room," ordered the Paymaster. "Then fall in outside."

Within two hours of General Breckenridge's arrival all was prepared and each man stood ready to thrust his hand through the open living room window and receive his pay. When the last man had been paid empty boxes were cast aside while those still containing monies were reloaded onto the wagons.

"See you boys in Washington," the General said, mounting his horse and raising his hand in a farewell salute.

"God bless you sir," a voice shouted from the crowd and a spontaneous cheer broke out as Breckenridge rode past the line and down the drive leading to the road. Each man he left behind now jingled twenty six dollars and twenty five cents of real money in his pocket.

In the few days we had been away Washington had changed for the worse. Our earlier visit had been greeted by half-hearted cheering. Now, only a few brave souls wandered the streets and, even they, turned their backs on us as though we carried the plague.

Empty of all feeling, except a gnawing hunger, we trudged wearily along the deserted, dirt strewn streets towards the old branch bank of the State of Georgia. Here we were commanded to stack the heavy chests in the bank vaults and await further orders. We could never have foreseen the nature of these, when they eventually came.

Confederate Gold
The Missing Treasure

CHAPTER 7

With the treasure secure in the bank vault a single guard was thought to be sufficient and, on the morning of our second day in Washington, that duty fell to me. Pacing the stone-flag floor I thought about all that had happened in the four weeks since we had left Richmond determined to carry on the war. I wondered at the lack of action or, even worse, the lack of direction by our leaders which had turned our noble resolve into one of self preservation. Damn them, I thought, as I glanced out of one of the bank's iron-grilled windows.

Not certain I had seen aright I turned, blinked and looked back. Sure enough a horse was galloping across the square towards the bank, a single seat buggy bouncing dangerously behind. The sight of the caped driver bobbing and swaying precariously like a rag doll, at each wild lurch of the vehicle, fascinated me. I stood rooted to the spot as he continued to urge the horse on as though the devil himself were on his heels.

Just when it seemed horse and buggy must crash into the front of the building the driver hauled back on the reins. The horse reared and its forelegs thrashed the air, like a prize fighter, before dropping back onto four feet and skidding to a stop directly in front of the bank doors. The driver's face was hidden under a wide brimmed hat but something about his gait, as he climbed down and started to limp up the stone steps, seemed familiar. I had a strange feeling that I had seen him somewhere before. He rapped loudly on the bolted doors.

"Your name and state your business," I shouted.

"Military business," he said, continuing to beat on the doors. "In the name of the President of the Confederacy open up at once. I do not have time to waste."

The voice, although raspy, also had a familiar ring to it. I hesitated. Then quietly I slid back the iron bolts all the time wondering if I would have the courage to shoot this man if it proved necessary. While many might have died because of my actions during the war I had never actually killed anyone in cold blood. With the doors unbolted I stood back, loaded rifle pointed directly at their center, and prayed that I would not have to pull the trigger. Taking a deep breath I said, "Enter, hands in the air."

The doors flew open and in the sunlight that slanted in from outside I saw the man's face. Although more ravaged than I remembered there was no mistaking those twinkling eyes and wry smile. My jaw dropped in astonishment and my rifle followed.

"By all that's holy!" Sangster said, his voice rising as he stared me. "I've been trapped. I would never have dreamt you, of all people, would have joined the damned Yankees? As God is my witness I'll die before you'll take me."

Before I could recover from my shock he slipped to one side and I felt the muzzle of a revolver pressed against the side of my head. "Now drop that rifle you scum," he hissed in my ear.

I did as he said.

"Desertion I can understand in these times, but joining the blue-bellies. That I will never understand. In there," he said, prodding me in the direction of a small room on the right, "and tell me why."

I obeyed staring stupidly at my erstwhile Captain and friend while he stood with his revolver pointed steadily at my head. I wondered if his strange behavior might be the result of some war injury of which I was not aware.

"I'll kill you if you don't answer," Sangster said calmly, as though killing was an every day experience for him. "I'll probably kill you anyway," he added.

"What the hell's got into you," I said, finding my voice as my temper started to overcome my fear. "What's all this damned nonsense about deserting and joining the blue-bellies. How the hell can I answer anything when I don't know what the hell you're talking about."

Confederate Gold
The Missing Treasure

"That's a Yankee uniform shirt you're wearing unless my eyes deceive me," he said.

Despite the belligerent tone of his voice relief welled up inside me. Although I knew I was not yet out of danger I started to laugh. At first it was little more than a chuckle but as Sangster's look turned from anger to amazement my chuckling increased until it became a full throated guffaw. "You stupid old fool," I gasped, as tears poured down my cheeks. "Captain Parker found these in Abbeville and gave them to us. They're better than the ones we had. You should have looked below the shirt before going out of your mind. Do these look like part of a Yankee uniform?" I pointed down to the mud splattered, torn and darned Confederate navy pants which, less than four years ago, I had worn with pride.

A grin slowly spread across his worn features. "Go get your rifle," he said, slipping his revolver back in its battered holster with a practiced hand. "And while you're at it bolt the bank doors. The danged place could have been robbed while we've been fooling around in here."

"So what have you been doing for the cause since we last met?" Sangster said, as I returned.

Briefly I recounted the frustrating events of my last four weeks guarding the gold train.

"Not much of a life for a seafaring man," he said when I had finished.

"No," I agreed.

"How the hell did you finish in Richmond in the first place?"

"I was ordered there after we'd scuttled the old ship."

"Ah yes, that's right. I'd forgotten." His voice sounded far away and I guessed he was back on the *Carolina II*.

"What about you?" I asked. "I see you've changed the rolling decks for a rolling buggy."

"Yes," he said.

Bill Westhead

I waited hoping he would offer some explanation. "And that limp?" I continued when it was clear he would say no more. "Don't recall you limping the last time I saw you."

"Did a couple of runs on another ship after we sank the *Carolina II*. Unlucky enough to encounter a damned Yankee patrol the night we came ashore the second time," he said. He looked straight at me, a lively yet thoughtful glint in his eyes. "Stopped a bayonet in the scuffle but managed to avoid death in a Yankee prison camp. It wasn't serious. We've all seen worse. But it was enough to finish my days at sea. What was serious though was that we lost the whole cargo. Of all the danged bad luck in the world my final run finished as a miserable failure. Still that was another time and another place."

"So what are you doing here?" I asked.

"I told you military business," he said. "I have orders to take $86,000 in gold coin and bullion from the Confederacy funds and hold it for emergency purposes at a secret location."

"Still trying to run Yankee blockades then," I said, as he waved a signed paper under my nose.

He chuckled. "You might call it that," he said, "but come I haven't all day to stand around much as I might like to. We all know those blue-bellies are closing in fast and I have to move. Now where's this gold I'm here to collect?"

"I can't just hand it over like that," I said. "I'll have get the keys from Captain Clark who, as you must well know, is now Acting Treasurer for the Confederacy. He'll want to see your orders too before he'll open the vault."

"Well you'd best go find him then," Sangster said, his hands clasped behind his back as he paced the room. "I've got to be out of here and well on my way before dark. Go on, I'll stand guard until you get back."

"But —," I started to argue.

"No buts," Sangster cut in. "I'm authorized by the President himself, so go and get this Clark and let's get a move on."

"Why don't you get him?" I asked.

Confederate Gold
The Missing Treasure

"'cause I don't know him and don't know where to find him," Sangster snapped. "Now for God's sake go."

His demand put me in a dilemma. I would be ignoring the President's order if I delayed but damned by Captain Clark if I left my post. Deciding I would rather face the wrath of Clark than the President I set off at a run across the square, turned left at the end and headed in the direction of the house being occupied by the new Acting Treasurer.

"I need you at the bank, sir," I said, saluting Clark as he answered the door. "A Captain Sangster has orders to take $86,000 and hide it in a secret place for use in emergencies.

"What!" Clark shouted, struggling into his uniform jacket. "I have no knowledge of this. Where is this man Sangster?"

"Guarding the vault sir."

At this Clark's face turned bright red. He pushed past me, swearing loudly, to tear down the street and across the square as fast as his short legs and portly frame allowed. I followed. We entered to find Sangster standing by a window whistling. From the look on his face he had obviously enjoyed the spectacle of Captain Clark's run.

"Good day to you Captain Clark," Sangster drawled in his charming southern manner which, I knew, he could turn on and off at will. "I have here, sir, an official paper signed by President Jefferson Davis himself authorizing you to hand over $86,000 to me for safe keeping."

"Safe keeping indeed," blustered Clark, grabbing the paper that Sangster held out to him. The bushy eyebrows knitted together and the long nose twitched as he read and re-read the paper. His actions left no doubt of his reluctance to hand over the money.

"While I do not pretend to understand the reasons behind this action, everything seems to be in order for the transfer," he said officiously, thrusting the paper back into Sangster's hand. Oil lamp in hand Clark led the way down to the vault. Selecting a large key from a bunch he carried secured to his waist belt, he

Bill Westhead

inserted it in the heavy door. "Singleton, assist the Captain load the bullion," he ordered, as he swung the door open.

"Yes sir," I said.

Under the eagle eye of the Acting Treasurer, we carried four large chests out to the waiting buggy. To me it looked like any other buggy and I could not believe Sangster, for all his bravado, was witless enough to drive round the countryside with the chests on display for all to see.

Without warning he collapse over the floorboards.

"You all right?" I asked in alarm, laying a hand on his shoulder.

"Fine," he said, straightening up. His hands now held two lengths of wood which I realized had been framing the buggy floor. With these pieces removed he slid back the whole floor revealing a large cavity into which the chests were quickly stowed. With the floor boards replaced no one would ever guess the driver was sitting on a fortune.

He saw the surprise on my face. "Designed and built it myself," said he proudly, tapping the last piece of the framing into place. Satisfied everything was secure he climbed onto the running board, took up the reins and, with a nonchalant wave, cantered quietly across the square.

I marvelled at his daring and composure. But for all that, as the buggy disappeared from sight, I wondered if I would ever see my old skipper again. Silently I prayed he would make his destination safely, wherever that might be. Aloud I voiced the hope that once the present chaos had passed we might meet again under happier circumstances.

I was not to know that, at the very instant the buggy rounded the corner, decisions had finally been made that would profoundly effect me in the days ahead. At around mid- morning the following day, the few remaining troops were ordered to assemble in the square where Captain Clark would address them.

"The Cabinet has decided," he said in a deep voice that belied his small, plump stature, "that today, May 4th, the train

Confederate Gold
The Missing Treasure

will be split in two. The Confederate train will go south with the President, his staff and selected guards. The remainder will stay here under control of officers of the Richmond banks, until they decide what action to take."

Having made this brief announcement, he waved a bunch of keys over his head like a flag and ordered us to follow him down to vault.

"Those chests on the right belong to the banks, those on the left to the government," Clark said, as we crowded into the confined space. "Take all those on the left and load them on the three wagons you'll find waiting outside."

Without a word we set to work glad to be loading some of these unwieldy chests for the last time. We had loaded and unloaded them so often that we no longer cared about the contents. Long ago we had concluded they were going nowhere except, sooner or later, into the hands of the Yankees.

"Move," shouted Clark, as we slowly plied our way from vault to wagon and back. "We haven't got all day for you to slouch about your task. The President must continue his journey as soon as possible and you will not delay him, on pain of death."

To emphasize his words the Captain drew his revolver, waved it in the air, and fired into the roof of the vault. The explosion and reverberating echo in the confined space had the required effect.

Within the hour the loaded wagons headed out to join the Presidential party camped near the small town of Sandersville south of Washington.

What now, we wondered, as Captain Clark hurried across the square in the wake of the retreating wagons. The answer was not long in coming. Within a few minutes of the Acting Treasurer's departure a heavily built man, shoulders hunched as if against the cold, shuffled into the main room of the bank. His pallor was an unhealthy yellow and the dark brown eyes, which in earlier days must have been set in fleshy cheeks, now loomed large and staring from a sunken face. A sickly smell of scent flowed from his well-brushed grey hair, contrasting sharply with the dirty, crumpled civilian clothes that hung on his large boney frame.

"My name is Alexander Fisher," he said by way of introduction. "Thanks to the persuasive arguments of your Captain Clark, I now find myself in charge of the monies housed here," he added, as he slumped into a rickety chair that groaned under the weight.

Fisher was clearly at the end of his stamina. "I fear the Confederacy is finished and your duty to the cause is done," he said, gasping for breath. "You guards are forthwith dismissed. Go home to your loved ones." It was a statement not a command and, having delivered it, he leaned forward and buried his head in his hands.

For the second time in five days I felt myself abandoned at a time when I most needed companions. As I listened to Fisher the sour taste of bile filled my throat. My heart raced and my hands were damp with the sweat of fear at the thought of being forced to face the enemy alone. It was some minutes before I could trust myself to speak. "But you will need guards for your gold," I said, voicing the hopes of many that Fisher would change his mind and retain our services.

"We have all the guards we need," he mumbled without looking up. "We can't afford more, added to which we don't even have enough food to feed those who are staying on."

"But —," I started again in desperation.

Fisher waved his hand in dismissal. It was clear the decision was final. For us the war was over and we were now forced to face the task of fending for ourselves. It was the end of one war and the start of another. We had fought long and hard together. Now we were going home alone.

Dejected I, along with the others, ambled back to the camp. Here I stole what little food I could find and stuffed it into an old, worn knapsack I had scrounged in Abbeville. For some minutes I argued about taking my rifle. It would afford me some

Confederate Gold
The Missing Treasure

defense if attacked but, on the other hand, if I was caught by the Yankees I might fare better unarmed. Finally self defense won out. I slung my faithful friend over one shoulder my knapsack over the other and, with sufficient food for at least one decent meal, walked out of the camp.

I had no plans. I only knew I had to go south believing the further south I went the less my chances of encountering blue-bellies. The icy hand of fear held me in its grip. Thoughts of suffering starvation and disease in a northern prison camp filled my mind to the exclusion of all else. My hand tightened on my rifle. I would defend myself to the end, saving the last bullet for my own use.

Alone, scared, hungry and unwilling to trust anyone, I trudged down the hard baked mud track that served as the Warrenton road. All my worldly possessions were in my, almost empty, knapsack. I had no hope for today let alone tomorrow. For me the future did not exist.

CHAPTER 8

For the rest of the day I plodded steadily south with no more definite plan in mind than to put as much distance as possible between me and Washington. With only the food I had taken from the camp to keep me going I lived in hope that, somewhere along the way, I would find food and shelter in exchange for work. But the farther south I went the greater the devastation and the more forlorn that hope became.

Even six months after Sherman and his blue bellied cut throats had marched through Georgia the smell of burnt fields coupled with the reek of putrefying animal carcasses still hung in the air. I wondered if we would ever be rid of the stench. Sight of an occasional chimney, starkly outlined against the cloudless sky like a lone pine tree, showed all that remained of a once thriving farm. Such sights merely added to my misery. I crossed the remains of a railroad, the tracks bent and twisted into giant bows and hairpins. Everywhere was deserted and the silence screamed defeat. It seemed my present world had reverted to a time before man or beast.

As dusk fell I found shelter in a copse of scorched loblolly pines whose charred trunks pierced the night sky like eroding monoliths. Traces of ash still covered the ground. Unwilling to light a fire for fear of discovery, I ate the three slices of bread and four slivers of thin, dried meat I had brought with me. Not knowing when or where I would eat again, I savored each small bite and relished the dry saw-dust taste, chewing and rolling it around my mouth until I could chew and roll it no more. Supper finished I clutched the rifle to my side and, using my knapsack as a pillow, settled down to sleep.

Some hours later I was awakened by a strange wailing. I rolled onto my back and gazed up at the stars twinkling through the mosaic of tree trunks, like candles on a leafless Christmas

Confederate Gold
The Missing Treasure

tree. The sound came again from afar off and, as I listened, memories of the old plantation days suddenly flooded back. What I was hearing was an African shout. I had secretly attended such shouts with my mother but had not seen or heard one for many a year.

My whole being began to tingle as, without a thought, I slipped my arms through the knapsack straps, picked up the rifle and headed in the direction from which the noise came.

Moving cautiously between scarred and shattered trees I came at last to the edge of a clearing in the center of which some twenty or more negroes were gathered. A grey headed old man, bare foot and wearing threadbare pants seemed to be the leader of the group. He tapped his feet and clapped his hands beating out the time to his own song. Three similarly dressed young male singers took up the tempo while the women, in long skirts and head rags, formed a circle moving counter clockwise in an intricate shuffling gait clapping their hands and swaying to the rhythm. As I stood there I was a child again. Overcome by the fascinating chants and rhythms, I involuntarily started to tap my feet in time with the group. I longed to join them but some sixth sense warned me to keep out of sight. I strained my ears to hear the words of the songs but, unlike those I had known, the English was mixed with some language I did not understand.

It was still dark when the festivities finally came to an end. Some of the revellers passed very close to me as they left the clearing and from their conversation I learned the reason for their celebration. Freedom.

I had heard rumors of slaves being freed by Sherman and his troops as they marched to the sea and that many had been given arms in expectation of them creating havoc among the southern whites. Although I saw no sign of weapons a chill ran up my spine and I shivered at the thought this group might well be armed. There was no knowing what my end might be if caught by this or any other band of free and armed slaves. I wanted to run from this new danger but, like a fly trapped in a spider's

Bill Westhead

web, I was helpless to move. Minutes, that seemed like hours, crawled by as I crouched there unable to control my trembling body. Finally the last of the group melted into the darkness and I crept away from the clearing, taking to my heels as soon as it was out of sight. An overgrown ditch offered sanctuary and, without a second thought, I hurled myself down into its all-embracing grass and weeds. Fortunately the ditch was dry. Here I stayed, still fearing that any group of free slaves, armed or not, would have little truck for a white Confederate soldier, no matter his background.

The sun was well up before I plucked up sufficient courage to crawl out from my hiding place. Because of this late start I covered less than twenty miles before, in the slanting rays of the setting sun, I saw the silhouette of a burnt out farmhouse whose remains looked to offer some protection from weather and prying eyes. I was about to settle down in the corner between the smoke blackened stone chimney and partial wall when I was alerted by the sound of shuffling feet. Grabbing my rifle I pressed myself as far into the corner as possible and waited, hardly daring to breath for fear the noise betray my presence. The sounds came closer until, at length, dark shadows crept round the corner and along the wall.

"Stand where you are" I shouted from the safety of the shadows. "One more move and I fire."

The shadows stopped. With my loaded rifle trained in their direction, I advanced into the open and found myself face to face with a woman and three children. All four stood staring at me through desolate eyes. They made no effort to advance or to leave but merely waited as though resigned to whatever fate had in store for them. Despite their apparent apathy I remained wary knowing that in this day and age women and even children would kill if they felt it necessary. "Move out into the open," I commanded.

The woman made no move to obey but simply enveloped the children, as best she could, in her fleshless arms.

Confederate Gold
The Missing Treasure

They were a pitiful sight. Scrawny bodies and distended stomachs gave every indication of starvation, while their clothing, what there was of it, merely added to their wretched appearance. I guessed, from the age of the children, she was probably in her thirties but thin greying hair and wizened features made her looked nearer seventy. Although I kept my rifle trained on them I knew, no matter what happened, I could never pull the trigger.

"We have nowhere else to go," she said, her voice a lifeless monotone. "Shoot us if you must. Death might be a welcome relief."

At that I lowered my rifle.

"We have not eaten for days," she continued, releasing her hold on the children, "nor drunk for that matter. So what's the point of living."

"I've no food to give you," I said, "but there's water about."

"Oh yes, there's water about."

"Then why haven't you drunk?"

She seemed to ignore my question as she sank down her back against the stones. Once settled she looked up at me. "You don't know do you?" she said.

"Don't know what?"

"The damned Yankees poisoned the water when they came through. What wasn't poisoned became polluted by the dead animals they threw down our wells and into our lakes and rivers. No water around here is safe to drink."

Two of the children started to retch, their thin bodies clearly wracked with the pain.

"Dysentery," she said, nodding at the children. "We all have it. Maybe we'll live, maybe we won't. I don't much care either way. If we have to die I want us to die together, here on what was once our farm."

"Your farm!" I said, looking at the gaunt stack of stones that had once been a farm house.

"Yes. This was ours before the war."

75

Bill Westhead

A strange almost eerie silence fell over us. A minute passed then two. There was nothing I could say or do to break the stillness that enveloped us. She seemed to have drifted back into that lost world of only four years ago. I waited.

"My husband went off to fight," she finally said. "I tried to hold onto our few acres of land so he would have something to come back to. But he hasn't come back and never will."

"There's still time," I said.

"No. Time has run out for us." she said, then paused. "Don't suppose I shall ever know what happened to him but guess his mangled body is trampled into the mud and grime of some battle field somewhere far from here." Her voice broke as she finished and her mouth quivered and shook as she tried to recover herself. Then she began to cry.

"I'm sorry," I said. Although the words sounded inadequate even as I spoke them I could think of nothing else to say. We both knew she probably spoke the truth.

"What happened to the farm?" I asked and was immediately stunned by the intense hatred that flashed into her pale blue-grey eyes.

"I shall die a rebel," she almost shouted. "I could never, never, never be a part of the United States again. I swear I could never belong to any country that treats innocent people like they've treated us."

"But the farm," I prompted.

"They came. I remember standing there on the porch," she said, her emaciated arm indicating where the porch had once stood, "and watching. As far as the eye could see the heavens were lit by the ghostly flames of burning homes. Each new blaze marked the progress of the cowards and told of the sufferings of our friends and neighbors. Then they got here."

"And," I said quietly.

The hatred in her eyes seemed, if possible, to increase. "They tore into the place like demons. Any plea or argument was in vain. Into the smoke house, dairy, pantry and kitchen, breaking locks and anything else in their way. They were like a pack of rampaging wolves smashing everything as they went. Not men but uncontrolled wild beasts. What they couldn't carry in the way of meat, flour, lard, butter, eggs, pickles and wine they destroyed. Turkeys, hens, and pigs were shot down and left to rot. At one point I thought they were going to rape me but by then I didn't care. I'll tell you though I'd have killed any blue bellied bastard I might have given birth to."

"And the house?" I said, as she lapsed into silence.

"The last thing they did was to torch it," she said. "'Til the day I die I will hear the sound of their laughter as they set it alight. You see us as they left us and now, perhaps, understand why I will be a Rebel for the rest of my life."

I had no words of comfort for this woman and her children. Up to now I thought I had had a rough war, but my hardships were nothing compared with their sufferings. As I gazed at the scrawny creature sitting with her back against her own cold fireplace, all that was left of her dreams, I had visions of a happy family, but a few years ago, nestled by that same fireplace at the close of the day.

"This is your place ma'am," I said, bowing as if before royalty. "Would you permit a poor soldier to share it with you for one night."

A soft smile lit up her gaunt features and I saw that she had once been a pretty girl.

"You are most welcome sir, but we can offer you few comforts," she answered, trying to enter into my poor jest.

That night the five of us huddled together for warmth, partially shielded from the wind by the remains of the old farmhouse hearth.

"Thank you for your hospitality and may God be with you in the coming days," I said, as I readied myself to leave the following morning. "Hopefully these days will pass and the south will rise again."

"Amen," she said. "Although I doubt we shall live to see it."

Bill Westhead

I left quickly, trying to forget the sight of this pitiful family, but could not stop myself from one last backward glance. Four skinny arms were raised in salute. I waved back and, as the thought struck me I would probably never see them again, I felt my eyes begin to water. Sadness, shame and, above all, guilt at abandoning them to their fate overwhelmed me for I had little doubt they would soon starve to death.

It was some two hours later when, still lost in thought, I was nearly run down by a Union cavalry patrol and only just managed to dive into the woods before they clattered by looking neither left nor right. The bitter bile of hatred rose in my throat at the sight of the prancing horses, seemingly as arrogant as the troopers that sat them. It was easy to imagine such troops terrifying the woman and her children and I prayed they would not find them again.

Watching the patrol pass I realized the stupidity of travelling by day, particularly carrying a rifle. While slower, night travel would be safer and, as I was not held to any timetable, speed was unimportant. Although I knew my chances of begging for food during the hours of darkness would be markedly reduced I argued that the opportunities for stealing would be improved. My mind made up, I moved deeper into the woods and settled down to rest until dusk.

The next two nights travel proved uneventful. Knowing they were in complete control of the South, the Yankee patrols made no effort to hide their positions. As darkness fell they built huge camps fire which clearly marked their location and allowed me to bypass them with ease. I managed to keep up a steady pace but lack of food was becoming a problem. Sherman's army had devastated the countryside to such an extent that any food, no matter how small the amount, was so closely guarded stealing proved impossible. I would have chanced a shot at a wild rabbit or bird if any had been about, but the world seemed devoid of any wild life. Except for a few berries, I had not eaten for four days and nights and, mindful of the woman's warning, had drunk little. I was beginning to see and hear things that were not there - the sight and sound of running water or the cackle of hens. On one occasion I fired at a deer and saw it fall. But when I got to the spot there was nothing there. I wasted precious time searching for the carcass but never found it. I began to think I was losing my mind.

At dusk on the fifth night I shouldered my belongings as usual and within a few minutes settled down to a steady pace. The track I followed ran through a dense, untouched stand of trees. The light of the full moon filtering through the canopy of thick foliage caused strange shadows which, at times, gyrated in a silent dance so terrifying that I clung to the nearest tree trunk until the moment passed.

I must have been walking for about four hours before my sensitive hearing picked up the crack of twigs under foot and the sound of muffled voices. Believing the noise came from a Yankee patrol camped for the night I stole deeper into the woods until I found a suitable hiding place in the undergrowth. With my heart thumping as if to jump clean out of my mouth and the sweat of fear running down my insect- bitten neck, I lay there and listened. The voices rose and fell as the unseen beings roamed through the trees. I was so intent on trying to determine what was being said that I never heard the crunch of a boot close by until it was too late. Before I could move I was pinned face down in the dirt, my arms twisted behind my back and my hands tied.

Trussed up like a turkey ready for the oven I was prodded to my knees and then to my feet by the muzzle of a rifle thrust in my rib cage. Six dishevelled men surrounded me. Although they were dressed in an ill-assortment of thread-bare jackets and pants I noticed that each wore some tattered piece of clothing which, in better days, had been part of a proudly donned Confederate uniform.

"Thank God," I said breathing more easily. "I thought you were Yankees."

Bill Westhead

Hostile silence greeted my comment then, with a firm poke in the back, I was commanded to walk. Having no alternative I did as I was ordered. Johnny Reb or not, this group meant business and I had no doubt of my fate if I showed any sign of resistance. Bound as I was it proved difficult to keep my balance over the uneven ground. Several times I fell only to be hauled to my feet and forced forward with, what I now saw to be, my own rifle. Eventually we came to a clearing where four more of the gang sat round a small fire. A pot was hung over the embers and I smelt the glorious aroma of cooking meat.

"Food," I gasped, lurching towards the fire.

A blow to the side of the head sent me spinning to the ground. Lying there in a daze I slowly became aware of a musty smell that seemed to surround me. Opening one eye I saw a crowd of feet, some bare and swollen, others clad in boots held together with rags. It was a few minutes before I realized the stench was that of rotting flesh - gangrene which, without amputation, was a death knell to any and all who contracted the disease. I struggled to turn onto my back and let my eyes wander up passed ripped, mud spattered pants and shirts to hollow, sickly, unshaven faces. Some of the gang proudly wore their badge of honor, a dirty rag covering a stump where an arm or leg had once been.

"Who the hell are you?" A small, skeletal man leaned down and hissed in my ear.

"Josh Singleton" I said.

"And who the hell is Josh Singleton?"

"One time midshipman in the Confederate navy," I answered.

"Do you take us for fools?" he said, delivering a well aimed kick at my midriff which knocked the wind out of me. Though his foot was bare it was as hard as if he had worn boots. "Where the hell's your ship docked eh, and why aren't you on it?"

Confederate Gold
The Missing Treasure

The hollow laugh that greeted this last remark lacked any humor. I felt my heart pound and something seemed to crawl up my back as an uncontrolled shiver shook my whole body.

"My ship was scuttled when blockade running was abandoned," I said, fighting to control my voice.

The foot that crashed into my ribs this time was booted and an involuntary spasm shot through my body.

"Enough of your lies," the little man continued to hiss in my ear, while his eyes flashed dangerously. "I'll ask you again who you are and why you were spying on us?"

Every bone in my body ached as I struggled into a sitting position. Now, at least, I could face my accusers.

"Of late I have been a guard on the gold train," I gasped. Each word sent an agonizing jolt through me. "But," I continued, clenching my teeth, "five days ago they had no further need of my services and I was dismissed, along with the most of the other guards, and told to make my own way home. I reckoned that the farther south I went the less likely I was to be captured by the damned Yankees. I wasn't spying on you. How the hell could I be when I didn't even know you were here."

From the looks on the faces of the men encircling me it was clear not one among them believed a word I'd said. They may have fought for the cause in the past, I thought, but now each is fighting for his own survival. Killing has become a way of life for them whether the victim is young, old, man, woman, Yankee or Confederate.

"Tie him to that tree," my interrogator commanded. "Make sure he's gagged so he can't scream for help to any blue bellies that might be around."

With my hands still tied behind me, I was made to sit on the ground while they bound me securely to the trunk of a old pine tree and forced a gag into my mouth. Any movement, however slight, caused my shirt to rip on the rough ridged bark and after a while I felt the warmth of my own blood begin to trickle down my spine.

Bill Westhead

The night dragged by as I sat there on the damp ground. The only parts of my body I could move were my legs and then only to bend or straighten them. The moon moved so slowly across the sky I wondered if it had stopped altogether and began to doubt if the sun would ever rise again. I dozed fitfully, each time waking to the thought that I had slept my last in this world. I tried to relax and listen to the nocturnal sounds of the forest around me. The occasional hoot of an owl as it flew past on silent wings, the mixed croaking of frogs in some near yet unseen pond, the singing of the crickets and the skitterings of chipmunks as they grubbed in the earth for food. Although I envied them their freedom each sound offered me some small comfort. Perhaps life was returning to this blasted wilderness devastated by nature's deadliest enemy - man.

I kept a wary eye on the men gathered round the fire. While I could not see their faces or hear what they were saying, from the glances they occasionally shot in my direction, I was convinced they were planning the means of my disposal.

I've survived four years of hell to finish like this, I thought, as I watched them. Suddenly, like a cloud burst on a summer's day in Georgia, I felt my eyes water and tears of frustration began to course down my mud stained cheeks. At that moment I wished for some way to brush them away as I felt certain their telltale rivulets would only add to the gang's amusement when they finally decided how they would deal with me.

Slowly my frustration gave way to temper and I started to wriggle harder against the ropes that bound me. I was amazed at how much strength the ultimate fear of death generated in me. But the ropes held and I only succeeded in making my back bleed even more.

Finally I stopped wriggling and, resigning myself to my fate, prayed that whatever my end might be it would be quick.

CHAPTER 9

By the time the sky started to lighten in the east I had aged ten years. One of the men rose, wraith-like, from the forest floor and stirred the embers of the fire. Small flames sprouted upward as if welcoming the new day. I drooled as he added water and meat to the cooking pot and hung it back over the fire. As the early morning mist cleared, I watched the sun rise over the trees and climb up into a cloudless, blue sky like a large golden kite. I had never savored a dawn like this before. Believing this to be my last day on earth I took in every detail, the pine needles changing from black to olive green, tree trunks from grey to brown and the shadows shortening across the clearing as the new day sprang to life. It was as if God had done his wondrous best for my final hours.

The men roused themselves and lounged around the fire patiently waiting for the pot to boil. Apart from a few furtive glances in my direction they ignored me, although I was sure they had decided on the time, place and method of my execution. While I dreaded their announcement it was the waiting that caused the bile to rise in my throat and my heart to race.

Some time later, after they had all eaten, one of the gang came over with a metal bowl half filled with stew. The condemned man's last meal, I thought, as he untied my gag and with grime covered hands shoved small pieces of meat into my gaping mouth. It tasted like nectar and more than made up for my present suffering. With the meat finished he lifted the bowl to my mouth and, despite my spluttering, poured the lukewarm liquid down my throat until I was certain I would choke to death. He pushed the gag back into place holding it there with another equally dirty rag tied tightly round my head. Then he left me alone to contemplate my fate.

Bill Westhead

I guess it must have been mid-morning before a figure pushed its way through the undergrowth at the edge of the clearing. The newcomer was too far away for me to see his features, which in any case were shadowed under a broad brimmed hat, but his gait was unmistakable. I had seen that same swagger and limp only a few days ago. Though I had no idea why he was there his arrival filled me with hope.

Without pausing Sangster crossed the clearing towards me exchanging nods with each member of the gang as he passed. He was clearly on familiar terms with every man present. As he looked down at me there was a lively, yet strangely thoughtful, glint in his eyes. He played with his fingers cracking first one and then another as he always did when about to make a major decision, but it was several minutes before he spoke. "Don't make a sound or try to run when I free you," he finally said, as he bent to untie the rag that kept my gag in place. "because it will be the last thing you do." There was no mistaking the menace in his voice as, with a wicked looking knife, he cut the ropes that bound me.

Rolling my tongue around my dry mouth and rubbing the stiffness out of my arms and shoulders I staggered to my feet. No longer restrained my muscles twitched uncontrollably and I braced myself against the tree trunk that had held me. Uncertainly I extended a trembling hand. The gesture was ignored as my old commander eyed me with that cold, calculating stare he had previously reserved only for Yankees.

"What the hell are you doing here?" he said. "Last time I saw you, you were guarding the gold. Now my men find you spying on our camp." His tone was both belligerent and accusatory.

"I wasn't spy —,"

"I trusted you," he continued, ignoring my half-hearted protest. "Even though I had my doubts about you back in Washington, I still trusted you. I even believed your story. But now —."

Confederate Gold
The Missing Treasure

The unfinished sentence held its own threat. Even in my present state of confusion I knew, if I was to save myself, I had to convince this man that I was not spying. A silence fraught with meaning hung between us and it was some minutes before I dared myself to speak.

"The day after I last saw you," I said haltingly, "I was dismissed along with most of the other guards. I was heading south when I stumbled on your camp."

"A likely story. You expect me to believe that most of you were dismissed leaving only a few to guard that fortune. That's asking for trouble. You'd better have a better story than that if."

Again he stopped in mid-sentence.

"If what?" I asked.

"You want to live." His voice was flat.

By now the group had gathered round and were listening intently to my interrogation. The atmosphere was like the calm before an approaching storm and I sensed, beyond any doubt, the next few minutes would determine whether I lived or died.

"Well."

"You know me, sir," I started slowly. "I served with you on the *Carolina II*. and, if you remember, saved your life the night you were blown overboard." I paused knowing I had to use every argument I could think of to save myself. "I would remind you the last time we met," I said boldly, "was but a few days ago at the bank in Washington when I helped you load $86,000 into your buggy."

There was a general murmur of discontent from the men standing close by and Sangster's eyes flash dangerously.

"You still haven't answered the question," he snapped. "We haven't all day to mess with the likes of you. Either we're going to be satisfied and let you go or we bury you here, dead or alive."

The thought of being buried alive horrified me. I shivered as a river of ice ran through me. "For God's sake," I begged, collapsing to my knees as tears began to stream down my face and drip onto the pine-strawed ground, "shoot me if you must but don't bury me alive."

"Speak the truth then," Sangster said, his voice cutting through my babbling like a knife.

I struggled to my feet and, with closed eyes, leaned back against the tree praying to be shot. In the crushing silence I could feel the cold, damp earth being piled around me as I fought for my final breath. Again I shivered and at that same moment stained the only pair of pants I had. A vile stench rose from around my feet.

"For some years I served on the *Carolina II* with this man as skipper," I said, fighting to control myself as I pointed a wavering hand in Sangster's direction.

"That's true," Sangster said.

This small show of support persuaded me that perhaps all was not lost and, given time, I might yet save my skin.

"When blockade running was at an end we were commanded to scuttle the ship and I was ordered to Richmond," I continued, my eyes fixed on Sangster. My hope and confidence rose as he nodded in agreement. I paused to wipe my hand across my brow before going on to give an account of my actions guarding the gold train, being careful to omit any further reference to the $86,000. As I neared the end of my story my eyes searched the faces of the men around me, looking for any reaction to the story. Some showed slight interest, some disbelief but all still appeared sceptical.

Suddenly Sangster interrupted. "Why aren't you still with the gold train?"

"I've already told you," I said trying to control my voice. Despite my precarious situation I was beginning to tire of this repetitive questioning. "Because Captain Clark, the Acting Treasurer, dismissed me."

"Or was it because you were leading the train right into the hands of the damned Yankees?" Sangster said. "How much were they going to pay you when you delivered?"

Confederate Gold
The Missing Treasure

I wondered if this suggestion of my turning tail and betraying our cause was intended to make me loose my temper and say something that would spell my end.

"I didn't realize until the other day there were two gold trains that came out of Richmond," I continued calmly, determined not to play into their hands. "Anyway the President —,"

"Which one?" one of the men shouted.

The implication of treachery was still there.

"There is only one we recognize, President Jefferson Davis. President Jefferson Davis," I said, with emphasis on the name, "ordered the two trains separated. The Confederate train will be used to continue the war while the other has been handed back to the banks of Richmond. The banks had the final say in who stayed on as guards and who was dismissed."

"You're a liar and a fool," a voice from the back yelled. "You expect us to believe that when we know better."

"I'm no liar or fool, you boot-licker," I said my voice rising with each word. "No matter what you think you damn well know it happens to be the truth." I stopped, fighting to regain my self-control before continuing. "The banks only wanted a few guards and the money with President Jefferson Davis," again I shouted the name, "was to be guarded by the cavalry. So we were dismissed. As I told you I was making my way south when I stumbled on this camp and thought it was a Yankee patrol."

For some minutes no one spoke. Even the man I'd called a boot-licker was silent. Then Sangster said "That's it?"

"Yes," I said wearily. "That's it."

"Come with me," he ordered, abruptly turning about and limping off across the clearing. He never looked back and it was apparent he expected me to obey without question. For a moment I stood motionless wondering whether to follow or make a dash for the trees and possible freedom.

"You heard the Captain." The skeletal man who had questioned me the night before spoke quietly but there was no mistaking the threat in his voice. "Move." It was an order.

With serious misgivings I pushed my way through the undergrowth, following the track Sangster had taken. Within a few yards I stumbled across him sitting cross-legged under a large pine, his broad brimmed hat lying on his knees. As I glanced back towards the camp, I realized he must have witnessed my capture and treatment and wondered why he had waited so long before intervening.

Seeing him sitting there, I realized this was no longer the swashbuckling captain of a blockade runner nor even the more recent gallant confidant of the President. In the short time since I had last seen him in Washington he had aged several years. The wild fire was still in his eyes but there was also a strange uncertainty I had never seen before, as though he was wrestling with something he did not fully understand. "Sit down," he said.

Again this was an order not a polite invitation and, as in the past, I obeyed squatting on the ground beside him.

"Sorry about the welcome," he said, a flash of the old devil-may-care smile crossing his face. "We had to be sure you were still loyal to the south. I regret to say there are many Rebs wandering the country at this moment who would sell their old comrades to anyone for the price of a meal. While I can't say I blame them I would willingly kill any I caught. Although I didn't think you were one I had to be sure."

"Are you?" I asked cautiously.

"Yes."

"Thanks," I said, with a relief I could not describe. "So what happens now?"

"I've decided to offer you membership in the group."

"And?"

"You help us take the gold." The reply was so unemotional that it took me by surprise.

"The gold!"

Confederate Gold
The Missing Treasure

"Quiet, you fool," he whispered, clapping a hard hand over my mouth. "Listen. For days we've been planning how to stop any of that gold falling into Yankee hands. But until now we've hesitated as we thought taking the gold would jeopardize the South's ability to carry on the war and we didn't want to do that. Now your news solves our problem."

"How?" I asked.

"Because you've told us there are two separate trains. The Confederate train to be used to continue the fight was intact, you said, and guarded by the cavalry. Although I'm sure none of the bank gold will ever be used to support our cause we must stop it falling into enemy hands. Added to which we reckon we deserve payment for our services."

"But you've been paid haven't you?" I asked.

"In worthless Confederate money." Sangster said. A glob of spittle hit the ground several feet away. "Four years and what have we got to show for it. Nothing. Even the little we had before all this started has been lost. Have you anything, a home, money, a family, anything?"

I had to admit that all I had was what I carried.

"As I said," he continued, "none of that bank gold will ever be used for the cause. If the Yankees don't get it you can bet all you possess it will finish in the pockets of those who sat on their fat arses making vast profits from this bloody war. We're not going to let that happen. Maybe some day that gold can be used to build a new south. In the meantime it will help each of us live through the present disaster."

Sangster leaned back against the trunk of the pine and stared straight through me.

"Well?" he said.

"Makes sense," I said, impressed with the simple logic of Sangster's argument. "But can you do it with the motley group you've got?"

His face hardened and his eyes blazed at my question. "That motley group," he said icily, "consists of some of the best

Bill Westhead

soldiers and sailors this country has ever produced. You may think you're as good but you're certainly no better than they are. Look at yourself."

I glanced down at my soiled rags. "Sorry," I said. "I was not doubting their ability, but have you enough men and arms?"

"Surprise my boy. Surprise," Sangster said, his eyes crinkling at the corners. "Providing we have surprise on our side, numbers and arms become secondary."

Whatever my reservations Sangster's words had given me hope for the future. If we could just lay our hands on the gold our sufferings would not have been in vain. With it the South could rise out of the ashes of despair and throw off the yolk of Yankee oppression. I could see myself as a wealthy landowner with wife and family. It all depended on taking the gold.

"Well are you with us?"

"That I am, Captain," I said, pulling myself back to reality and thrusting my hand out in acceptance. Again it was ignored.

"Right," he said, rising to his feet. "Follow me."

This time I was right behind him as we pushed through the undergrowth back into the clearing. Every man present turned towards us as we approached. There was no mistaking the antagonism on each face and my newly found enthusiasm evaporated like water on a hot stove.

"This is our newest recruit, Josh Singleton. Having talked to him I am confident he remains a true Southerner." Sangster spoke quietly yet forcefully. His command was such that he found it unnecessary to raise his voice. "Kemper bring the book."

A tall, bearded man gave a half-hearted salute before shuffling over to a tattered bed roll near the fire. After a few moments rummaging in the bedroll he returned and, with an air of reverence, handed a dog-eared book to Sangster.

"Singleton,"

"Sir," I said and, following Kemper's example, saluted.

"Step forward."

Confederate Gold
The Missing Treasure

Each hollow cheeked face watched my every action as I walked to the center of the group and stood, expectantly, facing my old skipper.

"In front of these good comrades and witnesses," Sangster said, solemnly holding the book in his outstretched hand, "I want you to swear on this Holy Book that you will continue to fight to the death for the Southern cause. That you will willingly obey any orders and undertake any assignment given to you. That you will die in action rather than be taken prisoner but if taken you will never, even under threat of death, betray any of your comrades."

I laid my hand on the Bible and swore.

"Now," he said, as I withdrew my hand, "You will return to Washington and find out all you can about the gold. We want to know where it is, how it's guarded and when it's moved."

"Return to Washington!" I said. My jaw dropped and my voice was little more than a startled gasp. "But the Yankees are all over the place. Chances are I won't get there."

"Haven't you just taken an oath in front of your new comrades to obey orders," Sangster snapped. "This is an order."

"I don't need to go to Washington," I said. "I know where the gold is. It's in the old branch bank of the State of Georgia, right in the center of the town."

"Do you know if today the gold is guarded?" Sangster said. "If so how many guards are on duty at any one time? Do you know when they're changed? Do you know when they intend to move the gold? Well do you?"

I had to admit I could not answer these questions.

"Then go and find out."

"It'll take three or four days there and the same back, six to eight days in all," I said still hoping he would cancel the order. "How do I know you'll still be here when I get back?"

"You don't, and I don't expect to see you back here in six to eight days. There is no way we can take the gold while it's in the bank so we have to wait until it's moved." Sangster's eyes held

Bill Westhead

that dangerous sullen look. The irritation in his voice was apparent as he continued. "If we're forced to leave this camp I'll see you're contacted."

I opened my mouth to speak but before I could utter a word a stinging blow landed across my cheek. "I gave you a direct order. Now go." he snarled.

It was clear further argument was useless and the general mutterings warned me it was also endangering my acceptance by the group. But I needed to show them I was still my own man. I picked up my knapsack in a casual manner and with long, steady strides crossed to the remains of a deer carcass lying partially hidden on the edge of the clearing. My mouth watered as I cut off a large chunk of raw meat and carefully, almost reverently, stuffed it into the knapsack on top of my few worldly possessions.

"Where's my rifle?" I said, turning to face my new comrades with a calm deliberation I did not feel.

"What the hell do you want a rifle for?" Sangster shouted, clearly angry at my delaying tactics. "Do you see anyone round here carrying a rifle?"

I looked around. There was not a rifle in sight.

"Well?"

"No."

"And nor will you," he said, laying a heavy hand on my shoulder. "No Johnny Reb is allowed to carry a fire arm these days." His lips curled in disgust as he added, "If you're caught with a rifle you'll land in one of those hellish Yankee prison camps. For your own safety we have disposed of your weapon."

"But —," I said without thinking.

For the second time his right hand slammed across my face. "Stop your antics and in the name of God be on your way. I'm tired of your damned arguing.

Knowing I was beaten, I adjusted my knapsack straps, saluted and set out to retrace my steps northwards. Without my rifle I felt naked but deep down I knew Sangster was right. I

Confederate Gold
The Missing Treasure

would have a better chance of passing enemy patrols if I was unarmed.

In spite of my initial fears the trek proved uneventful. Travelling by night and avoiding the myriad of camp fires that sprang to life as each day ended, I made good progress. Approaching the area of the burnt out farmhouse I looked for the woman and her three children. In spite of the urgency of my mission I felt I had to find them again. But my search proved to be in vain. After an hour I was forced to assume death had overtaken the family and that at this very moment their rotting flesh was being consumed by some more fortunate creature. I moved on.

Three days later, as the rising sun fought its way through the overcast sky, I again entered Washington. It was the morning of May 10th. 1865.

CHAPTER 10

As I came into Washington I realized my problems were only just beginning. The last time I had been here I had been part of the Confederate forces and openly roamed the streets. Now, aware of my present situation, I was forced to skulk along those same streets feeling as if the words 'spy' and 'robber' were emblazoned across my forehead in large letters for all to see.

Added to this feeling of standing out among the locals, like an observation balloon in a clear blue sky, was the fact I had given no thought as to where I might lodge without arousing suspicion. Wherever it was it must allow me to keep an eye on the bank at all hours of the day and night. If, as I assumed, the gold was still in the vault then, I argued, the remaining guards were also here and any one of them might recognize me if I begged lodging at the wrong house. My problems were further compounded by my having only a few coins of any value and some worthless Confederate paper money to offer in exchange for any lodgings I might procure.

Throughout the day I wandered aimlessly in search of an empty building that might be suitable for my needs but to no avail. All the vacant buildings I found, and there were many, had been securely locked and barred by their owners before they fled the expected onslaught. Trying to force an entry to any one of them would only have drawn unwanted attention to myself. By the end of the day I was no nearer solving my dilemma and decided to spend the night in the open countryside outside the town.

At dusk I set out along the Abbeville road in the belief that the gold, if it had not already been moved, would eventually be going north and have to pass along this route. About a mile from the town I came across a dry ditch, covered by an overhanging hedge, which seemed ideal for my purpose. Climbing down I nestled into a bed of dry leaves, their softness acting like balm to my tired limbs. The earthy scent reminded me of my days on the plantation and, lulled by the breeze that whispered through the hedge and surrounding grass, I fell into a deep, dreamless sleep.

Sun-up saw me back in Washington, fervently hoping my luck would change. But the day proved no more successful than the one before. By evening I had still nowhere to stay and no confirmation as to the whereabouts of the gold. A feeling of acute hunger was now added to those of fear and guilt as I trudged back along the Abbeville road to my ditch. Five days had passed since I had left the camp and still I had nothing to report. Believing every moment was precious, if the robbery was to succeed, I was becoming desperate.

Staggering into the town on the third day I sensed a new wave of bitterness among the few brave souls who ventured onto the streets. People hustled past with heads bowed and their usual somber greetings were noticeable by their absence. The feeling that some new disaster had occurred grew as the day progressed. Eventually my curiosity overcame my reserve and I plucked up courage to approach a middle aged man leaning against the open door of what had once been a clothing store. His musty suit, too large for his scrawny body, spoke of respectability but inside the store shelves, racks and counter were covered in nothing but dust.

"Where have you been?" he said, gazing at the ground as though he expected it to open up at any moment. "Have you not heard the news?"

"What news?" I asked.

"President Davis."

"What about him?"

"He's been captured along with his family."

"When? Where?" I said, grabbing him by the lapels of his frock coat.

"Don't know anything do you?" he sneered, looking straight at me and then, with surprising strength, brushing my hands

Bill Westhead

aside. "Captured three days ago, at Irwinville. We had hopes that, in spite of Lee's surrender, the President would continue the fight. But that hope is gone. If I were you I'd be on my way. There's nothing more anyone can do. We're are finally, completely and utterly beaten."

His eyes glistened as he turned back into the bare store. Dazed by the news I continued down the street. On either side dogwood trees were in full bloom their small white flowers combined with ruby colored azaleas, yellow forsythia and blue wisteria announcing the approach of summer and the inevitable heat. Nature was radiating an aura of peace and tranquility which contrasted sharply with the icy grip of fear which showed on the faces of the people whose silence I found more frightening than any show of panic. Nature was already recovering from the tragedies of the last four years but I wondered if we humans ever would.

With the Confederacy finished and the Yankees raiding across our fair southland, I was convinced the Richmond banks would never consider their treasure safe in Washington. Having no evidence it was still in the vault I began to wonder if it had already left for the north. If so I dare not return to the camp and would be forced to spend more weary days and nights alone on the road. I found no comfort in the thought.

This third day proved as fruitless as the previous two, except that, down a side street, I came across a middle aged woman selling chicken legs. The style of her well darned, dress of faded velvet reminded me of those I had seen Mrs. Hampton wear when I was a boy on the plantation.

"How much ma'am?" I asked, pointing to the legs in her wicker basket.

"Fifty cents each," she said.

I handed over the precious coins and scoured the basket for the biggest leg I could find. I had devoured the deer meat on my trek back to Washington and other than a few berries and last

Confederate Gold
The Missing Treasure

years rotten nuts this was the first decent food I had tasted in three days.

"I thank you ma'am from the bottom of my heart," I said, as my teeth finished tearing at the juicy flesh. "But pray where did you find chicken?"

"Not chicken." Her eyes were downcast as she spoke. "Best we can do these days is rat."

"Well its wholesome fare and much appreciated," I said, sucking the last slivers of meat off the bone before tossing it on the ground. Food had never tasted so good.

"You're very welcome my son," she said. "May God be with you in the days ahead."

"And with you ma'am," I said, doffing my kepi as she picked up her basket and wandered on down the street.

As evening approached storm clouds gathered and I set out for my bed under the hedge a little earlier than usual. On the edge of town I happened to glance down one of the side streets to my right and saw a large man ambling towards me, his thin, sagging face topped by a shock of well-brushed red hair. Recognizing Mr. Fisher I dodged into the nearest doorway and prayed he would not see me. I held my breath as the heavy clump of his boots approached the end of the alley. The rhythm never changed. Looking neither right nor left he continued on his way, his unfaltering footsteps passing within ten feet of where I stood. My face pressed hard against the shuttered door I continued to wait, huddled like a squirrel in its dray, until I could no longer hear the crunch of his boots.

Scorning the rain which now drove in wicked shafts from the boiling, black clouds overhead I ran down the Abbeville road my spirits rising with every stride. It seemed I was not too late. If Fisher was here then, I argued, the gold must be here. With an overwhelming sense of relief at having made some progress I settled down into my soggy leaf bed. The hedge offered some little shelter and I lay there, face down, listening to the rains dripping off the leaves above me and splattering into the grasses.

Bill Westhead

For the next two days I scoured the streets, hoping to catch further sight of Mr. Fisher and so assure myself he and the gold were still in town, but with no success. It seemed the man had suddenly appeared to taunt me and equally suddenly disappeared. My feeling of uselessness returned.

"Your family live hereabouts soldier?"

The pleasant voice broke in on my dejected thoughts and I turned to find myself face to face with a dapper looking gentleman who I judged to be in his sixties. Underneath the unruly white hair and bushy eyebrows shone kindly eyes of deep blue. I gazed at his dress and appearance which stood in stark contrast to the ragged wretches that formed the major portion of the town's meagre population. It seemed as if the war had, somehow, passed him by.

"Are you addressing me, sir?" I asked, adopting the best cultured voice I could.

"And what other soldier do you see around?" he answered, a smile twitching at the corners of his mouth.

"What makes you think I am a soldier?" I replied curtly.

His smile irritated me.

"Ah come my boy," he continued kindly, apparently not the least put out by my abruptness. "Just take a look at yourself. Your clothing, partly blue, partly grey, torn and tattered. Obviously a uniform sometime in the past."

"I stole it from a dead soldier," I lied.

"Oh no," he answered without rancor. "It's yours. But that's not all. Your general demeanor gives you away. You have that lost and defeated look I have seen recently in the eyes of many of our brave boys as they wend their way back from the war. And your age, sir which, despite your appearance, I guess to be in the twenties. Anyone of that age must have fought in the war."

I had to admit the truth of his observations and my earlier doubts returned a hundred-fold. To avoid any awkward situations I had tried to blend into the Washington scene but this man seemed to have had no problem in recognizing me for what

Confederate Gold
The Missing Treasure

I had been. I prayed he would not recognize me for what I was now.

"Come answer my question. Does your family live hereabouts?" the friendly voice continued, cutting into my brooding.

"No sir," I said, hoping to escape from this prying stranger.

"Then where are you making for?" he asked, ignoring the sharpness of my response.

I wanted to walk away but, in my present nervous state, I was convinced that if I did I would arouse his suspicions and he would pursue me with more questions. I had no alternative but to bluff it out.

"My family, or what may be left of them after Sherman's murdering pigs have been through, live near Savannah, sir," I said. "I am trying to make my way there, but stopped here in the hope of finding a little food and rest."

The answer seemed to satisfy the gentleman as, with a sympathetic nod of understanding, he offered me both rest and sustenance. "I'm Doctor Robertson." he said by way of introduction.

"I am Jacob Joshua Henderson," I answered, extending my right hand. I thought it unwise to give my true name in case any of my old comrades were still in town. "But I would deem it an honor if you would just call me Josh. It is the name I have answered to these last four years."

"As you wish Josh," the Doctor said, laying a guiding hand on my arm. "Now if you would be good enough to accompany me we will see what we can do in the way of food and a change of clothes."

In silence he guided me first down one street and then along another heading in the direction of the town square. On entering the square he made straight towards the old branch bank.

"Here we are," he said, as we approached the stone steps leading up to the front door. I stopped and my jaw dropped.

Bill Westhead

"What's the matter?" Robertson asked. He sounded worried as he laid a cool hand on my sweating forehead. "Are you sick?"

"No," I gasped, as I continued to stare at the heavy oak doors.

"Come," he said, as he gripped my elbow and assisted me up the steps and through the doors. "You clearly need rest above all else."

Standing in the all to familiar hallway I remembered the last time I had been here. That was the day I had helped load the Confederate gold onto wagons for its continued flight south. It was also the last time I had seen the bank treasure securely locked in the vault below.

"I suppose you are wondering why I live here," Robertson said, leading me across the bare hall to a narrow stairway, "and not in a house of my own."

I nodded, afraid to open my mouth for fear of giving myself away.

"Well," he continued, as we started up the stairs, "most of our people have fled so the few of us that remain are trying to keep the town functioning. Among several duties I now perform is that of cashier of this bank. It was just two weeks ago that I accepted the responsibility when the true cashier and his family left for Florida. I then decided to live here because I deem it best, where money is concerned, to sleep on the job." He chuckled at his own wit.

Arriving at the top of the stairs the good doctor ushered me into a small room with clean, white-washed walls. The furniture was sparse, consisting of a single bed and wash-stand on which stood a plain jug half filled with water and a cracked hand basin.

"A room fit for the President," I said, staring longingly at the bed.

"Not quite," he chortled, "but better than you've had for some time I'll wager. Now I strongly advise rest." He left, closing the door behind him. I could still hear him chuckling as he descended the stairs.

Confederate Gold
The Missing Treasure

I took off my clothes and, pouring water into the basin, sloshed it all over my naked body watching, mesmerized, as the grime slid away onto the clean floor. I knew I should clean up the mess but, in that moment of shedding weeks of filth, nothing else seemed to matter. I had not felt so clean since Danville. How long ago was that, I wondered, sitting on the edge of the bed and staring at the foul collection of threadbare clothes on the floor.

I must have fallen asleep for suddenly the room was in semi-darkness the only light coming from a short, guttering candle that stood in a metal holder on the wash-stand. Climbing off the bed, I grabbed the candle and started to examine my surroundings more closely. The floor by the wash stand was now clean, the jug refilled and my pile of ragged clothing had gone. At the foot of the bed was a neat stack of good, clean clothes. I was embarrassed to think someone had been in this room while I slept naked. I prayed it was not some female servant or, even worse, the Doctor's wife if he was married. I dressed quickly in my new clothes and went downstairs. He was sitting at a small, scrubbed pine table in the back room playing cards with a companion.

"Come, sit yourself here, my boy," he said, gesturing towards a plain pine chair at the other end of the table. "Allow me to introduce you to my friend Doctor Stone. James, this is Jacob Joshua Henderson, or Josh as he prefers."

"I'm pleased to meet you," I said, as Stone levered himself up from the chair and extended a long fingered hand. I noticed his left leg was missing below the knee.

"Lost that little jewel in the Wilderness," he said, seeing my stare. "Fortunately it wasn't my hands. At least I can go back to being a surgeon, even if they have to prop me up at the table." He had an infectious high pitched squeak of a laugh.

"Please don't let me interrupt your game," I said, chuckling at his wry sense of humor.

"There's no urgency to finish," Stone said. "We're going to have plenty of time now while the Yankees decide what to do with us." The continued high pitched squeak took the sting out of his words. I had an instant liking and respect for this man that could laugh so readily at what others would have seen as a major catastrophe.

The two doctors settled back to their cards while I watched.

"Do you live here too Doctor Stone?" I asked, when the hand was finished.

"No," he said. "I have a small house, which also acts as a surgery, on the other side of town."

"So you live here by yourself Doctor Robertson?" I said, in an attempt to find out who had been in my room.

"Not exactly," he replied. "I have a woman comes in to look after the place."

I gasped. "Did she —." I was too flustered to finish the question.

A deep throated roar coupled with a high pitched squeak greeted my embarrassment and I saw both men had tears running down their faces as they looked at me. "No," Robertson finally gasped between guffaws. "I did your room. Believe me you were no sight to behold." His belly laugh started again. "Anyway the lady in question has been a nurse for many a year and I'm sure during the war saw sights far worse that you lying naked on a bed."

"My thanks for your kindness," I said with relief, "and I apologize for the mess I made upstairs."

"Think nothing of it. We'll discuss it no more. Come let's eat."

"Sorry I can't stay Charles," Stone said, struggling onto his one good leg. With the aid of a crude wooden crutch he made his way to the door. With his hand on the latch he turned and added, "I must be on my way as our friend here is occupying your only spare room and it's best not to be seen abroad late at night."

Confederate Gold
The Missing Treasure

The simple, but wholesome fare of corn and bean soup was eaten in silence. When we had finished, Robertson lit an old clay pipe, pushed his chair back, crossed his legs and proceeded to puff away contentedly.

"I would suggest you make the most of the bed upstairs my boy. Get all the rest you can. One never knows how soon you may have to be on your way again," he said. This good advice was given in a generous manner and his look from across the table was almost fatherly.

"With your permission then sir, I will retire," I replied, rising to my feet. "If there is nothing I can do to help you it only remains for me to thank you yet again for my new clothes and the excellent meal." I was trying to behave in a manner that befitted both my host and my surroundings.

"It was my pleasure to assist you and I'm only too gratified that they fit," he said, removing the pipe from his mouth and picking a tiny bit of tobacco from the tip of his tongue. "But no, there is nothing you can do. I intend to retire myself," he added, "once I have fulfilled my duties.

"But surely the bank is closed sir," I said, my senses alerted by the older man's comment.

"Oh yes," he replied. "But even then I still have duties. I check the vault first thing every morning and last thing every night to ensure nothing has been tampered with. I'll be mighty glad when the banks remove their gold and then perhaps I can sleep in peace."

"But is the gold not guarded day and night?" I asked, digging for every scrap of information I could find.

"No," he said. "It was at first but they reckoned, with the few guards remaining, they could do nothing if the Yankees came so they don't bother now. The gold is as secure as it can be."

I could not believe my luck. Here was my host openly telling me all I wanted to know.

"If that be the case sir, I will bid you a good night," I said, moving towards the door. I fought to keep a firm grip on my

Bill Westhead

emotions for fear of arousing suspicion but my heart was pounding as I mounted the stairs.

I could not remember when I had last spent a night in a bed but, despite the comfort, I could not sleep. Again and again my thoughts returned to the Doctor's parting words. Now I had definite confirmation the gold was still in the vault and, furthermore, it was unguarded. But how was I to get word to Sangster. I could only guess at his reaction if the gold was moved while I trekked back to the camp. The problem remained unsolved by the time sleep finally came.

I woke to the sun streaming through the narrow window. At first I thought I was under the hedge on the Abbeville road with a heavy mist hanging over the fields. Then, as my eyes began to focus, I realized I was staring at the whitewashed walls and ceiling of a room. It was clearly well past daybreak.

I tumbled out of bed, splashed water on my face and fell into my clothes. "What a fool I am," I muttered, drawing on my pants. "They could have moved the gold while I slept."

I took the stairs two at a time only to find my host had already gone about his business in the town. On the table was a pot containing the remains of the soup, obviously left for me. I placed it on the stove before scouring the bank to see if there were any tell-tale signs of activity, particularly around the vault doors. I found none and breathed a sigh of relief, knowing the gold was still there.

After eating a bowl of the soup I returned to my room, sat on the edge of the bed and bent my mind to the problem that continued to plague me.

"How the hell am I to let Sangster know?" I mumbled, constantly banging my forehead with the palms of my hands in a vague effort to drive a solution into my befuddled brain. If I went out I would have to stay close to the bank and that could arouse suspicion. If I stayed in I had no chance of communicating with anyone. At one point I even thought of

Confederate Gold
The Missing Treasure

kidnapping either Mr. Fisher or Dr. Robertson or both, but quickly discarded the idea as being a useless waste of time.

As the morning passed my frustration grew until I felt imprisoned by the walls of the room crowding in on me. I had to get out of the building. Despite all my mental effort the only idea that made any sense was to head back to the camp gambling that the gold would not be moved in my absence.

Leaving a note for my host thanking him for his hospitality and saying I had decided to leave for Savannah, I shouldered my worldly possessions and left. I crossed the square and was passing an abandoned storehouse when a trim, wiry little man stepped out from one of the doorways in front of me. I nodded a greeting as we passed.

"Keep walking and don't turn around."

Suddenly I felt the hard muzzle of a revolver thrust into my back and I sensed the hand that held it belonged to the man I had just passed. I had no alternative but to obey while, at the same time, wondering what he might want of me. I had nothing worth taking.

"Where's the gold?"

I stiffened. So that was it. He was after the gold too.

"Gold! What gold?" I tried to sound surprised and puzzled. I needed time to think.

"Don't try to play games with me you young fool. Just answer the question or you're dead." he said in the quiet cultivated voice of a Southern gentleman. At the same time the revolver was jabbed harder into my back to emphasize the threat. I was ashamed of the trickle of water that suddenly dribbled down my legs.

"I don't know what the hell you're talking about," I said loudly, hoping he would not hear the tremor in my voice.

"We'll see." The chuckle had a cruel ring to it as though he was enjoying the encounter.

"Down there," he commanded, slamming the butt of his revolver into my right shoulder numbing my arm and causing me

Bill Westhead

to turn into a narrow alley between two stores. The far end was blocked by a low roofed warehouse. There was no means of escape and suddenly my survival instincts took over. Without thinking I hunched low, turned and sprang at the voice behind me. My assailant proved more than equal to the attack. Dancing neatly aside he caught me a stunning blow on the side of the head as I sailed by. The wind was forced out of me as I crashed, face down, on the hard baked earth.

"Get up and no more heroics if you want to see the sun set," he said, and I heard the contempt in his voice.

Rolling onto my back and gasping for breath, I tried to focus bleary eyes on my attacker. Cavalry I guessed, as my eyes travelled the short distance to his neatly bearded face. Cold, black eyes that condoned no argument bored into me. Despite the heat in the alley, I shivered. With a smile that would have frozen the devil in his tracks, he brandished the revolver before returning it to its holster.

"Now, my fine hero," he mocked, hauling me to my feet. He was surprisingly strong. "I'll ask you again. Where is the gold?"

"I still don't know what the hell you're talking about," I stubbornly replied.

"They told me not to trust you," he said with a sigh. Slowly he pulled the revolver from its holster, his fingers caressing the barrel. This taunting caused a hollow feeling to hit the pit of my stomach.

"Who?" I asked, my eyes drawn to the long, slender fingers. The man could have been an artist or musician I thought.

"Captain Sangster's boys," he answered, continuing to stroke the weapon.

His reply blasted me out of my reverie "Who did you say?"

"Captain Sangster's boys," he said calmly, "or had you conveniently forgotten your comrades?"

"You're a liar. You were never in the camp." My voice echoed round the narrow alley leaping back at me from the walls and intensifying my acute sense of isolation.

Confederate Gold
The Missing Treasure

For a moment he hesitated but before I could follow up on my advantage he was back in command.

"I saw you dragged in but you probably didn't see me. I went foraging immediately afterwards." His black eyes continued to bore through me. "Well, now we've settled that little point, tell me about the gold."

"How do I know you're from Sangster's group?" I asked with more confidence than I felt.

"What does it take to convince you?"

"Describe him for a start," I said.

The description rang true, but I needed more.

"Were you with him at Vicksburg?" I asked.

"Don't you fool with me. He was never at Vicksburg. If you told us the truth back there you know full well he was a blockade runner."

The look he gave me clearly showed he was tired of bandying words with me. He wanted information and he wanted it fast. I had all the proof I was going to get. Whether I liked it or not I had to trust him.

"It's still in the vaults here," I said. "I wanted to get a message to the group but daren't leave in case they moved it while I was away."

"Anything else?"

"No. That's all I've managed to find out since I came here," I said. I still had doubts about this man and was not going to offer any more information than I thought necessary to save myself.

The little man nodded. "I suppose I've got to believe you," he said, "'cause you look too scared to lie. But I hope for your sake you've told me all you know."

"I have," I said, taking a deep breath and letting it out slowly.

"I sure hope so because you make one wrong move and you'll —." There was no need for him to complete the sentence, his low menacing voice was enough. We stood facing one an other, challenging each other, doubting each other. The alley was devoid of all sound and even the air seemed to stop moving.

"From now on I'm your only contact," he finally said, as he returned his revolver to its holster. "You're to stay here until they start to move the gold. We reckon they'll take the Abbeville road north but whether they do or not you follow them. Clear?"

I nodded.

"Now wait a few minutes."

Without another word the little cavalry dancer darted out of the alley. I looked up at the thin crack of sky between the buildings and uttered a short, silent prayer.

Returning to the bank I found the note where I had left it, unopened. Tearing it into small pieces, I stuffed them in my pocket and went up to my room. I still doubted my attacker had any connection with Sangster but it was too late to worry about that now. Only time would tell if I had betrayed the group.

CHAPTER 11

Monotonous days dragged into unending nights as I waited for something to happen. Nothing did. The gold stayed securely locked in the vault and boredom became so overpowering that I even began to wish for a second meeting with the little cavalry man. But he seemed to have vanished as quickly as he had come.

On the surface Washington was slowly returning to some degree of normality as each day a few more of those who had fled returned to open up their homes and businesses. Despite this an underlying tension was still present as the townsfolk waited to see what the damned Yankees would do. I spent my days wandering the streets and so it was, by chance, that I came upon Dr. Stone's house and surgery. Thinking a few hours in his company might help to alleviate the monotony I ambled up the weed-strewn path between rampant azalea bushes and knocked loudly on the solid wooden door. A clopping and shuffling sound issued from within before the door was thrown open and the doctor stood there leaning heavily on his home-made, T-shaped crutch.

"Well I'll be damned," he said. "You're the young man I met the other night at Charles' house aren't you? What are you doing here?"

My mind churned like a water wheel as I endeavored to think of some explanation for my unexpected visit.

"Are you sick?" he continued as I stood there, feet scuffing dust into the air.

"N-n-n no sir," I stammered.

"Well you will be if you come in here," he said brightly. "Got two bad cases of typhus in the back so, much as I'd like to swap a few stories with you, I'd advise you to be on your way."

"I'm sorry to have bothered you sir," I said haltingly, at the same time taking a step back as though trying to distance myself from the dreaded disease inside.

"No bother," he said. "Under other circumstances I would have invited you in but it's better you not enter. Come back again in a week, if you're still around. I reckon neither of my patients will last any longer poor devils." He let out a long, deep sigh. "What a waste."

"Thank you sir, I'll do that," I said, increasing my distance from him.

He raised his hand in a friendly salute before closing the door. Retracing my steps I imagined the doctor stumping around on his crutch administering to the needs of his two patients. I wondered how long it would be before he, too, fell victim to the dreaded disease. As events turned out I was never to know for I never saw him again.

Two weeks after my return to Washington I woke to the sound of shouts and tramping of feet. Leaping out of bed I rushed to the small frame window. There, below me, men dressed in rustic looking shirts and breeches were loading the familiar treasure boxes onto five wagons drawn up at the bank doors. Their random method of stacking puzzled me until they covered the first loaded wagon with a heavy cotton canvas. The finished result reminded me of the North Carolina apple vendor wagons which I had often seen trundling along the roads in the days before the war.

So that's how they expect to get through the Union lines, I thought, continuing to gaze down at the scene. It might just work.

My feeling of frustration dropped from me like pine needles in a gale as I turned my thoughts to the action that lay ahead. Although reluctant to leave this haven of rest and take to the road again I was thrilled that the monotonous wait was, at last, over.

Certain I would come under suspicion as soon as the robbery became known I felt I needed to delay discovery of my departure

Confederate Gold
The Missing Treasure

from Washington for as long as possible. To achieve this meant I must leave the bank today in the same manner as on each previous day. Clearly I could take nothing with me. With a last wistful look at the knapsack stacked in the corner of the room, I left.

Believing Robertson would be occupied in the vault, supervising the gold movement, I crept down the stairs and along the passage to the kitchen. The empty larder shelves told their own tale but underneath were two large barrels, one containing corn and the other beans. There were also four stale loaves of bread piled in a corner. With mixed feelings of guilt and excitement I filled my pockets with corn and beans, before breaking off a chunk of the bread and stuffing it down the front of my shirt. I genuinely regretted being unable to thank my host for his kindness but argued that one day, when the world returned to normal, I would come back and atone for my present actions.

Although the morning was cool my clothes stuck to me as I picked my way between the loaders to the front door. I was relieved the men were too busy to notice my strange gait or the bulging pockets which gave my hips and thighs a bloated appearance. About to step through the door I found my way blocked by a thick set man of angular feature who seemed to be in charge. Not being in uniform I could not tell his rank but, from his attitude, guessed I him to be a sergeant.

"Who are you?" he demanded, his dark eyes narrowing.

"Henderson," I said, moving to one side in a effort to avert his suspicious gaze.

"What are you doing here?"

"Returning home, if I have one left," I said, deciding to stick as close to the truth as possible. "Dr. Robertson has kindly given me food and shelter for the last few days."

"Stay where you are," he said, forcing me back against the wall. "Jackson," he continued, addressing a wizened little man whose grin showed several gaps in a row of rotten teeth, "ask Dr.

Bill Westhead

Robertson if he would be good enough to step up here a moment."

With a nod, Jackson ambled away in the direction of the vault.

The corn, beans and bread seemed to increase in both size and weight while sweat ran down my brow and into the corners of my eyes as I waited for the cashier. I was certain he would notice my peculiar shape as soon as he saw me. My heart thumped in my throat as Dr. Robertson appeared and my captor strode across the hall to meet him. They were too far away for me to hear their whispered conversation but from the gestures and glances in my direction I had high hopes the cashier was confirming my story. I was to be proved correct as soon as the sharp featured man returned.

"You can go," he said with a wave of dismissal, before turning back to direct the loading of the fourth wagon.

"Thank you,' I said. Then in an effort at friendliness added, "Reckon you're almost finished."

He stopped in mid stride and turned back on me. The look of suspicion was back in his narrow eyes. "How do you know how much we have to load," he snapped.

"Well there's only one empty wagon left," I said, peering through the open door while at the same time cursing my stupidity.

At that moment two men pushed between us carrying one of the treasure chests. "One wagon or not," he continued as we again stood face to face, "If I see you or hear of you hanging around this bank I'll have you shot. On your way."

I needed no second bidding. Like a lead ball leaving the muzzle of a rifle I was out the door, down the steps and passed the wagons before pausing to let out a great sigh of relief. I longed to look back to make sure I was not being followed then scamper across the square to the safety of the side streets. Instead I forced myself to look straight ahead and saunter across the

Confederate Gold
The Missing Treasure

square, all the while searching for a spot to observe the wagons without being noticed.

I have no idea how long it took before I found what I was looking for - a deserted store set back from the main street. Leaning on a rail fence, which ran along the front of the store, I was hidden from the bank by the corner of a protruding building which in better times, according to a faded sign, had housed Messrs. Trumble & Connor, Attorneys-at-Law. Chewing nonchalantly on a piece of straw I watched and waited.

Finally the loading was completed and the covered wagons trundled across the square at a slow walking pace. The scrawny horses, ribs clearly visible through dull, matted coats, strained under the load. From the condition of those horses they will not get far today, I thought, as I waited for them to disappear from view. As soon as they turned right at the end of the square onto the Abbeville road, I followed.

In the town it was easy enough to keep out of sight of the men sauntering alongside the wagons several doorways offering immediate concealment. As a precaution I occasionally turned down a side street, round a block, and back again. But once on the open road cover became more difficult and I was forced to crisscross grey, barren fields which, in normal times, should have been turning green with new crops. Sometimes I had to deliberately walk away from the convoy, although always keeping it in sight.

Five miles down the road the desolate fields gave way to wooded areas bursting into their summer glory. Able to move more quickly I was soon level with the convoy and had no problem keeping pace with the straining horses. By now the sun was directly overhead and I reckoned we had been travelling for about three hours. At this rate I calculated the convoy would haul up for the night about fifteen miles from Washington, if the horses could keep going that long.

For what I estimated to be the next two hours I was never more than a hundred yards from my quarry as it plodded painfully down the dry, rutted road. I was amazed at the steady pace of the gaunt beasts. The guards appeared to be in a trance-like state as they shuffled alongside the train paying little or no attention to either wagons or horses. Watching the convoy's progress from behind the trunk of a large laurel oak tree I thought of my time as guard on that same train only a few weeks ago.

"Thinking of taking it for yourself?"

Although the sneering voice was no more than a whisper it hit me in the gut like a rifle butt for I had heard no sound behind me. I wheeled round to face the wiry little cavalry man I had last seen in an alley in Washington. My temper rose and my fists clenched at the sight of him. The way he had bettered me that day still rankled.

"I'm doing exactly what I was told to do by you," I snapped.

"So be it my fine hero. But you can stop now. Your fearless work is done," he mocked. "There is nowhere that convoy can turn off this road so we'll catch up with it when we're ready." He turned and headed back into the woods away from the road. "Come with me."

As at our previous meeting the command brooked no argument. With a last backward glance at the convoy, I followed. He moved quickly and quietly gliding between the trees as though floating on air. His feet never seemed to touch the ground and he moved so easily it looked as though his limbs were tied together with loose rope. Despite my best effort it was impossible to keep up with him. The distance between us continued to widen until, without warning, I was slammed into the dank forest floor by, what felt like, a swarm of swirling bodies. The smell of rotting flesh again invaded my nostrils and memories of my reception at the rebel camp flooded back.

"Let him up boys," my tormentor said, chuckling at the spectacle. He need not have spoken for, by now, my attackers were scrabbling on the ground picking up the food that had spilled from my pockets and shirt and stuffing it into their gaping

Confederate Gold
The Missing Treasure

mouths. Gasping, I struggled to my feet, wondering if my back was broken or simply bruised.

"Just a precaution I forgot to remind you about," the little cavalry dancer said, as he doubled over with sadistic laughter. "We can't," he wheezed, "have all and sundry wandering into our new camp."

I longed, at that moment, for a few minutes alone with him. A few minutes where I could go at him bare knuckled without the threat of others interfering. But I knew this to be a futile hope and I kept my tongue and fists in check while he had his laugh.

This camp showed even more signs of human degradation and defeat than the previous one. The men were covered in dirt while festering sores were clearly visible through their ripped clothing. Their greasy hair and untrimmed beards seemed to shift continuously as lice crawled through each matted cluster. Food, in the form of a mutilated carcass, lay near the smoking embers of a fire. The raw flesh hanging from the skeleton appeared to move as scores of maggots consumed the remains. Save for the trees there was no cover of any sort against the elements. I guessed everyone slept as they were, where they were. The distinct smell of gangrene seemed to linger everywhere.

Even Sangster had suffered. He now walked with an exaggerated limp and the stoop of a beaten man. Only his eyes showed the same devil-may-care attitude that had made him a hero of the south and a scourge of the north. As I took in the scene my hopes of a fortune vanished. Despite the poor condition of the convoy this emaciated band would never have the strength to rob it.

"You'd best change," Sangster said, peering through hooded eyes at my clothing. "Can't have a gentleman involved with this gang of cut-throats, unless you're the leader."

"What is there to change into?" I asked.

"Why these," he said, indicating his own dirty garb.

Realizing this was no mere suggestion, I reluctantly undressed and donned the stinking rags Sangster had tossed on the ground at my feet. My greatest regret was having to give up my good boots in exchange for the soleless footwear Sangster had flung at me.

"That's better," he said, as he slipped his thin arms into my jacket. "Now you look like one of us and I'm dressed as befits my command. Tell me, what news of the gold? I've already learned some details from Doctor K." He nodded in the direction of the cavalry dancer. "Now I need to know about the guards. How many, how armed?"

"You still mean to take the gold train?" I said, staring at him in disbelief.

"Yes," he snapped, folding his arms impressively across his hollow chest.

"But this lot don't look capable of fending for themselves let alone robbing a gold train."

"Don't let our appearance fool you. I want no more of your defeatist talk. What I want is information if you please."

Even the general shuffle of rag-clothed feet was stilled as I told the group what I had seen. "With the condition of those horses," I concluded, "they'll be lucky to make fifteen miles by night fall."

"And the guards?" Sangster prompted.

"Probably about twenty, although to be honest I never counted them," I said. "Most have rifles but they seem a dejected lot. Doubt they have much fight in them."

"Right," he said, turning towards the group. "You heard it boys. We've run from the damned blue-bellies long enough. Tonight we have the opportunity to become rich. Then each and every one of you can flee this Yankee dominated hellhole and start a new life in some better place. There's enough for everyone and if you do as I tell you it will be ours."

A spontaneous rebel yell shattered the silence.

"Quiet you fools," Sangster snapped. "Do you want everyone from here to Abbeville to hear you?"

Confederate Gold
The Missing Treasure

The yell ceased as suddenly as it had begun. It was as if the group had been blasted to eternity by a cannon ball. The only sound that now broke the awesome stillness was the loud, repetitious chattering of a nearby mocking bird.

Fixing unwavering eyes on each man in turn Sangster continued. "From now on anyone disobeying orders will be shot." These last words made it clear the robbery would be a team effort and sounded the death knell for any individual schemes.

Furtive glances told me everyone knew the man meant what he said and that he would not hesitate to carry out his threat. Even the mocking bird was silent.

"Make ready," Sangster commanded. "We leave to catch up with the convoy." He seemed oblivious to the tension in the air as he continued to give his orders. "If any of you fall foul of Yankee patrols before or after the raid that is your own problem. There'll be no, I repeat no, attempt at rescue." He paused, took a deep breath and plunged on. "But woe betide you if you tell them anything. We'll travel in groups of three. Each group watch the one in front and the one behind. There must be no stragglers. Any questions?"

No one spoke. For four years these men had obeyed orders, some clear some confusing, but there was nothing confusing about the orders they had just been given. In a few minutes the fire was doused and the site abandoned for Mother Nature to reclaim as her own in her own good time.

I found myself in the lead party with Sangster in front and the hated Doctor K behind. In silence we trudged north through the sweltering woods that paralleled the road. By late afternoon we had caught up with the wagon train and I was not surprised to find its progress had slowed. Some guards heaved on the bits of the lead horses while others whipped them from behind in an effort to increase their pace, but to no avail. The heat of the day had wasted the animals. The convoy could not go much farther.

Bill Westhead

For another hour we slipped from tree to tree, our eyes riveted on our fortune. In that time our leaden-footed quarry, slowing with every step, covered about a mile.

As the sun started to slip from the cotton ball clouds towards the distant horizon the wagons turned in through an open gate and lumbered up a tree-lined drive towards a large house. Although there were signs of destruction at the stable end, the house itself seemed to have missed the ravages of war. A high sloping roof covered the second storey and balconies ran round three sides on both the first and second floors. The building had obviously been constructed in the days of Southern wealth. Now it stood mocking us. Another dismal reminder of all we had lost in the last four years.

"Come with me," Sangster whispered, tapping me on the shoulder. Together we crept forward. The evening breeze carried with it the sweet smell of the tall grasses as we lay at the edge of the woods little more than a hundred yards from our prize. My former skipper drew a telescope from inside his jacket and putting it to his right eye began to survey the scene as one of the guards approached the front door of the house.

"The man's a minister!" he murmured a moment later, staring at me in utter disbelief.

"What man?" I asked.

"The one answering the door. Here take a look." He passed me the telescope.

"Long time since I saw this," I said, taking the instrument from him. "I reckon it must have been back on the old *Carolina II.*

"Always kept it with me." A hint of a smile creased his haggard features. "Saved me many a time since I came ashore."

With my elbows propped on the ground I raised the telescope to my eye. Sure enough the man at the door wore the garb of a minister. Scanning down the tree-lined drive I read the carved wooden sign near the gate. "Guess it must be the Reverend Chennault," I said.

Confederate Gold
The Missing Treasure

"How do you know that?"

"Look to the left near the gate."

I passed the telescope back to him. "You're right," he said, training it on the tell-tale sign.

We watched for several minutes as soldier and minister stood, heads nodding, arms waving and hands pointing. Finally they seemed to reach some agreement for the guard returned to the convoy and the train shuffled off round the far side of the house. A few minutes later it reappeared heading for a large, strongly fenced horse lot. A double gate offered the only entrance.

"Guess they got permission to spend the night there," I said. "Looks a pretty good site."

"Not for us," Sangster said thoughtfully. "Difficult to surprise them out there. I'd reckoned on them making camp in the woods or somewhere along the roadside not in the middle of a danged open field."

In the final cloud splattered rays of the sun we watched as the wagons were formed into a close circle in the center of the field and the exhausted horses led off in the direction of the damaged stables. Remembering the sight of our fine cavalry at their peak, I felt a pang of remorse for those starving creatures and silently hoped they would be well recompensed for their heroic efforts.

The glow of the campfire within the circle increased as darkness fell. As if in sympathy, smaller fires began to spring up and glimmer in the woods surrounding us. Although we had not seen another living soul all day these modest fires proclaimed, like a town crier, the existence of bands of straggling Confederates resting here and there. Way off in the distance a much larger blaze indicated the likely presence of a Yankee force.

"I don't like the closeness of that house," Sangster muttered as, by the light of the wagon train fire, we observed four armed guards patrolling the fenced perimeter. "There could be Yankees

Bill Westhead

billeted there in which case we'll all be dead or worse, prisoners," he continued, as we crawled back into the shelter of the trees.

Scratching mosquito bites I knelt facing him and waited for his decision. Minutes ticked by in time with the rustling of leaves overhead while Sangster's eyes flitted from house to wagon train and back. For a long time he said nothing. Then, having apparently made up his mind, he looked straight at me. "We're not going to get a better chance," he said. "We'll attack tonight. Bring the lads over there." He nodded in the direction of a dense area of undergrowth away to our left.

Squatting on the ground in a tight semi-circle, we listened as our leader gave his final orders in the same crisp, clear delivery I had heard him use on other occasions when action was pending.

"You, you, you and you," he said, pointing to me and three other members of the group, "will silence the guards. Once that's done the four of you will gather behind the wagon furthest from the house and signal us to join you. We'll attack from there. Each will take what he can carry. We are to meet in Savannah in fifteen days time at the lodgings of Dr. Campbell-Johnson."

"What's the address?" I asked.

"You don't need to know," he said. "If you get caught the Yankees will force it out of you and that will put everyone else in danger. You'll have to use your wits to find it, but I will tell you it's over an Inn." There was a long pause as he glanced at each man in turn to ensure his orders were understood. "Those men are our brothers in arms who have fought for the cause," he finally said. "There will be no killing. No one, I repeat, no one will carry arms. If you have any you will bury them here and now."

This last was greeted with an angry murmur and three men brandishing revolvers rose ominously. They were not going to abandon a friend who had shared their trials and kept them safe for the last four years for anyone, least of all a sailor. They glowered at Sangster while the rest of us sat in stunned silence.

Confederate Gold
The Missing Treasure

He remained calm as he faced them. Only the set of his jaw showed his determination to be obeyed. He took a pace forward. "Now," he hissed.

In the face of this forceful show of resolve the dissidents hesitated then, with faces like pall bearers at a funeral, each knelt and buried his weapon.

With the danger passed, Sangster moved through the group shaking hands and having a private word with each man in turn. It was as though he knew that, for one reason or another, there were some he would never see again.

"You've been a true friend. May God go with you," he said, as he took my hand in that familiar, firm grip.

"Thanks," I said, placing my free hand on his shoulder. He smiled that old wicked smile I had come to know so well.

My eyes were bright with unshed tears as he limped through his bedraggled force. Probably the last force he will ever command, I thought. A sad end for a gallant gentleman who has given his all for a cause that is lost forever.

Watching his slow progress through the group I was suddenly back to those earlier days of the great adventure. A time when the Captain and crew of the *Carolina II* were feted in every southern port. No one would have imagined, in their wildest dreams, we could have sunk so low as this. Fate had dealt harshly with us in the past but now the stage was set for one final run and there was no turning back. I prayed that this time Fate would be a more kindly companion.

CHAPTER 12

Sangster and those of us chosen to silence the guards crept back to the edge of the trees. From there there was nothing but open space to the encamped train. For what seemed like an eternity we lay hugging the ground, our eyes fixed on the shadows moving in and about the wagons. Despite their arduous day, the guards appeared to be in no hurry to turn in. Time and again their fire dwindled only to blaze up again as more wood was piled on. We shivered as the cooling air forced moisture out of the clammy atmosphere. I tried to think about my target and visualize my attack. My fortune was so close and yet so far away.

All too slowly the distant camp fires died and I envied the victors and vanquished alike finding peace in sleep. At last the fire within the circle joined the others in death. Still Sangster gave no order to attack and we continued to lie in the damp grass becoming more and more restless as each moment passed.

"Go." Finally he gave the order and stealthily the four of us moved out from the shelter of the tree line. In the dim light, afforded by the cloud covered moon, we crept towards our respective targets.

My guard, as I now thought of him, patrolled the far side of the lot. To reach him while keeping out of sight of other guards and anyone in the house, I had to make a wide sweep to the right. I wanted to crawl but knew I did not have the time. I had to run. Slowly I rose to a crouch. Feeling exposed I froze listening for the alarm that would announce my discovery. But all remained quiet. Bent almost double, my feet hardly leaving the ground, I stumbled along tripping and falling several times over the uneven ground. Each fall sounded like a canon shot in my ear and each time I hugged the ground certain the explosive noise would be heard. Even at a run the detour took so long I began to

Confederate Gold
The Missing Treasure

worry that dawn would break before I ever reached my objective.

After what seemed like a lifetime spent crawling, crouching and running I was, at last, within twenty yards of my target and still there had been no alarm. Silhouetted in the pale grey moonlight he looked huge, at least six feet tall with broad shoulders. A large flowing cape, similar to those used in better days by the cavalry, enveloped his body.

I watched as he shambled back and forth along the post and rail fence, stopping occasionally to lean on the top rail and peer into the darkness. It seemed my best chance of success was to surprise him from the rear as he turned, but his shuffling movements were so erratic it was impossible to judge such an attack. Realizing there was no time to spare I crept forward every time he turned his back. At last I lay rigid alongside the bottom rail, face pressed to the ground and hands under me hiding the flesh color that would betray my presence. I was terrified my thunderous breathing would give me away and time, like my heart beat, stood still. I dared not look up but simply listened to the tramp of his feet coming toward me and then turning away again. In desperation I waited for those feet to pass by but each time they stopped short of where I lay.

The steady plodding must have hypnotized me for suddenly I heard the scrape of his boot on the middle rail. He was standing directly above me. A hollow feeling grabbed my gut as I imagined him staring out over the open ground. I offered up a silent prayer he would not look down.

How long he stood there I shall never know but eventually the boot scraped again and the grass squelched as he ambled off. As quickly as my stiffness allowed I climbed between the two lower rails and rose to my feet. He turned at the sound and at that exact moment I sprang swinging the edge of my right hand at his throat. He swayed to one side and the chop landed on the side of his neck doing little damage. Although handicapped by his cape his clenched fist shot out whistling over my head. I ducked and drove my knee between his legs. He let out an agonizing cry and clutched himself with both hands. Now his belly was defenseless and my fist smashed home driving the wind out of him. Before he could recover I slammed a second punch into his stomach forcing the last of the air out of his lungs before catching him with two solid blows to the head and a chop to the neck. He crumpled to the ground and lay still.

I wondered if I had killed him but, as I stood there regaining my breath, a moan escaped his lips. I had to immobilize him before he recovered. As he stirred I noticed the leather belt round his waist. Quickly unhooking the buckle I removed it, heaved him onto his face, and secured his hands behind his back. Then I pulled his pants down round his ankles, took off his boots and forced both his feet into one of the pant legs. Next I ripped off his shirt and tore it in two. One strip I stuffed into his gaping mouth holding it in place with the other tied securely round the back off his head. Lying there he reminded me of a trussed up turkey waiting to be slaughtered for Christmas.

I sat smiling at my handiwork when I noticed his boots. Discarding my own pathetic footwear I pulled them on. Although too big they were in good condition and I was sure would stand me in good stead on my trek to Savannah.

"You won't be going far tonight me boy," I said, gazing down at my former opponent. Now, fully recovered, he glared back at me with a look so full of hate that I prayed my makeshift bonds would hold.

Sloshing about in my new, oversize boots, I stumbled towards the appointed wagon amazed that, even now, no alarm had sounded.

As I moved into the faint shadow of the wagon a voice hissed "That you Singleton?"

"Yes. My man's out," I whispered.

"Not before damned time. Where the hell have you been."

"Sorry. Did it as fast as I could," I said. Now was not the time to argue or offer any explanation.

Confederate Gold
The Missing Treasure

"Well now we're all here I'll signal the rest," Alan Burns muttered, standing back from the wagon and waving both scrawny arms in the air.

The open ground seemed to move like a giant ant hill as the gang scrambled across the fields towards us.

"Everyone accounted for?" Sangster demanded, as he arrived behind the wagon.

The murmur that greeted this double-edged question confirmed that all the group were present and the guards had been dealt with.

"Now it's each man for himself," Sangster whispered. "In and out quickly taking only what you can carry. Don't forget the more you take, the heavier your load and the slower you'll travel. Savannah in fifteen days lads and we'll wait for no one. If you miss the rendezvous you're on your own. Good luck and may God go with you. Go."

Like ghosts we slipped from behind the wagon into the circle expecting to fight our way to the treasure. To our astonishment every one of the guards lay asleep, huddled in his blanket round the embers of the long dead fire. Taken completely by surprise they offered no resistance. Before they knew what had happened they were tied up and gagged.

To our amusement their faces registered shock and helplessness as they watched us tear the canvas covers off the wagons and heave the money chests to the ground. Those chests that did not split open on impact were smashed with the butts of the guards own rifles. Gold and silver coins flowed ankle deep around the wagons, glinting in the pale moonlight as though imitating the myriad of stars that now twinkled in the clearing sky. I had never seen, or even dreamed, of such wealth. We started to dance among the coins until we felt the lash of a knotted rope across our backs. Sangster never issued unnecessary orders, when the need arose he let the rope do the talking.

Bill Westhead

Our elation subdued everyone began stuffing their pockets with handfuls of the precious metals, only to find the degraded cloth could not hold the weight. Coins cascaded back onto the ground. Some of the luckier ones found cloth satchels among our captives' equipment and these they filled. Others, like me, tore clothing off the guards to tie into makeshift sacks. Into these we crammed as much wealth as we felt we could carry. There was so much money scattered on the ground that, despite our best efforts, we were unable take it all. One by one we reluctantly slipped away as quietly as we had come, leaving piles of coins, silver bricks and gold ingots lying where they had fallen.

Staggering like a drunkard under the weight of my sack I crossed the open ground into the welcoming darkness of the woods. With every lurching stride my load became heavier and I soon realized I would have to make a number of changes if I was to carry this fortune over one hundred miles to Savannah. Every bone in my body ached and I cried out for rest but fear of capture and the inevitable hangman's noose drove me to take one painful step after another. In spite of the chilling air, sweat poured down my body and blisters started to form on my feet slopping about in newly acquired boots.

When the sky greyed and the stars dimmed I seriously began to think of abandoning my treasure and returning to the comfort of Dr. Robertson's lodgings. But it was too late. I had made my choice and now must bear the consequences. I pushed deeper and deeper into the woods, each agonizing step increasing the distance between me and the gold train.

By the time the sun sailed upwards into a cloudless, azure sky I had to chomp down on my lower lip to prevent screaming out loud. My legs would not support me any longer. I sank to my knees crawling the last few yards into a clump of undergrowth which, to my befuddled mind, offered rest and concealment.

Removing my boots I stared in horror at my bleeding feet and wondered how they were ever going to carry me to Savannah. Overcome by agony and exhaustion I nestled down

Confederate Gold
The Missing Treasure

and hoped the smell of spring freshness, that oozed out of the earth, would revive my sagging spirits. My eyelids drooped but fear kept me from that deep sleep for which my body yearned. Each time my eyes closed I imagined myself encircled by leering troops who made short work of both me and my fortune. Sometimes they were Confederate but more often Yankee cavalry who, I was certain, would increase their patrols once the events of the night were discovered. One nightmare ran into another with no break as I tossed and turned on my prickly bed.

"I must sleep" I muttered, shifting my position for the umpteenth time. At each move the coins in the makeshift sack at my side jingled like a peel of church bells. I was certain the noise would invite the curiosity of anyone passing by. I wondered about emptying them on the ground but realized they would glitter in the sunlight and again arouse suspicion.

For much of the morning I lay there willing myself to sleep while at the same time struggling to find an answer to my problem.

As the heat of the day penetrated my hiding place an idea started to form. Very carefully, so as not to disturb the undergrowth, I undressed. Sitting naked, I sorted my tattered clothing into two meager piles, one to wear and the other to make another sack. Knotting the rags in the second pile together and using string from my pants to tie up the holes I soon had what I needed. As quietly as possible I opened my original sack and transferred half my fortune to the second one. Then I scraped away the earth until there was a hole big enough to bury both. After smoothing out the excess dirt I lay down again. Although nightmares continued to plague me they were now interspersed with dreamless periods and I settled into uneasy sleep.

The day was well advanced when some sixth sense roused me. I lay still, listening. There was no mistaking the sound of men's voices and the scything swish of undergrowth being beaten. Instantly I knew they were searching for me and the others like me. My mind screamed capture and inevitably death but my body, paralyzed with fear, refused to react to the fast approaching danger. The searchers must have been little more than two hundred yards away before self preservation finally came to my rescue. Falling into my rags and grabbing my boots, I crawled out of the far side of the undergrowth. In a crouch I scuttled from tree to tree praying the hunters' eyes would be glued to the area immediately around them.

My luck held and I had increased the distance to over three hundred yards before realizing that their suspicions would be aroused if they spotted me running away. Except for my boots, there was nothing to connect me to the robbery. Also I had no idea in which direction I was heading or what other, perhaps greater, dangers lay ahead. Pausing to catch my breath, I decided that my best hope was to try and bluff my way out.

From behind the trunk of a large white oak I heard the men cursing as they pounded their way ever closer to where I stood. There was no time to lose. Pushing my suffering feet into the oversized boots, I brushed myself down and limped towards them.

"You there, stay where you are." The shout came from a skinny, fair haired boy. I was relieved to see he wore a battered Confederate cap although he looked too young to have fought in the war. I judged him to be in his early teens. I stopped.

"You looking for something?" I asked, as he came abreast of me. I tried to appear calm but my heart pounded and my legs felt as though they could give way at any moment. He carried a dangerous looking, old flintlock musket. Attached to the end of the barrel was a long, angular bayonet which he now brandished a few inches from my gut.

"Yeah," he said, slowly lowering the gun. With the butt on the ground the tip of the bayonet was level with the top of his head. He looked straight at me, distrust in his grey flecked hazel eyes. Neither of us spoke or moved. We simply stood staring at each other. Clearly he did not know what to do and I was not about to help. It was up to him to make the next move.

Confederate Gold
The Missing Treasure

"Who are you?" he finally said, again heaving up his musket and pointing the wicked looking bayonet at my stomach.

"John Sullivan," I replied, hoping he would not hear the quaver in my voice. "Late of General Hood's army."

"You'd best come with me," he said, prodding me towards an older man who was poking through the undergrowth with a vicious looking pitch fork. I noticed the butt of a colt revolver jutting from his wide leather waist belt.

"Who have you got there Harry?" he snarled, as we approached.

"Claims he's called John Sullivan, Mr. Sowell" the boy answered. As the rest of the group gathered round I noticed they all carried some type of weapon.

From the deference my captor showed to the older man, I guessed Mr. Sowell was in charge. Pale blue eyes narrowed under straw colored bushy eyebrows as he looked me up and down, his mouth clamped shut in a thin line across his sallow face.

"So John Sullivan, if that is your name, what are you doing hereabouts?" he demanded, suddenly thrusting his full bearded face into mine.

"Going home," I replied, taking a step backwards. "We're finished. There's nothing left to fight for. The damned Yankees have beaten us. I just hope the old homestead is still standing."

"Everyone says that. I was proud to wear this once," he said, sticking his thumb into his dirty grey jacket. As he did so I noticed the Captain's badge on his sleeve. "But now," he continued, "its a sign of all we've lost. Who were you with?"

"Says he was with General Hood," my young guard said as I hesitated.

"Suppose you were like all the others caught up in the damned disasters in Tennessee and Georgia? Man had no sense," Captain Sowell said. There was bitterness in his voice.

This seemed harsh criticism of a man who, I had heard, had lost an arm and a leg in our cause but I knew nothing about the disasters in Tennessee and Georgia. I nodded in agreement and hoped that would satisfy him.

"Ah, it was rough there," he mused, "but I don't doubt we're heading for rougher times ahead. Well on your way and God's speed."

I thanked him and was about to move on when a voice from the back said "Shouldn't we search him before he goes?"

"Yea, I suppose we should," the Captain agreed.

"What are you looking for?" I asked, as two of the group approached and ran their hands up and down my body.

"What's it to you?" Sowell said, his eyes suddenly narrowing with suspicion. "You're not from hereabouts are you?"

"No," I answered.

"So where were you last night?"

Not for the first time I cursed myself for opening my mouth. Then, feeling a slight trickle down my left leg, wished I still wore something under my outer clothing.

Again I hesitated before answering. "I guess about ten or more miles north of here," I said finally. "I've been walking all day, so yes, it must be at least ten miles."

"You're not sure where the hell you were last night are you?" Sowell said. "You could have been in the same area as the gold train."

"Gold train?" I said feigning puzzlement and, at the same time, fighting to keep my voice calm. "What gold train?"

"The one that was robbed last night."

"A gold train robbed!"

"Yea. All hell broke loose today. It seems the thieves got clean away and now, we've heard, the Yankees are questioning the Chennault family, poor devils."

"The who?"

"Chennault. Seems the train camped in their horse lot last night. But none of us believe they'd anything to do with it."

Confederate Gold
The Missing Treasure

"Have they caught anyone yet?" I asked, holding my breath and hoping my comrades were still free.

"Not yet," he said.

I let out a quiet sigh, but my relief was short lived as he added, "But we'll continue the search until we do, because there'll be hell to pay if we don't. God knows what those poor, innocent Chennaults will suffer."

"You reckon you'll get them, then?" I persisted.

"We've got to catch 'em to save the Chennaults," he said firmly. "They can't have got far carrying all that weight so we'll just aim to keep watch on the roads. Sooner or later they'll be caught. God help 'em when that happens. Still better we catch them than the Yankees. At least they won't suffer before they die."

I agreed that capture by the Yankees would be the worst fate of all, but the look of pleasure on Sowell's face as he talked about a quick death made the small hairs on the back of my neck stir and a shiver ran down my spine.

"That was Confederate gold that belonged to all of us not just those damned rogues that took it," he said. "They robbed the south and that's why they'll die when we catch them."

Now I realized I could expect no mercy from either side. I had no friends only foes. I could trust no one. Strangely I found some small comfort in the thought of again being alone to fight the world.

"Enough of this talk," Sowell said. "We have a job to do and damn me we'd better do it or we might well find ourselves on the end of the hangman's noose." He waved at the group to spread out and continue the search.

I watched, horrified, as the men advanced through the woods. God help anyone in there, I thought, as they thrust their glinting bayonets and wicked pitch forks into the undergrowth. For a few minutes I stood, needing to find some landmark that would help me recognize my hiding place again. A clump of wild azaleas surrounding the base of a large oak, their buds

Bill Westhead

bursting into bright orange blooms, caught my eye. I was fixing the sight in my mind when I was interrupted by a loud yell.

"Are you going to go or join us?" Sowell shouted, pointing in my direction. "Those around here who are not with us must be against us, so make up your mind."

I was trapped. Armed only with a strong stick, I reluctantly joined the search party as they beat their way back through the woods towards scene of the robbery. For the rest of the day I was constantly on guard in case some inadvertent word or action on my part should give me away. Each time a bayonet or pitch fork was thrust into the undergrowth my heart missed a beat as I waited for one of my former comrades to be skewered and brought to light like a pig on a spit.

As the day advanced I began to relax my vigil in the belief that, come nightfall, I would be free to go my own way. I judged, by the sun, we had spent the day travelling westwards and my fortune lay well to the east. With any luck I could recover it this very night and be well away from the scene of the robbery by the morning.

"Where did you say you were making for?" The sudden challenge broke into my thoughts like a thunder clap.

What?" I asked. Lost in thoughts of escape I had failed to noticed one of the group had worked his way over and was standing at my shoulder. "What did you say?" My hands suddenly felt clammy.

"I asked where you were making for?" he said. "By the way I'm Jacob Hartley." His voice was quiet and reasonable but that did not stop the dreaded hollowness flooding back into my belly. "Well?" he said after a pause.

"To my home and family if either are still there," I said.

"And where may that be?"

"Between Augusta and Savannah."

"Maybe so and maybe not," he said, kicking a clump of undergrowth before unloading a shot into the middle of it. "And what are you going to do if you don't find them?" he added

Confederate Gold
The Missing Treasure

turning to face me, the smoking pistol grasped firmly in his right hand.

"Maybe come back here," I said lamely. In truth I had no idea what I would do if I had lost my fortune.

"I understand a lot of the area round there was burned by that red-headed dog Sherman but I hope you find them," said Hartley, a trace of sympathy in his voice.

"Thanks," I mumbled, stepping forward in hopes of putting an end to his prying, however well intentioned it might be.

"Ah," he grunted, as he strode away to continue his search for the fugitives.

Relieved I moved to widen the gap between us in case he suddenly found another line of questioning to throw my way.

The search continued for another hour before darkness overtook us and the hunt was abandoned for the day.

"Where are you spending the night?" Hartley asked, at the very moment I was about to leave the group.

"Here, in the woods I guess," I said heartily, while praying that he would go about his own business and leave me alone.

"No you won't, not with this search going on for the robbers," he said. "If the Yankees catch you sleeping in the woods alone you'll be in for a rough time trying to prove your innocence, if you can ever prove it. Believe me heads are going to roll for this one. You'd best sleep in my outhouse tonight.

"Thanks," I said, realizing I had no alternative and that he meant the offer kindly.

"Can't feed you 'cause we have nothing for ourselves," he continued. "So a good night's rest is the best I can do."

"I'll settle for that," I said, with a cheerfulness I did not feel. "I've many a mile to travel and rest will do me good."

We were half way across the fields making for what, even at that distance, appeared to be a dilapidated, grey colored, clapboard farm house when Hartley stopped. Turning to me he muttered, "Don't trust Sowell."

"Why?" I asked, my curiosity aroused.

Bill Westhead

"He's not what he claims to be. Wears that captain's jacket but never fired a shot in anger. Spent his war guarding prisoners. If I tell you he was at Andersonville, you'll know what I mean."

Although I had heard stories of Andersonville, I thought the place to be no worse than many a Yankee prison camp.

"Someone had to do it," I said defensively, believing Sowell was only doing his duty. "He was probably sent there like we were all sent places we didn't want to be."

"Not him," Hartley said, a hard edge to his voice. "I've heard tell he volunteered for the job, made a fortune and then turned against his own to save his neck."

"Do you reckon those in command at Andersonville will hang?"

"Some probably will and in my opinion Sowell should be among them. Not that our camps were any worse than those our boys suffered in the north," he continued, echoing my earlier thoughts. "Trouble is we lost the war. But I'm telling you don't trust him. He'll do anything to line his pockets and save his neck."

"Why do you work with him then?" I asked.

"So we know what he's up to," Hartley said, giving me a sly wink. "There's always one of us with him so there's nothing the bastard can do that we don't know about."

"Well thanks for the warning," I said. "I'll certainly keep my eye open for him."

"And I'll tell you another thing." Hartley said, placing a friendly arm round my shoulder. "He'll do his best to catch those poor devils that robbed the train just to keep in with the Yankees. For your own sake you keep away from him."

"Is he really as dangerous as all that?" I said, wondering if the warning meant Hartley suspected I was one of those poor devils.

"Every bit." His voice dripped pure hatred.

As we neared the desolate farmhouse I saw that the grey color I had noticed from afar was not paint but smoke grime.

Confederate Gold
The Missing Treasure

"A little reminder of those northern bastards," Hartley said, noting my stare. "But I suppose we were luckier than most. They looted the farm, took the animals and grain but, for some unknown reason, only burnt the outbuildings."

The outhouse, to which he led me, was a disaster. The roof was gone together with two of the walls. The remaining two walls, being of stone, had withstood the fire. The floor was heaped with ash and partly burnt timbers, yet it offered more shelter than the undergrowth of the previous night.

"Best I can do," he said apologetically, "but probably better than you've had for some nights, eh."

"Yes," I said nodding. Although not what I had hoped for, I had to admit it was the best I had found since leaving Dr. Robertson's.

"I'll see if there's anything for a bed," Hartley said, levering up the remains of a small beam, and pushing it out of the way. By the time I had scraped away the ash in the corner of the two standing walls, Hartley had returned with a pile of straw, which he scattered in the cleaned area.

"'night," he said as he left.

Removing my boots I was pleased to see my feet, although still blistered and bleeding, were no worse. Slowly my tired body relaxed back into the straw. The ash, stirred by a light breeze, invaded my mouth and nostrils causing the same stifling sensation I recalled from days spent in the dry, dusty cotton fields of my childhood. But this time it was coupled with the reek of burnt wood and my thoughts drifted back to my final hours in Richmond.

My stomach ached for lack of food. Not for the first time I wondered if the risk of trying to carry my fortune to Savannah was worth the price. What did I have to look forward to - the hangman's noose, starvation or simply to wander this desolate countryside for the rest of my life avoiding every living soul. In short, no matter what I did there was no future. Even the blowing ash seemed, at that moment, to condemn me to an endless existence in a living hell.

Confederate Gold
The Missing Treasure

CHAPTER 13

Rays from the rising sun shafted through the clear blue sky, pierced my eyelids and caused my eyes to water. In the instant of waking my mouth felt dry and gritty and my empty belly ached. The clucking sound of a hen on the other side of the stone wall only added to my hunger. Shaking the ash out of my boots, I carefully pulled them on before brushing myself down and walking out into the yard. A bare footed woman, wearing a long dark dress and poke bonnet, was shuffling across the yard her head lowered. The dress, which had seen better days, hung limply from narrow boney shoulders while the poke bonnet hid her face making it difficult to determine her age. Three hens fussed about her.

"Morning ma'am," I said.

She stopped and slowly raised pale slate grey eyes to stare at me. The scrawny neck and bloodless face topped by long dank hair gave her the appearance of a scarecrow.

"Who are you?" she asked in a quavering voice.

"Miz Hartley?" I said, ignoring her question for I had forgotten the name I had used the previous day.

She nodded.

"I met the search party yesterday and last night your husband offered me your outhouse for the night," I continued, by way of explaining my presence. "I'm on my way home."

If I was expecting a reaction I was to be disappointed. She simply ignored me and continued her search. I guessed she was looking for eggs and the thought increased the ache in my belly until I almost doubled over with the pain.

"With your permission ma'am," I gasped, as I struggled to stand straight, "I would like to use your well."

"There's no water in it," she said without looking up.

"No water," I echoed, unable to believe her words.

Bill Westhead

"Those blue-bellied Yankees poisoned the well before smashing in the sides," she said.

"In that case, I shall be on my way faster than I thought." I said, hoping that my remark would bring a smile to her worn features. But again there was no response. Despite what Hartley had told me the night before, I wondered if I dare ask for food and was contemplating the question when Hartley, himself strode out into the yard.

"You still here?" he said, his face registering concern. "I'd suggest you be well on your way before Sowell arrives to continue the search for those robbers."

In my longing for food and water I had forgotten about his earlier warning. Again I wondered if he had guessed I was one of them and my heart missed a beat.

"Yes but —" I started to say.

"Didn't I tell you he was a suspicious bastard," he said, cutting me off. "Don't suppose you noticed how he watched you all the time you were with us yesterday. He'll haul someone in before he's finished, guilty or not, and that someone might well be you."

"But —," I began again.

"Look I want no 'buts' I just want you out of here." he said, laying a fatherly hand on my shoulder. "Trust me. Sowell let thousands die in Andersonville. What's a few more deaths to him if it saves his scrawny neck. That scum has no conscience. You're not from round here so believe me he'll take you if he can't find anyone else."

His words struck me like a lightening bolt and I knew, beyond any doubt, I had to get away but my rumbling, aching belly told me I could not go far without food.

"Food," I whispered. "Anything."

He looked at me sadly before crossing the yard to the woman who was now scrabbling on the ground. I could not hear what was said but they appeared to be arguing before she, reluctantly, thrust something into his hand.

Confederate Gold
The Missing Treasure

"Here, take this," he said, returning to me and pushing an egg into my hand. I guessed it may have been the only egg the woman had found that morning and could understand her resentment. They were starving themselves and yet were giving me possibly all they had to help me on my way. I wished I could have given them some of my silver in return but that was impossible.

Guilt-ridden, I broke the precious shell and let the slippery contents slither down my parched throat. It hit the bottom of my stomach like a rock and I immediately felt sick.

"Thanks," I muttered through clenched teeth.

"Now go and God be with you," Hartley said, slapping me on the shoulder.

"Which way to Augusta?" I asked, fighting the bile rising in my throat.

"That way," he said, pointing to the right of the sun. "Its a good two days walk but looking at the state of you I reckon it'll take you at least three, maybe four."

"My thanks to you and your wife for everything," I said, taking his hand. "Don't know what I'd have done without you."

"Glad we could help," he said. "Now make for those woods and be out of sight before Sowell gets here."

Although neither Jacob nor his wife had said anything I suddenly realized that if Sowell arrested me as a suspect he would, in all probability, detain the Hartleys for aiding me. The longer I stayed around the farm the greater their danger. With this thought uppermost I in my mind I limped off towards the woods. At the edge I looked back at the two figures standing in the yard. Slowly I raised my hand in salute but there was no response. Mentally I added their names to the list of people I needed to come back and thank when Georgia returned to normal.

I struggled on for a time before coming across a narrow stream. Its waters, rippling and dancing over small stones, reminded me of the miniature bells that used to swing from trees at Christmas in that time before the great adventure. As I knelt to drink the precious liquid I remembered the warning and, despite the temptation, knew I dare not risk being poisoned. Splashing this nectar over my face and arms had to be sufficient. Finally I removed my boots and dangled my feet in the cool, soothing flow.

Lying in paradise, eyes closed, my mind flitted back over the events of the last days from the gold of the wagon train to the gold of azalea bushes. At this last thought I opened my eyes. Enticing as this little Eden was I dare not stay. Eyes skinned for my landmark oak tree and ears acutely tuned for any noise of search parties I stumbled on through the trees.

In a short time the balmy effect of the water began to wear off and the pain in my feet and gut increased with each step until they were almost unbearable. I felt worse than I had done the night of the robbery and I still had the trek to Savannah before me. Biting my lips till they bled and punching forward with clenched fists I stumbled on resting frequently against one of the hundreds of tree trunks that barred my progress. I had just decided to give up this idiotic search when, through a gap in the trees, I recognized the Chennault house in the distance. The glint of Yankee cavalry prancing round the wagons still stationed in the horse lot filled me with horror. As fast as my weary legs would carry me I staggered deeper into the woods, tripping, falling, rising and falling again. The nightmare of my flight from the gold train two nights ago was repeating itself, only this time it was worse. Every muscle in my body cried out. My feet screamed stop. Unending pain throbbed in my empty belly. Fear hammered in my head like the pounding hoofs of pursuing cavalry. Again I tripped and fell.

Unable to rise I lay as I had fallen, head resting on my arms certain that this was the end of my journey. Damn the gold, damn Sangster, I thought. I'll lie here, surrounded by the blessed woods of Georgia, until death puts and end to my misery. The late afternoon sun filtered through the trees and I lifted my head

Confederate Gold
The Missing Treasure

for what, I reckoned, would be my last view of this earth. Were my eyes deceiving me or was there a hint of glittering gold ahead. Slowly I rose to my knees. From this position the gold appeared to turn orange and out of its midst sprang a large tree. I closed my eyes against this cruel mirage, but when I opened them again the scene remained unchanged. Luck or misfortune had brought me within a hundred yards of my treasure. I scrambled to my feet and at a shambling run headed for the undergrowth. Aches and pains faded as I collapsed onto the prickly bed and immediately fell into a deep, dreamless sleep of exhaustion.

It was dark when I awoke to raindrops splattering on my face. The sound of lightening crackled in the distance followed by drum rolls of thunder. Explosive flares seemed to light the sky reminding me of my last day in Richmond. Wind whipped the rain around me as I scrambled out of my hiding place and stood letting my ragged clothing soak up this manna from heaven. Then I stripped naked and wrung the water out of my drenched clothing into my mouth. Here was water, pure water, water I could drink without the ever present fear of poison. The storm rumbled past and the blackness gave way to a tumbling grey overcast. I dressed and for the first time in weeks felt clean and refreshed. Now I had the will to go on although my belly still ached for food.

Searching round the area I found some wild blueberries just beginning to ripen and I stuffed handfuls of them into my mouth. Although good to chew they did little to assuage my hunger and I longed for a squirrel or rabbit to fill the void. But even if there had been one about I had no means of catching it.

Returning to the undergrowth I unearthed my fortune. Now my luck had turned visions of mansions and servants again floated before my eyes. I settled back on the damp ground, the sacks either side of me, and waited for the glorious cover of night.

Bill Westhead

Heavy clouds and the thick overhead foliage blotted out the faint light of the new moon. I could only see a few feet ahead of me as I crawled out of the undergrowth. Despite this I knew I had to move for I had already lost one night of travel and now only had fourteen left to make the rendezvous which lay well over a hundred miles away.

Although the challenge seemed impossible I clutched the two sacks to me as though my life depended on them and inched my weary legs and worn feet towards Augusta. Starvation coupled with the weight of the sacks made for slow going and my progress slowed even more as the night wore on. As dawn broke I heard the low, hoarse rattle of red-bellied woodpeckers and seeing their red heads flash back and forth as they searched for breakfast, I prayed that I too might find food. By the time I crawled into a thicket to rest I reckoned I had covered about twelve miles. In a state of utter weariness I was, once more, ready to abandon my fortune and accept what few benefits, if any, life might still offer.

After burying the sacks I slept. Dreams of being hunted down by merciless bands, sometimes Yankees, sometimes Rebs, came and went. I awoke with a start, unrefreshed. Sweat poured off me, a combination of fear and the unmerciful heat of the sun. I knew I had to find food but did not have the energy to rouse myself. Instead I lay there talking and chuckling to myself while plucking stalks of grass and stuffing them in my mouth.

It was a long time before I came to my senses and realized the futility of my actions. Leaving my fortune well hidden I crawled out of the thicket and wandered off aimlessly in hopes of finding some small farm or even a plantation that had escaped the ravages of Sherman's march. But all I found were stone foundations, bare chimneys and barren fields, all that remained of what had once been flourishing farms. Everywhere the scene was the same and the faint stench of burning still lingered in the sultry air.

Confederate Gold
The Missing Treasure

Even more distressing than the devastation was the lack of life. Where the countryside should have been teeming with people, tame and wild animals, there was nothing. I wondered if I was the only one left alive after the holocaust.

It was late in the day before I found a small cabin which had miraculously survived. For several minutes I stood closing and opening my eyes to ensure it was not a figment of my imagination. But each time I looked it was still there. Terrified that it might vanish at any moment I staggered across the parched field and, on hands and knees, crawled up two wooden steps onto a narrow porch. As I raised my hand to knock the porch suddenly began to spin around me and a long, bright tunnel opened up. A door creaked and a blue apparition began to spin with the rest. The whirling increased twisting first one way then the other until I was swept, headlong, down the long tunnel and into sickening blackness.

CHAPTER 14

Although a thick, heavy blanket of nothingness enveloped my brain I sensed cool, refreshing water dribbling down my parched throat. At times the corner of the blanket seemed to lift and I could see beyond then, almost immediately, the dull effect descended again and I was powerless to shrug it off. In one of my more lucid moments I thought I had reached Savannah but could not remember anything of the journey, could not recall where I had hidden the gold. Above all where was this precious water coming from? I longed for wakefulness to seep back into my befuddled brain but everything remained a blur. I gave up the unequal struggle and lapsed back into oblivion.

The next time I regained consciousness I felt my arms and legs in the grasp of some huge, unrelenting hand. Unable to move I lay there and concentrated on a single bright star that shone way up in the heavens. This star coupled with the darkness of my surroundings now led me to believe I was in the woods, not Savannah. I needed to be on my way but no matter how hard I struggled I could not rid myself of that unseen, restraining hand. Finally I lay back exhausted and soaked in sweat from my efforts. As my mind became more clear I realized I was lying in a pile of straw on an uneven plank floor, tightly wrapped in an old quilt. The shining light was no longer a star but a lone candle set on a rough hewed table, its flickering light throwing shadows on smoke blackened wooden walls.

A faint smell of something cooking pervaded the air and jolted the gnawing agony in my stomach. Turning my head in the direction of the smell I saw her standing in front of a stone fireplace on the far side of the room. A motley array of pots hung from hooks along the wall. Her back was towards me. I tried to attract her attention but only a groan escaped my cracked lips.

Confederate Gold
The Missing Treasure

Still it served the purpose. She turned and seemed to float across the room to where I lay.

"Ah you're awake," she said.

She wore a blue blouse buttoned up to the neck and an old fashioned bell shaped skirt of similar color hung from her narrow waist, the hem dusting the floor. She looked, as I imagined an angel would look, hovering over me.

"Are you feeling better?" Her voice sounded soft and caring.

"Yes thank you, ma'am." The words were clear in my head but took a long time to form on my tongue.

"Just rest yourself and I'll have some food for you shortly." she said, turning back to the fire. "You're really in a mess, but we'll have you back on your feet in few days."

Her words shot through my confused brain like a rifle bullet. I did not have a few days. I had to be on my way. I struggled to get to my feet.

"No use trying to do that," she said, hearing the noise. "You'd never make it to the door. Stay where you are and rest."

I had no alternative. Trussed up like a chicken I collapsed back into straw and let my mind grapple with the problem of reaching Savannah in time. I had no idea how long I had been here, wherever here was. Maybe it was already too late.

Within a few minutes she knelt beside me carefully spooning hot squirrel stew into my mouth. As I gulped it down it hit my gut like a stone hitting the bottom of a deep well, making the ache worse than before. Unwittingly I let out a moan and curled up into a fetal position. She stopped, waiting for me to recover.

"More," I managed to gasp.

"Yes," she said, "but not now. Wait a while and then you can have more. You'll only throw up if you have too much too quickly."

As the pain eased I saw her clearly for the first time. Long, dark, unkempt hair straggled to her shoulders, framing angular features and setting off a sharp chin. Not a pretty face but attractive in its strength. Her green eyes seemed to hold a hint of

Bill Westhead

sadness. Unashamed I let my gaze wander from her head to her feet. Hidden under the blouse and well darned blue dress her body, like her face, appeared strong and firm. But it was the smile, lighting up her face, that held my attention. I guessed she was in her twenties.

"We need to get you cleaned up," she said, hanging the stew pot back over the fire. "A shave would do you a world of good."

Before I had time to object she miraculously produced a pair of rusty scissors and an old razor. With the aid of home-made lye soap and a little water, she set about removing the bearded growth of several weeks.

"How did you let yourself get into this state?" she asked, as she cut and scraped away.

"Walking home," I said, finally finding my voice. "With the war over all I want to do is to get home and forget. What happens after that is anybody's guess."

"How far do have to go?"

"Between Augusta and Savannah," I said. My answer was purposely vague for, although she had probably saved my life, I was not about to trust her.

"Well you've all the time in the world to make it," she said. "So you'd best stay here until you're fit to travel and then we'll see if we can help you on your way."

I started at the mention of time. "What's the date?" I asked, trying to keep the panic out of my voice.

"Well I know it's Sunday," she said, counting on her fingers, "so it must be the 28th of May." She looked at me a puzzled frown creasing her forehead. "Why?" she asked.

Only ten more days to make the rendezvous and at this moment I could not even stand on my own two throbbing feet, let alone walk.

"Well," I said, after a long pause, "in my father's last letter he told me my mother was not expected to live. I must make it home, if I can, before she dies." The lies were becoming easier each time.

Confederate Gold
The Missing Treasure

A look of sympathy flashed across her face. "I know what you mean," she said quietly. "I lost my husband at Bull Run in '61. Life has not been the same since, nor will it ever be. But I find working helps. I keep this place going in memory of him."

"I thought you said we a moment ago," I said.

"Oh that's just habit," she replied. "We'd known each other since childhood. It was always we."

"And you keep this place by yourself?" I asked, trying to veer away from the subject as tears started in the corner of her remarkable eyes.

"What else am I to do?" she said.

"Is there no one else around, family or someone, who could help?"

"No one. I'm here by myself," she said, her voice trailing off into silence.

She sat for some minutes staring into space before suddenly springing to her feet. "Ah, enough of this moping," she said. "This is not going to get you well again and on your way to see your poor mother. Now let's get those clothes washed."

Without hesitation she stripped off the quilt and, before I could object, deftly removed my shirt and pants. My face flushed with embarrassment but she did not seem to notice. Without a word she carried my rags outside while I struggled to pull the quilt up over my gaunt, naked body. A short time later she returned carrying a jar of, what appeared to be, grease in her wet hands.

"This will ease your aches and pains," she said, as she ripped off the quilt. Gently but firmly she worked the unguent into my aching muscles. She seemed completely unflustered by my nakedness. Although it smelled vile, the results were incredible and the pain seemed to disappear through her soothing fingers.

Her firm hands, massaging my legs, suddenly caused an unwitting movement between my thighs reminding me that I had not been with a woman since Richmond. My reaction increased with the realization we were alone. Forgetting my acute embarrassment I reached up with both arms and encircled her waist. Gaining strength, from some unknown source, I dragged her down onto the straw beside me. She offered little resistance and I sensed the tension seep out of her as my hands slowly roamed over her body. But as I began drawing up her skirt she put her hands on my chest and steadily pushed me away.

"Sorry," I mumbled, ashamed at my action.

"Don't be," she whispered, getting to her feet and looking down at me. "With all the men being killed I never thought this would happen again after I lost Thomas."

Tantalizingly she started to unbutton her blouse revealing firm breasts, before slowly dropping her skirt. Like me she wore no under garments. Pain vanished as my body reacted to her every movement and I could hardly control myself as she lay down beside me and snuggled her head into my shoulder. Her warm flesh against mine drove all thoughts of Savannah out of my head. Instant longing took hold and my arm tightened around that narrow waist pulling her closer until, at last, we both gave freedom to our pent up emotions.

I awoke the following morning as the sun dipped through the narrow window of the cabin and swept across my face. For a moment I wondered where I was. Then I felt her body still nestled close to mine. Memories of the previous night came flooding back and I lay there, reluctant to break the spell, letting my eyes and mind wander. There was a freshness about the place which even the faint smell of the ointment failed to dim. I felt utterly contented. The war and its aftermath was in another time and another place.

The likelihood of making Savannah in time is now so remote, I thought, why not stay here and use the gold to rebuild the farm. Then I wondered what her reaction might be when she learned how I came by it. Would she accept my offer or would the memory of her husband and the cause he had died for result in her denouncing a Confederate robber.

Confederate Gold
The Missing Treasure

These thoughts were still racing through my mind when she turned on her back, opened her eyes and smiled at me. I wanted to take her again.

"Food first," she said, holding up a restraining hand.

"All right," I said, as she quickly donned her crumpled skirt and blouse. I sighed.

"You know," I said, turning on my side so I could watch her every movement, "we've been together all night and I don't even know your name."

"You never asked. Your mind was on other things," she said coyly. "Still if it makes you feel any better it's Jane, Jane Harrison. What's yours?"

"Josh Singleton," I said without thinking, then quietly cursed myself for being stupid enough to give my real name. But the damage, if damage there be, was done.

"Josh," she mused, as she busied herself around the fire. "I suppose that's short for Joshua, as in the Bible."

"I suppose so," I said, "but what about this food that you seem to think we need more than love."

"It's coming."

"Well before I eat I would like my clothes back if it's not too much trouble ma'am," I said, playing along with her teasing game.

"I wondered how long you were going to lie naked in that straw," she said, tossing my tattered, but now clean, clothing at me. "Breakfast is ready if you feel up to it."

"I'm up to anything," I said, struggling unsteadily to my feet and dressing.

"Later, my boy," she said, placing a wooden platter of hog and hominy on the table in front of me.

"How in God's name did you find this?" I asked. "It's a meal fit for a king." Then looking at the amount she had served added, "and probably his court."

"I managed to get the corn in last year before those bluebellies came through. The hogs were hidden in the woods."

Bill Westhead

"But didn't they take everything when they were here?"

"I was one of the lucky ones," she answered, a strange look in her eyes. "The officer in charge of the raiding party was a rare Yankee gentleman. He took my horse, two cows and the hens but he left me my home. He never found the corn."

"And the hogs?" I asked.

"Ah, I let them think they'd got all I had," she said. "I've become a very good liar over the last few months. Now enough of your prying questions. Be thankful for the food and eat."

"Yes ma'am,"

The pain in my stomach had eased and I was ready to eat my fill. In silence I devoured the meal while trying to decide my future. Should I still try and make Savannah or stay here with this loving angel calmly sitting opposite me.

"Your very quiet," she said, as I licked the last scraps from the platter.

"I've a lot on my mind," I said, looking down. I dared not meet her eyes for fear of giving myself away.

"Well rest yourself and maybe things will be clearer tomorrow," she said, rummaging on a small shelf in the far corner. Incredibly she produced a pipe and small tin of tobacco which she handed to me.

"You're full of surprises," I said, prodding the dry, crumbling tobacco into the bowl. "Where ever did you find this?"

"It was my husband's," she said quietly, as she passed me a lighted taper. "Never been used since he went away for good. The tobacco's stale but it's the best I can do."

"You're a wonder," I said, leaning back on the chair and puffing away contentedly. Although hot burning it was the best smoke I had ever tasted and I said so. She smiled.

We sat for some time in intimate silence before Jane got up to clear the table. Without thinking, I grabbed her arm as she passed and pulled her down onto my knee and into a long and

Confederate Gold
The Missing Treasure

passionate embrace. When we finally parted I had made up my mind.

"I'm going to tell you something," I said, "but before doing so I need your solemn promise, as a Confederate, that you will never breathe a word of this to anyone on pain of death."

"Pain of death," she repeated, trying to stifle the laugh that sprang to her lips. "Sounds very serious."

"It is serious," I said. "So hush your laughter and listen carefully."

The laughter died and her eyes opened wide at the harshness of my voice..

"A few days ago a Confederate wagon train of gold was robbed," I continued, then paused. Her reaction to this news would determine what I said next.

"Damned Yankees," she muttered. It was enough.

"Rebs, not Yankees," I said. "We did it to save the gold falling into enemy hands. I know where part of that treasure is hidden and if you will help me on my way some of it can be yours. What do you say?"

She stared at me for a long time. Her initial look suggested she wanted to believe me but clearly wondered if fever had turned my brain. Then her eyes narrowed as she stood up and wandered over to the door. My body tensed and I held myself ready to grab her if she showed any sign of running. Our passion of a few minutes earlier had been replaced by an overpowering silence. There was no clock in the cabin, but if there had been it would have surely stopped.

My mouth went dry at the thought of having to kill her to prevent her screaming my secret to the world. I had witnessed death in many forms during the war but this would be different. This would be murder and I knew, in an instance, I could never do it. I felt suspended in my own private zone of silence and prayed for her to say something. The waiting became unbearable.

Bill Westhead

At last she turned back into the room. "So this story about your dying mother was a lie," she said, her green eyes blazing.

"Yes," I said. "She died many years ago."

With a look of contempt she turned back again and walked out onto the porch. In two strides I was at the door but she made no attempt to run. Instead she stood there, her work-worn hands resting on the rail, gazing across the fields. The silence that now lay between us seemed as overwhelming as the black storm clouds racing towards us.

"Well," I finally said, unable to stand the stillness any longer.

"I don't know that I want to help a liar and a thief," she said. Her voice sounded flat as she continued to stare at the approaching storm. "I need time to think."

"You have the rest of the day," I said slowly and deliberately. "But I need to know by nightfall." I longed to take her in my arms but this was not the moment. "There's gold for you if you help me on my way to Savannah," I reminded her. "But if you won't —." I shrugged my shoulders, leaving the sentence unfinished.

"What if I won't or can't?" she asked, thrusting out her chin and glaring at me.

"You'll have to come with me and there will be no gold."

"Why? Despite what you've done I could never betray you, a Reb, to the Yankees."

"I can't trust anyone. Not even you," I said. "I daren't even let you out of my sight."

Tears sprang into her eyes. "I wish you'd never come here and, above all, I wish you'd never told me," she sobbed. "You know I can't leave here after all I've fought for. It's all I have in the world."

"Please yourself," I said. "Those are the conditions." I spoke harshly to cover my uneasiness.

For the rest of the day I watched her every move. Time and again I longed to make love to her but my ultimatum had killed

Confederate Gold
The Missing Treasure

everything between us. We only spoke when absolutely necessary and, even then, the words were stilted.

As the watery-yellow sun dipped away in the west we stood at either end of the porch the distance between us indicative of the gulf that now separated us.

"Well," I said, "have you decided what you're going to do?"

She looked across at me, her eyes full of loathing. "I've nursed you, fed you, housed you and given myself to you," she said, "and what have I got in return. Nothing but trouble. What gives you the right to tell me I must risk my neck for you and your damned gold or lose everything I have struggled to keep."

She grabbed a broom and swung it viciously at my head. I ducked, but her action showed how she had held the place together throughout the war. She was a fighter.

"You still haven't answered my question," I said as calmly as I could.

"I've risked my neck before to save this place," she screamed, "and I'll do it again. So, God help me, I'll try and get you to Augusta. But from there on you're on your own and out of my life."

I let out a long pent up sigh of relief before asking how she planned to do this.

"What does it matter to someone who only thinks of himself and gold," she snapped.

"Don't forget," I said. "I promised you gold if you helped me. I need to know so I can keep that promise."

Her eyes blazed and it was some time before she spoke. "Every now and again I take a small load of corn to Augusta in hopes of selling it to buy other food," she finally said, in a voice as cold as death. "I'll hide you in the wagon. It's all I can do to save my farm and your damned neck." She spat out the last three words.

I nodded. The idea of riding to Augusta was appealing. "When do we start?" I asked.

Bill Westhead

"First light, day after tomorrow" she said. "It takes the best part of a day to Augusta what with Yankee patrols stopping you all the time. As if they weren't enough, there are also roaming bands of cutthroats, both white and black, who'll set upon anybody at any time for anything and God help you if they do."

"Why not tomorrow?" I asked, eager to be moving.

"Firstly you wouldn't get very far in your condition. You'll be surprised what another day's rest will do for you," she said. "Secondly. If I'm risking my neck and farm for you, I want to see that gold before we leave."

The cold calculating look she gave me froze me in my tracks. In that instant I realized I was completely in her power and she knew it. The realization did nothing to relieve my anxiety but there was nothing I could do about it. I nodded my agreement and together we waited in silence for the darkness.

As the cabin sank into blackness I got to my feet. "You're coming with me," I said.

"Why?" she asked. "What do you need me for?"

"Don't argue," I said. "You think I'm fool enough to leave you here. Who knows but what the Yankees might be waiting for me when I get back. Now move."

She tossed her head and without a word followed me out into the pale moonlight. She did not object when I took her hand, but there was no intimacy in the cold fingers. It was some time before I found my bearings but, once found, we made good progress to the thicket. Cautiously we circled the area to make sure we were alone before crawling into the brush. The ground looked to be undisturbed. Jane squatted and watched me unearth the two sacks and refill the hole.

"That it?" she said when I had finished.

"That's it,"

"Now what?"

"Back to your farm."

Confederate Gold
The Missing Treasure

We approached the cabin from the rear and cautiously peered through the window. In the dim light the room seemed just as we had left it.

"Well show me your precious gold," she said, as I closed the back door. There was no mistaking the sarcasm in her voice.

While she lit a candle I untied the knots and let my wealth fall to the floor. The pile of gold and silver glittered dully in the glimmering light. Her eyes were wide in astonishment and her hands trembled. "My God!" she breathed.

"Put that light out," I whispered savagely. "Do you want the whole Yankee army to descend on us with this in the middle of the floor?"

Sheepishly she extinguished the light. "Sorry," she said, as the flame died.

"We'll have to hide your share somewhere," I said, ignoring her apology. "Where would you suggest?"

"Under the cabin," she answered without hesitation.

Quickly I divided the horde into two roughly equal piles. Covering one with the quilt, I scooped the other back into my underwear sack and warily opened the door. Thankful that at that moment the moon was covered by a thick layer of cloud and gave little light, I crawled under the cabin. Here the earth was soft and in a few minutes I had scraped out three shallow holes burying a portion of the treasure in each.

"I've split it into three lots," I said, brushing the sand off my clothes as I came into the cabin. "In that way if someone should stumble on one they may not think of looking any further. Now for my part of the fortune."

For the first time that day, Jane smiled. "You're a good man at heart even if you are a liar and a thief," she said, as I started to scoop the remainder of my treasure back into the other sack. My heart rose at her words. Perhaps tonight would be the same as last night, I thought, and my body started to respond. But instead of coming towards me, as I had hoped, she wandered over to the

Bill Westhead

kitchen area and started poking about in one of the cupboards. Almost at once she produced two well worn saddle bags.

"They belonged to my husband," she said quietly. "It will be easier for you to carry your treasure in these than in that homemade sack you've got."

The remark and the broad smile that accompanied it suggested all was well again. I moved to take her hand and lead her to the straw, but she pulled away.

"Not tonight," she said, her voice firm. "While I think you mean well I'll never forgive you for threatening this farm. We can be friends, but that's all."

"Where are you going to sleep then?" I asked.

"Over by the fire on the quilt. You take the straw," she said.

The lonely night passed slowly as I lay listening to her steady breathing from across the room. The pain of wanting her next to me was more than I could bear and thoughts of taking her in her sleep crossed my mind as I tossed and turned in the straw. I got up and went outside into the cool, damp air to sit on the porch. Finally I fell asleep my back propped up against the outside wall of the cabin.

The following day Jane remained aloof, firmly rebuffing any attempt by me to penetrate the barrier she had built around herself. Much of the time I spent wandering around outside unable to stand the confines of the cabin.

"Food up," she shouted through the window, as I sat on the porch steps at the end of the day.

"Why not bring it out here where its cool?" I said.

She made no reply but in a few minutes appeared carrying two wooden platters and sat down besides me.

"I've been thinking," I said through a mouthful of grits.

"Not again. Not another bright idea," she mocked.

"I believe you when you say you would not give me away to the Yankees," I continued, ignoring her gibes. "So why not let me drive myself to Augusta."

Confederate Gold
The Missing Treasure

"You," she spluttered. "Don't be stupid. What makes you think you would fare any better than me. Don't forget I do the journey regularly and know many of the folks along the way. You don't. Added to which how would I get my horse and cart back if you went alone?"

"Horse!" I said in amazement. "I thought you told me that Yankee officer had taken your horse."

"I did," she said, a knowing smile creasing the corners of her mouth. "But who do you think is going to pull the cart? Me? For a robber you are not very bright."

Her reminder was like a knife in my gut. I winced.

"Before you ask any more stupid questions," she continued, "I have a small pony hidden in the woods. He's too small and looks too frail to be of any use to a soldier, so if anyone spots him they leave him alone. But he's much stronger than he looks and can pull that cart all day if necessary."

"You never cease to amaze me," I said.

For the first time that day she laughed out loud and her eyes shone with pleasure. I dared to slip my arm round her shoulders. She did not pull away but inclined her head slightly towards me. Neither spoke as we sat there on the steps gazing into the vast night sky where stars, as big as scuppernongs, started to twinkle in the endless canopy.

It was some time before either of us moved. Then taking her hand I led her inside to the straw. All bitterness seemed to be forgotten as we clung to each other. Dawn would come soon enough. In the meantime nothing mattered in the world except the two of us entwined as one. My dreams of Savannah and fortune paled into oblivion. The morrow would take care of itself.

CHAPTER 15

The grate of the door latch must have roused me. In a daze I reached for Jane reckoning it would be the last time I would hold her. I was reluctant to waste those final, precious moments. Only straw scratched my bare arm. Lifting my head I looked over at the kitchen area but that, like the rest of the room, was empty. It was as though she had never been. Suddenly the thought struck me like the slave master's whip that, despite her assurances, she might yet betray me. Her condemnation of me as a liar and thief echoed in my head. Leaping to my feet I dressed, all the time keeping my ears open for any noise that might warn me of approaching danger.

The piles of gold and silver coins were still where we had left them hidden under the quilt. My mind in turmoil I quickly stuffed them into the two saddle bags. Part of me longed for Jane's return while common sense screamed at me to go. Finally the screaming beat out the longing and I shouldered the saddle bags. Warily I cracked open the door and peered out into the bright sunlight. Then I saw her emerging from the far woods leading what, at that distance, appeared to be a large, long haired dog. As she drew nearer I saw it was a pony, its shaggy head slightly below Jane's shoulder. My heart sank as I watched them approach the cabin. The pony was so small I doubted it could pull an empty cart to Augusta let alone one with two people aboard not to mention a load of corn.

"Morning," she said, as she tethered the pony to the porch rail.

"Is that what you call your horse?" I said, dropping the saddle bags on the floor in despair.

"Yeah," she said. "You got a problem with him?" The look on her face and exaggerated southern drawl warned me to hold my tongue.

Confederate Gold
The Missing Treasure

"No," I muttered, still staring in disbelief at the animal.

"Good," she said. "This is Traveller, named after Robert E. Lee's horse." She scratched the pony's head between the ears and ran her fingers through his mane. "Not as big I grant you, but just as beautiful and just as strong."

If ever an animal expressed love Traveller did at that moment thrusting his muzzle into her shoulder and gazing at her with large brown eyes. It was as though he knew she would protect him and in return he would give his all for her. But I doubted his all would be enough.

"That's my boy, Traveller," she said softly, putting her arm round his neck and pressing her face into his forehead. Despite the passing of time, I dared not break the spell that bound girl and pony. I simply stood, watched and waited.

"Don't just stand there," she said finally. "There's work to be done if we are to make Augusta. Go get the wagon from the shed round back." She pointed behind her.

Rounding the corner of the cabin I noticed, for the first time, a low wooden structure some two hundred yards away, partly hidden in a small grove of wild Cherry Laurel. The faint outline of a track led towards the building. As I drew nearer I saw the roof and two of the walls had already collapsed and the two remaining walls looked ready to fall at the slightest breath of wind.

If my hopes had sunk at the sight of the pony they were dashed completely by the sight of the two-wheeled cart inside the remains of the shed. All three sides and tailboard were pitted and rotten while the floor boards were riddled with holes. I wondered how she managed to haul corn without dropping ears all along the way. The only consolation was that the wheels and shafts appeared sound and the harness, although black with age, was smooth and supple. I'd be faster walking than going in this thing, I thought, as I manhandled the decrepit vehicle back to the porch where Jane and Traveller remained locked in a loving embrace.

Bill Westhead

I lowered the shafts carefully to prevent the shock of impact causing the cart to disintegrate. "Here," I said.

"Go and get the quilt and those saddle bags," she ordered, as she expertly backed Traveller between the shafts. By the time I returned she had the pony fully harnessed. Grabbing the quilt she spread it out over the cart floor.

"Now we're ready," she said, leading the pony and cart round to the far back corner of the cabin. I followed and watched as she unpegged a single corner board from the siding and slid out four horizontal wooden planks to reveal a cleverly concealed dry storage space.

"My husband built this cabin," she said, as she worked. "Even at the start of the war he had doubts about the outcome and so built this as a hide-away. I use it now to store any food that I can lay my hands on."

"The gold would have been safer in here than under the cabin," I said, admiring the ingenuity of her dead husband.

"Food is worth more than gold these days," she said. "Besides it's always possible the Yankees might return and burn this place. Then where would the gold be. No it's best where it is."

"But the war's over."

"The war's over but the fighting isn't," she spat back. "No one is safe these days. We were safer during the war than now. At least then we knew who the enemy was, but today —." Her voice trailed away.

"I suppose you're right."

"Of course I'm right," she continued, and for the first time that day she smiled. "Now let's get loaded and on our way."

Peering through the hole where the planks had been I saw ears of corn piled neatly on the floor. Each mound looked to be dry and, considering its age, in good condition.

"Where did you get all this?"

"I've grown it over the last two years," she said, clambering into the storage space.

Confederate Gold
The Missing Treasure

"If you're hungry eat these," she said, throwing the ears out onto the ground. "Haven't time to cook this morning."

"Thanks," I said, grabbing a couple of ears from the rapidly building pile.

Finally she emerged into the sunlight. "Now," she said, starting to replace the planks, "go pick up your saddle bags and lie down on the cart floor."

I did as she bid, wriggling about to make myself as comfortable as possible. I knew I would be there for several hours. The quilt helped but the rotten floor poked its unevenness into every part of my thin body. She watched in silence, a stoney expression on her face, while I turned this way and that. Finally I found the most comfortable position was stretched out on my back.

"That won't do," she said. "Your feet are hanging over the edge. You'll have to lie on your side and bend your legs."

I started to writhe again until I had exhausted every possible position hoping to find one that would allow me some modicum of comfort. But it was not to be.

That's enough," she said, making no effort to hide her exasperation. "Where you are is where you'll have to stay."

Without further warning she hooked on the back board and started to pile the corn around and on top of me until I was fully covered. The extra irritation caused by the uneven pressure of the hard ears merely added to my torment.

"Don't move," she said, as the uncontrolled jerking of my tensed muscles caused the corn to shift. "And above all do not make a sound."

Tears trickled down my face as I fought to control my twitching body. Then I heard the scrape of her feet as she climbed onto the seat followed by a jolt as the cart began to move. I had been uncomfortable with the cart stationary, but now its rolling movement made my situation many times worse. At every lurch, the floor seemed to dig deeper into my bones and the corn packed down in such a way that it soon proved impossible to move any part of my body. I longed to cry out for her to stop but held my tongue knowing this was my last hope of making Savannah on time. Even when I reached Augusta I still had over a hundred miles to go and reckoned I only had eight days left.

To take my mind off my present agonies I tried to reason that each creaking turn of the wheels meant one moment less in my cramped condition. I was also making up for time lost. I tried to force myself to plan the rest of my journey, but to no avail. My brain refused to focus on anything but my immediate suffering.

By now my nose and throat were filled with dust from the cart floor and the dry husks surrounding me. Attempting to stifle a sneeze, I started to choke and strangled coughs racked my imprisoned body. Even in my misery I knew the corn must be shaking as if an earthquake had struck the cart, but there was no word from Jane.

Suddenly, through my spluttering, I heard the distinct thud of galloping horses hoofs and the distant jingle of harnesses. The sounds came closer and the rolling of the cart slowed then stopped. I prayed we had just pulled over to let the horsemen pass, but some sixth sense warned me we were in imminent danger of being searched by Yankee cavalry. I lay still, fear welling up in me like the dark of a pit shaft. I hardly dared breathe and the next cough froze in my throat.

"What have we here ma'am?" Although the enquiry was polite, the coarse, grating Northern accent sent a river of ice through me. I had never been so close to the enemy before and felt certain that my life on earth was about to end. Time stood still. My world, like my breath, stopped as I waited for Jane's response. It seemed so long in coming I began to wonder if she was still there. My muscles started cramping again and I fought to control the involuntary twitching that threatened to give away my hiding place.

Confederate Gold
The Missing Treasure

At last she spoke. "Why sir," she said, drawing out each word in her best southern drawl, "I have orders from a major in the Union army to deliver this corn to the quartermaster in Augusta."

I imagined her eyes open wide in innocence and a telling smile being flashed in the direction of the cavalry commander. I prayed that he would succumb to her charms and let us pass, but my prayers went unanswered.

"And who might the major be ma'am?" This time I heard a doubt in the rasping voice.

This is the end, I thought. She has no hope of answering that. The pressure in my bladder increased ten-fold and I suddenly found my pants and the quilt soaked. I only hoped no one would notice the trickle of pale yellow liquid that I felt sure must be dripping through the cart floor.

"I regret Captain that I do not know his name." I was amazed at how helpless she sounded. "Now the South is defeated we do not, nay dare not, ask questions when orders are given."

The captain grunted. "Well be on your way and make sure you deliver that corn safely. There's still many a danger on this road from wandering Johnny Rebs who have nothing to lose. They've been known to kill for food. Have you any means of protecting yourself?"

"No sir," she said. From the sound of her voice I imagined her eyelids fluttering coyly.

"Then we will ride part of the way with you."

"Why, thank you Captain."

I cursed at her ready acceptance. Why the hell could she not refuse. Then I realized to decline such an offer would immediately arouse suspicion.

The cart jolted forward and above the creaking of the wheels I heard the dreaded clop of horses hoofs and the clink of harnesses alongside. For some miles these sounds served as a constant reminder of the danger surrounding both of us.

Bill Westhead

The sun beat down and my jail reeked. I dreaded one of the Yankees getting too close to the cart and recognizing the stink. If that happened the cart would be searched. Within minutes I would be discovered and both of us taken captive. The thought sent shivers racing through my aching body.

The cart bumped along the rutted, dirt road. Stabbing pains shot through my limbs and it was only the fear of what would happen to Jane that stopped me surrendering. For a time I lay there, soaked in a vile mixture of sweat and pee, silently choking on the dust that saturated what little air there was around me. Finally I reached the point where I could endure this hell no longer and, despite the consequences, was on the verge of giving myself up when the jolting suddenly stopped.

"We must leave you here ma'am and patrol south. I wish you a safe journey."

"Why thank you sir for your protection this far," Jane said, in a voice that suggested she meant it.

My relief knew no bounds as the sound of our escort faded. The cart jerked as Jane urged Traveller forward. With the departure of the patrol the tension in my muscles eased, my breathing returned to normal and the pain in my legs and arms slowly decreased. With time I became less sensitive to the jolting and managed to turn my thoughts to the future. Visions flashed before me of vast fields of cotton and my own columned plantation house with Jane sitting on the shaded porch, surrounded by our children. Life would be the best it had ever been.

"Halt."

The harsh accent pulled me back to the ever present dangers of the real world and I was immediately immobilized as if by a snake bite. I held my breath and as the cart jolted to a stop the aches and pains returned, firing though me like darts. My stomach turned over.

"Get down."

I heard the scuffing of feet as Jane obeyed.

Confederate Gold
The Missing Treasure

"What's this?"

Something hard suddenly struck the cart causing it to rattle and the corn to shift. I was petrified that the side would collapse if it was hit again. But Jane sounded unfazed by these blue-bellied bullies. In a calm voice I heard her tell the same monstrous lies she had told the earlier patrol and marvelled at her self control. I expected at any moment they too would let her pass but in the next second my hopes were dashed.

"If that's to feed our boys, as you claim ma'am," he said with an arrogant chuckle, "we'll save you the journey to Augusta."

"What do you mean sir?" Jane said and, for the first time, I heard a slight tremor in her voice.

"Why ma'am, my boys are hungry so we'll eat that corn right here. Pull over by that tree."

I heard the sound of scraping feet as Jane climbed back onto the cart. Then the all too familiar rocking motion started again. What an appropriate place, I thought, convinced that in a few minutes I would be discovered and then both of us would be strung up from one of the boughs. Now the end was near fear melted away and a strange calm came over me. In the short time it took to reach the tree I had resigned myself to my fate but fervently prayed that, when the time came, I would have the strength to save Jane.

"Major." As if on cue Jane's voice suddenly cut into my musing. "If you steal this corn someone will be answering to General Wilde and I don't guess it will be me."

"You never said the General ordered the delivery." The major spoke slowly and I sensed that mention of the General's name had given him cause to think again. What a hell of a girl she was. Quick witted and fearless.

"In that case you'd best be on your way ma'am and may God go with you."

You hypocritical bastard, I thought, as I felt the cart turn. Now we were out of immediate danger my fear returned. I lay clutching the two saddle bags, as though my life depended on them while my lips moved, this time in a silent prayer of thanks to the Lord for our deliverance.

After what seemed like an eternity of bouncing and rocking we stopped again and, as before, I heard the scrape of Jane's feet as she climbed down. I had heard no challenge and wondered if she was watering Traveller or if we had, at last, reached the end of our journey.

"Stay were you are and I'll be back in a minute," she hissed at me through the corn cobs.

While my hopes soared at the thought of being in Augusta the aches and pains of my confinement returned with a vengeance. Then, miraculously, I felt the weight of the corn start to shift and realized it was being unloaded. In a few minutes I was able to uncoil from my fetal position and, in agony, push myself off the back of the cart. My legs were numb and gave way under me. I hit the ground. Without a word Jane helped me up, slung the two saddle bags over her shoulder, and supported me as we staggered across a moss covered stone courtyard towards a dilapidated shack.

The place appeared to have been quickly and roughly thrown together using pieces of wood and boards, many of which showed severe scorch marks. Inside the hard packed earth floor was smooth. Two broken-down easy chairs leaning against the far wall constituted the total furnishings. The atmosphere was stifling, heightened by the smoke from the remains of a small open fire in one corner.

"Not what you expected eh?". The tall woman who addressed me in a husky voice looked to be in her fifties. Her grey hair, severely pulled back into a neat bun at the nape of her neck, seemed to exaggerate the narrow, straight nose and wide-set, pale blue eyes. As she bent towards me, I noticed the long thin, aristocratic fingers of a pianist, but the hand she offered felt rough and calloused. Her dark green taffeta dress, although patched, suggested she had known better days.

"No," I said, placing my hands on her shoulders to prevent myself from falling. "But these days one is grateful for any shelter."

Her thin lips broke into a smile.

"This is Mrs. Rebecca Parslow," Jane said, nodding in the direction of the older woman. "She will help you on your way to Savannah. Now I must go and sell my corn. Maybe we'll meet again when the world returns to normal but, in the meantime, God bless you and keep you Josh."

I could not believe we were going to part with so few words after all we had meant to each other. Removing my hands from Mrs. Parslow's shoulders I tottered over to where Jane was standing and, taking her in my arms, placed a long, hungry kiss on her mouth.

"I love you," I said, as our lips parted. "I mean that with all my heart. Tell me you love me too."

"It's the times, Josh," she whispered. "I am very fond of you but do not love you. Who knows what will happen between now and whenever. For our own safety we must part, but I shall always remember you."

"And I shall always remember you and everything you have done for me. May God be with you until I come back to claim you," I said.

She gazed up at me and smiled. Unspoken words hung between us and I knew I would never forget her or the moment. Slowly she reached back and parted my hands that encircled her waist. With eyes lowered and a faint blush on her cheeks she tossed the saddle bags on the floor before walking out of the shack. Mrs. Parslow followed.

I collapsed on the floor and, unashamed, let the tears pour down my face. I longed to run after her but my legs would not carry me. I also knew in my heart she was right. By pursuing her I could endanger all three of us. I had to let her go at least for the time being.

"Welcome to my home," Mrs. Parslow said, on her return.

"Your home!"

"Ah, I haven't always lived like this," she said, with a genteel wave that indicated the shack and its contents.

Unable to think of anything suitable to say I simply nodded and waited as she glided over the earthen floor to one of the easy chairs. She sat on the edge, her back as straight as a ramrod much, I imagined, as she might have done presiding over a gathering in her drawing room years ago.

"Before the war my husband was a cotton merchant and we had the best of everything," she said, her voice calm. "He was an Englishman. When the war started he remained here organizing supplies of cotton for his family's mills in Lancashire. But as our Southern cause began to falter he decided to return to England." She paused, her hands twisting together in her lap.

"Why didn't you go with him?"

"He wanted me to but how could I leave the South in her hour of peril."

"Have you heard from him since he left?"

"Oh yes, that is until these last few months when its been impossible to get letters from abroad. He arrived safely and in every letter since he's begged me to join him. Some day I will."

"What did you do after he'd gone?"

"Helped the cause as best I could," she said. "Our boys needed medical supplies so I organized the collection and local distribution of snakeroot, pokeweed, skunk cabbage, dandelions and other herbs.

"And this place," I said, my arms opening wide.

"Last December when the Yankees came through they burnt our house to the ground along with many others that stood in their way. We, who had everything, suddenly found ourselves with nothing."

By now Rebecca Parslow needed no prompting from me. A distant look in her eyes she kept talking as though, having once started, she had to unburden her soul of all that had happened. I

Confederate Gold
The Missing Treasure

took the opportunity to push the saddle bags out of sight under one of the chairs.

"We banded together and between us salvaged pieces of wood, board and any thing else from the wreckage of several houses. With these we built a number of huts, similar to this, and furnished each with whatever we could retrieve from our devastated homes. There's quite a colony of us around here. Although far different from what I've been accustomed to I must say I'm thankful these days for any mercy however small." She spoke quietly, seemingly accepting her fate without bitterness.

"But —," I began.

"I've talked enough," she said, holding up her hand before moving over to the fire and poking the embers. "First we must eat and then decide how we're going to help you on your way. In the meantime, dear sir, make yourself at home."

With an impish smile, she gave me a mock curtsey and pointed to one of the easy chairs.

"Thank you ma'am," I replied, bowing low. "Your kindness overwhelms me."

At this she burst into a tinkling laugh. "I can see we're going to get along just fine," she said.

While I sat and watched, she put a number of vegetables into a small stew pot and hung it over the fire.

"Don't ask what we are eating," she said, turning back to me, "because I don't know what to call it. I put in anything I can find that is edible, no matter what its age, then wait to see what comes out. My husband might have called it broth, but more likely he would have thrown it out." The lightness was still in her voice and I began to wonder what she was conjuring up for my journey.

She was right about the broth. Although no doubt nourishing, it proved to have no taste and a strange smell.

"How I long for salt," she said, as she spooned the watery liquid into her mouth. "At least it would make this taste of something. But such is not to be."

Bill Westhead

We ate the rest of the meal in silence. "Coffee?" she asked, as we finished. "Oh it's not the real stuff," she added, as I dropped my spoon in surprise. "In fact it's made out of a mixture of okra and acorns, but better than nothing."

She crossed to the fire and filled two cracked mugs. She handed me one. Like the broth it was tasteless and looked more like dirty water than coffee. But, as she herself had said, it was better than nothing.

"How would you like to be my son?" she suddenly asked, as I drank.

My face must have registered the shock I felt for she went off into peals of laughter. Holding her sides, tears rolling down her cheeks, coffee sloshing over her dress and down the chair, she continued to laugh for several minutes.

"I thought you were going to help me get to Savannah." Her laughing annoyed me and I spoke sharply.

"So I am my boy. So I am," she said, collapsing back into the chair. "But dear oh dear that was so funny. You should have seen the look on your face."

"What would you expect with a question like that? Anyway what was the point?"

"Because that's how I'm going to help you," she said, regaining control. "We're going to travel together as mother and son."

I was about to protest that having a woman of her age along would slow me down, when she placed a hand on my knee and looked straight into my eyes.

"I want to join my husband," she said quietly, "and to do that I have to make for a port. Savannah is the nearest but I dare not travel alone in these times. Apart from Yankees and free slaves roaming the countryside I hear some southern whites have formed a new, secret society. Nobody knows who they are but it's rumored it can cost you your life if you fall foul of them.'

"Haven't heard of them," I said. "What do they want?"

Confederate Gold
The Missing Treasure

"Nobody knows for sure." Her look told me she was clearly frightened of them. "I've heard it said they are for keeping the black slaves in their place."

"Well you're not a slave so why should they bother you?" I said, feeling more comfortable.

"As I told you." She paused. "Nobody really knows what they want, but from what I've heard they put the fear of God in me."

"What have you heard?"

"Enough. It would be unwise of me to say more," she said. Her eyes darted round the shack as if she expected a member of the society to leap out of the walls.

It was clear that I would learn nothing further so, deciding to change the subject, I asked her if she thought she was up to walking as far as Savannah. It was her turn to look surprised.

"Whoever said anything about walking," she said. "I may look destitute in this hovel but there is money elsewhere. If I can buy a horse or two we can travel together in style as mother and son. This gets you to Savannah to meet your old comrades and gives me some protection on the way. You see it meets both our needs."

The plan seemed sound except, I thought, for two drawbacks. I needed better clothes if I was to pass as her son and somehow I had to conceal my fortune about my person. As my toes touched the two saddle bags I wondered how much Mrs. Parslow knew about my comrades and the stolen gold.

"Come, what do you say?" she said, rising and coming over to where I sat.

Unable to think immediately of an alternative plan, and knowing I only had a few days left to make the rendezvous, I agreed.

"Good. Now you stay here and I'll be back presently. If you want more broth or coffee help yourself," she said, as she slipped out through the doorless opening.

Left alone, I brooded over the problems of the saddle bags and how much Mrs. Parslow knew of my situation. I wondered whether or not I could trust her with the truth. She could even now, I reasoned, be denouncing me to the authorities. An icy clamp clutched my body at the thought and, despite the oppressive heat in the shack, I shivered. Should I leave at once or chance staying? For some time I pondered this question before deciding to stay. As a precaution I pulled one of the chairs close to the doorless opening. From here I could remain hidden but still have a good view of anyone approaching the shack.

Here I sat and waited, while my heart continued to pound and my mind raced with one uncertainty after another. Whether I made Savannah with prospects of a long and happy future or become a prisoner with no future at all would, I thought, be determined in the next few hours.

CHAPTER 16

Time hung like a noose around my neck as I waited for Mrs. Parslow's return. At times I sat and at others paced back and forth across the shack, all the while keeping a close watch on the opening. For something to do, I downed another mug of the tasteless coffee while continuing to try and solve the problem of the saddle bags. Slowly the sun dipped, until its last rays topped the surrounding hovels and slanted in through the entrance. At least the sunset bodes well for the morrow, I thought wryly, as I once more settled in the chair.

By the time she got back the sun had long since slipped behind the skyline of the makeshift town and stars flashed, like so many diamonds, in the sapphire blue of the evening sky.

"Come see what I've got," she said. There was no mistaking the pride in her voice as she bustled into the shack.

My excitement rose as I followed her outside, hoping to find two fine horses. But any thoughts of a quick journey to Savannah vanished at the sight that met my eyes. Standing there nuzzling in the damp earth for nonexistent grass, stood a half starved mule, its mangy coat unable to hide the protruding ribs. Tied across its back was a bundle of clothes.

"Best I could do and I had to haggle for hours to get that," she said, seeing the look on my face. "Even then it cost me over seven hundred dollars. But you have to admit its better than nothing."

"I suppose so," I said, making no effort to hide my disappointment. "But I doubt he'll get us very far."

"I've told you before we can't be choosers these days." She was clearly annoyed at my sullenness. "Now don't just stand there, get him inside."

"Why?" I asked, still staring at the mule.

"You ought to know," she said, grabbing the rope and leading the animal into the lean-to. "What do you think would happen if I left him outside for the night? I'll tell you straight, he'd be gone in no time."

Floundering between moods of guilt, fury and despair I followed her inside and watched as she tethered the animal to the leg of one of the arm chairs.

"Now let's get you changed and those rags out of the way," she said, untying the bundle of clothes from the mule's back and tossing them at my feet. "Here."

While I changed, she busied herself at the fire, stirring the embers and adding more bits to the broth pot.

"That's better," she said, turning to look at me now dressed in a pair of well-worn light brown pants, a dark shirt, with one arm missing and a short frock coat that had clearly been a feast for moths. I reddened under her lively gaze but had to admit she was right.

Although there was a glint in her eyes, they seemed to be thoughtful as she continued to stand and stare at me, arms folded across her bosom. "I still don't know what to do with those saddle bags," she said suddenly. "If we take them like they are they're bound to arouse suspicion if we're stopped, and yet we can't leave that money behind."

"How do you know what's in them?" I snapped.

"Oh I guessed," she said, turning back to the broth pot, "from the way you've kept them with you all the time, never letting them out of your sight. Then, of course," she added, waving her stirring stick at me like a school teacher, "there was a jingling noise whenever you moved them."

In a strange way I felt relieved that she knew my secret and had not, as far as I knew, made any attempt to steal the gold or give me away to the authorities. But shame at not offering to pay for the mule tempered my relief for I was sure I had more money than she had. For a while neither of us spoke. Mrs. Parslow knelt by the fire and, like a witch hovering over her cauldron,

Confederate Gold
The Missing Treasure

continued to stir the pot. Finally she rose and announced the meal was ready.

"Of course!" I said, as she floated across the floor, her dress flowing in line with her aristocratic movements. "That's it."

"What did you say?" she said, coming up to me.

"I said that's it,"

"What?"

"That skirt of yours would be a great hiding place." I started to explain. "If we made some small bags we could hang them under your dress."

"I'm not sure that would work," she said, pouring the thin, flavorless soup into two wooden bowls. "It's going to make me very bulky, not to mention the weight."

"Not if we make several small bags and tie them all the way round your waist like a belt," I persisted. "And you'll be riding the mule anyway."

"Well, I have to admit its the best idea we've had to date," she said, handing me one of the bowls. "Eat first then we'll give it a try."

I spooned the broth down as fast as I could and as soon as I had finished began tearing my old, discarded shirt into several pieces. Onto each I placed a number of gold and silver coins then tied the corners together tightly to prevent the coins clinking when moved. The work finished I went outside while Mrs. Parslow took herself off into the darkest corner of the shack and, with the aid of a piece of stout string, tied the bags round her narrow waist.

"Well what do you think," she said from the doorway.

I was delighted with the result. Although her waist line had increased markedly she had retained her figure. I felt sure that even those who had known her before would hardly guess she now carried a fortune.

"Marvellous," I said, and in my excitement aimed to throw my arms round her.

"Yes," she said, cleverly sliding away from my embrace. "I think the idea will work, although it does little for my comfort. Now you stay here until I free myself of this burden." She slipped back inside while I gazed up at the heavens and asked the Lord to help us.

Suddenly the inside of the hut seemed to catch fire. In a panic I rushed in only to find Mrs. Parslow standing by the leaping flames.

"You all right?" I asked, dashing up to her.

"Oh yes," she said calmly. "There's no cause for alarm. I am just burning your old clothes. Don't want to leave any trace do we?""

"But you could have burnt down the whole place."

"That would have been no great loss," she said. Her fire-lit face creased into a smile. "I've seen bigger and better fires than this in the last few months. Anyway its all under control."

Silently we stood and watched as the fire began to die down. "Now to sleep," she said, when only the smoldering embers remained. "This may be the last good night we have for some time. We need to be away from here by first light."

True to her words she settled into one of the rickety arm chairs and in a few minutes was sound asleep. Not for the first time I marvelled at the woman whose spirit, despite all the hardships that had befallen her, remained undimmed. If all Southerners have the same spirit, I thought, we might have lost the war but we will never be beaten.

While Mrs. Parslow slept I tossed and turned restlessly in the other chair, occasionally getting up to check on the mule. I could not wait to be away from the moldy smell and smoke blackened walls that enclosed me. It seemed the sun would never rise as the hours of darkness drifted by at funereal pace. All the while the sound of my companion's deep, steady breathing rumbled round our abode like distant thunder.

At last the sky started to lighten in the east and the fuzzy outline of the surrounding shacks became visible through the

Confederate Gold
The Missing Treasure

early morning haze. Despite my lack of sleep I was wide awake and ready to move by the time Mrs. Parslow stirred.

"We'll finish that broth," she said, straightening up from the chair and brushing herself down. "Then we're on our way."

The broth had been poor fare when hot. Now, stone cold, it proved difficult to swallow the watery, tangled mess she poured into the two unwashed bowls. But swallow it I did, for I was eager to start. Mrs. Parslow also seemed to have a renewed energy about her. As I led the mule outside she started to string the belt of coin bags round her waist. Minutes later she mounted side-saddle and, without a backward glance, pronounced herself ready to leave.

Leading the mule I set out for the river. This, we had decided earlier, was the most direct route to Savannah as well as providing a constant supply of fresh water for our journey. We knew no matter which route we took we would have to beg or forage for food.

For the first two hours we trudged steadily across barren, untilled fields seeing neither sight nor sound of any human being. It seemed we were back in the time before man first walked the planet. Only the slush of my feet and the clop of the mule as he plodded along unwillingly at the end of his rope broke the oppressive silence. We had named him Archibald after Mrs. Parslow's husband.

Under the unmerciful sun the stagnant air was hot and steamy and my body was soon bathed in sweat. The forsaken terrain emphasized the bleakness of our prospects. At last the dusty fields gave way to a beaten path and the ground began to slope gently towards the sound of rippling water.

The sweet, icy water of the Savannah river struck the backs of our throats in little tart explosions. We drank slowly savoring each mouthful before splashing the cooling water over arms and faces. Refreshed we sat for a few minutes on the bank and in the clear light that can only be reflected from water, stared across at the wooded slopes on the far side.

Bill Westhead

The track alongside the river made for easier going and, despite frequent stops to refresh ourselves in the chilling waters, we made steady headway. As the day progressed vaporous clouds, first white then darkening, began to blow in from the direction of the sea chasing across the face of the sun like sheep on fields of misty sky. A welcome soft, drenching rain began to fall and large, cleansing and reviving droplets splashed down from the heavy foliage overhead. As evening approached a light breeze stirred the air. The rain lessened and finally stopped. We pulled off into the woods for the night and, after tethering the mule, I set out to find food.

Except for a handful of unripe plums, the sourness of which made our mouths pucker, my search proved futile. Following this sparse meal and a long, refreshing drink from the river we lay quietly in the undergrowth, staring up through a leafy canopy at the faintly glimmering stars. Finally the whispering of the breeze through the branches lulled us to sleep.

The following morning dawned with wisps of white feather-like clouds drifting aimlessly across a starch blue sky. There seemed little point in wasting time foraging after the efforts of the previous night so, with the last vestiges of sleep whisked away by the cold river water, we took to the path. The rope was slack as Archibald, refreshed by his night's rest and tree bark meal, contentedly ambled along behind me.

As the sun climbed higher in the sky the temperature rose and, despite the shade of the leafy trees that lined our route, it was not long before we were again soaked in our own sweat. The path dipped and rose at random following the contours of the land. Sometimes we were tree shaded and level with the river and at other times exposed on high bluffs with the waters far below us. We stopped frequently to refresh ourselves, splashing about in the lazy eddies like children. We ignored the few unripe plums we found afraid that eating too many would result in stomach cramps, something neither of us could afford if we were to make Savannah in time.

Confederate Gold
The Missing Treasure

As on the previous day we saw no sign or heard any sound of human life. In the all encompassing silence my mind wandered off into thoughts of the good times that, if our luck held, might lie ahead. Glancing back at Mrs. Parslow sitting bolt upright and staring out at the river, I was reminded of a beautiful picture Mrs. Hampton had shown me one Christmas day back at the plantation of Joseph and Mary on their way to Bethlehem. I wondered if they too had travelled in companionable silence and whether this was a good omen for the success of our journey. The thought lifted my sagging spirits and lightened my step.

By the time we made camp that evening a feeling of tranquility had settled over me. As if in a dream I set out once more in search of much needed food.

I had covered about two miles without finding anything when a faint sound caught my attention. I stopped and listened. When the sound came again I recognized it for what it was - a muffled human scream, like that of a beaten slave or mortally wounded soldier. It was a cry of agony and hidden somewhere in its depths was the sound of sheer terror. In an instant I was back in the real world, a world where imminent danger lurked round every corner and in every shadow.

I knew, for my own sake as well as that of Mrs. Parslow, I should avoid the area and continue my foraging some place else. But I could not help myself. Something inside was driving me to find the source of the screams.

They became louder and more frequent as I stealthily inched from tree to tree, my heart racing and my stomach tightening with each step. Watching the ground around me, to avoid stepping on anything that might give me away, I almost blundered into a small clearing where a group of negroes, in a motley collection of what appeared to be military uniforms, brandished lighted torches and danced wildly round something suspended from the branch of a large tree. At first I thought I was watching some type of religious ceremony until one of the soldiers pranced up to the object and thrust his torch into it. A fearful, penetrating shriek rent the air and the stench of burnt hair and scorched flesh reached my nostrils. Bile rose in my throat and the blood froze in my veins but I could not tear my eyes away from the scene. Suddenly the group stopped their devilish dance and, as if in some satanic ritual, slowly advanced to beat out their torches on the victim's body. There was one final ear-piercing scream, which I vowed I would hear to my dying day, then silence. A knife flashed and the corpse fell to the ground in a heap. In an instant the tormentors were gone, vanishing into the trees like phantoms of a by-gone age.

I waited for several minutes on the edge of the clearing, hardly daring to move or even breathe, before plucking up enough courage to cross to the tree. In the pale moonlight I could make out what remained of a half naked white man, his hands and feet tightly bound by ropes. Burns, so deep that in places bone was visible, covered most of his upper body and the hair on his head was burnt to a crisp stubble. Empty eye sockets gazed into the night sky. I bent over and retched at the gruesome sight, my empty stomach heaving and heaving until it could heave no more.

I sank to the ground and, leaning back against the tree trunk, wondered what the victim had done in life to warrant such a death. A slave auctioneer perhaps, a bounty hunter or maybe a plantation overseer. Whatever it was I felt sure he had not deserved this fate. I looked again at the contorted thing that had once been human and shuddered. It could have been my father, I thought, and silently blessed the day he had been killed at Vicksburg. Brother striking brother in war was bad enough, I reflected, but what I had just witnessed was savage murder. Had I not seen it for myself I would not have believed it possible. Now I understood, only too well, Mrs. Parslow's fear of travelling to Savannah alone.

Alone. The thought entered my mind like a meat skewer. Unsteadily I got to feet and started to run back along the way I had come. At this very moment Mrs. Parslow was alone with my fortune and I had no doubt what her end would be if this same group found her. In my haste I stumbled over the uneven ground and tree roots, constantly falling and rising again oblivious of the cuts and bruises or the noise I was creating. My breath came in rasping gasps as I pushed on knowing I had to keep going as fast as my legs would carry me.

"Whatever's the matter?" she said, opening her eyes in astonishment as I burst into our little camp area. "A gang of negroes," I gulped. "We must move at once."

"Move? Now? But its the middle of the night. Come, come now, calm yourself," she said, laying a hand on my shoulder.

I realized I was making no sense to her. With an effort I pulled myself together and told her what I had witnessed. My words had an immediate effect and within minutes we were moving out, pulling a reluctant mule behind.

I decided to stay on the path as this was relatively free from twigs and branches the crack of which might, at any moment, alert our pursuers. I sensed an eeriness in the silence that surrounded us. The pale moonlight filtering through the Spanish moss covered trees cast dark, flickering shadows along the trail. Sometimes these seemed to resemble human forms striking us with fear and causing us to freeze in our tracks. We moved in fits and starts for the rest of that horror filled night until the grey dawn finally extinguished the pestilent moonlight and the world took on a more merciful canopy. By then I reckoned it was safe to call a halt.

Finding a small clearing in the trees to the side of the path we made camp. By now food was becoming our primary concern for, apart from the unripe plums, we had eaten nothing since leaving Augusta. But the events of the previous night had taken their toll and I needed rest before venturing on another foraging expedition.

The sun was high overhead when I woke with an aching gut and hollow rumbling in my belly. My companion still slept soundly while Archibald contentedly nibbled at a small area of

Bill Westhead

grass. Lying on my back I listened to the mating calls of mocking birds and watched the flashes of white as they flitted through the trees. Every now and again a bright red streak at the edge of the woods announced the presence of a Cardinal. How I envied them their carefree life. The heavy scent of pine wafted over me borne on the humid breeze. These were the sights, sounds and smells of a world at peace and I was reluctant to break the spell. But the ache in my empty gut remained and, although she had not complained, I knew Mrs. Parslow must be suffering the same pangs of hunger. Not for the first time I wished I had gained the knowledge to live off the land like the Indians.

Grudgingly I got to my feet and wandered down to the river in the vain hope that a drink might relieve my aches and pains. Sitting on the bank, staring into a deep, quiet pool, I was suddenly mesmerized by the sight of fish. Here was food right on our doorstep and I wondered why I had not thought of it before. How long ago was it I had spent evenings alone, fishing in the river that ran by the plantation? All I needed was a long, pointed spear. Hurrying back to the camp I searched the area until I found what I was looking for, a thin, straight, supple tree limb about five feet long. With difficulty I broke it off and then, finding a rock, began grinding a point on one end.

"What are you doing?" Mrs. Parslow asked, levering herself up on one elbow.

"Making a fishing spear."

"The way you're grinding that you'll never get a point on it," she said. "Much better use a knife,"

"Yep," I drawled, continuing to grind away. "I would if we had one."

"We have," she said, rummaging down the front of her dress. "I never travel without a knife. It offers me some small protection." She withdrew her hand and held out a small hunting knife.

Confederate Gold
The Missing Treasure

"I suppose you carry matches too in case we want to start a fire," I said, never ceasing to wonder at this amazing woman.

"As a matter of fact I do," she said, slipping her hand again down the front of her dress and producing a tin match box. Opening the lid she proudly displayed some half dozen pine matches about two and a half inches long with very small red tips. "There now, anything else?" she said, her eyes twinkling in amusement.

"No thank you ma'am," I said. "I think you've done enough, the rest is up to me."

Within a few minutes I had sharpened the spear to a fine point and was back down to the pool. The task of spearing fish, so easy as a boy, proved more difficult than I remembered. Several times I missed my mark but finally eye, hand and spear became better coordinated and soon four good size fish lay on the bank. By the time I arrived back at the camp with my catch Mrs. Parslow had a fire going. It only took a few minutes before we were feasting on fresh, juicy flesh.

"More?" I said jokingly, as I swallowed the final mouthful.

"I don't think so," she said, with a smile as she shook her head. "But I do want to hear more about last night."

My mind flashed back to that satanic clearing and, with halting tongue, I tried to describe what I had seen. I wanted to spare her the most gruesome details, but she would have none of it. A hush descended on us as I finished my story. Even the birds became silent as though paying their last respects to the dead. Mrs. Parslow sat, her unfocused eyes staring into the distance, her thoughts clearly elsewhere. Only the tinkling sound of the river broke the stillness.

"Perhaps the white group are better," she said finally.

"What did you say?" Her voice had been so low that I was not sure I had heard correctly.

"That group," she said, louder this time. "You remember what I told you back in Augusta about a secret group the white folks were forming to keep the black slaves in their place.

Bill Westhead

Perhaps after what you've just told me they may be the lesser of two evils."

I wondered why, after four years of bloody conflict, we were being forced to choose between the lesser of two evils. Perhaps now the war was over the true killing was about to begin and, if so, I wanted no part of it.

"I'm sure," she said finally, "that most members of that white group are good, church going men but not averse to lynching a negro or two if they think it necessary."

My mind churned with mixed emotions. Memories of the white corpse and the negro soldiers jumbled with thoughts of my long dead negro mother. If she were still alive her life would be threatened by this newly formed gang. But despite this, after seeing the menace of freed negroes, it seemed there was good reason to form this new group and I said so.

"Each to their own opinion," Rebecca Parslow said, a thinly veiled tone of disgust in her voice. "I've been on this God-forsaken earth many more years than you. One day you'll come to realize there's no right or wrong, just grey. It all depends on which side you're on."

"Well," I began, and then thought better of it. I decided to change the subject. "We should be on our way," I said, after a long pause. "We still have several hours of daylight left."

"You're right," she answered, rising to her feet. "For our own safety we must travel together and arguing about the rights and wrongs of folk is not going to help."

In a few minutes we had scattered the ashes in a wide circle, and buried the remains of our meal. Then with Mrs. Parslow again mounted on Archibald we left.

As we ambled along I kept wondering how we were going to avoid the double peril caused by roaming bands of free negroes on the one hand and the newly formed white group on the other. So deep were my thoughts that they blotted out the beauty of nature that surrounded us. I no longer heard the birds or smelt

Confederate Gold
The Missing Treasure

the pine. Instead unknown, leering faces flashed before me coupled with screams of agony and the scent of burnt flesh.

"I've been thinking," I said as, late in the day, we stopped one more time to refresh ourselves at the river's edge.

Mrs. Parslow looked up her cupped hands stopping half way to her mouth, her forehead creased in curiosity.

"The most dangerous period seems to be from darkness to the middle of the night," I continued. "That's when we must stay awake. So why don't we travel from mid-day to mid- night?"

She thought about this for some minutes, seeming to turn it over, in her mind before saying, "Sounds sensible to me, although night travelling will be slower. Still I suppose it's better to be slow and safe."

That evening we plodded on into the ever deepening darkness. Our pace was slower than I expected and I began to wonder if we had made the right decision. It was probably well after mid-night before, exhausted, we finally gave up and dragged ourselves into the trees to rest and await the new day.

CHAPTER 17

We woke to the sweltering heat of the mid-day sun. Not a cloud could be seen through the overhanging trees whose leaves drooped in the suffocating heat. Every living thing, except ourselves, seemed to be cloaked in sleep. Our small world was filled with an overwhelming stillness. It was time to be on our way.

Reluctantly I scrambled to my feet, brushed the pine straw off my clothes, and untethered Archibald. Mrs. Parslow stirred and in a few minutes we were back on the path, now hazed in the noon-day heat, slogging against a solid wall of muggy air. The only sound was the steady clop of the mule's unwilling feet. Minutes dragged into hours, which seemed like days, as we plodded towards our destination. The sting of salted sweat ran down my face and into my eyes and mouth. Soaked clothing clung to my body like a tight skin. At every step it rubbed against the inside of my thighs and crotch until my flesh was raw and my gait became a stiff-legged, lurching stride.

Glancing back at my companion I saw she was in little better condition. Her clothes too were sweat stained and the once neatly tied bun of grey hair at the nape of her neck had gone. In its place long, wet locks clung to either side of her thin, flushed face, fell to her shoulders and disappeared down her back. Even the mule was suffering. Head down and tongue lolling out of the side of his mouth he dragged one foot after another as if each step would be his last. It was the worst travelling day we had yet encountered, the more so, as the path now ran across an exposed bluff far above the ever tempting river.

I longed for a breeze or even a few clouds to shield us from the sun's rays, but no relief came. The only consolation was that we met no other human being and I began to think that, despite

Confederate Gold
The Missing Treasure

the conditions, our decision to travel from mid-day to mid-night had been correct.

With the approach of evening the trail dipped as if mocking our suffering. Our pace quickened on the downward slope and, without pausing, we splashed into the exhilarating waters shouting and laughing like children. For a while Archibald lay on the bank, his long tongue lashing water into his gaping mouth, before he too joined in the romp.

Our spirits revived by the cleansing river and the arrival of a light breeze that suddenly sprang up out of nowhere we moved on into the descending gloom of night.

It was about two hours later that we were halted in our tracks by a blinding explosion off to our right that lit up the darkening sky and cast wavering shadows across our path. The fear, that had gnawed at me for so long, struck again and I felt that all too familiar hollow in my gut. No matter how small the fire might be now I knew, from my days on the plantation, the dry woods around us could be engulfed by flames within minutes. Our only hope was to make for the river, some fifty feet below.

"Off the mule and down to the river," I shouted.

There was no response from Mrs. Parslow. She simply sat the mule as though mesmerized by the blaze.

"Down to the river," I shouted again, as I dragged her off the animal and shook her until her eyes began to focus.

"But —," she started to say, then fell silent.

"Follow me," I ordered, pulling Archibald towards the steep slope that lay between us and safety.

Unable to keep our footing we slipped and slithered down the dry, dusty slope like skaters on ice. The murky waters rushed towards us. Before we could regain our footing we slid into the swirling eddies and found ourselves being swept out into the main current. Fighting to keep my head above water I saw Mrs. Parslow struggling to swim towards the bank but her progress was severely hindered by her long dress and my treasure. Somehow I managed to hang onto the rope which a frightened

Bill Westhead

mule at the other end was fighting to tear from my grasp. I kicked my legs wildly in an effort to reach the bank but was dragged back by the frantic animal. Fighting for breath and trying to control my terror, I was about to sacrifice the mule for my own safety when I felt a hand grab my shoulder and saw the blurred vision of a grey head bobbing beside me. Together, wide eyed and ashen faced, we wrestled against the current and mule. Several times the churning waters closed over our heads but finally our feet touched solid ground.

"You all right," Mrs. Parslow gasped, as we scrambled onto the bank. I heard the concern in her husky voice. "I've managed to tie poor Archibald to that rock over there."

"Good," I spluttered, lying face down while spewing up gallons of Savannah river water. Then slowly raising my head I saw she had discarded her dress and sat there in the moonlight wearing no more than a torn woolen petticoat, red with black stripes, over a chemise the top of which clung to her thin, upper body like a sheath. I was relieved to see her bulging waist line which meant the bags of gold and silver still hung there.

"Oh dear," she said, leaping up in embarrassment. "You should not see me like this young man. You must promise to keep your eyes tightly closed while I dress again."

I did as she bid, but could not help smiling. Without a thought for her own safety she had just saved my life and yet was now mortified at my seeing her without a dress. As I waited for her to release me from my promise, I wondered if I would ever understand the conventions of southern women.

"You can open your eyes now," she said, squelching toward me along the bank.

"I can never thank you enough for saving my life out there," I said, pointing over the river, "and I apologize if I have embarrassed you. I certainly didn't intend to."

"It was as much my fault as yours," she said, "so let's just forget it ever happened. Now, what do we do?"

Confederate Gold
The Missing Treasure

"I need to find out about that fire," I said, scrambling to my feet. "You stay here and keep an eye on the mule. I'll be back as soon as I can."

Without waiting for a reply, I scrambled up the slope on hands and knees. Coming so soon after my fight with the river the climb exhausted me and, on gaining the path, I collapsed heart pounding and lungs gulping in the night air. It was some time before I felt strong enough to stand. At first sight the distant conflagration did not appear to have increased in size and this gave me hope as I set out cautiously to investigate.

I was within fifty paces of the fire before I saw the blaze was not coming from the trees and undergrowth as I expected, but from an enormous cross stuck between two small mounds of earth. Flames leapt skyward from both post and cross-piece in an eerie ruddy glow lighting the heavy overcast that had replaced the cloudless sky of earlier in the day. Around the cross, in slow measured steps, circled a group of specters clothed in dark, ground length capes. Their features were hidden behind fearsome three pointed masks made all the more frightening by the incandescent light from the fire. Each held a long, wicked looking whip. Every now and again one of the phantoms would flail the two mounds of earth, the thong of the whip flicking out and back like a striking rattle snake.

This strange ceremony intrigued me and I watched for some time before I saw one of the mounds move. In that moment I realized the mounds were not earth but naked human beings, their dark bodies pressed close to the ground, as if trying to avoid the cutting lash. I had seen similar lashings administered to slaves on the plantation, only they had been tied to a post, not grovelling on the ground. I wondered what these two might have done to deserve this unusual punishment.

Suddenly one of the robed figures held up his hand and all movement stopped. He advanced on the cowering negroes who made no sound although his whip continued to bite into their naked backs. I had seen cruelty before but this sight made me sick.

The sepulchral tones of the advancing, hooded figure shattered the silence. "We're spirits from another world come to tell you the white race reigns supreme," he chanted, in a voice like that of religious minister. He paused to let his words sink into the minds of his victims. "Repeat after me," he continued, "The white race reigns supreme."

A frightened murmur rose up from the two prostrate figures, so low I could not hear the words, but it seemed to satisfy their tormentor. Slowly he raised his arms to the heavens and in a tone which resonated round the clearing said, "Remember our justice is swift and sure. If you are still here by sundown tomorrow we will find you and burn you on our sacred cross."

What the whip could not achieve this final threat did. Almost in unison the two negroes lifted their heads and let out a high pitched scream of abject terror before, once more, prostrating themselves at the feet of their captors.

Satisfied that their order would be obeyed the ghostly figures faded into the woods and, a few minutes later, my ears picked up the sound of muffled hoof beats rapidly fading into the distance.

Teeth clenched, heart beating like a battle drum, I waited a few minutes before crossing the clearing. The negroes still lay prone, their faces pressed into the sandy soil their backs bleeding from deep cuts. As I stood looking down at them I felt a surge of pity at their plight until I recalled the action of their brothers. At least the lives of these negroes had been spared, even if only for a day, while my compatriot had been tortured to death.

Bits of the flaming cross were starting to break off, falling in a shower of sparks on the pine-straw covered ground. Fearful that this might start a forest fire I spent some time stamping out the stray sparks, stepping over and around the two bodies still hugging the ground.

"Go. For God's sake get out of here," I finally said.

Confederate Gold
The Missing Treasure

Two pairs of terrified eyes, those of a man and those of a woman, stared up at me. "Did you hear me," I shouted, as they made no effort to move. It seemed fear had frozen them in time and place.

With a feeling of frustration I bent down grabbed the man by his arm and hauled him to his feet. He stared at me the whites of his wild eyes shining in the light from the dying flames. Then, as if the sight of a white man was too much for him, his body went limp and his chin dropped onto his chest. The smell of terror oozed from his bleeding back. It was all I could do to hold him up.

"Go. For God's sake go," I shouted. "Get to hell out of here if you value your lives." For a moment his sagging body remained motionless. Then, as if my words had finally penetrated his dulled brain, he pulled the woman to her feet and, together, they headed for the trees.

The burning cross was all but extinguished and I felt it safe to leave the clearing. In a daze I made my way back, wondering who the ghostly apparitions were.

Digging my heels into the dry slope so as to avoid another bout with the river I arrived to find Mrs. Parslow asleep, her feet firmly planted against the rock to which Archibald was tied. The day's travelling was over. Scraping a hollow to prevent myself from slipping into the water while I slept, I settled down. Sleep came slowly as the sight of the burning cross constantly played before my eyes.

I awoke shivering in the early morning mist. I lay there as scenes from the last two days floated before me. Closing my eyes I tried to block them out but it was no use. They remained there, swirling ghouls mocking me out of the river haze. I scrambled to my feet rubbing the sleep from my eyes. Only then did I see Mrs. Parslow kneeling perilously close to the river's edge thrusting my long fishing spear in and out of the water. I watched as, time after time, she plunged the spear into the eddy only to see its rise again fishless.

Bill Westhead

"Here let me try," I said, coming up behind her.

She started at the sound of my voice and would have fallen in had I not grabbed her shoulder.

"Oh, you gave me such a fright," she said, her hands grabbing the slippery grass and holding on as though her life depended on it.

"Sorry," I said. "I was only trying to help. You don't seem to be catching anything."

"You're right," she said, handing me the spear. I've been here for ages and not hit one fish. Every time I try I slip and the fish just glides away."

I soon found out what she meant. The dampness in the air made the narrow bank so slippery it was almost impossible to launch the spear without sliding into the river. It took several attempts before I finally succeeded in landing two medium size fish. With the aid of her precious matches Mrs. Parslow had already started a small fire and soon the fish, speared on twigs, were sizzling over the flames.

Breakfast finished we lounged in pleasurable silence for some time before untying Archibald. Trying to climb the slope back to the path was like trying to skate uphill and we made little progress. The mule proved more adept than either of us and it was due to his efforts rather than our own that we finally arrived at the top close to where we had, so ignominiously, departed the previous night. Exhausted by our efforts we decided to take a short rest before continuing our trek to Savannah.

Squatting on my haunches in the shade of the trees my mind again turned to the sight of the burning cross and cowering negroes. "Last night," I began, then fell silent.

"Last night, what?" Mrs. Parslow asked, settling down, her back against the scaly trunk of a River Birch.

I paused before answering. "You made mention of that secret white group formed to keep slaves in place."

It was her turn to hesitate. "Yes," she said, drawing the word out as if begging the question.

Confederate Gold
The Missing Treasure

I took a deep breath. "The flames last night were not caused by a forest fire. It was a burning cross."

A slight gasp escaped her lips. "I knew it," she said.

"Knew what?"

"They'd be around here somewhere. No matter what they stand for they still put the fear of God in me. Tell me what happened."

I recounted what I had seen. "What do you really know about them?" I added, when I had finished.

"I think I've told you too much already," she said, her eyes downcast as if afraid to look at me.

"But you've told me nothing," I persisted.

"The less you know the better."

"Look ma'am," I said, standing over her. "Last night I nearly walked in on a strange happening and God help me if I had. I need to know what these people are about so I can, at least, be on my guard."

She looked up at me and, for the first time since I had met her, there was terror in her pale eyes. "Nobody knows who they are or what they're about," she whispered, in a voice that hinted she was afraid the trees might hear and repeat her words. "But have heard tell that when the blue-bellies came through they clothed and armed many of the slaves encouraging them to revolt. Many didn't but some did. The group you saw the other night in their motley uniforms torturing that white man might be some of those who, drunk on whiskey, are now bent on revenge." She paused, her pleading eyes begging me not to pursue the matter further. But for our own safety I had to know.

"What else happened," I said, ignoring her entreaty.

"The Yankees promised to divide up the plantations and give every free slave forty acres and a mule. Coming on top of everything else this promise has so enraged the owners that they have banded together and sworn to retake what they believe is rightfully theirs and keep the slaves in their place. Both sides preach if you're not with them you must be against them." She

Bill Westhead

paused, pushing back an unruly lock of grey hair that fell over her eyes. "I no longer know who's right or who's wrong or even if there is a right or wrong. All I know is I'm not for either side and live in mortal fear of both of them."

As she finished I drew a long breath, held it deep in my lungs before letting it out in a long, slow whistle. Inside I floundered between relief and despair. It seemed inevitable we would be caught by one side or the other but, given a choice, I hoped it would be the whites. I reckoned we stood a better chance with them. They had no way of knowing my mother had been a negro slave.

For a long time we sat in silence lost in our own thoughts, while the sun climbed higher in the heavens. In the peaceful shade of the trees, listening to the sound of the river lazily lapping the bank, it was hard to believe mutilation and death could be so near.

"We should move," I said finally, after what seemed like an eternity.

Mrs. Parslow nodded and, without looking up, slowly got to her feet.

Neither spoke as we loaded the mule and started down the track, ears peeled for the slightest sound that might warn of approaching danger. Throughout the rest of the day and into the night no words passed between us. It seemed as if neither was prepared to breach the brooding blanket of silence that enveloped us. It was no different the following day. Only when it proved absolutely necessary did either speak and then in short, terse sentences.

It was not until the morning of the sixth day the agonizing and unnatural quiet was finally broken by the sound of church bells calling the faithful to prayer.

"Those sound very much like the bells of the old Saltzburger church," Mrs. Parslow said, as the deep, mellow clang rang out over the countryside. "I haven't heard them for years."

Confederate Gold
The Missing Treasure

At the cheerful sound of her voice I turned and saw her face light up as peel after peel echoed through the trees. "If I'm right we're close to Savannah," she continued, dismounting from the mule and smiling in the direction of the sound.

At that moment, I swear, the sun threw a halo round her grey head and tears glistened in her eyes. The frown that had creased her forehead for the last two days had disappeared, replaced by a look of complete serenity.

My heart raced. "Did I hear you right?" I said, trying to keep the excitement out of my voice.

"That we are near Savannah?"

"Yes."

"Well," she said, still smiling "if I am right about those bells then yes we are close. Oh how I would love to attend church one more time before I leave here for good."

"Maybe you will," I said, dropping the mule rope and running back to where she stood. We hugged and, in that instant, our fears were forgotten and our friendship sealed.

"We must move on," she said, breaking my encircling arms "We're close but we're not there yet." She paused before adding with a chuckle, "So back to work, son."

She remounted the mule and I picked up the rope. Now my feet sprang over the hard packed dirt surface and I felt I was walking on air. By early in the afternoon the light breeze that rustled the leaves bore on it the faint, but familiar, tang of salt water reminding me of my days at sea. As dusk descended we had our first glimpse of Savannah.

Under broken cloud its buildings glinted in the splintered rays of the setting sun. From this distance I was surprised to see the city looked little different from the Savannah of my childhood. It was not the heap of smoking rubble I had expected but a beautiful sight that I knew would forever live in my memory. If, at that moment, I could have chosen any scene in the world to paint this would have been it.

Bill Westhead

"What a fine sight and apparently untouched," I sighed. "Thank God this is the end of our journey."

A tinkling laugh, that I had not heard for several days, greeted my remark.

"Was it all that bad having me along?" Mrs Parslow asked.

I smiled. "No. You choose to misunderstand me."

"Not really," she said, still laughing. "I know what you mean and I feel the same way. This is a wonderful but sad moment. Wonderful that we have arrived and tomorrow will go our separate ways. Sad because I doubt we shall ever see each other again. But no matter what the future holds I will always remember our journey together and this moment."

"Yes," I said, "so will I."

There was nothing more to be said. In companionable silence we gazed on a sight neither of us ever expected to see. As I offered up a prayer I felt a tear trickle down my cheek washing aside the dust and grime. Embarrassed, I turned my back on my companion and gazed across the river, that had been our friend and guide for the last seven days, towards the vast marshlands on the South Carolina side. Smells I remembered from my boyhood wafted across the water and my thoughts turned to the men who had fought and died for our cause. Beloved faces flew past me like chaff in a strong wind. How long I stood there, lost in yesteryears, I do not know.

The sound of Mrs. Parslow talking softly to Archibald broke my reverie.

"What are you going to do with him?" I asked, as I watched her tether the mule for what was probably the last time.

"Oh there will be plenty of offers for a good mule in Savannah," she said, hugging the shaggy head. "I can't take him with me, much as I would like to, so I'll sell him and put the money towards my passage to England. Don't worry, I'll find him a good home."

Confederate Gold
The Missing Treasure

"I hope so," I said, looking sadly at the faithful beast that, unknowingly, had shared our fears and now unwittingly shared our triumph.

Suggesting we needed something better than fish to celebrate the evening, I left the camp in search of food. Exhilarated by the sight of Savannah I whistled as I went, all thoughts of white gangs or freed slaves fading like the setting sun. Within minutes I came upon a small clearing and there, as if by divine providence, a scrawny hen rooted in the ground clucking with delight at every scrap she found. Without a second thought I hurled myself at her, caught her and, in no time, had wrung her neck. Delighted with my success I hurried back to camp proudly clutching my, still fluttering, prize.

As had become our custom Mrs. Parslow had a small fire burning by the time I got back. Eagerly I plucked and gutted the bird before hanging it over the flames on a wooden spit. The aroma of the cooking flesh made my mouth water and I constantly wiped my hand across my saliva covered chin. Only resolute willpower stopped me tearing the half cooked bird from the spit. We ate without saying a word, out teeth ripping every morsel of tough flesh from the bones.

After dousing the fire I lay back and watched the dusky shadows creep up the river. Listening to the night creatures skittering through their domain I wondered how the other members of our gang had fared.

CHAPTER 18

I shivered in the chill of the early morning air. Drops of water fell from moisture laden leaves and the dank odor of rotting vegetation overwhelmed the sweet scent of pine tar. My aura of well-being seemed to soak away in the damp earth, replaced by frightening visions of my trying to enter Savannah and find Campbell-Johnson's lodgings. So near and yet so far, I thought, as I made my way down to the river.

The cool cleansing water did nothing to raise my spirits and I noticed, not for the first time, the sores that covered my arms and most of my body. These had started as irritating red spots back in Augusta but I had ignored them. Now they were open, suppurating lesions that showed no sign of healing. I felt the boil on the back of my neck that constantly oozed pus. Almost at the end of my journey I suddenly lacked the will to make the final push.

"You seem far away this morning," Mrs. Parslow said, as I returned to our camp site. Although her grey hair straggled down her back and dark stains of sweat and earth marred her worn, green taffeta dress, I thought she had managed to keep her appearance remarkably well despite the rigors of our flight. I said so.

A faint blush rose in her cheeks. "What a nice gentlemanly thing to say," she giggled. Clumsily she twisted her aristocratic fingers together like a young girl receiving her first compliment. It was then I noticed the swollen knuckles of her reddened hands and the pain, she had never once spoken of on our entire journey, was reflected in her eyes.

"Oh just a touch of arthritis," she said, seeing my look of concern.

"Why didn't you say something?" I asked.

"What could you have done if I had."

Confederate Gold
The Missing Treasure

"Nothing," I admitted.

"Well then there was no point in mentioning it was there? Anyway," she continued, "you have your own medical problems and I can do no more for you than you can for me." She turned away and appeared to dismiss the matter altogether. "I'll just go and freshen up."

I was sitting on the ground thinking about the day ahead when she returned.

"You're worried about today aren't you," she said, coming over to sit beside me.

"Yes," I replied, "and this damned depressing weather doesn't help."

"Well getting down hearted is not going to help either." she said with surprising harshness. "We've come this far and we'll see it through to the end. Now get a hold of yourself."

Unable to look at her I stared ahead saying nothing. There was nothing I could say. I knew she was right.

"I think I ought to go into the city alone and spy out the land," she continued, getting to her feet. "because the Yankees are less of a danger to me than they are to you. Trying to find passage on a ship to England seems to be a legitimate reason for my being there."

The more I thought about her proposal the more sense it made but, at the same time, I felt ashamed at my willingness to let her face this final hurdle alone.

"So that's settled then," she said, taking my silence for acceptance.

"Are you going to walk or take the mule?" I asked. For some unknown reason I felt desperately tired.

"I'll take the mule," she said, starting to untether the animal. Suddenly she stopped and, turning to face me, said "I'd best leave your money here or people might start asking awkward questions if they accidently come upon it. Here, hold Archibald a minute while I unfasten these bags."

Bill Westhead

I clambered to my feet and took the rope from her hand. I could not resist smiling as she discreetly hid behind a tree. In a few minutes she was back, her waist restored and her inflamed hands clutching the small bags of gold and silver. With difficulty she unclenched her long fingers dropping the bags on the ground. Then she mounted the mule.

"I'll be back before night fall," she said as, with a cheery wave, she rode off in direction of Savannah.

By now the sun had started to take the chill out of the air and slow the mournful dripping from the leaves. Left alone my depression deepened and, despite all my efforts, I could not shake it off. To keep myself occupied I tried to make another fishing spear but without the knife found it impossible to fashion a satisfactory point. I wandered through the trees to no purpose then swam in the river. None of these activities did anything to raise my spirits. The sun hung motionless in the sky seemingly locked in place. Time and my world stood still. Immovable. I walked to nowhere and back, turned and walked the same path again. Finally I gave up and resigned myself to a day of utter inactive loneliness.

I was lying on the ground, mixed thoughts of success or failure churning through my overactive brain, when I heard the steady clop of hoofs. In a flash I was on my feet rushing down the track. At the glorious sight of woman and mule my despondency vanished into the velvet blue evening sky.

"Well, what of the city?" I asked, grabbing the rope from her hand.

"There's much to tell," she said patiently. "But it has been a long day and I would like to eat first."

"Yes ma'am," I said, handing the rope back to her before sprinting back to our little camp site. By the time she had tethered the mule, washed and brushed herself down I had speared two modest fish and had them cooking over a small fire.

"Now, tell me everything that happened today," I said eagerly, as we finished our meal and doused the fire.

Confederate Gold
The Missing Treasure

"Well," she said, a broad smile lighting her face. "It's difficult to know where to begin. The best news of all is the city is not destroyed."

"I don't believe you,"

"It's true whether you believe it or not," she continued, ignoring my interruption. "The Yankees took Fort McAllister early last December. Everyone knew that devil Sherman would destroy Savannah just as he had destroyed Atlanta and everything in between. So to save the city, I was told, old Joe Johnson's forces slipped away across the river and the city fathers surrendered on December 21st without a shot being fired."

My jaw dropped in amazement. Try as I might I could not imagine Savannah being untouched. I had seen the horrific aftermath as this self-appointed Yankee avenger had swept across Georgia driving helpless women and children from their homes and torching the buildings.

"I find that unbelievable," I said.

"Well it's true. I've seen it for myself. Most of the buildings still stand with little or no damage. What's more there are only a few Yankee troops and officials about. The main part of their army has crossed into South Carolina to wreak havoc there."

I whistled in surprise, still unable to accept what I was hearing. In one way I felt pleased the city had been spared and yet, in another, ashamed at it's surrender.

"I still can't believe it," I said, fighting to control my excitement. "You're telling me nothing stands in our way."

"I wouldn't say nothing," she said. Her smile faded and her brow puckered.

"There's more?"

"Oh yes. You've only heard the part of it. Despite what I have told you conditions in the city are not good."

"Go on then," I said, as she gazed up at the early stars that peeked through the foliage.

She took a deep breath before plunging on to tell of the terrible cost of things; boots and shoes at two hundred dollars a pair and butter at eight dollars a pound, if it could be found. With Confederate money worthless few, if any, could afford these prices. The city's supply of rice was infested with bugs and starvation was rampant. Those few unlucky enough to lose their homes were now huddled together for shelter in makeshift tents. Worse still the Yankees had taken over eight hundred Confederate prisoners, the rearguard of Joe Johnson's force, confiscated all locomotives and steamers not to mention thirty thousand bales of cotton.

"Despite being spared mass destruction," Mrs. Parslow concluded, "Savannah, like the rest of the South, has been brought to heel by Sherman and his blue-bellies."

This account of the hardships suffered by the people of Savannah in no way blunted my eagerness to be in the city. Compared with many an account I had heard or scene I had witnessed since leaving Richmond it seemed they had fared better than most.

"Why don't we leave for the city right now?" I asked, leaping to my feet ready to run the three miles that stood between us and our final destination.

"Don't be foolish," she snapped in the same tone of voice in which she might have addressed a naughty child. "There's a curfew. If you want to be caught just try walking the streets at night. We go in the morning."

In all the days we had been together she had never spoken to me like this and, shamefaced, I retreated to the edge of the clearing. She made no attempt to follow and apologize for the rebuke. Sitting by the dead fire, her back ramrod straight, she stared through me as though I did not exist. Finally, more to break the overwhelming silence than any concern for her well being, I asked if she had managed to book passage to England.

"Regrettably I was not successful in that," she said quietly. "Time did not allow me to make any enquiries."

Confederate Gold
The Missing Treasure

"What are you going to do?" I said, suddenly fearful that she might expect me to stay with her until such times as she could sail.

"You have no need to worry," she said, hearing the concern in my voice. "All is not lost. Quite by chance I met an elderly couple and, in the course of conversation, found that before the war the gentleman had traded with my husband. On hearing of my problem they very kindly offered me a room in their house on Broughton Street for as long as I cared to stay which, all being well, will only be but a few weeks."

"Broughton Street," I said, trying to recall the layout of the city. "That's not far from the waterfront is it?"

"I am not certain, but believe it's close by," she said.

I wondered if I too might obtain temporary lodgings in this same house on Broughton Street. If so it would allow me to keep an eye on Mrs. Parslow as she carried my money into the heart of the city and also give me time to find Dr. Campbell-Johnson's lodgings. The more I thought about it the more the idea appealed.

"Did you happen to mention your son to these people?" I asked, as I moved back to the area of the fire.

"Oh no," she said, a look of surprise on her face. "I was so pleased at my good fortune I forgot to mention you. Why?"

"I was just thinking."

"What about?"

Trying to sound as indifferent to the idea as possible I outlined my plans and concluded by saying "I could then go off and search for my friends without fear of being caught with the money. But —,"

"But what?" she said.

"You never mentioned you were travelling with your son. Won't they think it strange if you suddenly arrive with him, not having mentioned it before?"

"They probably will," she said, her brow knitted in a thoughtful frown. Then her face brightened. "Why don't we drop the family relationship. You are simply a friend who has helped me on the journey from Augusta. I think they'll fall for that and it makes things easier because it's the truth."

Her solution stunned me with its simplicity.

"Will you still carry the bags?" I asked, as we settled down for our last night on the trail.

"Of course," she said with a chuckle.

As I lay there listening to the whip-poor-will's nocturnal songs I had mixed feelings about what the immediate future held. I was elated that I had made Savannah in time but my rejoicing was tinged with an element of sorrow at our parting. Tomorrow we would go our separate ways, she to England and me to wherever my fortune led.

As the sun rose we prepared for the final leg of our trek. The light breeze of the previous evening had stiffened into a gale, bending the tops of the trees. I felt, as much as saw, the ominous beauty of the iron grey clouds scudding across the sky. There was no dawn chorus, the birds silence heralding the coming storm.

"Hope we make Broughton Street before that lot hits us," I said, pointing away to the south where inky black clouds rolled over each other as if fighting for supremacy.

The mule seemed unconcerned about the approaching deluge. Stubbornly he resisted all my efforts to increase the pace seemingly in no mood to rush until a clap of thunder immediately overhead roused him from his lethargy. The first drops of rain hit us as we entered the outskirts of the city.

At that hour the streets were almost deserted. What few people were about ignored us as they leaned their gaunt bodies against the wind and hurried for shelter. The streets were littered with horse carcasses and we were forced to hold our noses against the sickening stench of rotting flesh. An aura of dejection hung in the air and the sour taste of defeat assailed us at every turn. If this was the price of surrender I wondered what the cost must have been to other towns and cities along the route that had

Confederate Gold
The Missing Treasure

resisted Sherman's onslaught. At least most of these people still had a roof over their heads.

As these thoughts churned through my head I began to lose patience with the forlorn looking citizens who shuffled along the side walks, heads down and hands plunged deep into coat pockets. From the look on their faces it seemed to me that, even in their hour of defeat, their only thought was of money and whatever means were available to them to recoup lost fortunes. But then, I recalled, Savannah had always been a law unto itself and who was I to criticize others for doing exactly what I was doing.

The initial downpour provided a welcome change from the heat of previous days. But the intensity of the storm rapidly increased and the wind began to whip the rain around us. Lightening spiked the sky above the roof tops and thunder exploded like a battery of cannons. At each explosion the mule stopped in his tracks and quivered, refusing to take another step until the noise had died away. The howling wind tore though our clothing chilling our very bones and the driven rain pricked our eyes like a thousand tiny darts. In frustration, I suggested we would be quicker if we abandoned the mule and made our way on foot but Mrs. Parslow would have none of it.

"He means money to me," she screamed, above the noise of the wind.

I laughed at her thinking of the few dollars she might get for him compared with the fortune she had tied round her waist.

Following her directions we found the house on Broughton Street. This proved to be a two-storied building in dire need of attention. Much of the paint had peeled from the siding exposing large areas of original timber which gave the appearance of a map with creamy-yellow land and dark grey seas. Several of the glassless windows were covered with pieces of cloth of varied design. A porch topped with bits of faded blue gingerbread work ran the full width of the house. The unadorned balconies along the front and down both sides gave the impression of having been added later. The whole structure had the appearance of a happening rather than a designed residence.

Dismounting from the mule, Mrs. Parslow climbed the five steps leading to the porch and knocked firmly on the front door which, like the rest of the house, was in urgent need of paint. Almost immediately it opened to reveal a small, pale faced woman, her white hair parted down the middle and pulled back into a fashionable, net covered coil at the nape of her scrawny neck. Her long black hooped skirt was topped with a white blouse that hung on her thin frame.

"Come in my dear, come in." Despite her frail appearance her voice, raised against the gale, had a generous ring as she grabbed Mrs. Parslow by the arm and pulled her inside.

"But my friend and the mule," Mrs. Parslow said, waving her hand towards me as I stood ankle-deep in a torrent of water that gushed down the street.

"Of course. Tell them to go round the back. Old Moses will take care of them."

Mrs. Parslow turned to convey the message which I had already heard. Raising my hand in acknowledgment, I turned and led the mule down a narrow alley alongside the house and into a back yard. An old, white haired negro, his body bent almost double, hobbled across the stones to greet me.

"I'll see to him massa," he said, taking the mule's rope. "You get yo'self inside." He pointed to the door of a single story building set apart from the main house and connected to it by a covered passageway.

Gratefully I did as he bid. A comforting blast of warm air and the smell of cooking hit me as I opened the door. In the center of the room stood a long, solid wooden table littered with an amazing array of pans and dishes. Around the walls were numerous shelves which in days gone by had undoubtedly been crammed with jars of fruit and spices. Now they held only three small jugs of molasses. A large iron stove occupied the far

Confederate Gold
The Missing Treasure

corner, its door partly open, giving a glimpse of a glowing, dull red fire.

After the hardships of my travels this was paradise. I stood with my back to the stove to dry my drenched clothing and had been there some time, soaking up the heat, when the lady of the house entered followed by Mrs. Parslow.

I stared in amazement at the sight of her. Gone was the bulky, travel-worn taffeta dress. In its place she wore a slimmer styled blue one which, although too short, suited her. The grey hair was neatly pulled back in the style she had worn when I first met her. She looked so refreshed that I could hardly believe this was the same woman who had entered Savannah in the midst of a violent thunder storm only a short time ago.

"Ah, there you are," Mrs. Parslow said. Then turning to our hostess, added, "Allow me to introduce you. This is Josh, the gentleman that accompanied me to Savannah."

Josh! I was stunned for not once since leaving Augusta had she addressed me by name. In fact Mrs. Parslow had never known my full name and, in her wisdom, had never asked. Then I remembered, Jane had called me Josh when we parted.

"Ma'am," I said, with a small bow in the direction of the lady of the house.

"Well now," she said, "and what are we going to do with you?"

"Oh, he's going to try and find his family," Mrs. Parslow butted in, before I had time to reply.

"Yes ma'am," I said, picking up on the cue. "If I may stay for a little while to dry out, I will be on my way."

The lady smiled and her wan face lit up recapturing, in that instant, a long-faded beauty. "By all means. Now come my dear," she said, turning to Mrs. Parslow "and let us discuss how we my help you be reunited with that husband of yours."

As they moved towards the door I realized I was being separated from my fortune. There was little I could do without giving myself away but I had to take that risk.

"Mrs. Parslow," I said, "I need to ask you about —"

"I will talk with you later," she cut in, and her look told me to say no more.

As the kitchen door closed behind them I felt sure all my efforts had been in vain and that my fortune would now be used to buy Mrs. Parslow's passage to England. I was in Savannah with my fortune only a few feet away and yet it might as well have been on another planet. I stood staring at the closed door while considering the possible use of force to regain what was rightfully mine. But I had no doubt what the consequences of such an action would be. I was still pondering the problem when the lady of the house returned.

"If you don't find your family today, you are welcome to rest here." She pointed to a rocking chair in the corner.

"That's very kind of you ma'am," I said.

"But," she continued, ignoring my thanks, "you must be back by curfew for we lock all the doors then."

"What time is that ma'am?"

"Dusk, unless you have a pass and good reason to be abroad at night." With that she closed the door and I heard her dainty footsteps rapping down the uncarpeted corridor.

I sat in the rocking chair, trying to decide what to do. Although it seemed unlikely Mrs. Parslow would venture out in the storm to book her passage I had no time to lose. Wet and cold as I might be I knew I must recover my fortune and make the rendezvous before that night's curfew.

CHAPTER 19

"Where do you think you're going?"

The sound of the rasping voice arrested my hand as I reached for the door latch. I turned and was shocked at the sight that met my eyes. Above an old-fashioned high neck collar and cravat the face was nothing more than pock-marked skin stretched over a skull. Broken, grey-brown teeth leered through lips that seemed too thin to meet, while tufts of white hair sprouted from the top of his head. Long, boney hands protruded from the sleeves of a dark velvet jacket that hung like a sack from his narrow shoulders. At just over six feet tall he probably weighed less than a hundred pounds. I stood transfixed, unable to tear my eyes away from this sight and equally unable to answer his question.

"The sight of me shocks you?" he said, in the same strange grating voice.

"I'm sorry," I said, finally finding my tongue. "I was expecting to see someone else."

"No need to apologize," the apparition continued. "I shock many people round here. But then they have no idea what the inside of a Yankee prison camp was like."

"You were a prisoner?"

He nodded.

"Where were you taken?" I asked, my curiosity aroused.

"Gettysburg. I was fortunate enough to live through Pickett's charge, although there's been many a time when I've regretted surviving."

"That was back in '63!" I said. "So you were in some Federal hell-hole for almost two years."

"You're right calling it a hell-hole," he said, moving over to sit in the rocking chair. "I finished in Rock Island, Illinois. We lost thousands of good men up there with the smallpox. It nearly got me." His hands moved automatically across his face and his large eyes stared at some distant horror only he could see.

"How did you get here?" I asked, trying to awaken him from these harrowing memories.

"Walked," he said. "How else?"

"But why here?" I persisted.

"This is my home," he answered wearily. "Like many of us me and my brother rallied to the flag back in '61. Joined the 4th. Regiment of Georgia. It was all a great adventure until —."

I waited as he struggled to find the right words. I sensed he needed to talk and, despite wanting to be on my way, I felt I owed him the respect of listening.

"My brother was killed at Chancellorsville and after that nothing went right," he said, after a long pause. "Now look at us. My father dying. My mother trying to live as she did five years ago although, if the truth be told, she's starving in poverty because there's nothing left. All my friends are gone. What have I got to live for?"

I had no answer. Instead I stood and watched as he slowly levered himself out of the rocking chair and, without another word or even a glance in my direction, left the room. And you, Josh Singleton, reckon you had a tough war, I thought, as the door closed behind him. I left the house by the kitchen door and sprinted down the narrow alley, all the while cursing myself for wasting valuable time. Dark clouds continued to race across the sky, but the rain had stopped and here and there the sun's rays broke through the overcast. Far from cleansing the air, the rain had only increased the stench from the rotting carcasses and piles of debris.

This part of Savannah was strange to me and on reaching the street I stopped wondering which way to go. I recalled that Campbell-Johnson's lodgings were over an inn and, as sailors liked their drink more than most, I reasoned many of the inns would be in or near the dock area. As we had never crossed the river I guessed the docks must be on my left.

Confederate Gold
The Missing Treasure

In an attempt to blend with the local inhabitants I thrust my hands in my pockets, bowed my head and shuffled dejectedly along Broughton Street until I found an alley leading off in the direction I wanted to go. Once in the alley I took to my heels. Soaked in sweat, my heart thudding against my ribs and my lungs ready to explode I pounded along the slippery, wet sand as fast as I could while fighting to keep my feet.

I had almost reached the end when the stooped figure of a woman, head and shoulders covered by a shawl, appeared from behind a pile of refuse. In one hand she held a small club with which she poked the pile while in the other hand she carried a sack. I skidded to a stop as a large wharf rat scurried out. In a flash the club descended crushing the animal's skull. The woman giggled with delight as she picked up the body by the tail and dropped it into the sack. Mesmerized I watched as rat after rat met its fate and the sack filled.

"Food," she said simply, looking up and noticing me for the first time. "Do you want a couple? Make good eating."

"Thank you no, ma'am."

"Please yourself," she said, returning to her task.

"If you please ma'am," I said, speaking to her bent back, "could you direct me to the docks."

"Running away are we?" she said, straightening up and facing me. The tone was both accusatory and belligerent.

"No ma'am," I said. "But I do need to find work."

"Work!" she scoffed. "Apart from a few merchants that seem to be doing all right for themselves there's no work to be had. Still you can try. Straight down there." She pointed on down the alley.

"Thank you ma'am," I said politely. I might have saved myself the trouble for she had already dismissed me and was, once more, engrossed in her search for food.

The early afternoon sky continued to brighten with the clouds now lit by a hidden sun. May be it was my imagination,

Bill Westhead

but as I continued down the alley I was certain the salt tang of the sea and scent of marshland grew stronger.

The alley opened onto a busy thoroughfare on one side of which were numerous large buildings. Signs on the walls or over the entrance ways showed them to be occupied by merchants, traders or shippers. The more signs I read the more familiar my surroundings became. Now there was no mistaking the salt tang of the sea and scent of marshland that pervaded the air. I had trodden this very street on earlier visits to Savannah and knew, beyond any shadow of doubt, that behind these buildings stood vast warehouses, their lower floors level with the wharfs that dotted the waterfront.

The cobbled street that led down to the waterfront was steep. As my hand slid along the damp surface of the walls that rose on either side I was reminded that these very bricks and stones had, at one time, been ballast in ships sailing the great Atlantic. What a tale they could tell if they could only speak, I thought, as I stumbled on down.

Arriving dockside I was stunned by the sight that met my eyes. When I had first gone to sea the river had been crammed with ships their tall masts looking like a forest of pine trees springing out of the sullen waters. The wharfs had bustled with activity as men scurried about loading bales of cotton onto those same vessels bound for the four corners of the earth. Now only a few ships were tied up, their rigging flapping idly in the wind and the waves slapping lazily against their hulls. The river beyond was empty.

Some cotton bales were being loaded, but far fewer than I remembered. Gone was the bustle of earlier days and a sullen lethargy hung over the whole area. The loaders showed no urgency as they hefted huge iron hooks into the randomly stacked bales while others lolled around as though waiting for something to happen. Here and there men wearing white shirts and dark striped pants, held up by suspenders, shouted orders and berated those around them but to no apparent effect. Even

Confederate Gold
The Missing Treasure

the few Yankee soldiers dotted in groups along the river front appeared bored. Some were even squatting on the ground passing the time playing cards.

Only the gulls screeching overhead, whirling and twirling about the ships masts and perching on the bales, showed any signs of energy. The war had not changed them. They alone were still free in this damned world. How I envied them their liberty.

I ambled towards the east end of the docks my pace in keeping with the those about me. Although my dress contrasted sharply with that of everyone around no one paid any attention. Despite this each shouted order caused my heart to miss a beat and my stomach felt as tight as a fist. On occasions I stopped to inspect a bale of cotton in an attempt to show I had a legitimate reason for being there. It also gave me a chance to better view the buildings in the immediate vicinity for any that might be seen to have lodgings above them. But by the time I got to the end of the docks I had seen nothing. I turned to retrace my steps forcing myself to continue strolling along the wharf checking cotton bales at random. The tightness in my stomach crept up to envelop my chest. Now my breath came in short gasps.

I was well past half way when my eye was drawn to a horse and buggy tethered to a hitching post outside the Ship Inn. For a moment I stopped and stared. Something about the carriage looked familiar. Then, remembering I was inspecting cotton bales, I moved on towards the western end of the docks. Ships, cotton bales and men became a blur as I tried to think what had attracted my attention to that horse and buggy. Suddenly an uncontrollable shiver ran through my body. I had loaded that same vehicle, or one just like it, with $86,000 in coin and bullion.

I walked to the far end of the dock area before turning. Resisting the urge to run I forced myself to meander back, continuing to stop every now and again to examine a bale of cotton, until I was once again opposite the Ship Inn. Fortunately there were a several bales close by and I gave these a cursory

Bill Westhead

inspection while focusing my attention on the building on the other side of the street. My excitement grew as I gazed up. There above the ground floor were two small, white-washed windows either side of a paint-peeled door that opened onto a small side balcony. The proximity of the buggy and what appeared to be lodgings above the Inn was too much of a coincidence. No matter the risk I determined to check it out.

There were no steps I could see leading up to the balcony which led me to assume that the only access to the floor above must be through the Ship Inn itself. Warily glancing left and right, I crossed the street. Large beads of sweat formed on my forehead as, with clammy palms, I pushed open the inn door. A dense cloud of tobacco smoke hit me taking my breath away and causing my eyes to water. In contrast with the sunlight outside, the darkness of the room dropped over me like a blanket. I started as something soft tickled my face. Slowly my eyes grew accustomed to the blackness and I saw I was in a large room, its a low beamed ceiling festooned with cobwebs. What little daylight penetrated the small, grime covered windows fell on a long bar around which a crowd was gathered.

Judging from their appearance most were sailors. Drink seemed to be in short supply, or service slow, for several men were shouting and banging empty mugs on the bar top. Through the smoke haze I noticed the rest of the room was taken up with tables and chairs, around which a number of civilians mingled with a few soldiers wearing the dreaded blue uniform. Scantily clad women of various shapes and sizes, their large breasts bursting out of tight fitting bodices, wandered between the seated customers and the bar.

From the way I was dressed, I should have taken a seat at one of the tables but instead made directly for the bar. I quickly regretted the mistake.

"'ere's someone we could use." The heavy hand of a bearded sailor slammed across my shoulders causing my festering sores to sting and bring tears to my eyes. I staggered under the blow

Confederate Gold
The Missing Treasure

and only saved myself from falling by grabbing the edge of the bar. "Looks like this gentleman might be falling on 'ard times," he continued, addressing the crowd before grabbing the lapels of my moth-eaten coat. "Would tha like to make an 'onest penny?" he asked, thrusting his weather-beaten face into mine. His breath stank of ale and stale tobacco.

"Doing what," I answered, trying to control the tremor in my voice.

"Why as a bloody sailor" he said, relaxing his hold and moving so that his enormous body pinned me to the bar. "We're three short and we 'ave to sail on't next tide." His strange accent gave me cause for concern.

"Where are you bound for?" The question was out before I could stop myself.

"Why England and 'ome to Liverpool," he said. "You joining us?"

"No," I said with a laugh. "I've already signed on so you'll have to look elsewhere." I had hoped the laugh would be convincing but it was too high pitched and, to my horror, sounded more like a squeak.

"Oh aye," he said, peering at me closely. "Then why the 'ell ask where we were bound?"

"Just curious," I said. "Like all sailors."

"That's as may be." He eyed me suspiciously. "Them old, but fine, clothes makes me think tha might be an officer."

"No, just a midshipman," I answered, feeling on safer ground.

"Well then me lad, 'ow about a pint of ale to see thee on tha way," he said, seemingly satisfied with my answer. "That's if we can ever get one," he continued. "Ale 'ere's poor and't service worse." He moved over banging his mug on the bar and shouting at the buxom serving woman.

"Wait your turn Albert," she screamed at him.

"Now Betsy me pretty," he cajoled. "How about a pint for me friend 'ere and another one for me."

"Told you, wait your turn," Betsy answered, gathering three mugs in one large hand and holding them under a barrel.

Albert continued to chide her. After serving several customers she slammed two full mugs of ale in front of us with such force half their contents slopped over the bar top.

"Wasting good ale," Albert said, tossing over a coin which Betsy whipped into her apron with a well practiced hand.

"Shipping out soon?" Albert asked, as I raised the mug to my lips. I took a long swig wondering how to answer him.

"Yes," I finally said, lowering the mug.

"Well now, where's tha bound for?"

I took another long swig while my mind raced. Albert was becoming too inquisitive and dangerous. I had to get away before things got out of hand. Not only could I not answer his question but I was certain he would expect me to buy the next round and I here I was, a sailor in port, with no money. He would find that very strange.

"Not certain yet," I said, pretending to take a third swig of ale, while frantically searching the room for a means of escape.

"Not sure!" he echoed, surprise all over his leathery face. "Howd'ya mean? Any sailor worth 'is salt must know where he's going or he'll never get there. Eh lads," he shouted, "young fellow 'ere shipping out and don't know where the 'ell he's bound for."

The remark was greeted with a roar of laughter and I sensed the temperature in the room instantly rise. Behind the mug I flicked my tongue over dry lips and tried to swallow a lump that had suddenly risen in my throat. If I could not free myself of this man I was certain I would end up aboard a ship bound for a destination unknown or, worse still, be knifed in some dockside alley.

My eyes frantically searched the room for any door that might lead to the lodging rooms above. I found only one, apart from that by which I had entered, and it was over in the far corner. That must be the one, I thought, letting the ale filter slowly through clenched teeth.

"Might sound strange to you Albert," I said finally, setting my mug down, "but the truth is I'm here to get our sailing instructions and if I don't get about my business I might well be shipping out with you. I was told the fellow lives in lodgings above here. When I've talked to him I'll know where we are going."

"What's your ship?" Albert said. Doubt was back in his voice.

"We'll talk when I get back," I said, downing the last drop of ale before pushing my way through the crowd towards the door I had spotted earlier. Although I could feel his eyes boring into me he made no attempt to follow and I did not look back.

With a sigh of relief I pulled it open and found myself in a long, narrow, windowless passageway with several curtained doors leading off on either side. The only light came from a large, single candle at the far end that threw wavering shadows across a heavy, red velvet curtain. Ignoring the deep grunts and high-pitched giggles that came from behind almost every door I strode down the passageway searching for stairs that, I felt sure, must be there. But there were no stairs. My last hope lay behind the curtain. With heart beating like a drum and breath coming in expectant gasps I whipped the velvet aside only to find a solid, blank, wooden wall. There was no way of reaching the upstairs rooms from the corridor. I was trapped. No wonder Albert had not followed. He would be waiting for me at the bar his suspicions fully roused while Betsy, who I guessed acted as madam, would demand payment for the doubtful delights offered by her establishment. I would be unable to satisfy either but, given a choice, I felt safer facing Betsy than Albert.

I decided to stay where I was for a while hoping Albert would have left by the time I returned to the bar. Blowing out the candle, I squeezed between the red curtain and wooden wall hardly daring to breathe. The dust from the curtain dried my

Bill Westhead

mouth and irritated my nose. I was trying to stifle a sneeze when a door slammed.

"You rotten stinking whore." a coarse male voice shouted. "I paid good money and what did I get, a sack of damned rotten potatoes. I've had better with some of the young lads on board."

A witch-like cackle greeted this tirade before the dull thud of flesh on flesh abruptly changed it to a howl.

"Even the damned candle's out," the man continued.

"Well you'd best come back in here if you can't see," the woman screamed. "I promise I'm great with blind men and it won't cost you much more."

"Come back. If I come back I'll kill you, you witch."

Any response to this threat was cut short by the door being slammed again. Heavy footsteps pounded down the passage. Then there was the crash of a second door.

I had tarried long enough. It was safer to face Albert and his prying questions than be caught where I was. Feeling my way from door to door I crept back down the passage. Half way along I heard a woman sobbing and guessed she was the one who had been verbally and physically abused. Although I felt sorry for her I had no inclination to stop and help.

Any hopes Albert might have returned to his ship were immediately dashed as soon as I entered the bar. There he was, leaning against the counter, just as I had left him.

"Work fast don't you boy!' he taunted me, as I stepped into the room. "Surprising what you can get back there but I'll wager tha still doesn't know where tha's going." His guffaw caused heads to turn.

"Got in the wrong place," I said, pretending to join the laughter. "Didn't waste my time though. Had myself a bit of fun." I scratched my crotch.

"Bet tha did," he continued, doubled over with laughter. "I'd also wager if tha doesn't know where tha's going tha at least knows where tha's been."

Confederate Gold
The Missing Treasure

I said nothing, letting him enjoy the joke at my expense. "Now," he finally said, straightening up and locking his narrow eyes on me, "who art thou and what does tha want?"

"I've told you."

Despite his size I was tired of being harassed by this man. I could feel my temper begin to rise and had to bite my tongue before continuing. "All right," I said. "First time here and I made a mistake. Not regretting it mind you but I do need to be about my business." I placed a hand on his broad shoulder in what I hoped was a friendly manner. "Now, do me a favor and tell me how I find the upstairs of this place."

"You're a good lad and can take a joke," he said. "Maybe you are and maybe you ain't a sailor but —"

"Out the door turn left, left again and up the stairs at the far end," Betsy cut in.

I could have thrown my arms round her ample waist and kissed her at that moment, but all I said was "Thanks."

"I trust you paid her well," she said, ignoring my expression of gratitude. "It's their living and God help any that treat 'em bad for I won't."

"She seemed satisfied," I mumbled, as I pushed my way through the crowd, fearing at any moment one of the women would appear and Betsy would question her.

"Good sailing Albert," I shouted, as I reached the door.

He frowned as he stared at me but said nothing. With a long sigh of relief I was back in the muggy air of a typical spring afternoon in Georgia. From the position of the sun I reckoned I still had plenty of time before curfew. Following Betsy's instructions I found the stairs and mounted them two at a time. Facing the paint-peeled door I wondered if this would prove to be the lodgings I sought or another trap.

With shaking hand I rapped lightly on the decaying wood. There was no answer. My heart sank. I knocked again more firmly. Again there was no answer. Frustrated, I raised both fists and pounded on the door causing the heavy hinges to rattle and bits of rotten framework to fly off. This time I heard the sound of footsteps then heavy bolts being withdrawn. The door creaked open a few inches and a face appeared.

Although the head was bald the rest of the face was almost totally covered by an unkempt grey beard. Blue-gray stones peered from beneath bushy eyebrows which seemed to be a continuation of the beard. He blinked in the sunlight before fixing me with a stare that penetrated my very soul. We faced each other neither saying a word. Then the head withdrew. Bewitched by his stare, I made no attempt to stop the door being closed in my face. From somewhere within I heard the clank of bolts being shot into place.

Confederate Gold
The Missing Treasure

CHAPTER 20

Recovering my senses I stood staring at the bolted door and wondered if the face had been that of Campbell-Johnson. I steeled myself and hammered on the door again. Once more pieces, larger this time, splintered from the framework. I continued to pound away and was making so much noise I failed to hear the sound of bolts being withdrawn. Suddenly the door cracked open and, for the second time, the bearded head of the occupant appeared.

This time I was ready. "Are these the lodgings of Dr. Campbell-Johnson?" I said, sticking my foot between the door and the jamb.

"Who wants to know?"

The was no mistaking the Scottish burr. Jock MacGregor, who hailed from Glasgow, had been a mate on my first ship and had spoken with the same accent. The man before me was certainly Scottish and I became even more convinced that these were the lodgings I sought.

"Josh Singleton," I said. "Looking for the lodgings of a Campbell-Johnson." Tears welled up in my eyes as he leaned against the door, crushing my foot. "I believe you may know the whereabouts of a Confederate naval captain, name of Sangster," I gasped through the pain.

"Come you in, laddie. Come you in," he said, throwing the door wide open and grabbing my arm in a huge, hairy hand. With amazing strength he hurled me into the room. Stumbling across the uneven floor, I tripped and fell, the wooden boards slamming into my sores like a thousand needles.

"Now who did you say you wanted?" he demanded.

I rolled over and looked up at the man standing over me. He was enormous, well over six feet tall with shoulders to match. Little fringes of grey hair sprouted around the dome of his bald head. I judged him to be in his fifties. His piercing eyes reflected the light from the candle he held over me and told me I was in dire trouble if, perchance, I was in the wrong place. An involuntary shudder wracked my body.

"You got a fever, laddie?" he asked, seeing the shiver.

"No."

"No," he said, clapping his free hand to my forehead. I was surprised to find his touch gentle. "You're hot but it's no fever heat. So tell me again why you're looking for me."

"We-, we-, well," I stammered, moving my hands and arms in front of me as protection should one of his great boots be aimed at my rib cage. "I believe you might know where I could find Captain Sangster."

"It's all right Ian, he's one of mine."

At the sound of the familiar voice from out the darkness I suddenly felt lightheaded. I scrambled to my feet and, in the dim glow afforded by both the candle and what little light filtered through the white-washed windows, saw the silhouette of my friend. While the voice had not changed I was stunned by his appearance. This was a mere shadow of the man I had served with on the *Carolina II*, the man whose buggy I had loaded, the man I had last seen in a horse lot outside Washington. His back, once so straight, was hunched so that his neck seemed to disappear into his shoulders and I doubted he weighed over a hundred pounds.

"Apart from me," Sangster continued, "he's the only one that's made it on time, poor devil. Name's Josh Singleton."

"Aye, that's what he told me," Campbell-Johnson said. "Pleased to meet you Josh." He extended his massive hand. "Welcome to my lodgings. Make yourself at home."

"Thanks," I said, as my hand was swallowed up. "But why didn't you say something the first time you opened the door?"

"I wasn't going to speak until you told me your business," he said, "and you didn't say a word. Scared you did I?" Suddenly

Confederate Gold
The Missing Treasure

the beard parted as he let out a huge belly laugh and the blue-grey eyes mellowed. "Anyway here you are."

As my eyes become accustomed to the dim light I was struck by the fact the room was smaller than I had expected. I also noticed the rotten door through which I had entered was covered by a heavy internal door secured in place by three enormous bolts. Someone had clearly gone to a lot of trouble to make this room secure.

"Come, sit yourself down," Campbell-Johnson said amiably, as he pushed more than guided me to a simple spindle backed chair alongside a small table.

Apart from a large sea chest and three similar chairs arranged one on each side of the table, there was no other furniture in the room. Peering at the chest I could just make out the letters C-J (DOCTOR) roughly carved on the side which was sufficient to tell me Campbell-Johnson was a ship's physician. Two rumpled blankets along one wall indicated how the two men had spent the previous night.

"But for your voice I would not have recognized you Captain," I said, as I sat down. "The last weeks must have treated you badly."

"That they did Josh," Sangster said, taking the chair opposite me. "But now it's all worth while. What of your journey?"

Before I could say a word the doctor spread his large frame over the chair at the head of the table, leaned back and folded his arms across his massive chest. Fascinated I waited for the chair to collapse under the weight.

"Well," Sangster said. There was no mistaking the eagerness in his voice.

I related my experiences since the robbery, taking care to omit certain parts and down play others. I felt that neither man would take kindly to my affair with Jane, nor my stupidity in the bar below. I left out much of the first and skimmed over the second.

"You've done well," Sangster said, as I concluded my story. Campbell-Johnson nodded in agreement.

"And how about yourself?" I asked.

"I made it as you can see. Truth to tell it was not the best journey I've ever made but I got the buggy through."

"I noticed it," I said. "In fact that was the first clue I had that you might be here. But I don't recall seeing it in the camp or during the robbery."

"No. But it was hidden close by," Sangster said, a smile of amusement creasing his care-worn face. "Thought at that time it would be a quick, pleasant jaunt to Savannah. How wrong I was. Still the dumb Yankees never found the secret."

"So what of your journey?"

The old devil-may-care look was back in his eyes. "Not much to tell," he said, leaning back in his chair. "Apart from little food and water for five days, plus two days as a prisoner of the blue-bellies little else happened."

"How the hell did you finish up a prisoner?" I asked.

"Oh that's a long story," he said. "Maybe I'll tell you one day."

I dropped the subject. If Sangster ever told me it would be in his own good time. "Any news of the others?" I asked.

"Aye," he said, rising slowly then shuffling back and forth across the room, "and none of it good. Seems many ran foul of the damned Yankees one way and another."

There was a long, dead moment. I felt a wave of bile well up from my gut as I recalled him saying we were the only two to make it so far. I wanted to know what had happened yet feared the answer. Finally I plucked up courage to ask.

Sangster sat back in the chair. White knuckled hands gripped the edge of the table. His eyes gazed round the room, as though searching for something, before finally coming to rest on the two of us. Then he hunched forward his hands slipping off the table to hang between his legs while his elbows rested on his thighs.

Confederate Gold
The Missing Treasure

"The guards freed themselves, gave the alarm and General Alexander came after us." His spoke in a quiet monotone, so low as to be little more than a whisper. I had to lean forward to hear. "Within a short time he'd captured six of our boys each foolishly trying to carry too much. He ordered a group of reluctant ex-Confederates to guard his prisoners while he continued the search. Once he'd left our lads appealed to the guards and offered their fortunes for a chance to escape.

"Could have been worse," I mumbled.

"What was that?"

I repeated my comment, louder this time.

"You don't know that because you've only heard the half of it." Sangster's voice rose in anger. "I'll thank you to keep your damned thoughts to yourself until I've finished."

This violent outburst together with the grim look silenced me. I sat still waiting to hear the rest of the story.

"General Wilde sent a detachment to arrest all suspected parties," Sangster said, after several minutes. "Not only did this pig recapture those who had just bought their freedom but he caught all but three of the rest red-handed in a barn near the scene of the robbery. I guess they'd decided to lie low until things quietened down." He paused before adding wistfully, "If only they'd had the sense to get away from the scene we might be having a joyful reunion now."

"What —?" I faltered, still not sure I wanted to know. "What happened to them?"

Slowly Sangster rose and shuffled over to the window, vacant eyes staring into space and mouth clamped tight. He stood like that for some minutes before turning and glaring at me. "He murdered every one of them!" he croaked, fighting to control the loathing that welled up inside him. "Every one of them. My boys, who fought so gallantly for our just and noble cause, were strung up like common criminals."

The blood throbbed wildly in my temple as I waited for him to go on which, I sensed, he would do once he had recovered his composure. For a long time he stood in the middle of the room staring, unseeingly, at the blank walls.

"Murder. Murder," he suddenly screamed hysterically, then paused before saying in a voice which now embodied pure hatred, "Like all bloody Yankees, that damned man Wilde is not fit to swill out pigs."

"How?" I asked quietly.

"He tied their hands behind their backs and strung them up by their thumbs until they confessed. Like men true to the cause no one confessed so, one by one, they were cut down dead."

Slowly the image of what I had just heard permeated my senses. In horror I visualized my comrades, as I now thought of them, hanging there until death released them from their sufferings. My thumbs felt numb and a terrible ache crept across my shoulders. Although not a religious man I could not help likening their deaths to the crucifixion. Not one of them deserved such a fate. We had only taken what rightfully belonged to us rather than let it fall into Yankee hands.

"What of the three that got away?" I asked, arching my shoulders as the pain increased. "Any news of them?"

"None," Sangster said. "It seems they avoided Wilde, but I've no idea where they are."

"How do you know all this?" I asked, curiosity at last overcoming my anger.

"Never forget, my boy, despite Appomatox Court House we are still the Confederacy and we will rise again," Sangster said. "Perhaps not in our life time but, make no mistake about it, we will rise again. Many still remain loyal to the South and news travels fast. I'll say no more." He looked desperately tired as he rubbed his hands across his eyes.

Campbell-Johnson heaved himself off the chair. "You'd best be getting your things together and down to the ship laddie," he said, placing a hand on my shoulder. "We'll —." He stopped and I sensed him staring down at me.

Confederate Gold
The Missing Treasure

My muscles tensed as his massive hands gripped my head and thrust it forward. As I hit the table I felt sure my time had come, although I had no idea why. He ran his fingers over my neck and down my back as though toying with me. The lightness of his touch added to my panic. In that moment fear lent me the strength to push the chair back and leap to my feet. I had not come through the last four years to be butchered by this unknown giant. If I had to die I would, at least, go down fighting.

Turning to face him I saw my move had caught him by surprise. Following up my advantage I sprang but, with remarkable speed for so big a man, he side stepped my rush and I staggered across the room. I regained my balance and turned back to face him.

"Hold it laddie," he said, taking a step towards me. "I'm just looking at those sores on your back and neck."

I felt my face redden as I straightened up from my crouch position. "Sorry," I said.

"No matter," he continued. "There's nothing I can do about them. Enough of doctoring for one day we've more important business to attend to. As I said we'd best get our things together and down to the ship."

"You're right," Sangster said, leaping up from his chair. Immediately he became the man of action I had known for many years. His stride showed renewed energy as he crossed the room and, removing three boards from the far wall, opened up a wide, shallow closet. Here was further proof this room was no ordinary lodging but a carefully constructed hiding place. My mind flashed back to our blockade running days. It was the sort of room that might have been built during the war to smuggle men and materials in and out of the Confederacy.

The two men dragged four boxes out of the closet. They were the same four boxes I had helped load into the buggy back in Washington. I marveled at the audacity of the man who had taken $86,000 of Confederate gold from under the very noses of the officials and driven it over one hundred miles, through countryside infested with Yankee troops. If someone had told me this I would not have believed it but there was no denying the evidence standing in the middle of the floor.

"Don't just stand there laddie," Campbell-Johnson growled. "Help the Captain. You'd better put your fortune in as well."

"I eh, I don't have it with me," I stammered.

Sangster turned. "Where in the name of God is it?" he demanded, his face flushed.

"In a house on Broughton Street."

"What the hell's it doing there," he said. Then before I had time to answer added, "How long is it going to take you to get it here?"

There was a long pause while I tried to estimate the time needed to search the house. "About an hour to an hour and a half," I finally said.

"Well you'd best be sharp about it laddie," Campbell-Johnson butted in. "Because we sail tonight with the tide."

I gawked at him in disbelief. "Sail!" I said.

"As God is my witness, you didn't expect us to stay here with half the Yankee army searching for us," Sangster stormed. "It's all arranged. We sail on the *Heron*, tonight. Now go and don't waste any more valuable time."

Campbell-Johnson unbolted the inside door and I stepped through the dilapidated front door into a blistering wall of muggy air. My breath caught in the back of my throat and sweat immediately started to run down the back of my neck.

"I'll leave this here," I said, pealing off the short frock coat and handing it to Campbell-Johnson standing like Atlas in the darkness of the doorway. "Haven't had that off my back for many a day."

"If you're not back in time we go without you." he said, taking the coat. The door slammed shut behind me.

Looking to the west I saw the eye-searing sun had already started to slip down the cloudless sky, warning me that I had no

Confederate Gold
The Missing Treasure

time to waste if I was to be back before curfew. I took the steep cobble road at a sprint and in a few minutes reached the main thoroughfare. Here men were starting to leave their places of business at the end of the day's work. Heads bent, as though in deep thought, feet scuffing the hard surface of the road they wended their way homewards in the same zombie-like manner I had noted on first entering the city.

I paused to regain my breath. Then adopting the same attitude as those around me I shuffled off looking to find the narrow alley that led onto Broughton Street. Within a few minutes I found it. Now hidden from prying eyes I raced along its sandy surface, past the rat infested refuse pile, as fast as my weary legs would carry me. Emerging onto Broughton Street I was surprised to see a number of ladies, heads held high, strolling along in the late afternoon sun much as I recalled them doing before the war. Only their drab clothing told of the changed times. Despite the urgency I forced myself to stroll the short distance to the house while frantically wondering how to avoid the watchful eye of Moses.

My heart thumped in my throat as if to jump clean out of my mouth as I rounded the corner. A sigh of relief escaped my lips on finding the yard empty. Slipping into the kitchen I closed the door quietly behind me. Although, truth to tell, I was only about to take what was rightfully mine I felt like a thief in the night.

With clothes clinging to me and salt-ladened sweat stinging my eyes I tiptoed across the kitchen and entered the uncarpeted corridor that led to the front of the house. There was no sound of voices from any of the downstairs rooms. The place seemed deserted. My foot was on the bottom step of the stairs when a faint shuffling sound caused me to turn. I half expected to see the skeletal figure of the son and was surprised to find old Moses had followed me down the hallway, a worried frown creasing his leather-like face.

"You want something massa?"

"I'm looking for Mrs. Parslow," I said, trying to keep my voice level. "Do you know where she might be?"

"They all gone out for a walk," the old servant said. "The mistress told me they be back in an hour. Young Massa Charles he like to get out in the fresh air for a short time every day. Says it helps him and Lor' he need it poor soul."

"An hour!" I said. "How long have they been gone?"

"Oh a little while," said Moses. "But they be back soon. You want to wait? I'se sure the mistress not mind you waiting in here." He opened the door into the front living room.

"Thank you Moses," I said, hoping he would catch the hint of dismissal in my voice.

"You all right massa?" Moses asked, as I took a seat by the window overlooking the street.

"Just a little tired," I said. "But don't worry about me. You go about your business." I spoke harshly. I needed Moses out of the way.

With a slight inclination of his head he backed out closing the door behind him. The old man means well, I thought, as I listened to the sound of him shuffling down the corridor. Alone, I wondered what Mrs. Parslow might have done with my fortune. It seemed unlikely she would have taken it with her so I guessed she had hidden it in her room, wherever that might be. There was no time to waste.

Two doors, either side, opened off the upstairs landing. I tried each in turn and, on opening the third, saw her green taffeta dress thrown carelessly across the four-poster bed. The room smelt musty as though it had not been used for some time. The wall paper and drapes were old and faded.

Apart from the bed there were only three other pieces of furniture in the room, an ornate cedar chest under the window, a large maple closet along one wall and a wash table complete with jug and bowl in the far corner. The sparse furnishings looked expensive although they bore the marks of neglect, lacking the sheen of earlier days. Only the bed seemed to have

Confederate Gold
The Missing Treasure

had any care lavished on it. A single picture hung on one wall and I stopped for a second to glance at the Savannah river front of a few years ago.

I quickly dispensed with the wash table before turning my attention to the bed. It revealed nothing. The closet held two old suits, that I guessed belonged to Charles or his brother, but nothing more. Only the chest remained as a possible hiding place. If my gold was not there I would have no alternative but to await Mrs. Parslow's return.

Lifting the lid I saw the uniform of a Confederate officer, neatly laid out with hat at one end and cavalry boots at the other. A sword and revolver lay on top, together with a folded Confederate flag. In wonder I stared into this bodiless coffin. No doubt it was a private memorial to the son and brother who had fallen at Chancellorsville.

Reverently I lifted the contents out of the chest and laid them carefully on the bed. The base of the chest appeared to be split but the line seemed too straight to be an age crack. My pulse quickened as I scratched at the crack until my finger nails were broken and bleeding but the base would not move. I needed something to pry it open. Defeated, I was about to replace the uniform and return to the living room when I remembered the knife Mrs. Parslow carried in her green taffeta dress. It was still there, the sheath carefully sewn inside the bodice. In seconds I removed the board and there, stacked in a small recess, lay my treasure. My hands shook as I lifted out the bags, still strung together, and laid them on the bed. Carefully I replaced the two boards and put the uniform, weapons and flag back in their original positions.

On returning to the kitchen I realized I could not walk out of the house carrying the treasure bags in my arms. Quickly I dropped my pants and tied the bags round my waist but then found the pants would not fasten. I cursed at leaving my coat with Campbell-Johnson. In desperation I tied the bottom of my pants and stuffed the bags down my legs. Now my walk became a stiff-legged limp.

I stumbled about the kitchen as Moses hobbled past the window currycomb in hand. The sight of him solved my problem. Grabbing a stick from the hallway stand I limped after him across the yard to the stable. To avoid raising any alarm I thought it best to tell the old servant I was leaving and somehow to let Mrs. Parslow know I had taken the gold. Leaning against the stable door, stick behind my back, I watched as he started grooming the mule.

"Moses," I said.

"Yes massa," he replied, wielding the comb with a well practiced hand.

"I cannot wait any longer. Please tell Mrs. Parslow I have found my family and friends and taken my belongings."

Without looking up, Moses nodded. "That I will massa."

The continuous swish of the comb along the mule's hide was music to my ears. I turned to leave. If my luck held Moses would be too busy for the next few minutes to notice my sudden disability. As fast as my weighted legs allowed I hobbled down the alley and onto Broughton Street. A few passers-by gave me a sympathetic look no doubt believing my peculiar gait was the result of war wounds. Most simply ignored me as being but one crippled soldier among many.

By the time I rapped on the decaying door of Campbell-Johnson's lodgings dusky shadows had gathered across the river and lightening spiked the distant sky.

"You've only just made it, laddie," Campbell-Johnson said, closing the creaking door behind me and shooting the bolts of the internal door into place. He was dressed in uniform and clearly ready to leave. "Put your fortune in there." he continued, indicating the chest which was half packed with a few civilian clothes and a surgeon's apron.

"In here?" I asked.

"Yes, laddie. In there."

Confederate Gold
The Missing Treasure

"But —,"

"We don't have time to argue," Sangster cut in. "Just count your fortune and then do as he's told you."

I pulled out the bags from my pants and, opening each, carefully counted the contents. Satisfied I put the coins back in the bags and laid them on top of the clothes. The doctor pressed them down firmly before laying a tray of gruesome looking surgical instruments on top. Although the tray completely covered the clothing beneath it did not seem to me a very secure hiding place but I refrained from saying anything.

"How much did you gain for your night's work?" Sangster asked, as Campbell-Johnson closed the heavy lid, secured the large iron clasps and bound the whole with strong cord.

"Five thousand, five hundred and forty dollars," I said, making no effort to hide the excitement in my voice. In my wildest moments I had never dreamed of having so much money. "Oh and fifty dollars," I added.

"Why, and fifty dollars?" Sangster's voice was sharp.

"I've got five gold eagles in my pocket," I said, still dazed at the amount of my fortune. "I'm tired of begging and stealing. From now on I'll pay as I go, at least for a time."

"You fool," Sangster hissed. "How the hell are you going to spend those coins without arousing suspicion. If you're caught with them on you you'll be done for. Put them in the chest with the rest."

"No. They're mine and I'll take my chance."

"Then you'll take it alone," Sangster said. "If you don't do as I order you'll travel to Mexico by yourself. We'll have no part of it."

"Mexico!" My jaw dropped.

"We sail for Tampico tonight, with or without you. Keep the money and ride or give it up and sail? I doubt you'll ever meet up with us again if you ride."

For a few moments I stared at Sangster in disbelief, stunned both by his threat and the thought of leaving my homeland.

Then stubbornness won out. "I'm keeping the fifty dollars," I said.

Sangster glared at me but said nothing. Campbell-Johnson bent over the chest. Fascinated I watched the muscles in his huge arms bulge as, in one clean movement, he swept it onto his back as easily as I might have heaved a knapsack.

"Right," he said, straightening up and heading for the door, "I'm ready for the open sea again."

I was at the top of the steps before Sangster laid a restraining hand on my arm. "Not with those five eagles on you, you don't," he said coldly. "You stay here. Clear everything into the closet and close the wall before you leave. We don't want anyone to know we've been here."

Although familiar with his quixotic mood changes, I was still stunned by his attitude over my gold coins which, to me, seemed totally unreasonable.

"You'll find a knapsack and some food in there," he added, pointing to the closet. "It might be of use to you."

I never saw the blow that felled me.

By the time I came round my two companions and my fortune had disappeared. I needed to run after them along the wharf but as I clambered to my feet a thousand lights flashed before me like a meteor shower and I collapsed again. I do not know how long I lay there, eyes closed, before managing to crawl back into the room where, still dazed, I struggled to close and bolt the inner door.

Confederate Gold
The Missing Treasure

CHAPTER 21

Elbows on the table, aching head cradled in both hands, I cursed myself for my obstinacy. As the minutes extended into hours I thought of all the questions I had not asked. Tampico was in Mexico, but I had no idea where. When was the ship due to dock? How long would they stay there? If I did not make it in time, where were they going?" Despite Sangster's threat there had to be a way of catching up with them. But it was too late now. Once more my fortune was in the hands of others but this time I had no idea how to get it back. Slowly I fingered the five gold coins that had been the cause of my present predicament.

The room was shrouded in darkness by the time it dawned on me I had to solve one problem at a time. First I needed food and rest. Then in the morning, after cleaning the room, I would try to find a horse and head inland. What happened after that was, at this moment, beyond thought.

Feeling my way round the closet I found the knapsack and inside, among several bits of clothing, a tin box containing matches. Lighting the remains of the candle I searched the rest of the recess. It was empty except for a small wooden box containing three pieces of hard tack some pork and a tin canteen. The hard tack was stale and infested with weevils while the meat tasted of nothing but salt. Despite this, I wolfed down the food finishing my meal with a long swig of muddy tasting water from the canteen.

My hunger only slightly appeased I turned my attention to the knapsack. It was made of canvas supported on a wooden frame. By the flickering light of the candle I saw a large 7 stencilled on the front which, I suspected, referred to the original owner's regiment. Emptying it onto the table I saw, to my astonishment, the cap, jacket and pants of a Yankee uniform. The sleeve bore sergeant chevrons and down the side of the

Bill Westhead

pants ran the crimson stripe of the ordnance. So that was how he did it, I thought, staring at the uniform sure that a Yankee, clad only in his under clothes, lay dead somewhere along one of the roads to Savannah. I smiled at the arrogance of my late skipper who, like a chameleon, could change colors to meet any situation. I loathed touching the hated cloth and a strange tingling sensation ran through me as I stuffed it into the darkest corner of the closet.

Apart from the uniform the knapsack yielded seven more pieces of hard tack, a wicked looking hunting knife with a six inch curved blade and the very jacket and pants I had acquired from Dr. Robertson. I changed, piled the knife, canteen and hardtack on the table then hid the knapsack and my cast-off clothing in the recess. Next I stowed the chairs but the table proved too wide for the shallow closet no matter how I turned it. The legs had to be broken off. It would be easy and quick to smash it against the floor or walls but I dared not do this for fear the noise would arouse the curiosity of those in the bar below.

The table proved more solidly built than its appearance suggested. All four legs had been set firmly into the top and try as I might I could not loosen them. The room became stifling and sweat ran off me like water, puddling on the floor. My arms ached and my breath came in loud rasping gasps as I continued to struggle. The candle died long before I remembered the knife. Even then the first leg proved equal to the knife edge and my frustration grew. The splintering of wood as I hacked away sounded like the rattle of machine gun fire. Finally the leg shattered and I froze certain the noise must have been heard below. With the knife clasped firmly in my right hand I waited for the knock I felt sure would come. The threat of discovery made my throat, already dry from the salt meat and hardtack, feel worse.

I waited for several minutes but no sound disturbed the silence other than my gasping breath. Finally convinced my fears were unfounded, I set about the second leg. By the time all four

Confederate Gold
The Missing Treasure

legs were removed and stowed in the closet, together with the table top, I was utterly exhausted. Leaving the knife and wood chips where they lay I grabbed the canteen and pressed it to my lips only to be teased by a trickle of water. At that moment I would willingly have given my five gold coins for a good thirst-quenching drink.

Satisfied I had carried out Sangster's instructions to the letter I crawled over to the blankets. Despite a feeling of exhaustion I tossed and turned my mind racing back over the day's events. Unable to sleep I got up gathered the wood chips together, wrapped them in one of the blankets, and stuffed the whole into the closet. This done I forced myself lie down again.

I must have finally slept, for the distant rumble of thunder roused me. The strong sunlight filtering through the grimy white-washed windows showed the day to be well advanced. It was time to move. I threw the blanket into the closet, replaced the boards and closed the wall for the last time. Brushing myself down I thought of all that had happened since I had last worn Dr. Robertson's clothes and wondered what fate might have in store for me before I changed again. After a final inspection of the empty room I grabbed the hardtack, canteen and knife, cautiously pulled back the bolts and opened the door.

The lethargy of those working on the wharf contrasted sharply with the energy of the sun's rays glistening and dancing off the river's surface like candlelit diamonds in a tiara. From my vantage point at the top of the steps I counted the ships berthed close by. They were all there except one and, sadly, I knew she had slipped safely away while I slept. My gaze wandered slowly along the riverfront and on out to the horizon. Then I saw it. A distant plume of smoke interspersed with licking flames, announced a disaster in the shipping channel that led to the open sea. In that moment I knew it was not thunder that had aroused me. Gripped with foreboding, I hurled myself down the steps two at a time.

Bill Westhead

"What's happened?" I shouted, grabbing the first person I saw and pointing in the direction of the smoke.

"Don't know for sure," he said, shrugging his shoulders before hefting his large metal hook into a bale of cotton. "Hear they've launched a cutter to investigate. Some say it's that ship that slipped out early this morning. May have hit one of those torpedoes we put in the channel three years ago to keep the damned Yankee navy out. We thought they'd all been cleared."

Stunned, I gazed at the spiraling smoke certain I was now the only one of the group left. I had done everything I could. There was nothing else to do here in Savannah. Cursing the world I went in search of the horse and buggy I had seen the previous night. It was still where the owner had left it and he was not coming back. Taking advantage of a horse trough nearby I splashed my face and quenched my raging thirst. Never had water felt and tasted so good. Refreshed, I filled the canteen, unhitched the horse and mounted. Don't rush, I reminded myself as I guided the horse down the wharf and up an alley leading to the main street.

At this hour the street was deserted except for a few clerks hurrying to and from their paper-littered desks in the counting houses. Heads bent, eyes seemingly glued to the sidewalk, they ignored me. Plodding along the cobbled street that formed the main thoroughfare I cursed the war and the final disaster it had wrought on me. In spite of the events of the previous night the loss of my closest wartime companion proved hard accept. We had shared many an adventure together and, until this moment, I had believed him to be indestructible. The hurt was doubly painful when my thoughts turned to the five thousand, five hundred and forty dollars of gold and silver coin lying on the sea-bed. The slow, steady clop of the horse's hoofs seemed to beat time with my depressed state of mind as I recalled details of my futile trek to Savannah.

Suddenly I remembered Jane and the fortune I had buried under her cabin. My hands quivered as, in my imagination, I felt

Confederate Gold
The Missing Treasure

every contour of her young, firm body. "There's still hope," I muttered, closing my eyes in an attempt to hang on to the vision. With them life still offered love and luxury without the need to leave the south or face the dangers of a trek to Tampico. I felt a stiffening in my groin and, kicking the horse into a canter, rode out of Savannah my spirits revived.

The day proved to be typical of June in Georgia with the sun beating down unmercifully from a cloudless sky and the temperature rising by the minute. There was no wind, not even a breeze to rustle the leaves. The only cooling, if cooling it be, was caused by our movement disturbing the listless air around us. The faint but constant odor of burnt earth was now coupled with the stench of rotting vegetation.

Although eager to find Jane and my fortune, I slowed the mare to a steady walk knowing she would suffer in the heat if pushed too hard. To ease the going I had decided to follow the main roads to Augusta but giving a wide berth to all cities and towns along the way.

Confidence restored I let my thoughts wander into the future. Every now and again I fingered the five gold coins in my pocket. Touching them made me feel like a plantation owner. I whistled snatches of 'Dixie' and the horse, pricking up her ears, seemed to move in time with the melody. At one point I leaned forward and whispered in her ear, "The south will rise again and we'll both be part of it." She whinnied as though she understood and agreed. She was a true Rebel.

Except for the overpowering heat and foul smell the day passed quietly and, as the sun started to slip down the sapphire blue sky, I searched for a safe place to spend the night. I had done this so often recently it was now second nature and it was not long before I spotted a small pond surrounded by trees some two hundred yards from the road. Although mosquitoes infested the stagnant waters it seemed like an oasis in the wilderness. I dismounted amazed at finding the place deserted. We sank to our knees and drank our fill from the warm but invigorating water.

Then I tied Dixie, as I had called the horse, in the shade where she could eat her fill of the long, sweet grass that grew beside the pond.

After eating my ration of one piece of hard tack I lay on the bank in my own silent world my eyes closed against the brilliance of the dying sun. Not even the biting insects could dampen my spirits in this idyllic spot. The war and its aftermath was far away. I felt like primitive man simply living out each day with little memory of the past or need to care what happened in the future.

The following morning found us eager to be on our way. After another piece of hard tack and long drink, I turned Dixie's head towards the road. With hard packed earth underfoot we made good progress, each step carrying us ever closer to Jane. The weather was a repeat of the previous day. Sweat poured off me and the constant chafing of my pants as I rose and fell in time with Dixie's gait rubbed my thighs raw. But we did not stop. Finding Jane and the rest of my fortune remained uppermost in my mind.

Nightfall found us camped alongside a fast running stream into which I plunged, fully clothed, only to come up gasping as the cooling waters took my breath away. Despite the heat of the evening I shivered as I climbed out and sat leaning against the scaly bark of an old water oak. But for the first time in days I felt clean and refreshed. Supper consisted of another precious piece of hard tack washed down with a long drink from the stream. If only Jane were here I would have all I wanted in this world, I thought, as I settled down to sleep under the clear star filled sky.

Heavy drops of rain dripping from the broad three lobed leaves above woke me. Low, dark clouds crashed and raced across the sky driven on a strong wind. My clothes offered little protection against the storm and the remaining four pieces of hard tack in my pocket were wet and soggy. Feeling dejected, I stuffed a handful of sodden crumbs into my mouth and prepared to face the elements.

Confederate Gold
The Missing Treasure

Dixie seemed to relish the rain and cooler temperature and she set out at a steady trot. I began to feel better as the miles slipped by and whistled a few bars from Stephen Foster's songs as my thoughts wandered into the future. I was so engrossed that I failed to hear the muffled sound of hoofs galloping over the rain sodden ground.

"Stay where you are."

The command sent a river of icy water through me. I shivered. There was no mistaking the coarse northern accent. The five gold coins in my pocket suddenly weighed like boulders and Sangster's words rang in my ears. Under my breath I swore at my own stupidity. For weeks I had taken every precaution to avoid Yankee patrols, but thoughts of a future with Jane had driven all caution from my mind and I had ridden straight into a trap. Reining Dixie to a halt I turned to face six horsemen, each wearing Yankee cavalry uniform. My initial reaction was to try and make a break for it but one look at the condition of their horses and the carbines buckled to the off side of their saddles was enough to tell me the futility of such a move. I forced myself to look them straight in the eye while, at the same time, trying to control the tremors that rippled through my body.

"Who are you and where are you going Reb?" demanded the young, clean shaven officer who wore the insignia of a lieutenant. He looked little more than a boy compared to the bearded, battle hardened sergeant on his left. I wondered if the lad had ever seen action.

"Alan, heading for north Georgia," I said after a moment's hesitation.

"Alan who?"

This time the pause was longer. Then Jane's name leapt to mind. "Harrison," I said.

"Sir, when you speak to me," the young lieutenant snapped. "Where have you come from.?"

"Savannah," I said, then waited a moment before adding "sir", dragging the word out in typical southern style. His face colored and his knuckles holding the reins visibly tightened at the intended insult. Whether or not he had seen action, I needed to be more careful. If he lost his temper I would be the one to suffer.

"What business did you have in Savannah?"

"Trying to find work, sir," I said. "But there's no work to be had for the likes of me. So I'm going home to farm what little land has been left to us." I was surprised at the ease with which these half truths tumbled from my lips.

"I don't believe you, Reb." Although his color had returned to normal and his hands relaxed his voice remained menacing. "Where did you get that horse?"

"I was an officer during the war, sir. I bought her when I volunteered and she has been with me for three years. When we surrendered, I was allowed to keep her."

"Officer," he barked. "You and the likes of you were all damned traitors." As if to emphasize his words he leaned out of his saddle and spat on the ground. "Pity was we left you any land at all," he continued, prodding me in the shoulder. Dixie bucked at this sudden movement and I tightened my grip on her rein.

"Dismount."

Knowing resistance was useless I slid to the ground as slowly as I dared. My left hand held Dixie's rein, while my right hand, plunged deep in my pants pocket, clutched the five gold coins.

"Search him."

"Sir," the sergeant said, dismounting and snapping his hand up in a smart salute. Although short in stature, he had powerful shoulders. He ambled towards me like an ape, one hand resting on his sabre the other rubbing his bearded chin, as though deep in thought. As he neared me his piggy eyes narrowed and his mouth twisted into a sadistic grin. I backed away pulling Dixie with me. Unhurriedly he followed. Time was on his side.

A chill ran up my spine and my knees quaked. I had to get rid of the coins. There was no doubt in my mind that if he found

Confederate Gold
The Missing Treasure

them on me I would not only lose them but my life as well. At the risk of being shot, or worse still, hacked to death I half turned my back on the advancing sergeant. At the same time I slowly withdrew my right hand and, as I rubbed Dixie's chest, let the coins drop into the grass verge. I prayed the grass would swallow them up and thanked God there was no sun to glint off their polished surfaces.

"Get on with the job," the officer ordered, as I turned back to face the group.

With surprising speed the sergeant's large, hairy hand shot out and sweeping the hunting knife from my waist pointed it at my chest. Spittle oozed from his mouth and dribbled down his beard while his gloating face told me he longed to plunge the weapon home. My skin crawled at the diabolical chuckle that gurgled in his throat and I flinched as the blade pricked my flesh.

"Stand still Reb," he snarled, slashing an imaginary X across my chest before sticking the knife in his belt. The devil was enjoying himself. He ran his hands all over me and, purposely ripped one of the lapels off Dr. Robertson's jacket. Then he plunged his hand deep into my pocket and squeezed me in a vicelike grip. I doubled over in agony and, despite all my efforts at control, could not stop a dribble running down my pants leg.

"You're a dirty boy Reb," he sneered, splitting the pant seam as he withdrew his hand. He stood back, maliciously surveying my torn and stained clothing. This was no search but simple humiliation and this man was an expert.

"Search completed sir," the sergeant said, saluting. "Beg to report he's clear."

The younger man's face flushed with rage. "Damn it,' he said, "thought we might have found something worth the taking." Then he noticed the canteen. "Search that," he ordered.

Slowly the sergeant lifted the strap over my head, taking pleasure in smashing his elbows into me in the process. Undoing the top he drained the precious water onto the ground before hurling the canteen to one side.

Bill Westhead

"Nothing sir. Only thing he has worth taking is the horse."

"That nag," the lieutenant scoffed. "Doubt she's fit for anything but the glue pot."

I glanced at Dixie and saw what he meant. She looked a poor sight with her head hanging low. Compared to their mounts she was little more than skin and bone but I knew that with care, she would recover. I needed to keep her if at all possible.

"Sir," I begged, "she has carried me faithfully over the years and I pray you'll let me keep her in her last days."

"Oh, hell keep the damned thing," the officer said, a touch of boredom creeping in to his voice. "I'll bet you'll be carrying her home before she'll carry you, although in all honesty you look little better than she does."

"I thank you sir," I said as politely as I could.

"Think yourself lucky we haven't strung you up, Reb," he said, wheeling his horse round. Then he stopped and looked back. "Sergeant," he snapped. "Remind this Reb who won the damn war he and his like started."

"Sir." Again the sergeant's hand swept upwards in salute. But this time it did not stop at his brow. As though mesmerized I watched it continue round until he buried his clenched fist in my gut. The force of the blow knocked all the wind out of me. As I doubled up, hands clutching my stomach, a second blow slammed into the side of my head. My brain erupted in a terrifying explosion, a myriad of colors flashed before my eyes and as a third blow landed on my chin I hurtled into the depths of an inky black abyss.

The rain had stopped by the time I came round and found myself lying face down in my own vomit. My head burst as I struggled painfully into a sitting position. I felt dizzy and as I opened my eyes everything swam back and forth in a circular motion. Gingerly I tried to scrape the dirt, grass and vomit from my face. My mouth was bone-dry and tasted of blood while my tongue found gaps where teeth should have been. Slowly my eyes began to focus and I saw Dixie nibbling the grass close by. I

Confederate Gold
The Missing Treasure

tried to go to her but the moment I stood everything began to spin again. I collapsed into the soft, sweet smelling grass and waited for my senses to return to normal. Time did not matter.

At last I managed to stand long enough to take stock of my situation. Above all else I needed water. The canteen lay a few feet away, its side dented by contact with a rock. I stumbled over, picked it up and, holding it like a precious jewel, shook it expecting to hear the slosh of water. There was no noise and I stared in disbelief. I felt sure I had filled it earlier in the day. Vague recollections of my painful encounter with the Yankee patrol began to return and, as they did so, my hands strayed to my pockets. The damp, mushy hard tack was still there but the other pocket was empty. Panic gripped me.

"Where the hell are they," I said, leaning on Dixie's neck as another bout of dizziness hit me. As if trying to offer help she raised her head and nuzzled me like a long lost friend. I stood leaning against her flanks until the intermittent spells of lightheadedness finally stopped. Only then I remembered the sequence of events. Quickly I dropped to my knees.

After what seemed like hours of frantic searching I had found four coins but, despite delving into every tussock, I could not find the fifth. Knowing time was precious I reluctantly gave up and, with four coins safely in my pocket, mounted Dixie.

"Sorry Dixie, but after what's happened we can't stay on the road," I said, applying pressure to her left flank. At a leisurely pace we crossed the wasted fields to the tree line.

The pale blue sky studded with ash grey, watery clouds reflected my misery. Because of the rough ground, sudden spells of dizziness, blurred vision and nausea that occasionally overcame me we travelled slowly for the rest of the day. At times I wondered if these attacks were from the blows to my head or whether I had suffered some other injury from the blow to my gut. Sunset found us on the edge of a small copse of tall elms. Although there was hardly any grazing, I was too sore and weary to go on. The empty canteen swinging at my side mocked my parched throat, and added to my agony.

Confident Dixie would not stray I left her free to feed while I scoured the ground for a soft place to rest my aching body. By now the vomit had dried on my clothes and, as I futilely tried to scrape off the offensive mess, I wished I had brought my other clothes with me instead of leaving them stuffed in the hidden closet of Campbell-Johnson's lodgings.

In the end I gave up the unequal struggle and, after a mouthful of soggy hard tack, settled down at the base of a tree where large gnarled roots gave support to my aching limbs. Lying there and hearing the silence I longed for the deep sleep that would swallow up the pain in my battered body and the agonizing thirst in my throat. But the night dragged by while my ever-open eyes gazed at the moon and stars as they made their lingering way across the heavens.

The dawn sky promised rain, a most welcome gift in our present condition. My eyes closed I prayed for the heavens to open and, as I did so, the first drips splattered on the ground. Grabbing the canteen I held it under the leaves in an effort to catch each precious drop before it hit the ground. But the downpour was short lived and I gulped down what little water I had managed to collect. Far from slaking my raging thirst the taste of water only increased it. Tears of frustration trickled down my grime covered face as I stared up at the unmerciful sun breaking through the life-giving clouds until Dixie's muzzle in my back brought me to my senses.

"We need to find the river." I spoke aloud although as far as I knew there was no other human being near.

As if she understood the horse neighed agreement.

We pushed on through trees and over barren fields while the pitiless sun beat down from a cloudless June sky. The stench from my clothes, a mixture of old vomit and new sweat, turned my gut but there was nothing I could do until we found water. Despite the leisurely pace Dixie was foaming at the mouth by

Confederate Gold
The Missing Treasure

mid-afternoon and I was passed caring whether we made the river or not. One day, I thought, someone will come across our sun-bleached bones out here in this God forsaken wilderness.

Finally Dixie stopped and, despite all my efforts, refused to take another step. She had come to the end. Slipping off her back I put my arms round her shaggy neck. "Come on old girl. Don't give up. We'll make it," I urged.

She turned her head and looked at me through large, pain-filled, brown eyes which told me she had nothing more to give. Unable to help her I walked away with a heavy heart. I had only gone some twenty yards before I heard her uneven clop behind me. Looking back I saw the pitiful sight of her staggering after me, her head so low that her muzzle almost dragged the ground.

In this manner we stumbled on, me leading and Dixie following, stopping every now and again to lean silently on each other for support. Nothing but the mimicking songs of mocking birds, flitting across the open ground, broke the stillness until, in a daze, I thought I heard the faint sound of running water. I stood stock still for several minutes fearful the life-saving sound might simply be in my imagination. The silence was overwhelming. Even the birds stopped their singing as I strained my ears trying, once more, to catch the sound. When it did eventually come I knew it was for real. There was running water somewhere beyond the stand of cottonwood trees that faced us. Summoning the last of my energy I hobbled across the intervening ground and through the trees. A few more paces and I stood on the sloping banks of the river as it glinted in the last rays of the dying sun.

In my eagerness I hurtled down the shallow bank into its cool, refreshing flow. Coming to the surface I gasped in surprise and pleasure to see Dixie kneeling on the bank, her sweat soaked flanks heaving furiously, as she drank her fill. I clambered out and laid a hand on her mane while aloud I thanked God for our deliverance.

Bill Westhead

Over the next two days we retraced part of the route I had taken with Mrs. Parslow. Memories flooded back as we ambled passed familiar spots although it seemed months, if not years, since I had last set foot in these parts. I hoped by now she had gained passage to England.

With a constant supply of water, fish to alleviate my dwindling diet of mushy hard tack and grasses for Dixie we seemed to be travelling through paradise. We were in a world of our own with never a sight of human soul. Only the birds accompanied us, flitting through the trees or darting across the surface of the river. Their constant singing cheered us on our way while the trees, cloaked in shimmering green, gave welcomed protection from the unrelenting sun.

On the third day we came to the place where Mrs. Parslow and I had first joined the river path. After a final wash and drink I reluctantly turned Dixie's head away from the river and struck off across country towards Augusta, the only starting point I had in my search for Jane.

I knew the cabin lay somewhere to the west within a day's ride but had no knowledge of the route and no landmarks to guide me. Not much to go on, I thought, as Dixie's steadily plodding feet stirred up small clouds of dust. Occasionally a clump of trees dotted our way offering us a few minutes respite from the sun's glare. Bile still rose in my throat every time I saw a burnt out farm or home and I loudly cursed the damned Yankees.

Towards mid-day, on our second day after leaving the river, I spotted what looked like a lone cabin in the far distance. It seemed promising, rising out of the scorched earth like a mirage, and my heart leapt. The nearer we got the more certain I became this was the place I was looking for. As we crossed the last field my heart pounded with excitement its rapid thumping sounding like a drum roll. My breath came in short, quick gasps and my body reacted at the thought of my love lying behind those walls.

Confederate Gold
The Missing Treasure

I stood on the well-remembered porch and knocked on the door. In a moment I felt sure it would open onto a new life. There was no response. Certain she was there and determined to make her hear I hammered and shouted until my fists were sore and my voice croaked. But the door remained closed. Frustrated, I ran down the side of the cabin to the narrow shuttered window that looked into the main room but it, like the door, was closed.

"Jane, it's me, Josh," I screamed through the crack in the shutters. The only answer was the echo of my own voice.

There was no sign of life at the back of the cabin or in the back field although the decrepit cart still stood in the partially collapsed shed. Even the concealed storage place proved to be deserted. It was impossible to believe Jane had willingly abandoned the cabin after fighting so hard during the war years to keep it. I began to worry that in my absence some disaster had overtaken her.

At last I tried the cabin door and to my surprise found it unlocked. Dreading what might lie beyond I cautiously pushed it open. In the dim light from the shuttered window everything seemed to be as I remembered - the hearth where I had watched her prepare breakfast, the motley array of cooking vessels, the table, now bare, and the straw bed, with its loving memories, in the corner. Everything was neatly and tidily stored just as it had been the day I left. There was no sign my love had been attacked or that she had left in a hurry. Despite this, she was nowhere to be found.

I had been so intent on finding Jane I had forgotten all about my treasure. If it is still where I buried it, I thought, then for certain she will be back. I crawled under the cabin and, finding the ground undisturbed, let out a long sigh of relief.

After tying Dixie to the porch rail I went back inside and settled down to wait. Sitting at the table, head cupped in my hands, I longed for her with every bone in my body. At every sound, however slight, I rushed outside hoping to see her, only to find Dixie brushing along the rail or some small animal rooting in the ground. To occupy myself I cleaned the, already clean, cabin and re-arranged the straw all the while visualizing Jane lying there. At times I wandered across the fields hoping when I got back she would be there. But the cabin remained empty.

With mixed feelings of frustration and fear I stood on the porch and poured my heart out to Dixie, while my eyes continued to search the darkening horizon. I was still standing there waiting and watching as the faint rays of the new moon struggled in vain to penetrate the inky blackness.

CHAPTER 22

All my hopes of the last few days were being ground to dust and thrown out like grain pouring through the hole of a millstone. Leaning against the porch upright I continued to gaze into the eternal night until my eyelids drooped.

"Standing here won't make her come any quicker," I said, my voice sounding strained in the ghostly silence.

Reluctantly I went back inside. No light penetrated the open door and while the blackness of the cabin put me in mind of a cave I had once taken shelter in during my blockade running days it also fitted my mood. Too dispirited to bother lighting a candle I sat at the table holding my head in my hands.

"Might as well rest," I muttered. My voice seemed to mock me as it bounced off the still walls to echo round the deserted cabin. Stripping off my clothes I lay, naked, in the straw.

With my eyes closed I could sense Jane lying next to me. It was so real I could actually feel the smoothness of her body, but as soon as I opened my eyes she was gone and I was alone. The unending silence gnawed at my very soul. I tossed and turned scattering straw out over the floor. Everything seemed worse lying there without her. Lying in the very place we had made love. On occasions I called her name. At every sound I expected to see her silhouette against the charcoal grey of the night sky. But she never came. I had never felt as depressed as I felt that night.

Unable to sleep I got up, dressed and went back outside to stand and stare. The night was one of the darkest I could remember with only an occasional star managing to peep through the leaden overcast. Not until the pale grey of dawn started to light the eastern sky did I give up my useless vigil. With a feeling of utter emptiness I went inside, shut the door and sat, elbows propped on knees, face buried in my hands.

I must have fallen asleep for the next thing I remember was being woken by the spear-like rays of the sun slashing through the open door into the cabin. In that moment of waking I was consumed by a strange sense of dread. But the moment passed as quickly as it had come and in its place an acute gnawing sensation grabbed my gut.

Still believing Jane would return, I crossed to the hearth to find a potato or corn, a few peas or beans, anything she had grown in the field out back. There was nothing, not even the remains of a fire. Clearly she intended to be away for several days. As I slammed my fist into the wall the cabin door burst open. I turned instinctively my arms reaching out to greet her. Then I froze.

It was not Jane staring back at me but a stranger who towered over me by some six inches. His thinning hair was heavily streaked with grey while restless green eyes, above hollow cheeks, darted about the cabin as if he were afraid that some evil was about to leap out and devour him. A straggly grey beard almost reached his waist and covered a thin, straight set line of a mouth. His clothing, caked in dirt and grime, was just recognizable as having once been a Confederate officer's uniform. A stain on the empty right sleeve might have once been blood red but was now so old as to appear dark brown or black. Thin legs protruded from cut- off pants and ended at feet wrapped in an assortment of rags.

"Who the hell are you?" the stranger suddenly demanded. I was taken aback by the strength of the voice and, despite his pitiable appearance, some instinct warned me to be wary.

"Josh Singleton, late of the Confederate navy," I said, deciding to start off with the truth. "Like you, I guess, I'm making my way home, hoping to find peace and a future in this God forsaken world we are now forced to live in."

"Ah!" he grunted, moving across the room towards me. The piercing look in those startling green eyes told me he did not

Confederate Gold
The Missing Treasure

believe me, I took a step backwards. Suddenly he turned and began to pace up and down the cabin floor.

For a while I stood and watched this odd behavior waiting for him to speak. He said nothing but continued to pace, his eyes flicking from side to side as if searching every inch of the cabin. He seemed to be trying to resolve some internal conflict. At last he stopped and stood over me. His hand shot out and long, thin, boney fingers seized my shoulder in a vise-like grip.

"I suppose you're like all the others, waiting for her," he said, a thinly veiled tone of contempt in his voice. I shook my head, not in denial, but in a effort to collect my thoughts. At the same time I felt my temper rise at his insulting remark.

"If you're talking about Jane Harrison," I said, with all the arrogance I could muster, "yes I'm waiting for her. But what the hell has that got to do with you?"

I put my hands up to protect myself from the blow I expected, but his hand never moved. Instead his grip on my shoulder lightened, becoming more friendly than aggressive. Without warning he burst into a deep, sarcastic laugh. It seemed to come up from his rag-covered feet, through his belly and roar out through his bearded mouth.

"Thought that might be the case, you poor damned fool," he roared. His face was so close that I could smell the staleness of his breath, like stagnant swamp water, and see the few rotten teeth that clung to his bloodied gums. "If I'd been here," he continued, dropping his hand to his side, "I'd have flogged you alive with my one good hand to knock some damned sense into you. But then I wasn't and it's too late now."

I gaped at him, sure he was out of his mind. "What the hell are you talking about?" I said.

He gestured me to the table. "Come," he said, "I can see you're in shock so let's discuss this like the gentlemen we once were."

I sat, while he stretched out on the chair opposite, his good arm slung across his sunken chest. Although his haggard appearance suggested he was much older I guessed, from the way he moved, he was in his thirties. I waited for him to speak but he said nothing. For a few minutes he sat there, head bowed. When he eventually looked up there was an emptiness in his eyes as though the man inside was somewhere else.

We continued to face each other for several minutes until, unable to bear the oppressive silence any longer, I asked him what there was to discuss.

"Not what, who," he said, after a moment's hesitation.

"Who then."

"Jane."

"What about her?" I asked, my pulse quickening.

"You were a fool," he continued, quietly rocking back and forth. "But not the only one I'll wager."

"What the hell do you mean?" I said, leaning forward and looking straight into those faraway eyes.

"You mean you don't know?"

"Don't know what?"

"She took you in like all the others," he said, tilting the chair back at so precarious an angle I was sure he would lose his balance as he had lost his mind.

"Yes she took me in and helped me," I said, as he brought the chair forward again, "You're going to tell me she helped others returning from the war. That doesn't surprise me. She was that sort of girl."

"You're right, she was that sort of girl." The scorn was back in his voice and it cut through me like a knife.

"Look, I don't know who the hell you are, why the hell you're here or what the hell you're trying to tell me. So let's stop playing this stupid game," I said, slamming my fists on the table. "I met Jane a few weeks ago while making my way home. I was sick and she cared for me. I spent a few days here until strong enough to travel. Then she helped me on my way. Satisfied?"

Confederate Gold
The Missing Treasure

He did not seem the least put out by my show of temper. "I'm sure you spent a few days here," he said calmly then, with a sneer added, "with her."

I leapt to my feet ready to fight this intruder for insulting my loved one but, before I could say a word, he too rose and leaning across the table said, "Gave you what you wanted I'll be bound." His eyes pivoted for a moment to the straw bed. "Snug as a bug in a rug. She would so long as she got something in return. Appeared to help a lot of folk but really only helped herself."

"You're a damned liar," I shouted, reaching over to grab him. "I've sat here for a coon's age listening to you insult her and I've had enough."

"Sit down," he said, easily avoiding my grasping hands. Still standing, he put his one hand on the table and held me with an unblinking stare. "Just control your temper for a minute and listen. I must apologize for not introducing myself but finding you here drove such things out of my mind. I'm Major Robert Harrison, of Jeb Stuart's cavalry. At least I was until the battle of Yellow Tavern where he lost his life and I lost my horse and this." He nodded at the empty sleeve. "For the last year I've been walking and fighting, fighting and walking until I arrived here a few days ago to find the place empty."

"I thought her husband was dead!" I said. My voice cracked as I slumped back in the chair. "Least that's what she told me."

"Her husband is dead," Harrison said. "That's probably the only true thing she told you. I'm her brother. Did she tell where he died?"

"I think she said Bull Run."

"That's also true. But didn't you find that name a little strange for a Southerner."

"What's strange about Bull Run?" I asked.

"Only that south of the Mason Dixon line we generally call it Manassas."

"So, she used the northern name. I don't see that as a crime. I've heard both used in the south."

Bill Westhead

"I suppose you're right," he said, gazing up at the ceiling.

Looking at the man opposite I saw, for the first time, the resemblance to Jane. If I had not been surprised by his sudden arrival I might have guessed earlier from the unusual eyes. As I studied him more closely I could see, under the straggly beard, he had the same angular features.

"Now I know who you are and why you're here," I said, "but I still don't know what you're trying to tell me about your sister."

He lowered his head and his eyes again locked on mine. "Although everything has changed in the last four years," he said, his face showing a mixture of sorrow and fatigue, "I still find it difficult to talk about my family to a complete stranger."

"I understand," I said, realizing that Robert Harrison was struggling for words. "But hopefully, if you can tell me where Jane is, we won't be strangers any longer."

"Why?"

"Because I intend to marry her, if she'll have me."

This last statement breached the dam and his words came tumbling out in a torrent. "Ever since she was a little girl Jane yearned for the gracious living. She'd have done anything to be the wife, or mistress, of a plantation owner. But we are, or were, just ordinary folk making enough of a living from our farm here to keep the five of us, father, mother, Jane, Harry and me."

There was a far away look in his eyes as he turned and walked out onto the porch. I followed.

"We lost Harry at Antietam," he said, gazing into the distance. "Father and mother never got over it and both died the following year." He sounded detached as if reporting some insignificant event but his face told a different story. "But nothing," he said, his voice suddenly rising, "was ever enough for Jane. At fourteen she ran away to Savannah in hopes of finding a rich husband. We heard later she hurled herself at every eligible man she could find, but nothing came of it. Then came the war and she, like many of us poor wretches, got caught up in

Confederate Gold
The Missing Treasure

the glamour of the times." A long, low sigh escaped his lips. "If only we'd known then what we know now."

The pause that followed did not invite questions but offered a moment to reflect on what might have been and what was. I waited for him to continue.

"In the midst of all the excitement everyone fell in love and many married," he finally said. "Not to be outdone Jane married her cousin Thomas Harrison. Don't know if she ever loved him, poor soul, but she certainly loved the uniform and basked in the respect she received as the wife of a brave and loyal Confederate officer." He paused and looked at me as though unsure whether or not to go on.

"And," I prompted.

"We once owned the land around here," he sighed, his voice little more than a whisper. "Father gave Jane and Tom a few acres as a wedding present and Tom, Harry and me built this cabin. But the marriage didn't last long. As she told you poor Tom was killed a few months later at Manassas."

Robert turned his head and again gazed out over the land he had known and loved as both man and boy. His eyes, saddened beyond tears, mirrored his thoughts. It was land he had fought for and lost. Land he would continue to fight for against a new breed of men called carpetbaggers who, even now, were descending on the south to pillage and plunder in the name of reparation. He stood in silence for some time before going back inside.

"After Manassas Jane moved to Savannah, wallowed in the accolades heaped on her brave husband and played the part of the grieving war widow to perfection," he said, when we were once more seated at the table. "Of course, at that time she was one of a few. Regrettably she soon became one of many and her life changed. No longer was she invited to the grand balls and other functions organized to raise funds for the troops. As time past things got worse and, little more than a year after Tom's death, she stopped associating with anything connected to the war. She became more and more convinced the south had lost. Eventually she left Savannah and returned here to await the final outcome."

"Poor girl," I said quietly, at the same time thinking how inadequately the words expressed my feelings for Jane at that moment in her life.

"Yes," Robert muttered. "That's what everyone said. For a time they left her alone thinking she was grieving for Tom and believing, if the south lost, she would think his death had been for naught. Of course her friends called whenever they could to keep an eye on her and see she was all right. It was not until the war ended anyone realized that amidst all the devastation Jane remained besotted with the idea of wealth and would stop at nothing to achieve it."

Robert leaned forward. "Did you never wonder," he said, grinding the words out through clenched teeth, "why this place remained standing when everything around, even her old home, had been ransacked and burned by Sherman's troops?"

I was stunned by the question. "No," I said, swallowing a lump that suddenly rose in my throat. "I was so thankful to find the place I never thought about it."

"I suppose you can guess how my sister saved it?" Robert said, staring straight at me. There was no denying the implication in his voice. I knew his next words would damn my hopes and I did not want to hear them. My mind was in turmoil as wild scenes careened through my brain. The low-ceilinged room suddenly became suffocating and the stench from the man on the other side of the table unbearable. I leapt to my feet and rushed out the door, fearing I would be sick if I stayed.

Holding onto the porch rail I closed my eyes. I knew, beyond any doubt, she had saved the cabin and land by giving herself to Yankee and Reb alike, and I was one of many. I recalled the journey to Augusta and how I wanted to laugh at the clever way she had dealt with the Yankee patrols. It was no longer funny and I felt sickened at the thought she might have known one or

Confederate Gold
The Missing Treasure

other or even all of them intimately. But I still longed for her and believed I could win her if only I could find her. The war was over. We would start again leaving what had happened where it belonged, in the past.

Memories of the few glorious days we had spent together flitted through my mind and led me on to thoughts of Mrs. Parslow. I vividly remembered the shack in Augusta. The war had cost her everything she had. Would she now, like Jane, do whatever was necessary to regain her wealth. Was it possible she would betray me in exchange for a passage to England. Maybe at this very moment Yankee patrols were scouring the countryside searching for me.

"You'll never outrun your fate, you damned fool," I screamed.

"Who's a damned fool?" Robert shouted from inside.

"Sorry," I said returning to the table, too scared to watch the horizon for fear of what I might see. "I reckon I must have been talking to myself."

"More like shouting to the world."

"Do you know a Mrs. Parslow, in Augusta?" I asked.

If Robert heard the quaver in my voice he chose to ignore it. "No," he said, "but then we traded with a lot of people in Augusta before the war."

"Could Jane have spied for the Yankees to save this farm?"

"No she wasn't for either side," he said. "I'm certain she used nothing but her body to get what she wanted. The folks around here have said nothing and they'd know. Anyway whether she did or not shouldn't bother you. The Yankees aren't after you are they?" He gave me a searching look.

"No," I said guardedly. "But you never know these days."

"You're right," he agreed, "But they're not likely to do more than harass you unless they think you've something to hide."

In spite of the oppressive heat and stifling humidity I could not stop shaking. Clearly he knew nothing of my past and, to my relief, did not seem to care.

Bill Westhead

"Anyway spy or not she'll bother us no more. She's far away from here." He spoke quietly and, despite all he had said earlier, I noted a certain sadness in his voice. "Neighbors tell me she went north with her last lover, a major in the Yankee infantry."

The room spun and a cold fist squeezed my heart. "Why?" I groaned, as I buried my head in my hands. Now she was utterly lost to me my longing for her was greater than I ever thought possible. "Why would she go off with a Yankee, officer or not, when they killed her husband and ruined her life?" I pleaded, fighting to compose myself.

Robert did not bother to reply. There was no need. His raised brow and quizzical eyes told me I already knew the answer - social position and wealth.

The thought of wealth suddenly brought to mind the gold buried under the cabin. Although the ground had appeared undisturbed, I wondered.

"It seems that apart from saving her land and home, my sister made money by her trade." Robert's far away voice cut in on my thoughts.

I felt the sweat on my hands. "What do you mean?"

"When I heard she'd left I searched this place from top to bottom for any clue as to her whereabouts. Under this very floor I found three holes scraped in the sand. I reckon that was where she hid her money. From the size of them I guess she must have had a tidy fortune hidden away."

"Several thousand," I moaned. Now all I had from the fortune, that more than once had almost cost me my life and still left me a hunted man, were the four coins in my pocket.

Robert either did not hear or chose to ignore my mumbling. "I filled in the holes and leveled out the ground so there would be no questions asked, should the Yankees come here," he continued, his thoughts clearly elsewhere. "You don't know, these days, what might arouse suspicion. The simple fact this cabin still stands might well be enough."

Confederate Gold
The Missing Treasure

The room closed in on me. I had to be by myself. As if he understood, Robert made no move to stop me as I staggered through the door onto the porch. There, in the bright sunlight, the future which I had imagined only the day before turned from a dream to a nightmare. After all my suffering half my fortune lay at the bottom of the sea and the rest somewhere in the north. The fact I could tell no one of my loss without telling them how I came by such a fortune only served to increase my agony. I clutched the four coins in my sweaty hand and let my passions run riot, from love to hate and back again.

"Well that's the story of my sister and your lost love," Robert said, startling me as he placed a friendly arm round my shoulder. "I can never approve of what she's done, but I suppose I must be grateful she saved this land. At least it gives me a chance to regain my sanity after four years of living hell."

"I suppose so," I said, my voice a lifeless monotone.

As he dropped his arm I turned and looked at the profile that reminded me so much of Jane and the future I had hoped to build with her on this land. Now the future of this paradise rested with Robert. There was no part in it for me. My dream was dead and the sooner I moved on the better.

"I suppose you want to be on your way," he said, as though reading my thoughts, "but there's no hurry. In fact I would appreciate it if you'd stay for a while. Help me get this place in some sort of order. I'd also welcome the company."

I heard the pleading in his voice and saw him furtively wipe his eye on the tattered grey fabric of his sleeve. Whatever he might think Jane was still his sister and I realized his suffering was at least as great as mine. There was no way I could bring myself to just walk out on him. I felt trapped as I put my arm round his slumped shoulders.

"I'll stay the night and see what the morrow brings," I said.

"Thanks." He grasped my other hand firmly.

In companionable silence we stared over the landscape. It was a view that would never be painted but would always live in my memory. After some time he turned, went inside, and closed the door behind him. Alone on the porch I wondered what the morrow would bring.

CHAPTER 23

When I awoke the following morning Robert was still seated at the table, head resting on his arm, snoring steadily. Brushing straw from my clothes I crept across the cabin and out the door. The sight of Dixie tethered to the rail made me realized the events of the previous day had driven all thoughts of her from my mind. I needed to make amends.

"Sorry old girl," I said, as I wandered over to pat her head. "It's just the two of us now."

She gave a plaintive nicker, nestled her soft nose into my shoulder, and regarded me with large, baleful eyes. I could not believe that less than two days ago I had ridden up here thinking my love and fortune were all but in my hands. In that short time my world had been shattered beyond repair and now, age twenty five, I was right back where I started in life, unwanted, a nobody. The only difference between then and now was that back then I had a home which, although not to my liking was, nevertheless, a place to rest my head.

Dixie's muzzle prodded my shoulder and brought me out of my melancholy. I untied the rope and led her into the back field where, in times past, Jane had grown corn. Here I left her to roam in hope the stubble and weed would satisfy her hunger.

Robert stirred as I entered the cabin, wiping the sleeve of his arm across sleep-filled eyes. "I need to water Dixie. Where would you suggest I take her?" I asked.

"There's a stream back behind the old barn there," he said, pointing through the open window. Then with a touch of nostalgia in his voice added, "We use to play there as kids."

Sitting on the ground under a cloudless Georgia June sky I contemplated the dismal future I saw ahead of me. Dixie crunched weeds and stubble, her mouth working like a grindstone, until she had had her fill. Then I led her down to the stream.

On the way back I stopped by the derelict barn. Sight of the two-wheeled wagon reminded me of the trek to Augusta and as I ran my hands over the pitted and rotten boards I felt again the aches and pains of that journey. The smell of corn was still there and, when I closed my eyes, I imagined the sound of feet scraping the sides as Jane climbed aboard. Although short lived the illusion was vivid enough for me to realize I could not stay here. Painful as it may be I knew I had to put the past to rest and go on.

Robert sat on the porch busily twisting one end of a long wire back on itself to form a loop before bending the other end round his feet and back through the loop. I wrapped Dixie's rope round the rail and watched, fascinated by his one-handed dexterity. Having completed the task he looked up. "You find the stream?" he asked.

"Oh, yes," I said, embarrassed that he had caught me staring at him.

"Good," he said, bending down to pick up another piece of wire.

"What are you doing?" I asked, looking at the small pile of loops strewn about the floor.

"Making traps," he said, continuing to twist and bend the wires.

"Where the hell did you find wire?" I asked. "I thought it had all been seized for the war effort."

"Ah," he said, with a knowing wink. "I guess Tom bought this before the war to fence off his land. Before he left he must have stashed the rolls in his hide-away because I found them under what was left of the corn."

"Thank God for Tom," I said, watching the pile of wicked looking nooses grow.

"We're going to need food 'cause all I've found is corn and a few shrivelled beans," he said, a smile creasing his worn features. "I hope with these," he continued, waving his latest snare in the air, "we can not only improve our food supply but vary our diet at the same time."

At the mention of food my stomach rumbled and my mouth watered reminding me I had not eaten since arriving at the cabin. "We need to eat first," I said. "I'll scratch around and see if I can find anything to go with the corn and beans."

"You can try." Robert tossed another finished loop onto the pile. "But I've looked everywhere and only found dried up corn and beans. Still in our present state I suppose that's better than nothing. He paused before adding, "As the old saying goes beggars can't be choosers."

"Are there any fish in that stream?" I asked.

"Never seen any," he said. "Anyway we've no pole so don't waste your time. Get the fire lit. You'll find kindling and logs stacked out back."

Armed with the dry wood and a match from a tin box I found on the shelf I soon had the fire going. As I put the box back on the shelf I noticed "United Machine and Supply Co. N.Y." stamped on the back. My heart lurched at the thought this very box might have belonged to Jane's major. As though touching it might have fouled my hands, I wiped them down my pants.

While waiting for the fire to warm up I ambled down to the stream and filled a large pot with water. To this I added the corn and wizened beans then put it on the fire and waited for it to boil. Before long two steaming bowls of watery stock were on the table. I smiled as the sight of them reminded me of Mrs. Parslow's broth.

"Robert," I began, as I sipped a mouthful of the tasteless soup.

His green eyes narrowed as he looked at me. "Yeeez," he said in his best Southern drawl.

"Since last night I've done nothing but mull over what you said about my staying on here for a while but there's too much of your sister in this place."

"I guessed memories of her would drive you away," he said, without looking up. "I understand your feelings, but I'm truly sorry. When do you intend to leave?"

"I'm sorry too," I said. "But I have to get away from here, at least for the time being. Maybe I'll be back one day, if you'll have me."

"Maybe I will and maybe I won't," he answered, his face creasing into a rueful smile. "But you still haven't answered my question. When are you going?"

"If it suits you I'll stay the night and leave at first light tomorrow, unless there's anything pressing I can help you with."

"There's plenty to be done," he said, "but nothing that you can do in a day or even two or three. Just help me with those traps before you go."

We cleared the table before setting out across the barren field for the tree line. As we entered the woods I recalled Jane had hidden her gallant little pony Traveller beneath these very trees and I wondered what had happened to him. It seemed unlikely she would take him with her, so I reckoned he had been sold or turned loose to fend for himself. Just another of God's creatures she probably hurt, I thought, as we set the traps.

"What are you hoping to catch?" I asked, as we sprinkled a few grains of dry corn around one of the traps.

"Anything that's stupid enough to walk into one of these," Robert said, carefully placing another trap in the roots of a water oak.

With the traps set we spent the rest of the day lazing on the porch. We exchanged s few war stories but most of the time we sat watching the birds. Bright blue jays and scarlet cardinals mingled with the white flashing wings of mocking birds. Their colors brought to mind the flag we had fought under while the solid black plumage of crows circling above us seemed to foreshadow our future. Not for the first time I envied the birds and their world which, unlike mine, had not been turned upside down by the stupidity of man. I could not remember when I had

Confederate Gold
The Missing Treasure

last spent such an agreeable time and cursed the emotions that were forcing me to leave this behind.

As dusk approached we returned to the woods, praying that the twisted wire killers would provide meat for the table. We were not disappointed. We had caught as many squirrels as we had laid traps. That night we ate like kings and, with bellies full, slept like the dead.

"Take this with you my friend," Robert said next morning, as he handed me a small sack containing six of the squirrels we had caught the day before. He had also thrown in some of the dry corn. "It'll help sustain you on your journey to wherever."

"Thanks," I said, "but what about you?"

"There's plenty left for me," he said, "so be on your way and God be with you." His extended hand took mine in its vise-like grip. For a moment we stood face to face, each seemingly supported by the others handshake, reluctant to let go of the present. Time stopped and unspoken words hung between us. At last we broke and as I rode off I felt Robert's eyes boring into me. I gritted my teeth, afraid to look back.

At the tree line I turned south, believing the farther south I went the less the likelihood of harassment by Yankee patrols. Little did I know or care where this decision would lead me. As far as possible I kept away from the main, hard packed roads having already learned my lesson. Water remained my main concern and at every stream or pond we came across we quenched our thirst and I filled the canteen. At a leisurely pace we crossed land savagely crushed under the vicious heel of the victorious blue-bellies. Scenes of devastation were everywhere. Lonesome chimney stacks stood, like abandoned telegraph poles, above the cinders and dust of burnt out buildings. Fields, which at this time of year should have been green with emerging crops, were a reddish grey mixture of Georgia clay, stubble and ash. Here and there we received sullen greetings from a few brave souls who had filtered back to their wasted land. People were finding the transition from war to submissive peace far more difficult than the earlier transition from peace to war. Everyone knew now the only law in existence was the law of strength and that law resided in the hands of our northern conquerors.

Despite the never ending devastation that surrounded me, the landscape became more and more familiar the further south I travelled. Certain features began to stir childhood memories and it was no surprise when topping a rise, early on the third day, I saw all that was left of the old plantation house. At that distance the pride and joy of the Strong and Hampton families seemed to thrust its stark walls towards the cloudless sky as if challenging the South to rise again.

Coming closer I saw tangles of unattended creeper threatened the crumbling, black-sooted brick work. Tendrils wafted in the light breeze, climbing ever upwards to where the roof had once been. Unhindered sunlight shone through eyeless windows and glinted off shards of glass that hung in the charred frames. There was nothing where the slave cabins had once been. The haunted appearance of the ruin sent a shiver down my spine.

A powerful, yet unseen, hand drew me across the weed infested garden and grassless lawn that the hoofs of a million trampling horses had churned into a plowed field. For the first time in my life I entered by the main doorway now no more than a gaping hole in the brick work. The ground floor was littered with ash and bits of burnt wood where the upstairs pine floors had burned and collapsed. Supporting beams hung at drunken angles from their sockets in the walls. Other charred remains told the fate of the furniture that had once graced the house. With every step dust rose in clouds to penetrate eyes and nostrils making seeing and breathing difficult. Scuffing my feet in the debris I was amazed to find many of the ground floor oak timbers, though heavily pitted by fire, were still intact.

"You looking for something?"

The challenge came from outside the house. I looked up to see a shriveled black head topped with frizzy grey hair. Dark, deep set, unblinking eyes stared at me through the window opening and added to the eeriness I had felt on first entering the ruin.

"No," I said, backing away and hoping the vision would disappear as fast as it had come.

"Then what you doing here?" Despite the quaver there was challenge in the voice.

"Just a sentimental journey to see my old home," I said, realizing the creature would not go away until she was satisfied.

"You use to live here?" Her voice was curious now.

"Yes. back in the days when Mr. Strong owned the plantation."

"What was you called?"

"They just called me Josh when I was here. My father was the plantation overseer back then. My mother worked in this house."

"You'se Emma's boy?" she said.

"Yes," I murmured. At the mention of my mother's name I was instantly back to that time in my life when I had lived in and around this very house. "You knew her?"

"Why yes. Emma and Rose be the best of friends. Never knew what happened to her boy after you ran off. So now you back and the Good Lord be praised. Maybe you get this place going again for us poor folk to work."

A dull, empty ache gnawed at my gut as I moved through the filth towards her. "There's no hope of that," I said, at the same time wishing there was some way I could help. "Like everyone else, I've got nothing."

"I dreamed the Good Lord send someone to help us but never guessed it be Emma's boy," Rose said, as tears started to run down her hollow cheeks. "But now you say you like all the rest of us poor folk."

Without thinking, I reached through the opening and put my arms round the fleshless shoulders of the old slave. Her tired head dropped down onto my arm and she wept. We embraced for some minutes before her withered arms suddenly encircled my neck and she looked up.

"You say you ain't got nothing, but I'se know where the old family hide their treasure," she said, her tears replaced by a wan smile that added deep creases to her care-worn face.

"You do?" I said, my interest aroused.

"The lady had us bury all them goods in this garden."

"Ah, but the Yankees have been here since then. They probably dug them up and took them," I said, looking at the myriad of hoof marks. "Even if they didn't we would have to dig up the whole garden to find that treasure and I don't have the time."

"You'se leaving so soon?" she asked. Her eyes were downcast and her thin arms fell to her side.

"Yes." There was a long pause while I searched frantically for words which might appease and comfort the old woman. Finally I said, "Look at this place Rose. There's nothing here for anyone."

"You'se right Josh. I hated being a slave but now I'se free I'se worse off. We slaves had friends, cover for the night and food. Now I'se got nothing. But you'se must look to you'se self," she said, patting my hand, "and I pray the Good Lord go with you."

For a moment her tearful eyes met mine. Then she turned and limped across the garden, head held high, as if refusing to show her disappointment in Emma's boy. I watched as my mother's old friend became a dot in the distance. Then I mounted Dixie and turned my back on the ravaged home of my childhood.

I decided to change direction and make towards the west. Somewhere way out there was land where I might forget the past and make a new start. For several days I ambled aimlessly towards the setting sun.

The food Robert had given me was long gone and I was forced to beg or steal from any dwelling I came across. Some answered my begging and shared whatever they had. Others

Confederate Gold
The Missing Treasure

refused saying they had nothing for themselves. When that happened I returned, under cover of darkness, and stole whatever I could find - a few potatoes, some corn, peas or beans and, if lucky, a chicken. I often felt ashamed on such occasions but needs must when the devil drives. I knew I would fare better if I offered to pay for food with one of my coins but this I dare not do for fear that it might fall into the wrong hands.

After several days begging my way across the country I stumbled on a decrepit looking two-storied farm house. Part of the roof on the near side sagged dangerously and all the windows had been boarded up as if in preparation for a siege. The place looked deserted except for a thin wisp of smoke issuing from the stone chimney.

Dismounting I climbed the broken steps to a rickety porch that swayed under me. Large gaps showed between the front door and frame giving the impression the door had been roughly hacked to size to fill the opening. From inside came the sound of low voices and shuffling feet. I was about to knock when the door slowly creaked open on rusty hinges and I found myself staring down the barrel of a flintlock musket. Gnarled hands held the gun steady, while piercing blue eyes squinted down the long barrel. I raised my hands, knowing that, old as it might be, the flintlock would be lethal at this short range.

"What y'all want?" I heard a slight tremor in the gruff voice and realized the man was scared, which made the musket even more dangerous.

"Food and water, if you can spare it, for a weary Confederate soldier and his horse," I said.

"You don't look like a soldier," he said. This time there was no tremor only suspicion in his voice as his eyes roamed over my clothing. "What's your name?"

"Josh."

"Josh who?"

"Singleton."

"Where're you from?"

"Richmond."

"Um," he grunted. "Where's your home?"

"East of here," I said, deciding to stay with the truth as far as I could. "Burnt to the ground like many another place hereabouts."

"And your family. What of them?"

"Don't have a family any more. My mother died before the war and my father fell at Vicksburg. Never had any sisters or brothers." Even as I spoke I thought how lame the story sounded and guessed he had probably heard similar tales from hundreds of others.

"You look more like a down and out clerk than a soldier." His unblinking eyes continued to stare at me.

Suddenly the voice of a frightened woman echoed from somewhere within the house. "He's not a Yankee is he Sam?"

"Not sure," the man answered, "but we'll find out." He thrust the muzzle further through the crack until it touched my chest. "Now you just stand back there nice and quiet," he said, hooking the door wider with his foot. Never taking my eyes off the musket, I backed down the steps as he came out onto the porch.

Sam stood a little over five feet and his once broad shoulders were now stooped. Older than his voice suggested, I guessed he was in his late sixties which accounted for him being here and not tramping back from the battlefields like so many. His neck was so short that his bald head seemed to rest directly on his stocky shoulders, while his swollen fingers continued to play dangerously around the trigger of the musket. I wondered if he had had time to load it, but from the look in those penetrating eyes, I was not prepared to risk finding out. He stood stock still, looking me over before his eyes strayed to Dixie.

"Where'd you get the horse?"

"A friend gave her to me," I said, slowly moving a little closer to Dixie in case he made an attempt to steal her.

Confederate Gold
The Missing Treasure

"Well you look as though you've travelled rough for some days," he said, after a long pause. "Not like those smart looking Yankees we see about here all the time. Perhaps you're what you say you are so you'd best come in." Sam waved the musket in the direction of the door and I entered with the gun in the middle of my back.

Although old and well used, everything inside the house was spotless, in contrast to the outside appearance. The fresh odor of lye hit me as I walked in. Compared with other places I had been in since leaving Richmond this was a haven of cleanliness with the split plank, pine wood floor scrubbed white. The room itself was neatly furnished with four high back chairs set around a table, while in the far corner stood an old carved chest. Narrow stairs along the side wall led to the upper part of the house. Through a partly open door on the left was a smaller room where an elderly woman fussed over the coarse grey cloths that covered the backs of two well used easy chairs. I reckoned the door at the far end of the room led out to the kitchen area.

"Sit yourself down," Sam said, pointing his musket to one of the high back chairs. "Now tell me about yourself."

"I'm not going attack anyone so I'd prefer it if you'd put that thing down," I said, indicating the musket. "It's so old it may go off at any moment without you knowing."

Sam's weathered face crinkled into a smile. "Aye it might at that," he said, taking the chair opposite and leaning the gun against his thigh. "It's killed a good many folks in its time and frightened more. Now about yourself?"

Briefly I told him about my life as a blockade runner and my time in Richmond. Then I paused, eyes downcast, while I wondered what to say next.

"And when Richmond fell?" he prompted.

"Well er," I hesitated. "We were ordered to move south and join any Confederate unit we could find." I said, shrugging my shoulders.

"And," he persisted.

"General Lee surrendered before I found a unit so." I paused again, then for some unknown reason remembered Simon Price and that fateful morning in Richmond. "There was a comrade of mine. Together we walked to his home in North Carolina. That's where he found me the horse you saw outside. My own home was in the path of Sherman's bloody march to Savannah so when I discovered it burnt to the ground I decided to head west and here I am."

I heaved a huge sigh of relief as I finished, praying he would believe me.

"Same story as many I've heard," he said wistfully. "Our two boys went but never had a chance to walk back. One fell at Shiloh and the other in the Wilderness."

I sat there hearing the silence and it was several minutes before he spoke again. "Don't know why we keep this place. It's too much for the two of us and there's no one left to follow." He rose, crossed to the open door, and gazed across the stark fields that, in better days, had provided his family's livelihood. "Use to raise cotton," he said, "but look at it now."

I felt a need to ease his pain by changing the subject. "That's a nice chest you've got there," I said.

"Ah yes," he said, returning to his chair. "Been in the family over a hundred years. My grandfather brought it from England back in 1740." He paused, his eyes distant. "Wouldn't part with that if it was the last thing I had." Suddenly he turned and stared straight at me, his eyes narrowing. "What is it to you?" he demanded.

"Nothing," I said. "Just trying to be friendly. Look I know you don't trust me, but I am what I claim to be and I'll do whatever you want to prove it."

Lost in thoughts of what might have been and what was, I sat silently staring at the chest waiting for his answer.

"You're right," he said, after a long moment. "I don't trust you. Fact is I don't trust anyone these days and there's nothing you can do to change that."

Confederate Gold
The Missing Treasure

I liked the honesty of this gruff old man and felt I could trust him, even if he could not trust me. "You just told me you don't know why you keep this place on with only the two of you and no one to follow," I said. "What would you say if I offered to help you work it for nothing, except board and keep."

He sat bolt upright. "Ah," he said slowly, "how do I know you won't take off in the middle of the night with whatever you can carry like many have done round here."

"You don't," I said. "But trust has to start somewhere. How do I know that, some dark night, you won't blow my brains out with that musket of yours and steal my horse."

For the first time since we met Sam laughed, a high pitched cackle that echoed round the room like a clutch of broody hens with a fox about. "It's not loaded. Truth is it hasn't been loaded for years 'cause I've nothing to load it with." He shook his head and continued to chuckle. "Still it keeps off the unwanteds. I guess I'd probably kill myself if I ever fired the thing."

"Well do you accept my offer?"

"Don't seem to have much choice do I?" he replied, extending his hand. "But be warned. I'll be keeping a close eye on you and so will the folks hereabouts so don't cause any trouble. Sarah," he shouted, drowning out my words of thanks.

The woman I had seen earlier entered so quickly that I guessed she had been listening behind the door. She was taller than her husband but thin as a whip snake. The black dress that covered her from skinny neck to thin ankle, hung about her like an empty sack and thick locks of grey hair straggled below her mob cap. Fear sat in her light brown eyes as she looked pleadingly at her husband.

"My wife Sarah," he said, nodding in the woman's direction.

Her hands clenched and unclenched while her gaunt face registered shock as she looked at me. Until that moment I had given no thought to my appearance. Now I realized my unkempt hair and beard together with my torn and travel stained clothing would be frightening to someone who had not seen, first hand, the horrors of war.

If Sam saw the look on his wife's face he chose to ignore it as he continued his terse introductions. "This is Josh Singleton." Then, by way of further explanation, added "He's staying to help with the farm in exchange for his keep."

"Oh!," Sarah said. Now her long fingers played nervously with the folds in her dress. "I suppose you want me to get that room ready. I thought we weren't ever going to use it again after —." A fleeting look of despair passed between man and wife before Sarah turned, crossed the room and disappeared up the stairs.

"It was our older boy's room. The one we lost in the Wilderness," Sam explained quietly, his eyes softening as he gazed after his departing wife. "She never got over losing the boys and never will. Come to that neither will I. Just the two of us now." He fought back unbidden tears.

"Is there somewhere I can feed and stable my horse?" I finally asked, trying to break the tension that hung over us like a thunder cloud.

"We ain't got no stable," he said, still staring after his wife. "You'd best tie her to the rail behind the kitchen house."

There were a few blades of coarse grass alongside the rail and a horse trough close by. "Not the best, old girl," I said, looping the rope over the rail. "But at least there's a bit of food and some water."

Returning to the house I gaped in amazement at the plate of ham and grits that awaited me. I longed to ask where it came from but these days you did not ask questions, merely accepted whatever blessings came your way. I fell upon the meal, pushing forkful after forkful in my mouth while Sam and Sarah sat and watched. Within minutes the plate looked as though it had just been washed.

"Finest meal I've ever had," I said, wiping my mouth on my sleeve.

Confederate Gold
The Missing Treasure

"Best cook in the world," Sam said, placing a loving hand on his wife's shoulder. "She can make a meal out of little or nothing and little or nothing's what we have. Still she'll put some flesh on those bones of yours. You can bet your life on that."

"But ham!" I said.

"Just a little we put by," Sam answered with a sly look. "But that's the last of it."

To cover my embarrassment at having eaten the last of their ham, I picked up my plate and fork and made for the door. For several minutes I swilled the plate and fork in the water trough while recovering my composure. When I returned Sam and Sarah were sitting at the table facing each other, hands touching. An air of tranquility hung over the room. They indicated I should join them and as their hands moved across the table to touch mine I felt a contentment I had not known since before the war.

"There's work to be done on the morrow," Sam finally said, rising slowly from his chair and stretching, "and I for one am ready for my bed." His wife obediently followed and I watched them climb the stairs, hand in hand. I thought of the two sons that had been taken from them and wondered what other tragedies they might have suffered in the last four years. Yet I sensed each drew strength from the other and in this way rose above their own personal disasters.

I lay awake, hands behind my head, excited by my good fortune in finding this place and grateful to have been born a Southerner. With people like Sam and Sarah, Robert and even Rose, we would overcome these hard times. The past was past. The South would rise, stronger than before, and regain its former glory. Those we had lost had not died in vain. Before I fell asleep I prayed that the morrow would prove to be the first day of my new life.

CHAPTER 24

September 1912

"And was it?" I said, closing my note book and laying aside the pencil. My sudden question broke the silence.

A look of bewilderment crossed old Josh Singleton's face. "Was it what?" he asked.

"Was it the first day of your new life?"

"Aye," he mused.

I could see by the distant gaze in his twinkling blue eyes, he was still reliving those far off days of 1865. Somehow I had to bring him back to the present.

"So what happened after that?" I prompted him, finally breaking another long silence.

"Ah the Jacksons were the most Christian couple you could ever wish to meet. Completely devoted to each other. Did I mention they lost both their sons in the war."

I nodded.

"They were a bit guarded at first, especially Sarah, but as they said, the farm was too big for Sam to run by himself and they knew it. So I did whatever Sam asked of me and kept out of trouble. In time they began to trust me and —".

His eyes looked beyond me and once more he lapsed into silence. His lips moved but emitted no sound. His body was there but his voice, like his mind, was somewhere else. I picked up my pencil and opened my notebook again hoping the movement would jar him back to the present. But there was still no sound. "And?" I finally said.

He shook his head as if coming out of a deep sleep. "After some months we started to become a family," he said. "Those were bad times. Despite the surrender the war dragged on, one way and another, until the main planting season was over. By the

Confederate Gold
The Missing Treasure

time our exhausted boys finally made it back it was too late." Again he paused, his eyes vacant as though in a daydream. "Those that had stayed behind, like old Sam, had done the best they could but the crops were pitiful. We knew we were facing starvation in the months ahead."

"I never realized the South starved after the war," I muttered ruefully.

Suddenly he was back in the present, his eyes focused in a penetrating stare. "Don't suppose you young folk gave it any thought did you?" he snapped. "Just assumed everything was fine once the fighting stopped. Well believe me it wasn't. While we fought everyone pulled together, but once we stopped it was every man for himself."

"And you?"

"We were no different from the rest. Our only concern was to make sure we had food."

"How did you do that?" I asked.

"We used Dixie and a hand-made plow to till some of the land for planting. Course we were late and didn't get much. A few potatoes, some corn and a few beans and peas, that's all. But that winter we were thankful for anything we could get."

"Is that what saw you through?"

"Yes." The reply was terse.

"And after that?" I hated to be continually prompting him. While he told me his story of the robbery I had not had to say word but now, in the aftermath, he seemed reluctant to talk. Although he appeared alert I wondered if he was tired and if I should wait until the next day. With no hope of finding any gold I could afford to let Josh Singleton finish his story in his own time.

"The next year was different." Suddenly his voice regained its earlier vigor. "We plowed the land in early winter ready for planting. Seed was difficult to get but Sam had his contacts and we did pretty well. The next summer, I remember, we exchanged some of our crops for a couple of hogs and started back into a bit of cotton."

"So soon?" I said, and immediately cursed myself for interrupting him.

"Thought you'd studied the history," he said.

"I did," I snapped, then added "but mostly the period before the war."

"Ah well," he said, dismissing my comment with a wave of his hand, "you probably know we tried to force England and France to come in on our side by stopping shipments of cotton. We'd burn it before we'd ship it. Didn't help. But in the end those Europeans were so desperate they'd pay a king's ransom for good Southern cotton. You know within five years the cotton crop in Georgia was almost back to where it had been before the war. The South was determined to rise again and we did." A steely look of defiance crossed his face.

Astounded, I had to ask who picked the crop. I had picked cotton as a school boy and found it backbreaking work. It was hard, if not impossible, to believe three people, two of them old, could pick enough cotton to make it worthwhile.

"In spite of Lincoln and the lure of the north," he said, "a lot of slaves stayed in the South. They were free but had nowhere to go and were only too happy to pick cotton for food and a little pay." He chuckled before adding, "Especially if the Klan was around."

I was stunned by the hint of cruelty in his laugh which suggested that, despite his mother, he condoned keeping slaves in their place. I could not help asking if he had ever been a member of the Klan.

"At the beginning I was despite what I saw on the way to Savannah," he said, thoughtfully rubbing his chin. "Like many I was angry at the government's so-called reconstruction plans and scared of the power that some former slaves seemed to be getting. We all respected General Bedford Forrest so when he became Imperial Wizard in '67 we reckoned the Klan was all

Confederate Gold
The Missing Treasure

right. But when they started the killing it became too much for many that had seen the bloody slaughter of war. I never really left the Klan, just faded out."

To the best of my knowledge this was the first man I had met who admitted to being a founder member of the Klan and it roused my curiosity. "Are you still a member?" I asked.

He shrugged his shoulders. "Don't suppose so," he drawled. "Too old and anyway things are different now-a-days."

I let that pass and, after referring back to my notes, asked what had happened to the Strongs. I needed to tie up all the lose ends for my newspaper story.

"Don't know," he said, rocking back in his chair. "Never saw them again. Not sorry about anything that happened to Hampton, he deserved it." He paused, before adding wistfully, "But I hope his wife Jane was all right. That dear lady was a saint and deserved better than that bastard Mark Hampton."

The mention of Jane reminded me I needed to know more about the love of his life. But the hatred in his voice and the way he spat out the last three words startled me and I hesitated before asking the question.

He did not need to answer. The yearning in his eyes told me all I wanted to know. Despite everything she had done he still loved her and, it seemed to me, the intervening years had done nothing to shake his passion.

"She was the only one I ever loved," he said wistfully, "but I never saw or heard from her again after Augusta."

"And Robert?" I prompted.

He looked up and smiled. "Robert was different."

"Was he?"

"We became close friends," he continued, as though I had not spoken. "Old Sam Jackson was good to me. Whenever he could he'd give me a few days off and I'd ride over and help Robert."

"So he kept the farm?"

"Oh yes," he said. "By late '68 he'd tilled most of his land and, like the Jacksons, got into cotton. Then he married a local girl, Melissa Brown. It only seems like yesterday when he told me." His voice faded. Again he was reliving those tumultuous days of his youth. There was a long dead moment before he continued. "I remember when he told me. We were having a smoke on his porch as we always did at the end of the day's work. I should have been pleased for him but I wasn't. We'd become closer than brothers and it upset me to think of someone coming between us. But that was the way of it. It was the last time we sat together by ourselves although I still saw a lot of both of them afterwards."

Not even the birds broke the silence as the old warrior gazed into his past world. At that instant the present did not exist for him.

"Looking back I think those were the happiest years of his short life," he finally said, swallowing his words in the emotion of the moment. "The last time I saw him was the fall of '73 and he looked in the best of health. Then suddenly he upped and died. They said it was something he'd picked up during the war."

The tears were not in my imagination.

He looked desperately tired as he rubbed the knuckles of both hands into his eyes. I felt embarrassed intruding on these private memories and, with flushed cheeks, turned away to allow Josh Singleton time to recover his composure.

"Both me and Melissa were in shock," he said, haltingly. "After Robert's death I still visited the farm. Mark you it was never a love match but we found comfort in each other's company. In time, she married again, sold the farm and went to live in Charleston. I only saw her once or twice after that when she came to visit her relatives this side of Athens. But I haven't seen her now for some years."

"And Mrs. Parslow?"

"Oh it was some time later. I was in Savannah arranging for a shipment of my cotton so I called at the house on Broughton

Confederate Gold
The Missing Treasure

Street. The elderly couple and their son had gone, but the people next door remembered her. They told me it was several months before she gained passage to England but, as far as they knew, she made it safely." He paused, then added with that deep manly chuckle, "I guess she must have had some money after all because she did it without my fortune."

"And what about your mother's old friend Rose and the treasure she told you the Strongs had buried?" I asked, looking though the list of names I had jotted down in my note book.

"Ah," he said. His eyes crinkled knowingly under their bushy brows. "Reckoned you'd get round to her sooner or later. I've seen you ticking off names and every now and again your face has given you away.

I shriveled up in the chair, wondering why the mention of Rose had aroused his suspicions.

"You might be a reporter but you can't fool me," he said, leaning forward and thrusting out his chin. "Despite what you said young man I knew you'd hoped to find my, or someone else's, treasure one way or another."

Before I could utter a word of denial he went on, his voice growing harsher with every word. "You expected me, in my old age, to tell you where it was didn't you?"

His gnarled hand shot out with surprising speed hitting my knee and knocking my note book to the ground. I bent down to pick it up and as I did so he leaned back in his rocker. "I'm sorry for you," he said, "because, believe me, there's no happiness in gold. Even if you could get at it you'd be better off not trying. There are other things in life more important." There was a spiteful edge to his voice. "Reckon I've been wasting my time telling you my story, haven't I?"

Trying to hide my humiliation which, I felt sure, must be plastered all over my burning face I wanted to look anywhere but at him.

"I admit finding the gold was my first thought," I muttered. Then in an attempt to explain myself added, "You see I want to start my own newspaper. But, I've not lost interest in your story. Look at all these notes I've taken." I handed him the note book.

"Well at least you're honest," he said, as he leafed through the pages. "Perhaps I was a bit harsh on you but you deserved it. You know you and your Harry Hopkins are not the only ones interested in that fortune." He paused, still studying my notes. "The Yankees recovered some as you know," he said without looking up, "but there's still a lot missing. For years there have been rumors about where it's hidden but that's all they've been, rumors. No one, not even the Government, has managed to find anything."

"Well you know where some of it is," I said, trying to conceal my embarrassment.

"Yes and so do you," he said, then quickly added, "and you are the only one I've ever told. Can't think why I did because you're no different from the rest. You're all gold diggers. Maybe it cleared my conscience. I don't know."

"Do you want it to remain a secret?" I asked, in an attempt to regain our earlier friendly rapport.

"What's it matter now," he said. "All my friends have gone long since. If anyone wants to search for the *Heron* so be it. It's your word against mine and I'm still the only one that knows the truth. You've no proof I haven't made the whole thing up."

His words stunned me. I had been convinced his story was true. Now in a few words he had cast serious doubts in my mind as to its validity. I wondered if I should tell Harry Hopkins not to publish it.

To hide my confusion I bent down to retrieve my notes from the floor where Josh Singleton had dropped them. "Can we get back to Rose?" I asked, after straightening up and settling back in my chair.

"What about her?" he said. He leaned back in his rocker and smiled knowingly.

"I wondered if you ever saw her again?"

Confederate Gold
The Missing Treasure

"Yes," he said. "I saw her again. A few times. Look around you."

In the fading light I got up, stretched, then wandered along the porch but saw nothing that bore any connection to his mother's old friend.

"Sorry," I said regaining my seat. "I don't understand."

Suddenly his mouth widened into a grin and the deep lines at the corners of his eyes creased in amusement. This change in expression led me to hope I had regained his trust. But I knew I still had to word my questions carefully if I expected to complete the interview. Despite his age I reckoned he would try to fling me off the porch and tear up my note book if I gave any further hint, facial or verbal, of wanting to find lost treasure.

"For a reporter you've got a poor memory," he chortled, clearly taking pleasure in the puzzled expression on my face.

As a reporter I prided myself on having a retentive memory so what was I missing that was so obvious? Again I looked around but, with the best will in the world, could not see any connection with Rose.

He levered himself out of the chair and hobbled across the porch waving his hand for me to follow. As I joined him he threw open the front door. "There," he said.

I stared at the rug in the center of the polished hardwood floor. Suddenly I recalled his comment of the previous night that carpetbaggers weren't the only ones that knew their way around. Without admitting anything he was showing me evidence he and Rose had found the Strong fortune.

"At last," he said, seeing the light of understanding dawn in my face. "For about a year," he continued, carefully lowering himself back into the rocking chair, "I wondered where the Strong's might have buried their treasure." He paused as though struggling to find the right words. "After a while," he said slowly, "I remembered how much Mrs. Hampton loved her rose garden and how, as a boy, I had helped her tend the blooms. The more I thought about it the more convinced I became that the rose garden would be the place to start. Rose had worked as a field hand all her life and, despite her age, could handle a spade with the best of them. For many a night we dug side by side, without speaking or even breaking for a rest. Then one night we unearthed a wooden box and found it held some of the family silver. According to Rose there was more but as we both needed money fast we decided to leave the rest for later.

"What did you do with it?"

"Sold it all to a bloody Yankee and gave Rose half. With my half I bought food, seed and plants for the Jacksons," he said.

"Wasn't that stealing?"

"Hell no. They'd abandoned it. At that time, whatever you could find was fair game."

"What did Rose do with her share?"

"I don't know," Josh said, a catch in his throat. "Never saw her again. Heard she died sometime in the early '80's. Just plain worn out poor soul."

"When did you move here?"

"Damn, I thought you understood," he said, shaking his head in disbelief. "This is the Jackson place. I told you they looked on me as family. When Sarah Jackson died, about two years after her husband, she left me the farm. That's where Sam stuck his old musket in my chest," he said, pointing to the front door, "and this is where I tied Dixie." He patted the rail alongside and his eyes softened. "She was the best horse I ever had," he muttered, "Lived to a good old age."

"What about the floor inside?" I asked referring to my notes. "You told me, when you came, it was split pine."

"So it was but the plantation house was never rebuilt. Over time, I hauled the least damaged parts of the old oak flooring over here."

"But I don't see any burn marks on it," I said.

"You wouldn't," he answered. "When I laid it I turned the boards over so any burn marks would be underneath."

Confederate Gold
The Missing Treasure

"And are the carpet and drapes from the plantation house also?" I asked.

"No," he laughed. "They were all destroyed in the fire. I bought those later. Of course, over time, I've made some changes to the old place such as building a couple of barns out back for storage." He pushed himself up out of the rocker. "Now," he said, looking down at me, "if you've no more questions I reckon I need to eat, even if you don't."

"Just one final question, sir," I said.

"Josh," he reminded me.

"It's one of curiosity not fortune hunting so please don't take it the wrong way," I said.

"Well?"

"How did you spend those four gold coins?"

"Never did," he said with the, now familiar, chuckle. "Always reckoned I would keep them for a rainy day and that day never came." The vacant look that flickered in his eyes told me that he was back again in his world of yesteryear.

"Food," he finally said, snapping back into the present and limping off towards the front door.

I followed. As we crossed to the kitchen I gazed with renewed interest at the things around me. If only the walls and floor of this house could speak I wondered what they might add to the story.

"Time's gone by faster than I realized," Josh Singleton said, as he prodded the smoldering embers in the stove. "Reckon you'd best stay tonight as well." This time it was not an order just a simple statement.

"Thanks." I paused before adding, "Josh". I still felt uncomfortable using his given name. "What can I do?"

"Go draw water from the well out there," he said, handing me a wooden pail while he busied himself about the kitchen. Soon two pots filled with corn and black-eyed peas, were bubbling away on the stove. From the larder he took a ham and sliced off several thick chunks, all the time whistling 'Dixie'. He seemed to have everything under control and there was nothing I could do, except stand and watch. Preparation of the meal seemed to occupy his full attention and I wondered if this was a throw-back to the days when he was starving.

"Pull up your chair," he said, as he drained off the water and tipped a large helping of corn and peas over the ham on my plate.

As we ate, Singleton extolled the virtues of Eli Whitney and his cotton gin, problems of cotton picking with and without slave labor and the International Cotton Exposition he and Sam Jackson had seen in Atlanta in 1881. His memory of those days was as keen as ever. "King Cotton came back faster than anyone thought it would," he concluded, as we cleared the table and moved back outside.

We sat there soaking up the end of the day, silently relaxing in the cool breeze that fanned across the fields and played around the porch. It carried with it the smell of the land. It had been the working of that land that had become a major factor in the South's sufferings all those years ago. At the same time it also proved its salvation.

It was dark now and the stars twinkling in the clear heavens seemed so close you could almost reach up to touch them. Everything was so vast and so still it seemed we were the only two people alive on this earth.

I do not know how long we sat, before Josh Singleton's hand moved to his vest pocket and his arthritic fingers withdrew a watch. With some difficulty he flipped open the lid and stared at the face before speaking. "Reckon it's time for your bed young man."

"Guess you're right," I answered, stifling a yawn as I rose. "Again my thanks for your hospitality."

He gave me a dismissive nod.

On entering the house I looked back at the old man sitting in his favorite rocking chair, the watch open on his lap, his eyes staring down at its face. As I stood there he turned to gaze at the mountains of his native state then back to the watch. He appeared to be lost in a chaotic world I had heard about but, fortunately, never known. A world that I had, perhaps unwittingly, unlocked for him again.

I felt the note book in my pocket and knew, despite what Josh Singleton had implied earlier, I had a story to tell. Not of wealth, as I had expected when I first came here, but one of the South rising from the ashes of devastation. Of a people fighting against overwhelming odds to regain all they had lost. Of a people facing up to disasters and winning. Of friendship and courage. Tomorrow I would write that story, not perhaps as Harry Hopkins might envisage but as I knew it should be told.

CHAPTER 25

I awoke to the sound of rain pattering on the shingled roof. Opening the shutters I saw dark clouds scurrying across the valley and crashing into the distant mountains, as though bent upon their own destruction. The scene was depressing and I dressed slowly. It was my intention to take a leisurely breakfast, thank my host of the last two nights, and head back to Atlanta and the news office.

As I left my room a feeling of apprehension overtook me. It was so powerful I paused for a moment on the narrow landing trying to determine its cause. Everything about me appeared normal but the sense that something was wrong persisted.

I descended the stairs reluctantly fearing what I might find at the bottom. An uncanny stillness hung over the house, broken only by the sound of my footsteps. The silence became overwhelming. I crossed the walkway to the kitchen and pushed open the door. A prickling sensation ran up my spine. On the previous morning Josh Singleton had been bustling about preparing breakfast by the time I had risen. Today there was no sign of the old man and the stove was out. I wondered if, perhaps, he had been too tired last night and simply forgotten to bank the fire before retiring. Although I was not convinced by this thought I reckoned the least I could do was to light the stove and start preparing breakfast.

The wood was piled against the front of the house. As I stepped onto the porch I stopped in my tracks. The sight that met my eyes drove all thoughts of breakfast from my mind. There was my host sitting in the same position I had left him the night before. Rain trickled down his crinkled, weather-beaten face and large droplets dripped from his grey beard, soaking his clothing and collecting in a pool round the motionless rocker. Sightless eyes stared at the watch and I knew Josh Singleton would never tell his story again. I felt numb.

For several minutes I stood as though frozen in place, my hand clutching the door knob. Something about the way he sat and the position of the gnarled hand holding the watch implied he had been content at the moment of his passing. Slowly I approached stupidly wanting to put an arm round his shoulder and tell him all was well. Yet I feared to touch what, I sensed, would be cold, dank flesh. In the end I simply stood beside him. Letting my eyes follow his glassy stare I noticed something written on the watch cover. It was some minutes before curiosity overcame my fear of touching the dead. With an acute sense of loathing I reached down and carefully prised open the cold, stiff fingers. Now I could hold the watch close there was no mistaking a well-worn inscription on the cover. It took a little while, turning it this way and that in the dull grey light, before I could decipher the words. When I eventually did a long low whistle escaped my lips. I could not believe what I read - 'To my son James Sangster from Father, 1856'.

I looked, with renewed interest, at the body in the rocking chair then back at the watch cover. I wondered how Singleton had come by the watch. Had Sangster given it to him at some time in the past and if so why? From the way Josh Singleton had stared at it, the watch obviously meant a lot to him and yet he had never mentioned it in his story. Then I was struck by another thought. Was it possible Singleton was in fact Sangster and if so did Singleton ever exist? If he did what happened to him? Perhaps he, not Sangster, had gone down with the *Heron*. But if that were true, I argued, how would Sangster know of Singleton's adventures with Jane and Mrs. Parslow if, at the time, he had been driving the buggy to Savannah. I sat down, my eyes glued to the inscription just like the dead man opposite me had done, and wondered who I had been talking to.

"Who were you?" I spoke aloud, lifting my eyes to the lifeless figure opposite. "Were you James Sangster the

Confederate hero my grandfather talked about or were you, who you said you were, Josh Singleton?"

In this confused state I continued to fire questions, despite knowing there would be no answer from the rocking chair. Yet talking seemed to help. Although part of me hoped it had been Sangster, everything I had heard pointed to my host being Singleton. There was no way Sangster could have known all the details Singleton had given me over the last two days, particularly that of his parentage. No, it must have been Singleton, which meant that Sangster must have given him the watch at some time. Perhaps after the rescue on the *Carolina II*. While I had no doubt the treasure rested on the bottom of the Savannah river estuary I still remained uncertain who had told me.

I had been so engrossed in the watch that I failed to notice the dead man's left hand twisted inside his pant's pocket as though feeling for something. Curious, I worked my hand into the pocket although contact with the cold, wet, fish-like skin made my flesh crawl. Carefully I worked the screwed up material out of the clenched fingers and, as I did so, heard a faint jingle. A shiver of excitement ran through me as probed for and finally found four solid round objects. There was no doubt I had found all that was left of Josh Singleton's treasure.

For some time I gazed at the four gold eagles, dulled by age and handling, wishing they could talk. Then I dropped them, along with the watch, into my own pocket. A sickening feeling grabbed my gut as I carefully moved rocking chair and body into the house and closed the door before making for the main road.

By now the rain had stopped and a watery sun broke through the grey overcast. While standing waiting for the bus to carry me into Rome to report the death, I pondered the question of whose death I would report. My hands played with the four gold coins and watch in my pocket and I recalled the man I had interviewed telling me there was no happiness in gold. Suddenly I realized what he meant. Friends and honor, not wealth, made the world

Confederate Gold
The Missing Treasure

what it was and I had, over the last two days, found a fortune not of gold but of knowledge. I decided to stay for the funeral.

On the 1st. October 1912, in contrast to the day of his death, the sun shone warmly and small white clouds skittered past on a warm breeze. I stood with a small group of mourners in the local church yard. Lost in thought, I distantly heard the minister as he eulogized a gallant Confederate and hard working farmer from the hills of north Georgia. My hands continued to clasp the watch and coins as though, through them, I might somehow learn the truth. The tributes finished, I watched the coffin lowered slowly into the ground and continued to wonder whose body it contained. I knew the headstone, if there was to be one, would read Josh Singleton. But was it?

Gazing at the few who had gathered to pay their last respects my attention was caught by an elderly woman standing off to one side. She stood coatless, head bowed, her chin resting on the lace that topped the long, purple velvet dress that went down to her ankles. A choker of small pearls surrounded the thin neck. Her short grey hair was covered by a black hat with a wide brim which served to keep the sun off her pale complexion. She waited until everyone had filed past before moving. Then, leaning heavily on a stout cane, she approached the graveside and brushed a tear from her eye with a gloved hand.

"Though the times were hard, I would not have changed them even if I could. God keep you Josh." Even in the hush of the moment her voice was so low as to be scarcely audible. I moved closer to listen. "Now you will be with my Robert. May God take care of both of you."

I started at the words. The only human being in the world, I thought, who could link Josh Singleton with a Robert would be Melissa Brown. If so, this elderly woman was the only person who knew, beyond any doubt, who was in that coffin. Standing quietly by her side, I watched as she gazed down at the plain pine box six feet below her feet. Despite the anguish that wreathed her patrician face, she seemed bathed in an aura of tranquility as though she knew no further disaster could ever befall her.

"Excuse me ma'am," I said, as she finally turned and started to pick her way through the many grave stones that dotted the small cemetery. "I wonder if I may have a word with you."

"I'm afraid I don't know you, sir," she said. "Should I?" Her voice was soft but firm as she leaned on her cane and eyed me.

"No," I said. "My name is Tom Byars. I too was a friend of Josh Singleton, but a recent one, and I would appreciate an opportunity to talk with you. You clearly knew him long before I did."

"I don't consider this an appropriate time for such a discussion Mr Byars," she said pointedly. "You may or may not be aware I have just buried my oldest friend and I don't feel up to talking about him to you or anyone else at this time. Now if you will kindly excuse me."

"I do not mean to intrude on your sorrow ma'am," I said, "but —,"

"Not now sir, if you don't mind," she said, cutting me off before I had time to explain further.

"If you would just allow me a question, or two," I persisted, grabbing her thin arm in my eagerness.

"I can see I am not going to able to rid myself of you," she said, pulling her arm out of my grasp with surprising strength. "If I answer two questions, and no more mind you, may I then be allowed to grieve in peace?"

"Ma'am I too wish to grieve," I said quietly, trying to placate her obvious annoyance at my intrusion. "But I do need to ask you your name and then about a watch."

"My name, young man, is Mrs. Pugh. As for the second question, I have no idea what you are talking about." At that she turned her back on me and started to limp away.

"I gathered from your words at the graveside that you knew both the deceased and a Robert," I said, catching up to her. "Would that Robert be a Mr. Robert Harrison?"

Confederate Gold
The Missing Treasure

She stopped as though frozen in place. "Why yes," she said. Now her eyes were filled with the curiosity I had hoped to arouse in her. "How did you know about him?"

"Would you then be Melissa Brown, later Harrison and now Pugh?" I asked, ignoring her question.

She nodded, her eyes downcast. I felt sorry for her, but I had to go on.

"I mentioned earlier that I was a recent friend of the deceased. The last time we were together," I said, rushing on before she had a time to speak, "he told me about his friend Robert Harrison marrying a Melissa Brown. That was you wasn't it?."

"Yes that was me. It was a long time ago," she said. Her voice drifted off and her eyes looked into somewhere only she knew. She stared at the trees surrounding us, but did not see them. I sensed she was remembering the times of her youth, the 'hard times' she had spoken about to the silent grave a few minutes earlier.

I waited for her to return to the present before suggesting we sat down on a small iron bench at the entrance to the cemetery. She accepted my suggestion. Once seated I plunged headlong into the story I had gleaned over the last two days making only passing reference to the robbery and omitting any mention of the four gold coins. She listened intently, nodding every now and again, but saying nothing.

"Well that explains a lot Mr Byars," she said when I had finished. "From occasional remarks Josh made over the years I guessed he had been somehow involved in that robbery, but he never said so outright. I believe he was right to do it, otherwise that gold would have been taken by the Yankees. I expect to someone your age it all sounds like a romantic adventure." She paused and her grey eyes held me with their intensity.

"Today many people think of that war as one great romance," she continued. "Cavalry officers in bright uniforms, girls in crinolines, dances and parties. I suppose," she sighed, "it

Bill Westhead

was romantic to start with because none of us knew any better. We all thought it would be over in a few months. But it wasn't. It dragged on and on and in the end both sides suffered. Win or loose, every battle resulted in horrible wounds, disease and death. Even after the war was over the deaths continued. My Robert for one." Again her voice drifted away and a sad smile of remembrance flitted across her face. I waited and, once more, tried to visualize the hardships of that time. It was a few minutes before she found the courage to go on.

"Looking back," she said, "war never was and never will be romantic. I think it was the Almighty's way of punishing us for our sins. It was hell on earth. Ask those who were involved. I hope and pray we never see anything like it again."

She paused and looked keenly at me. "I'm sorry young man I got carried away for a moment," she said before lapsing into silence, which stretched into a minute, then two, then five.

"The watch?" I finally reminded her. "Do you know anything about a watch Josh Singleton carried."

"It's so long ago now that I can't say I remember him having a watch," she said, turning to face me.

"Well you see." I hesitated not sure how to explain my interest in the watch without giving away the fact that I had it and wanted to keep it. "The watch in question had an inscription inside which said 'To my son James Sangster from Father 1856!"

"Oh yes," Melissa Pugh said. "I remember now you mention it. You know I'd honestly forgotten all about it."

"Well," I said, "when I saw that inscription I wondered if Josh Singleton was really Josh Singleton or a name James Sangster had assumed after the robbery."

"Does it matter now?"

"No," I had to admit. "But it aroused my curiosity. I've thought about it for a long time and finally concluded that Josh Singleton was who he said he was and James Sangster gave him the watch at some time. Am I right?"

Confederate Gold
The Missing Treasure

"Sangster never gave anyone anything from what Josh told me," she said. "Certainly he never gave him a watch."

"How did he get it then if Singleton wasn't Sangster?" I asked, my hard won arguments shattered by her last remark.

"You remember when Sangster and Campbell-Johnson sailed on that fateful night?"

I nodded.

"Well what he didn't tell you, or forgot to tell you, was that in his rush to be out of the country Sangster, probably by mistake, left the watch in the clothes he left behind. Josh found it when he changed. He intended to give it back but Sangster drowned. Believe me young man, the person buried today was Josh Singleton, make no mistake about it."

"Thank you ma'am for your patience and kindness," I said, relieved that this final problem was now behind me.

She smiled. "Josh Singleton was a good man," she said. "Anyone he called a friend will always be a friend of mine."

For the first time I really looked at her. Even in old age she was a good looking woman in an aristocratic way. She must have been some beauty, I thought, all those years ago when she married Robert.

"And you ma'am?" I could not resist a final question as she started to rise. "How did you manage to get all the way from Charleston for the funeral."

"I didn't," she said, sitting down again and averting my gaze. "Mr. Pugh died recently and I was spending some time with friends over near Rome when I heard the news."

"I'm sorry," I said and, on the spur of the moment, put my arm round her thin shoulders. She moved to lean against me then withdrew. "We must not been seen like this," she said, a sad smile creeping across her face.

"Indeed not," I answered, trying to play along with the false joviality she endeavored to exude.

Bill Westhead

"Mr. Byars, I must be going," she said. "It's been a pleasure to talk to someone who knew Josh Singleton, although perhaps not very well."

"Again my grateful thanks ma'am," I said, as she levered herself upright with the aid of her cane.

"Since you reminded me of that watch I remember it so well now," she said, looking down at me. "With the three of us sitting round the old table Josh would occasionally pull it out. Each time you could see him thinking of his old Captain and their in and out, but never dead, friendship. After a while, he'd announce it was time for bed or for him to return to the Jacksons."

I knew as she spoke the watch meant more to her than it ever would to me. Pulling it from my pocket I stood and held it out to her. "Would you like to take this?" I asked. "I'm sure Josh would like you to have it."

Her whole body shook with emotion as she sat and gazed at the worn casing. "Thank you," she whispered, her fingers closing gently over it, as if around a fledgling bird, fearful of crushing it.

"Here is my address," I continued. "If I can help you in any way in the future please let me know."

She glanced at the torn scrap of paper before putting it in her small purse. "Please remember him kindly Mr. Byars."

Without a further word she limped slowly out of the cemetery gates, her head high. She never looked back. Still a Southern lady, I thought, despite all that has befallen her. Even in her old age she epitomized an unsubdued nation.

I sat on the bench for a long time, turning the four coins over in my hands and looking at the mound of earth alongside Josh Singleton's final resting place. Compelled by some force, over which I had no control, I wandered slowly back to the graveside. The pine box looked so small and insignificant at the bottom of the hole. Now the coins seemed to burn my hand. Then, as if drawn by a magnet, they slipped out of my grasp and dropped quietly down by the side of the coffin. In that instant I knew that was where they should be. The gentle breeze through the trees whispered my thoughts - you may still need those for that rainy day Josh Singleton.

It was over. In a trance I wandered back to the inn where I had been staying. Back from the turmoil of the Civil War years and into the peace of my own time.

Bill Westhead

ABOUT THE AUTHOR

Bill Westhead was born in Clitheroe, England and educated at Rossall School and Leeds University. After serving in the British Army he worked in the textile industry in Wales, England and N. Ireland before emigrating, with his family, to the United States in 1973. He reads extensively about the history of each area in which he lives. Knowing the history of the people or place, he claims, helps one understand their attitude and reasoning today. Small as well as large historical events can play a major role in shaping the attitude of people. 'Confederate Gold' is Bill Westhead's third novel. He first published 'Once in Old Frederica Town' in 1993 a story based on the founding of the state of Georgia. This was followed in 1999 by 'Clogs' dealing with the effect of mechanization on the textile industry in his home town at the time of the Industrial Revolution. He has also been published in 'Cricket' and 'Animal Tales' magazines as well as several trade journals.

CPSIA information can be obtained at www.ICGtesting.com
Printed in the USA
BVOW08s1658170214

345174BV00001B/13/P

9 780759 668522